R. D. Wingfield, who is married with one son and lives in Basildon, Essex, is a prolific writer of radio crime plays and comedy scripts, some for the late Kenneth Williams, star of the 'Carry On' films.

Winter Frost is the fifth book to feature DI Jack Frost. The series has been successfully adapted for television as *A Touch of Frost* starring David Jason.

Also by R. D. Wingfield

FROST AT CHRISTMAS
A TOUCH OF FROST
NIGHT FROST
HARD FROST

and published by Corgi Books

WINTER FROST

R. D. Wingfield

CORGI BOOKS

WINTER FROST
A CORGI BOOK : 0 552 14778 8

Originally published in Great Britain by
Constable & Company Limited

PRINTING HISTORY
Constable edition published 1999
Corgi edition published 2000

9 10 8

Set in 10/11pt Plantin by
Kestrel Data, Exeter, Devon.

Corgi Books are published by Transworld Publishers,
61–63 Uxbridge Road, London W5 5SA,
a division of The Random House Group Ltd,
in Australia by Random House Australia (Pty) Ltd,
20 Alfred Street, Milsons Point, Sydney, NSW 2061, Australia,
in New Zealand by Random House New Zealand Ltd,
18 Poland Road, Glenfield, Auckland 10, New Zealand
and in South Africa by Random House (Pty) Ltd,
Endulini, 5a Jubilee Road, Parktown 2193, South Africa.

Printed and bound in Great Britain by
Cox & Wyman Ltd, Reading, Berkshire.

WINTER FROST

Prologue

He had the photographs spread out on the table in front of him and was savouring them once again. Behind him the local television news was droning away unheeded.

Vicky . . . Vicky Stuart.

He froze. God! Someone was whispering her name. Heart hammering, he swung round. There, on the screen, was her picture. The little girl, eight years old, smiling, showing the gap in her teeth. He turned up the volume.

'. . . Denton police are holding a man in connection with the disappearance of eight-year-old Vicky Stuart who has not been seen since she left Denton Junior School for her home some nine weeks ago. According to a spokesman for Denton CID the man, who is in his early forties, is helping the police with their inquiries and no charges have yet been made . . .'

The picture on the TV screen, enlarged from a school group photograph, was not a good one, nowhere as clear and sharp as the photographs on the table before him where Vicky was staring at the camera, her terror shown in sharp focus.

A tapping at the front door. He frowned. He'd told her to use the back way. If anyone saw her coming . . .

He scooped up the photographs and stuffed them in the sideboard drawer, turning the key and testing to make sure it was firmly locked. Excitement made him sweat. He rubbed the palms of his hands down his trouser legs then opened the door. 'You look frozen,' he said. 'Come on in, I've got the fire on. We'll soon warm you up.'

She was seven years old, a few months younger than the other girl.

1

The bitter January wind butted the rusty 'Closed' sign and swung it on the chain which guarded the entrance to the abandoned petrol station. Closed for over eighteen months, it still reeked of stale sump oil, diesel fuel and the sweaty feet smell of old rubber. Parked untidily on the forecourt by the concrete bases where the petrol pumps once stood were two police cars and a mud-splattered Ford Sierra. Detective Inspector Jack Frost leant against the Sierra, a cigarette dangling from his lips in blatant defiance of the numerous 'No Smoking' notices, stamping his feet to get the circulation going. This was all a bloody waste of time. He had hoped to spend the rest of his shift back at the station, the radiator in his office going full blast while he fiddled his monthly expenses with the added bonus of his Divisional Commander, Superintendent Mullett, being away at Head Office so no chance of him bursting in when the ink on an allegedly month-old petrol receipt was still wet. Then later, feet up in the rest room, he had planned to watch a video of the big fight. What should have been a night of sheer bliss went right up the Swannee when that slimy bastard, Reginald Todd, had marched into the station to confess to the killing of eight-year-old Vicky Stuart. Todd was a minor child molester, exposing himself in front of kids or getting them to touch him in return for sweets, but now he was claiming he had gone up into the big time, that he had raped and killed the missing eight-year-old and hidden her body somewhere in this old service station . . . he couldn't remember exactly where . . . it was dark . . . he was confused . . . !

In the background, behind the fringe of trees, came the steady rumble of traffic on the new motorway, the motorway which had drained the life blood of trade from this once bustling service station. The derelict forecourt was now a waste ground, a convenient dumping place for unwanted mattresses, sofas and other rubbish.

Frost watched the uniforms manhandle an enormous treadless tyre and bounce it across the forecourt. He should be giving them all a hand but he knew they wouldn't find anything. That time-wasting, lying bastard Todd was a pathetic nobody, revelling in a chance to be the centre of attention. Frost shivered. Never mind about sharing the hardships with the troops, it was warmer inside the car. He climbed back, just in time to get the radio message from Control. 'Vicky's mother is here, Inspector . . . wants to see you.' Frost groaned.

She would have heard about the confession and be anxious for news . . . for good news. Mrs Stuart, a small bundle of nervous energy, stubbornly refused to face facts, and was convinced that even after nine weeks, her eight-year-old daughter would suddenly walk into the house, fit and well, hungry for her tea. Her fragile smile was always on the verge of crumbling, and she talked a lot so she wouldn't have to listen to other people telling her things she didn't want to hear. Frost suspected that when there was no-one to see, she cried a lot. He had tried to get her to accept that after nine weeks there could be little hope, but she wouldn't listen . . . 'Of course she's coming back, Inspector . . . I know it . . . I just know it.'

'Would you tell her . . .' he began and then his attention was attracted by the flashing of a torch. PC Jordan, grim-faced, over by the inspection pit was waving urgently, beckoning him over. Frost went cold. Control was still babbling away. 'Inspector . . . are you there?' He clicked over to transmit. 'Yes, I'm still here. Tell Mrs Stuart to go home. I'll call on her on the way back.' He took one last drag at his cigarette, then stepped out into the cold.

'Down there, Inspector.' Jordan directed the beam of his torch into the murk of filthy, oil-filmed water at the bottom of the inspection pit where discarded tyres and cans lurked. In the centre of the debris the torch lit up a sodden bundle of dark blue cloth. On that freezing cold November afternoon when Vicky Stuart waved goodbye to her schoolmates, she had been wearing a thick, warm, blue, winter coat. Frost poked another cigarette in his mouth and sighed. 'All right, lads. Let's get her out.'

It wasn't the girl. They had hauled out a bundle of evil-smelling rags. They took everything out of the inspection pit. Vicky wasn't there. She wasn't anywhere on the service station.

Vicky's mother was at the front door even before he got out of the car. She had been watching, peeking through the net curtains, hoping to see her daughter sitting in the passesnger seat next to Frost. At least, he told himself, this time he wouldn't be breaking bad news. He lived in dread of the day when he would have to. She would not face the possibility that her daughter was not coming back. She had even talked herself into believing that Frost shared her optimism. 'She's alive, Inspector. I know it and you know it. Vicky's alive.'

The brittle smile was there when she opened the door, but the eyes were anxious and she looked ten years older than when he had first seen her. 'It's good news, Inspector, isn't it . . . I can tell from your face that it's good news.'

If it was good news not to have found her daughter's dead body, then that's what it was. 'The man was lying, Mrs Stuart. He knows nothing about Vicky.'

'Of course he doesn't, Inspector. We both know she isn't dead, don't we?'

He said nothing. The coward's way out, but it was pointless trying to get her to face up to facts. She was still babbling away. 'You're going to find her. Any day now you're going to come to this door and you won't have to say a word – I'll see it from your face.' All the time she spoke her hands were worrying at her apron, twisting it, screwing it into tight balls of cloth.

Frost gave his non-committal nod. 'Marvellous if it happens, Mrs Stuart.' If it made her happy . . .

'And it will happen, Inspector. You and I both know it . . . it will happen.'

He walked back to the Sierra feeling drained. He wanted to take hold of her and shake some sense into her and shout, 'She's bloody dead, Mrs Stuart . . . a kid of eight can't go missing for nine weeks without a word and still be alive.' But he couldn't do it. He climbed back in the car and drove to the station ready to kick the shit out of Reggie bastard Todd.

Reggie Todd, sitting on the bunk in the police cell, noisily slurping down the cup of tea the sergeant had brought in for him, was a thin scrawny individual with a prominent nose and a large Adam's apple that clunked up and down as he swallowed.

A rattling of keys from outside and the cell door

crashed open. Detective Inspector Frost stood there, his eyes blazing.

Todd's Adam's apple moved up and down rapidly and he leapt to his feet, blurting out apologies before Frost could get a single word out. 'I'm sorry, Inspector. I'm truly sorry. I made a mistake . . . I must have dreamt it . . . It was so vivid I thought it was real.'

'You'll feel a vivid pain in the goolies in a minute,' snapped Frost, 'and it will be real.'

'I deserve it, Mr Frost . . . but please . . . I hate violence.'

'You didn't seem to hate it when you were telling us what you did to the kid. You were dribbling with excitement.'

Todd hung his head and said nothing.

Frost's lip curled with disgust. 'You will now make another statement withdrawing your phoney confession and you will then get the hell out of here and hope and pray that I don't bump into you on a dark night.' He turned on his heels and marched out of the cell.

Station Sergeant Bill Wells looked up as Frost pushed through the swing doors into the lobby. 'You should charge him with wasting police time.'

'He's wasted so much police time, I haven't got time to charge him for wasting it,' said Frost. He poked a cigarette in his mouth. 'I've got my car expenses to do. If anything important happens, like Lord Lucan walking in to give himself up, pass it over to Inspector Maud.' He looked around. 'Where is she, by the way?'

Wells gave a disdainful sniff. Detective Sergeant Liz Maud, posted to Denton a couple of months ago, had been made up to the temporary rank of inspector, while he, Bill Wells, after seventeen years in the force, was still only a sergeant. 'That jumped-up little cow . . . !'

Frost chuckled to himself. He loved winding the sergeant up. He tut-tutted reprovingly. 'That's no way to speak about your superior officer, Sergeant!'

Wells couldn't bite at the bait quickly enough. 'Superior? She's the same rank as me . . . a sergeant. She's done half the time I have, only been here five flaming minutes and she's made up to temporary inspector. What has she got that I haven't?'

'Big tits,' said Frost.

Wells jabbed a finger. 'You've hit the nail on the head there, Jack. It's sex discrimination in reverse.'

'I've never tried it in reverse,' said Frost, 'but where is she?'

'With a prisoner . . . a cab driver. He picked this woman up and, instead of taking her home, took her down a side street and raped her.'

'Bloody hell!' tutted Frost. 'I hope she didn't leave him a tip.'

His office was in darkness. He expected to find DC Morgan, newly posted from Lexington Division, hard at work with the crime figures, but the office was empty. He walked over to Morgan's desk and looked at the papers to check progress. They hadn't been touched since he left for the derelict filling station. Frost charged out into the corridor, almost bumping into PC Collier who was on his way to the lobby. 'Where's DC Morgan?'

'In the canteen, I think,' said Collier who knew damn well he was.

'Go up and drag the sod out. We don't pay him to drink bloody tea, we pay him to fiddle the crime figures.' His voice died. Over Collier's shoulder he could see into the open door of No. 2 interview room where a grim-faced woman in her late fifties sat bolt

14

upright, clutching a large brown plastic handbag to her bosom. She caught his gaze and snapped her head away to stare pointedly at the far wall. She had no wish to see that rude little man.

Frost pulled Collier to one side. 'What's old mother Beatty doing here?'

'Waiting for her statement to be typed,' said Collier. 'She's the rape victim.'

'Rape victim? In her bloody dreams!' snorted Frost. 'Where's DI Maud?'

Acting Detective Inspector Liz Maud, twenty-six years old, dark hair scragged back, stared at the man on the other side of the table who was lolling back in his chair, a look of amused contempt on his face. 'Let's go over it again from when you picked the woman up from the railway station . . .'

The man gave a resigned shrug. 'All right, but this is the last time. The old crow phones for a cab. I picked her up, took her to where she wanted to go, dropped her off and I drove away.'

'The woman tells a different story,' said Liz Maud. 'She claims you drove round to a side street and you raped her.'

'Do me a favour,' protested the man. 'I'm bleeding fussy who I rape.' He gave her a smirk. 'Now if it was you, darling—'

'If it was me,' Liz snapped, 'you wouldn't have anything left to rape with.' He mimed a mocking grimace of pain as she tugged a form sheet from its folder. 'You make a habit of assaulting female passengers, don't you?'

He expelled breath in exasperation. 'If you're referring to that slag of a prostitute, then we're talking ancient bloody history.'

'Nine months ago,' said Liz. 'Recent bloody history if you ask me.' She looked up in annoyance as the door creaked open and, without knocking, Frost walked in. What the hell did he want? She turned to the microphone. 'For the benefit of the tape, Detective Inspector Frost has entered the interview room.' She wiped a wisp of straggling hair from her forehead and glowered at him. 'Yes, Inspector?'

He beckoned her over to the door. 'A quick word.'

Her lips tightened. 'Later – I'm in the middle of an interview.'

'Now,' said Frost, stepping back into the corridor.

Eyes smouldering, she followed him out, closing the door firmly behind her. He had no business interfering in the middle of an interview. 'I very much resent—'

He held up a hand. 'Hear me out.' He lowered his voice. 'I don't think you're going to make this one stick, love.'

'No?' She gave him a superior smile. 'I've checked his form. He was convicted of assaulting two women in his cab. They couldn't pay the fare, so he beat them up – put one of them in hospital.'

Frost nodded. He knew all about that. 'But did you check the victim's form?'

She frowned. What was the fool on about? 'The victim?'

'Old mother Beatty. Acording to her, her drawers have been up and down more times than Tower Bridge. She's alleged rape and assault at least twelve times over the past two years, all of which have proved wishful thinking. She also reckons she gets heavy breathing phone calls, peeping Toms when she strips off in the scullery, and is being stalked.' He offered her the long computer print-out.

Liz flicked through it, lips tightening angrily. 'She sounded so genuine! I believed her.'

'She believes herself half the time,' said Frost.

Liz glowered at the interview room door. 'I could wring her bloody neck!'

'Don't be too hard on the poor cow. She's never had it . . . she's probably never going to get it so she has to imagine she's had it.'

'Never had it? Are you telling me she's a virgin?'

'So the doctor said the last three times she was raped.'

Liz handed back the print-out. 'So what do we do? If she insists, we've got to go ahead.'

'I'll go and sweet talk the old cow,' said Frost. 'You do a bit of back-pedalling with the cabbie: we don't want him suing for wrongful arrest.' It was then he noticed how tired and drawn she looked. 'Are you all right, love?'

She glared at him. 'Of course I'm all right. Why shouldn't I be?'

'You look a bit peaky.' He was sorry he had started this.

'Just tired . . . and fed up at having to waste my time on phoney rape charges.' Her eyes shot daggers down the corridor in the direction of the lobby where Sergeant Bill Wells, chin cupped in hand, was reading the evening paper. 'You'd have thought our Station Sergeant would have had the common decency to have told me.' She spun on her heels and went back into the interview room.

Doreen Beatty stared stone-faced at him as he entered the other interview room. He gave her a smile and got a sour grimace in return. 'I want nothing to do with you, Inspector Frost, thank you very much. I'm definitely pressing charges and there is no way you are going to talk me out of it.'

Frost tossed the withdrawal form over to Bill Wells. 'She's dropped the charges.'

Wells gawped at the form. 'How the hell did you get her to do that?'

17

Frost gave a modest smile. 'I told her he couldn't have raped her as he got his dick shot off in the Gulf War – friendly fire.'

'And she believed you?'

'Not at first, but I offered to show her the bit that was left and she gave me the benefit of the doubt.' He switched off the grin. 'Why didn't you tell Liz Maud the old biddy was in the *Guinness Book of Records* for multiple virgin rapes?'

Wells sniffed disdainfully. 'Not my place to tell my superior officer what to do.'

Running footsteps from the stairs to the canteen and Frost's temporary assistant, DC 'Taffy' Morgan, burst through the doors into the lobby. Morgan, a stocky, dark, curly-haired little Welshman in his late thirties, had sorrowful eyes and a heart-melting whipped puppy expression he could turn on at the drop of a hat which Frost found irritating, but women seemed to find irresistible. Morgan started when he saw Frost glowering at him. 'Just popped up for a quick cup of tea, guv,' he said in his 'oozing with sincerity', sing-song Welsh voice. 'I've nearly finished those figures.' Morgan was the only officer in the station who called Frost 'guv'. Frost reckoned he'd picked it up from the police series on the telly.

'Nearly finished?' said Frost. 'You haven't touched the bloody things since I went out. Let's get one thing straight, Taffy. There's only room for one lazy bastard in this station and that's going to be me. Understand?'

Morgan hung his head sheepishly. 'Sorry, guv. I'll get on to it right away, guv.'

The desk phone rang. Morgan paused while Wells answered it. Like Frost he hated figure work and hoped this might be a call that would take him away from it.

'I'll get someone over there right away,' said Wells, scribbling an address down on his pad as he hung up.

'Another pillow case burglary, Jack. Shall I give it to Morgan?'

'No. He's got his heart set on doing the crime figures. I'll take it.' He jerked a thumb to Taffy. 'On your way, Lloyd George.'

'Yes, guv,' said Morgan, making his disappointment very apparent.

Wells watched him go and sniffed disdainfully. 'How the hell do we get all the rubbish foisted on us? First Wonder Woman, now him.'

'I've known worse,' grunted Frost. 'What's the address of this burglary?' He had a quick look at his watch. If it didn't take too long he would have plenty of time to fiddle his expenses and see the videoed title fight with the rest of the shift. Life was a joy when your Divisional Commander was away.

Police Superintendent Mullett tapped his fingers happily on the steering wheel of his Rover as he drove back from County Headquarters. An excellent meeting under the chairmanship of the Chief Constable in which Denton Division came out very well, he thought. It was a meeting for all Divisional Commanders to discuss ways of maintaining an efficient force in the face of the draconian budget cuts that had been forced upon them. The Chief Constable – quite brilliantly, thought toadying Mullett – had suggested that more work with less manpower could be achieved by increased inter-Divisional co-operation with men being seconded from Division to Division as and when required. Some of the other officers had expressed their disquiet, feeling this could only reduce the efficiency of the supplying Divisions, but Mullett, not quite understanding what was involved, although sensing that nods of approval and not constructive criticism were required, had nodded until his head ached and had committed ten of his own officers to a

19

joint drugs operation. He was now basking in the euphoria of the Chief Constable's comments: 'It is the Denton spirit that's wanted throughout the County, gentlemen – an example to you all.' The sour glances fired at him by the rest of the meeting made it clear he was in a minority, but it was not the rest of the meeting he wanted to impress.

He pulled back the sleeve of his grey pin-stripe jacket to consult his Rolex. 9.58. The others would still be in the pub, drinking, drowning their sorrows, shaking their heads doubtfully over their beers and telling each other that it might look good on paper, but it just wouldn't work in practice. However, thought Mullett, if it did fail, it would be the Doubting Thomases who got the blame, not the wholeheartedly approving Denton Divisional Commander, determined to make a go of it.

As he spun the wheel to turn into the main road he had to brake sharply to avoid a mud-splattered Ford Sierra which had anticipated the traffic lights and roared across his path. He frowned. No mistaking the car or the driver. Frost! He'd have a word with him about careless driving when he got back to the office. As the Chief Constable had so rightly said at the meeting, supported by Mullett's unstinting noddings of approval, the police should always be setting an example, not bending the rules.

He took the short cut through the red light district as he wanted to check the current position. A deputation of some of the local residents, led by the vicar, had called on him demanding that the police clean up the streets. He had delegated the task to Frost who had insolently pretended that cleaning up the streets involved picking up empty crisp packets and cleaning away dogs' mess. Mullett's lips tightened. Frost might think that funny, but he wouldn't be laughing when Mullett got back to him.

The 'girls' were out in force, grinning, wiggling and

beckoning as he drove past. They had disappeared from their beats in a panic some two months ago when one of their number had been found beaten up and murdered, but had gradually drifted back.

He clicked on his radio for the local news. '. . . *Denton police have released without charge a man they had been questioning in connection with the disappearance some nine weeks ago of schoolgirl Vicky Stuart . . .*' Another frown. Frost hadn't had the common courtesy to contact him at County and tell him they had arrested a suspect. He had felt a proper fool at the meeting when the Chief questioned him about it and he had to phone the station to find out what it was about. He slowed down and stopped at the traffic lights. Someone tapped on the driver's window. A woman with dyed blond hair and a ridiculously low-cut dress. 'Want to be naughty, mister?'

'No I do not, madam,' he snapped, hastily jumping the lights and narrowly missing a collision to get away from her. Ignoring the angry hootings from other drivers, he turned into the Market Square. As he did so his mobile phone rang. Superintendent Harry Conley from Fenwick Division . . . probably still in the pub with the others, judging from the raucous laughter he could hear in the background.

'A spot of inter-Divisional co-operation wanted, Stan,' said Conley. 'Hope you can help?'

Mullett smirked happily. A chance to show what Denton could do. 'Certainly, Harry . . . fire away . . .'

A police car was parked outside the entrance to the apartment building and Frost slid his Sierra behind it. The burglary was at Flat 305 on the third floor. He thumbed the lift button, but nothing happened. A couple of swift kicks to the door hurt his foot, but failed to produce the lift, so it was the damn stairs. When he reached the third floor he saw that the lift doors had been wedged open with a piece of wood, preventing the lift from operating. On to Flat 305 where an angry-looking woman opened the door to his ring and beckoned him in. 'The more the bloody merrier,' she said bitterly. 'No-one here when he robs us, can't move for bleeding police when it's all over.' Frost grunted his sympathy. Two uniformed men, Jordan and Simms, were already in the flat, Simms questioning an irate man who was slumped in an armchair. 'First bleeding night we go out together for ages,' he was moaning, 'and this flaming well happens.'

PC Jordan briefed Frost. 'Mr and Mrs Plummer. Went out just before eight o'clock to see the film at the Premier, got back quarter of an hour ago to find they'd been burgled.'

'The whole bloody evening was a wash-out,' wailed Mrs Plummer. 'Moan, moan, moan from him because he was missing the match on the telly. When we get back the stinking lift is out of order so we have to walk up three flaming flights of stairs to find we've been robbed, and on top of that it was a lousy bleeding film.'

'If we'd stayed in to watch the match like I wanted,' said her husband, 'this wouldn't have happened.'

She turned on him angrily. 'Oh – so it's all my bleeding fault now, is it? Just because, for once in my life, I wanted to go out.'

Frost shut his ears to the row. 'Any sign of forced entry?'

'No.' Jordan took him over to the front door. 'The letter box is in line with the latch. He probably hooked a piece of wire through and opened it that way.'

Frost nodded his grudging admiration. 'He's a clever bastard. Did you see how he wedged open the lift doors to make sure they didn't come back too soon? Let's have a look at the conjugal nest.'

22

He followed Jordan into the bedroom and saw exactly what he expected. One of the pillows, taken from near the double bed's headboard, had been dumped half-way down in the centre of the powder blue quilt.

'Reminds me of my honeymoon,' grunted Frost.

Jordan grinned. 'A professional job . . . straight in the bedroom and in and out in a couple of seconds.'

'Still reminds me of my honeymoon,' said Frost. Jordan suppressed a snigger as the husband and wife came in. Crime victims rarely saw the funny side of things.

'Look,' shrieked the woman, pointing to the bed. 'Not content with pinching my jewellery, he's taken the bleeding pillow case.'

'He always does,' Frost told her. 'It's his trademark. He uses the pillow case to bag up the loot. He arrives empty-handed – nothing on him to arouse suspicion before the burglary. He makes straight for the bedroom – which is where most people keep their jewellery – grabs the pillow case, drops the loot inside, then . . .' Frost walked over to the bedroom window and raised it so he could look down. Two floors below was a grassed-over area. 'Chummy drops the pillow case with the loot out of the window and walks away. If he's stopped at this stage, and we haven't been that flaming lucky yet, he's got nothing on him to arouse suspicion. Then he calmly retrieves the loot and legs it away. He only takes small stuff that he can pocket. He must have been watching the place . . . saw you go out and took his chance. Did you notice anyone hanging around?'

The man and his wife both shook their heads.

'If it's any consolation,' said Frost, 'you're not alone. He's done about eight blocks of flats over the past three weeks; got away with thousands of pounds' worth of swag.'

'And you still haven't caught the bastard. Brilliant!' snarled the man.

'As soon as someone is observant enough to feed us with a description, we might have something to go on,' said Frost, 'but so far, no-one's come up with anything.' He gave the place one last look around before rebuttoning his mac, ready for the off. 'Don't touch anything . . . he hasn't left prints before, but there's always a first time. I'll send our lady Scenes of Crime Officer round first thing tomorrow morning to give the place the once-over.'

'Tomorrow?' shrieked Mrs Plummer. 'What about now? Time's bloody wasting.'

'She's off duty . . . and she's probably in bed with her pillow in the same position as yours but for a different reason. Tomorrow will be soon enough.'

Jordan's radio called. He listened and beckoned Frost over. 'Message for you from Control, Inspector. They've had a call from a couple on the next floor. Flat 410. Another burglary . . . sounds like the same man.'

Frost swore silently. 'You bet it's the same bloke. He's probably turned over half the flats in the building. He doesn't give a toss for what he's doing to our unsolved crime figures.' He checked his wrist-watch and groaned. At this rate he'd be working on his expenses into the small hours. 'Come on. Let's get it over with . . .'

The clock in the Market Square was chiming eleven as Frost nosed his Ford into the station car-park. It had been a sod of a night so far. Two more burglaries reported and investigated in the flats, making four in all . . . four lots of miserable people moaning about their rotten luck and what bloody use were the police who spent too much time harassing motorists for parking on double yellow lines and hardly any on the prevention of crime. Another four unsolved crimes for the monthly report and no further forward in catching the sod.

A list of the stolen jewellery was in his pocket, but Chummy was far too smart to use any of the local fences. Nothing from the previous break-ins had turned up.

Frost had switched his radio and his mobile phone off just in case some bright spark thought he was itching for more crimes to investigate. The rest of the night was expenses, crime figures, the big fight and then bed . . . He yawned. He could do with bed now. He'd been on duty since eight in the morning and was just about whacked.

At that time of night the station car-park should have been almost empty, but a large yellow and green motor coach was slewed across most of the parking spaces and he had to leave his Ford by the entrance. As he scrunched across the car-park the sound of drunken singing, shouting and the smashing of glass bellowed from inside the building. There must have been an affray at a pub somewhere. So much for peace and flaming quiet.

As he pushed open the rear doors the noise hit him like a punch in the face – drunken screeching laughter, bawdy singing, shouting and the yelling of Sergeant Wells demanding, but not getting, silence. Frost scuttled down the passage to the lobby and cautiously peeked inside. Drunks, men and youths, some near paralytic, others too full of bloody life, were sprawled all over the place and the noise was deafening. One man in the corner, eyes glazed, was performing a sinuous dance, with much pelvic thrusting, to music only he could hear. Another, egged on by the cheers of his mates, was standing on one of the benches, performing a strip-tease and was down to his bulging Y-fronts. In the corner, a sad-faced individual was quietly and copiously being sick. Red-faced and bellowing, Sergeant Wells was adding to the cacophony. 'Shut up all of you . . . bloody shut up!'

'What the hell is going on?' asked Frost. 'I thought I'd told Mullett not to bring his Rotary Club mates here any more.'

'Don't talk to me about flaming Mullett,' moaned Wells. 'This is all down to him!' He clapped his hands over his ears as the strip-tease finished and the applause rocked the room. 'Look at them . . . a coachload of football hooligans – just what I flaming well needed!' He took one of Frost's cigarettes. 'You should see what those animals have done to the toilets – you could float the *Titanic* on a sea of vomit and urine. There's over sixty of them and I haven't got anywhere to put them – the cells are all full.' He raised his eyes to the ceiling. 'Bloody, bleeding Mullett!'

'How does our beloved Divisional Commander come into it?' asked Frost, pushing away a drunk who was trying to put his arms round his neck. 'I'm already spoken for, mate.'

'This lot been up to town for the big match – though I expect most of them were too pissed to see it. They finish off all their booze on the way back, so they get the driver to stop at that all-night off-licence just outside Fenwick. They charge in, grab everything they can carry, wines, spirits, lager, packets of flaming pork scratchings, then belt back to the coach without paying. The manager and two of his staff try to stop them and get beaten up with bottles for their trouble. The manager's in hospital with a fractured skull.'

'Boyish high spirits!' murmured Frost. 'But how did we get involved? It's Fenwick Division's problem.'

'Tell me something I don't bleeding know, Jack. By the time the Fenwick area car turns up, they've all jammed into one of the coaches, left the driver behind and gone speeding off up the motorway. The area car follows, skids on some oil and overturns. So Fenwick now wants other Divisions to come to their rescue, stop the coach and hold the drunken sods until they can pick them up. All the other Divisional Commanders are boozing away somewhere. They don't want all the bleeding aggro so they ask Joe Soap Mullett. "We'll stop it," he says. "Denton will rise to the occasion as always." So we have to pull them in and now we're stuck with the sods. Mullett's mates must be laughing their bloody heads off.'

'Still,' grunted Frost, 'it's a fine example of inter-Departmental co-operation. Mr Mullett will be delighted.'

'Then Mr bleeding Mullett can come round with carbolic and a bucket and help swab up the mess. They're discharging from every flaming orifice in here.' He gaped and pointed. 'Look at that bastard. He's peeing on the floor.'

As Wells dashed over to stop the man Frost took the opportunity to beat a hasty retreat. His hand was on the door to his office when running footsteps and his name called made him turn round. An agitated PC Collier. 'What's up, son?'

Collier was panting and could just about get the words out. 'Quick, Inspector. A fight.'

Frost frowned. 'Nothing to do with me, son – tell Sergeant Wells, he's dying for something to do.'

'I think you'd prefer to handle it, Inspector.' Collier lowered his voice. 'One of the fighters is DC Morgan.'

Bloody Taffy! Frost hurried down the corridor after Collier, nearly tripping over a sleeping drunk on the way. Then, in the dim light, he saw them. Two dark shapes, rolling and thrashing about on the floor, each trying to get on top. One of them, a man with a long woollen football scarf twined round his neck, managed to pin the other's arms down with his knees, then began methodically banging his adversary's head on the stone floor. Frost squinted. Collier was right. The man underneath was DC Taffy Morgan and he was definitely losing.

Frost grabbed the two ends of the football scarf and pulled with all his might. The winner's face went red as the scarf tightened, eating into his neck. Choking, he released his grip on Taffy's hair to pull the scarf away. Frost jerked the man's head back, crooked an arm firmly round his neck and dragged him to his feet. 'Cuffs!' he barked. Collier snapped on the cuffs. Glowering, eyes blazing, the man watched as Frost helped Morgan to his feet. 'What the hell is going on, Taffy?'

Morgan looked sheepish. He brushed the dust down from his clothes, dabbed at blood that dribbled from his nose and gingerly touched the back of his head. 'Nothing, guv . . . A misunderstanding . . .'

'Misunderstanding?' croaked Frost. 'He understood what he was flaming well doing – he was trying to smash your Welsh head in.'

'Let me at him and I'll finish the bloody job,' screamed the handcuffed man, a shaven-headed lout in his late twenties who kept jerking his wrists, trying to snap the handcuffs apart.

Frost peered at him. 'Don't I know you, sunshine?' He clicked his fingers. 'Kenny Leyton . . . robbery with violence. I thought you were inside?'

'I came out last week.' Leyton's face was contorted with rage as he glared at Morgan.

'I hope you left your cell nice and clean because you'll be back again tomorrow,' said Frost. 'I'm charging you with assaulting a police officer.'

Morgan looked dismayed. He tugged at Frost's sleeve. 'No, guv. He was drunk. He didn't mean it.'

'You bet I bloody meant it,' shouted Leyton. He turned to Frost with a provocative grin. 'Come on, copper, charge me. I want to be charged. Let the court know why I want to beat his bleeding brains out.'

Frost's eyes swivelled from one to the other, Leyton furious, Morgan looking embarrassed and guilty. He jabbed a finger at Collier. 'Stay with Leyton. I'll be back in a minute.' Grabbing Morgan's arm, he pushed him into an empty office and slammed the door. 'Right, Taffy. What the flaming hell is going on?'

Morgan hung his head and mumbled to the pattern on the threadbare carpet. 'Nothing, guv. It's trivial. I don't want to press charges.'

'Trivial?' echoed Frost in disbelief. 'A convicted criminal bashing the living daylights out of a police officer? If you don't charge him, then I will.' He moved to the door, but Morgan called him back.

'Wait, guv . . .' The DC slumped down in a chair and put on his hangdog, little boy caught stealing the jam expression, the expression that made weak-kneed women take him to their hearts before taking him to their beds. 'It's a bit embarrassing, guv . . .'

'Then embarrass me,' said Frost, folding his arms and leaning against the wall.

'I met this woman, see. She seemed a nice type . . . I didn't know she was married. Honest, guv, I wouldn't have touched her with a barge pole if I thought she was married.'

'Barge pole!' exclaimed Frost, raising his eyes to the ceiling. 'I bet you touched her with something bigger than a bleeding barge pole.' Then the penny dropped. 'You're not trying to tell me she was Leyton's wife?'

Morgan gave a shamefaced nod.

'A known criminal?' croaked Frost. 'And while he was doing time, you was doing his old lady?'

'I never knew she was his wife, guv – cross my heart.'

'Where did you meet her?'

'The Raven's Arms. I went there for a quiet drink.'

Frost snorted. 'No-one goes to the Raven's Arms for a quiet drink. OK, let's hear the rest of this Mills and Boon love story. Did she take you to her place or was it the first shop doorway you came to?'

'We went to her place, guv.'

'Double bed or single?'

'Double, guv.'

'And you didn't think to ask who usually occupied the other half?'

'You know how it is, guv, the minute their knickers come off the last thing on your mind is asking personal questions.'

Frost sighed and poked a cigarette in his mouth. 'You're a bloody fool, Taffy. Knocking off the wife of a known criminal . . . If Mullett gets to hear of it you can kiss your job goodbye . . . and Leyton wants to cause trouble.'

'I know, guv. Sorry, guv.' Morgan gave Frost his soulful, wide-eyed expression.

'You're not sorry you did it, you're sorry the bastard found you out,' sniffed Frost. He pinched out the cigarette and dropped it in his pocket. 'All right – you nip back to the office and finish off those flaming crime figures. I'll see if I can get you off the hook with Leyton. And then I'm having a word with the canteen – I don't think they're putting enough bromide in your tea.'

Morgan grinned sheepishly and slunk out.

Leyton looked up belligerently as Frost entered the interview room, rubbing his wrists where the cuffs had been removed. 'I'm going to get that randy sod kicked out of the force,' he snarled.

Frost sat at the table then tugged a folded computer print-out from his pocket. 'Bit of advice, sonny. Don't mess about with the police. We can play dirtier than you and there's more of us.'

'He knocked off my wife.'

'He was the only man in Denton who hadn't up to then. It was his turn.'

'She's still my bloody wife.'

Frost unfolded the print-out. 'I've been looking at that electronics warehouse job we pulled you in for – the one where the old night-watchman got beaten up.'

Leyton leant back, arms folded, and smirked. 'You couldn't touch me . . . I had an alibi.'

'That's right,' agreed Frost. 'You said you were in bed with your wife and she backed you up. But what if my randy police officer suddenly remembers he was in bed with her at the time and although his mind was on other things, he was pretty certain you weren't in the bed as well? That would kick your alibi right up the arse. And then I could get a search warrant and make sure some of the stolen loot was found in your house. I could probably splash a bit of the night-watchman's blood on it just to make sure.'

'You bastard . . . You'd plant evidence?'

'Well – we both know you did it . . . I'd just be giving the wheels of justice a squirt of oil.'

Leyton leant across the table. 'All right. So what's the deal?'

'You made a mistake. You thought it was DC Morgan, but it wasn't. You apologize for hitting him and he graciously accepts your apology.'

'You bastard!' said Leyton.

'Apology accepted,' said Frost.

Morgan, suitably shamefaced, sat, lips moving silently, as he transferred figures from a stack of files to the large return that County sent out monthly to waste everyone's time. Opposite him, Frost sat staring again at his car expense claim. Mileage up on last month, but purchase of petrol down by almost half. He must

31

have made a silly mistake on last month's claim but no one in County had spotted it. Tapping the pencil against his teeth, he stared across to the facing wall for inspiration. Pinned up behind Morgan's desk was a poster displaying an enlarged photograph of eight-year-old Vicky Stuart smiling her trusting, gap-toothed smile. MISSING FROM HOME. It had been up nearly nine weeks and in spite of extensive searches and appeals over radio, TV and press, they were no further on in finding her than the day she went missing. The kid was now just another statistic for Taffy's unsolved crime return, the poster a permanent reminder of yet another of his failures. He tore his gaze away and found the bundle of blank petrol receipt forms he had accumulated from various petrol stations in the Division. He passed one over to Morgan. 'Make this out for seventeen gallons.'

Morgan squinted at it. 'Your car doesn't hold seventeen gallons, guv.'

'So I spilt some. Just do it.' Useless in many ways, nobody forged a better petrol receipt than Morgan who scribbled off the receipt, then dragged a tall, unsteady stack of files over towards him. Frost closed his eyes and waited for the inevitable to happen . . . A splatter of files falling all over the floor and the muttered 'Damn!' from Morgan.

'Mind you don't drop them,' murmured Frost, carefully changing a 7 to a 9.

Morgan scooped up the files. A photograph from one of them fluttered to the floor. He retrieved it, tut-tutting and shaking his head in disgust as he looked at it. 'The things some of these swines do to women never fails to shock me, guv.'

Frost took a look. 'Nasty! That's one of Inspector Allen's old cases . . .' The photograph was of a naked woman, on her back in long grass, mouth distorted by a tight gag, eyes open and bulging. Red indentations round the wrists and ankles showed where she had been tied down before being beaten, burnt with a cigarette, raped, then suffocated. 'Linda Roberts,' said Frost, 'a part-time prostitute – twenty-six years old. Allen reckons she picked up a punter who liked a spot of the old sado-masochism but it went too far.'

Morgan shuddered and stuffed the photograph back in the folder. 'Did we get the bloke who did it?'

Frost shook his head. 'Not a sniff. We were afraid he might have developed a taste for this sort of thing, but so far, poor old Linda is the one and only.'

The office door opened, letting in a solid blast of noise from the lobby and a perspiring Sergeant Wells. 'Where's Wonder Woman? I've got an armed robbery for her.'

Frost looked up. 'Haven't seen her for some time . . . Armed robbery?'

'As if we didn't have enough on our bleeding plates. A bloke with a shotgun holds up the all-night filling station and mini-mart near the Eastern Roundabout. This old age pensioner, armed with a shopping bag, decides to do a Clint Eastwood but gets shot in the legs for his trouble . . .' He frowned. 'What's this?' He was looking at the petrol receipt Frost had slapped in his hand.

'Alter that 5 into an 8.'

Wells snatched up a pen and made a quick alteration. Frost frowned. 'You're a lousy forger, Bill. No wonder you haven't got on in the force.' He flashed a sly wink across to Morgan then settled back to listen to the sergeant's knee-jerk reaction.

'The reason I haven't got on in the force,' replied Wells peevishly, 'is because that bastard Mullett blocks my promotion application at every turn.' He stopped dead in mid-splutter, his eyes widening in dismay as he stared out of the window into the car-park. 'Shit!' he croaked. 'What's he doing here at this time of night?'

Frost twisted his head round to see what Wells was staring at. A blue Rover was coasting into the car-park towards the Divisional Commander's designated parking space which was now blocked by the football supporters' coach. They watched, dumbstruck, as the car stopped, reversed, and was manoeuvred into a less prestigious position. Mullett got out, glared at the offending coach, then strode purposefully into the station looking for someone to blame.

Wells was about to dash off to warn everyone that the Divisional Commander was paying one of his sneaky visits when Liz Maud came in. 'I believe you are looking for me, Sergeant?'

'Yes, Acting Inspector, I was,' replied Wells, bridling because he detected she had over-emphasized the word 'sergeant' to rub his nose in the difference in their ranks.

Liz stabbed out an icy stare. 'In case you are un-aware of it, Sergeant, there is no such rank as acting inspector. The correct address is "Inspector". What have you got?'

Glowering, Wells filled her in with details of the armed robbery and watched her leave.

'Stuck-up bloody cow!' he snarled.

'She looks a bit peaky,' said Frost.

'Too much of the other, if you ask me!' said Wells.

A sage nod from Frost. 'Affects me the same way, Bill. I'm having to cut it down to five times a night now.'

Wells grinned and darted off to the lobby.

'A tasty bit of stuff that Liz Maud,' observed Morgan, head raised from his paperwork. 'Not a great looker, but you can sense hidden fires.'

'You'll feel hidden fires if she kicks you up the arse,'

34

said Frost. 'She's already spoken for, mate, so don't try anything on.' There had been a smouldering affair between Liz and DC Burton which seemed to have cooled off of late. 'Stick to ex-cons' wives, Taffy, they're more your mark.'

2

Police Superintendent Mullett, back ramrod straight, sat drumming his fingers on the satin mahogany surface of his desk in his wood-panelled office which Frost called the old log cabin. He could barely contain his annoyance. No parking space, the station like a bear garden and the unsolved crime statistics return he had expected to find in his in-tray so he could take it to County for the meeting in the morning was not there.

A tap at the door which opened to let in a blast of hysterical laughter from the lobby and a worried-looking Sergeant Wells. 'You wanted me, sir?'

Without deigning to look up, Mullett flicked a finger for Wells to close the door. He screwed his face up at the noise. 'What's going on out there, Sergeant – a drunken orgy?'

'Sorry about that, sir—' began Wells, but Mullett's raised hand cut him short.

'And my parking space – my clearly marked, plainly designated parking space – blocked! I was forced to park elsewhere.'

'We didn't think you'd be coming back tonight, sir—'

Another curt chop of the hand sliced him short. 'You didn't know I was coming, but equally you didn't know I was not coming. That is my parking space whether I am here or not. Do I make myself clear?'

'Perfectly clear, sir,' mumbled Wells. 'Sorry, sir.'

Mullett leant back in his chair. 'I presume there is some sort of explanation?'

'It's the coachload of drunks you asked us to detain on behalf of Fenwick Division, sir – inter-Divisional co-operation.'

'Don't use inter-Divisional co-operation as an excuse for sloppiness, Sergeant. Why are they still here? Surely you realize we were only holding them for collection, not keeping them here all night, blocking your Divisional Commander's personal parking area. I want them out!'

'Not quite so simple, sir,' protested Wells. 'Fenwick seem in no hurry to collect them.' He smiled hopefully. 'I was wondering if you might have a word with their Divisional Commander on our behalf . . . ?'

Mullett gave his superior smile. 'That would be an admission of your own failure, Sergeant, and as someone always pressing for promotion, I am sure that is the last thing you would want.'

'Yes, sir,' seethed Wells, moving to the door. 'Anything else, sir?'

'There is one thing,' beamed Mullett. 'Do you think you could rustle me up a cup of coffee . . . I'm parched.' He frowned as the sergeant's closing of the door seemed a little more vigorous than was necessary, then picked up his internal phone to find out what pathetic excuse Frost had for not providing him with the crime statistics.

'Working on them this very minute, Super,' said Frost, hanging up quickly. He returned his attention to Wells who was half-way through telling Frost what a nit-picking bastard Mullett was. 'What flaming figures is the silly sod talking about?'

'The unsolved crime return,' Wells told him. 'He's got to take them to County with him in the morning. He sent you a memo.'

'He knows I don't read bloody memos.' Frost called across to Morgan. 'Any chance you'll finish them tonight, Taffy?'

'As long as they don't have to be accurate, guv.'

'Statistics don't have to be accurate,' said Frost. 'Just give me something to keep him quiet.' The internal phone rang again. 'You'll have them in ten minutes, Super,' said Frost. 'Just checking them for accuracy. What . . . ? I'll tell him.' He put his hand again over the mouthpiece and looked up at Wells. 'Mr Mullett says would you hurry up with his coffee and he'd like some custard creams.'

Wells exploded. 'He can get stuffed. What the hell does he think I'm running here – a bloody café?' Frost took his hand from the mouthpiece. 'The sergeant suggests you should get stuffed, sir.'

Wells went as white as a sheet until he realized Frost had long since terminated the call and was speaking into a dead phone. 'You bastard, Jack! You frightened the life out of me.'

Frost beamed and looked over to Morgan. 'Hurry up, Taffy. The sooner he gets these figures, the sooner he'll go home and we can take the phones off the hook, flop down in the rest room and watch the big fight you're going to video for us.'

The outside phone rang. Fenwick division for Sergeant Wells. As Wells listened his face grew redder and redder. 'Tomorrow?' he shrieked, scarcely believing what he was hearing. 'No damn fear – you pick them up tonight. I haven't got room . . . I . . . And you, too, mate!' He slammed the phone down with such force Frost's paperclip trap leapt in the air and shed its contents all over the desk.

'Everything all right?' asked Frost innocently.

'No, it flaming well isn't. They haven't got anyone available to pick them up tonight so they want us to hang onto them until the morning.' A crashing sound, the shattering of more broken glass and a drunken cheer from the crowded lobby made him grit his teeth. 'They're wrecking the place. What am I going to do with them?'

'Bung them back in the coach,' suggested Frost. 'Then they can pee and puke to their hearts' content and Fenwick can have the pleasure of shovelling it out when they collect them tomorrow.'

Wells' face lit up. 'That, Jack, is genius . . . pure genius.' He rushed out of the office to make the arrangements as Mullett buzzed again demanding his coffee.

Liz Maud swung her car into the High Street, mentally disembowelling Sergeant Bill Wells for dropping her in it with the alleged rape. The illuminated 'Open' sign outside the all-night chemists flared red in her windscreen as she slowed down and stopped the car on the opposite side of the road. Carefully checking there was no-one to see her, she dashed across and entered the shop. The pregnancy kit, small enough to fit snugly in her handbag, cost £11.90. About to cut back across the road again, she had to jump back hurriedly to avoid a speeding car which was lurching from side to side. Flashing blue lights and the wail of a siren signalled the approach of a pursuing area car, hot on its tail. Jordan and Simms. She ducked back in the shadow until it sped past, then slunk over to her own vehicle and on to the scene of the armed robbery.

Wells gawped in disbelief as Jordan and Simms escorted the violently protesting drunken driver into the lobby. Most of the football hooligans were in the coach, but a hard core had refused to co-operate and were lying on the floor, having to be manhandled one by one by perspiring police officers. All a flaming game to them, but Wells was close approaching the end of his tether and now another bloody drunk.

'We've arrested him for drunken driving, Sergeant,' reported Jordan.

'Thank you very much,' croaked Wells. 'Another bleeding drunk – just what I'm short of.' He kicked out savagely at one of the prostrate football fans who was tugging at his trouser leg, trying to topple him over.

'He was veering all over the road, Sergeant – a danger to other motorists – and he refused to be breathalysed.'

The man squinted at Wells through drink-bleared eyes. 'I was coming here anyway, officer. I want to report a serious crime.'

Wells turned the page of the charge book. 'Hard luck – we've got all the crimes we can handle tonight . . . Name?'

'Never mind my name,' slurred the man. 'I've been robbed . . . over four hundred quid. I pay my rates – you bloody investigate.'

'Yes – you bloody well investigate,' yelled the man on the floor staggering to his feet. 'We're all witnesses. The gentleman's made a genuine complaint. He's entitled to justice.'

'You'll get justice round the bleeding ear-hole if you don't shut up,' snapped Wells, signalling for Collier to drag the man out to the coach before he flopped down again. He turned to the drunken driver. 'All right. What's your name?'

'Hughes. Henry Hughes.'

'And what happened?'

'She stole my wallet, all my credit cards and over four hundred quid in cash.'

40

'Who stole them?'

'This tom . . . this flaming tart.'

Frost, darting through the lobby on his way to the canteen, stopped and turned back. This sounded good for a laugh. 'A prostitute?' he asked.

Hughes nodded. 'The cow pinched my wallet.'

'Tell me about it.'

'She was swinging her handbag on the corner of King Street. She wants forty quid. I say OK, so we drive back to her place.'

'And where was her place?'

'Clayton Street.'

Frost nodded. A lot of toms did their business in short-let rooms in Clayton Street. 'What number?'

'I don't know. I just followed her in. I didn't look at the number. I wasn't going to write her a bleeding letter.'

'Then what?' prompted Wells who wanted to get this over.

'We had it away. Forty quid! She wasn't worth forty bleeding pence. I've had inflatable dolls with more reaction than her. Sod forty – I gave her twenty and that was generous.'

'I bet that pleased her?' murmured Frost.

The man blinked at the inspector. 'The cow started screaming and shouting. The names she called me . . . Anyway, I didn't want the hassle of clouting her one, so I ignored her and stamped out.'

'Then what?' asked Frost.

'I gets into my car and drives off. I'd just turned the corner when I realized my flaming wallet was missing. That cow had taken it!'

'Are you sure it was her who took it?' asked Wells.

'There was only me and her in the bleeding room. She must have nicked it from my jacket pocket while I was putting on my shoes.'

'What did you do then?'

'I was back there like a streak of greased lightning. She must have known I was coming back because the door was locked. I kicked and banged and swore, but she wouldn't open up.'

'Probably thought you were a Jehovah's Witness,' said Frost.

'It's not bloody funny,' snarled the man. 'I want her arrested and I want my money back.'

'Arrest her? You don't even know the number of her flat,' said Wells.

'I'd know it if I saw it again. Take me there.'

Wells jabbed a thumb at the two uniformed men. 'Take him there.'

Before they could move there came the sound of a struggle from the corridor and the thud of running feet. The man PC Collier had been dragging to the coach suddenly burst in and promptly sat himself down on the floor with his arms folded, a dishevelled PC Collier following, just too late to stop him. A roar of approval from other drunks on the floor. Wells winced and raised his eyes to heaven. The internal phone rang. He snatched it up. 'What is it?' he barked, quickly changing his tone when he realized it was the Divisional Commander. 'Oh. Sorry, sir. Yes, sir . . . I'm doing the best I can, sir . . . Yes, sir.' He banged the phone down. 'Bloody Mullett! He causes all the trouble, now he wants us to keep the noise down – it's giving him a headache. I'll give the bastard a headache.' He yelled for Jordan and Simms to bring Hughes back. 'Leave him and get these other sods into the coach.' He turned to Frost. 'And Mullett wants to know where the crime statistics return is.'

As if on cue, Morgan poked his head round the door and waved a sheaf of papers. 'I've done the return, guv. All you've got to do is sign it.'

Frost scribbled his signature, not bothering to check the figures which meant little to him anyway. 'Good

42

boy, Taff. As a reward you can visit a prostitute with this gentleman and get his wallet back.' He quickly filled him in. 'And bring her straight back here – no freebies on the way.'

'And bring him back as well,' called Wells, indicating Hughes. 'He's on a drunken driving charge.' He watched Jordan and Simms manhandle another football fan out. What a peaceful flaming night this was turning out to be . . . And it wasn't over yet.

The cashier at the petrol station mini-mart was shaking, sobbing and almost incoherent, so Liz had to rely on the statement taken from her by PC Lambert to find out what had happened. All she could remember was this man, his face covered by a black ski mask, suddenly bursting in with a shotgun, firing it up into the ceiling, then ordering her to empty the till into a carrier bag. An old man who was pottering about in the DIY section suddenly came charging down the aisle, hollering and shouting, hurling whatever came to hand from the shelves at the armed robber. He chucked a can of paint which shed its lid and spilt all over the robber's coat, then hurled himself at the man and tried to wrestle the gun away. In the struggle, the shotgun went off leaving the old boy writhing on the floor, screaming with pain. The robber snatched up the carrier bag of cash and fled. The cashier remembered hearing a sound of an impact as if the getaway car had hit something before roaring away.

The victim, grey-faced and clearly in shock, was being carefully lifted on to a stretcher. 'He's not too badly hurt,' one of the ambulance men told Liz. 'Give the hospital a ring in an hour or so after they've taken the pellets out. He should be able to talk to you then.'

Harding from Forensic was on his knees by the chalked outline of the shot man, carefully avoiding the pool of blood which had mingled with a puddle of white paint, tinging it pink. He beamed up at Liz. 'Clues galore. White paint over his clothes, of course – we'll be able to match it if you catch him – and I reckon the gunman got hit with some of his own shotgun pellets.'

'How do you know?' asked Liz, bending as he pointed to the main pool of blood.

'The victim was shot and fell here – this is his blood. But there's more blood further along.' He ringed with blue chalk some splashes of blood nearer the exit. 'We can safely assume this came from the gunman. Lucky for us we can match the DNA should you catch him. Unluckily for him, he's bleeding pretty badly and will almost certainly require medical attention.'

Liz radioed the station where Bill Wells, sighing audibly at being dragged away from something more important than a lousy armed robbery, reluctantly agreed to contact all hospitals and doctors.

PC Lambert, who had been chaining off the entrances to the service station to stop motorists driving in, reported that the post holding the Fina emblem had been damaged, probably hit by the getaway car. Harding hurried out to check, returning happily to announce there was plenty of dark blue paint scraped from the getaway car to keep him happy. 'Find the car and we can match the paint,' he said. Again Liz radioed the station.

'What is it now?' barked Wells, his voice raised against a background of shouts and crashes.

'All units to look out for a dark blue car with a damaged nearside wing, wanted in connection with an armed robbery,' she told him. 'Approach with caution . . . driver believed to be armed with a shotgun.' She had to repeat herself as Wells couldn't hear over the background. 'Those drunks still there?' she asked.

44

'Yes, they flaming well are!' snapped Wells, banging down the phone.

The ambulance men taking the wounded man to hospital were also taking the woman cashier who was still in a state of shock. As Liz watched the ambulance leave, she spotted the surveillance camera on the forecourt. Excitedly, she pointed it out to Lambert. 'Get the videotape.'

Lambert shook his head. 'Sorry Inspector, we've already checked. The recorder's up the spout. The tape's all snarled up inside and the cashier forgot to report it.'

'Very convenient for the robber,' muttered Liz significantly. She made a mental note to get Morgan to check on the cashier's background as soon as she got back to the station. Suddenly the aisle of shelves blurred in and out of focus and seemed to lurch to one side and there was a roaring in her ears, making her grab at Lambert for support.

'Are you all right?' asked Lambert with concern.

'Of course I'm all right,' she snapped, making an effort to pull herself together. 'Just a bit sick, that's all . . . something I ate.'

She coasted her car into the station car-park, keeping well clear of the coach into which a rabble of noisy drunks were being herded. As they spotted her they let out a torrent of wolf whistles, accompanied by crude gestures. Ignoring them she pushed her way through to her office, clutching her handbag tightly. She hoped to find Morgan in Frost's office as she wanted him to check on the cashier, but it was empty. Frost was in the lobby talking to Bill Wells who acknowledged her with a scowl. 'Any idea where DC Morgan is?'

'He's out getting a punter's wallet back from a tom,' Frost told her. 'He should be back soon.'

45

The explosive roar of the coach engine bursting into life and urgent shouts and yells from the car-park sent them charging down the corridor. Then came the teeth-setting sound of metal grinding against metal. They reached the rear entrance just in time to see the coach, its jeering passengers giving them the 'V' sign, weaving an erratic path to the exit, chased ineffectively by Collier, Simms and Jordan.

Wells' jaw dropped. 'They've driven off in the bloody coach,' he shrilled, staring accusingly at Frost whose idea it was in the first place.

Frost glared back at him. 'Didn't you think to check who had the flaming key?' They glowered at each other.

Giving up the chase and sucking air into spent lungs, Jordan and Simms made their way to the area car. 'We'll soon head them off, Sarge.'

'No, you bloody won't,' bellowed Wells. 'Let the next Division have the pleasure of catching the sods. Chase them until they reach our boundary, then get a puncture and radio that you've lost them.' He was grinning broadly at this happy outcome when the grin froze solid on his face. 'Look!' he croaked, pointing a wavering finger at Mullett's blue Rover, the Divisional Commander's pride and joy. It was now clear what the sound of metal grinding against metal had been. The rear wing was crumpled and the rear passenger door punched in. His mouth opened and closed. He could barely get the words out. 'Look what they've done to his motor!'

Frost looked and winced. 'Perhaps he won't notice.'

'Won't notice?' shrieked Wells. 'There's over a thousand quid's worth of damage there – of course he'll bloody notice!!'

Even before they reached the lobby they could hear the internal phone shrilling angrily. Wells stared at it. 'It's bloody Mullett. What shall I tell him?'

46

'Go on the offensive,' suggested Frost. 'Ask him why he hasn't made you to up inspector.'

Even at one o'clock on a cold winter's morning there were still people furtively scuttling along the back streets. A drunk clutching a lager can suddenly lurched in front of the car without warning and Morgan had to pound the horn and swerve violently to avoid hitting him. To express his gratitude the drunk jerked two fingers at the car, hurled the lager can at it and let off a stream of oaths before lumbering off into the dark. 'You should have run the bastard down,' grunted Hughes, who clearly had no fellow feeling for other drunks. Nearing their destination, they passed through the red light area where one lone prostitute, shivering in an artificial fur coat, forced a welcoming smile and moved forward hopefully as the car approached, slumping back against the wall as it drove past.

'She's a bit long in the tooth,' commented Morgan.

'Looks like the Queen bleeding Mum,' said Hughes, now staring ahead. 'It's down there!' He directed Morgan down a side street lined with parked cars. 'That's the place!' He indicated a three-storeyed building with a multitude of bell pushes alongside a front door which was swinging ajar. A couple of lights shone weakly from upstairs windows. Morgan parked behind a dark brown car which had its tyres slashed and the windscreen and side windows shattered. 'Nice neighbourhood,' he muttered. Hughes leapt out and bounded into the house. Morgan followed cautiously and slowly. If there was trouble, let Hughes have it. Some of these toms had long sharp fingernails and very short tempers.

He trotted behind Hughes, up uncarpeted stairs to the first landing where three doors faced them, each bearing a card affixed with a drawing pin showing the

47

name of the occupant. Hughes stopped outside the end door. The card read 'Lolita'. As he pounded it with his fist, it swung open. He charged in. The woman lying on the bed didn't look up. 'Where's my wallet, you cow!' She didn't move. He went over and shook her, then let out a cry and stared in horror and disgust at his hands. They were red and sticky with blood. 'Flaming hell.' He backed away from the bed, wiping his hands down the front of his jacket. 'Flaming hell!'

Morgan elbowed him out of the way. She was lying on her back, on top of the bedclothes, eyes wide open. A trickle of blood from her mouth had dribbled down to her chin. All she wore was a white bra and white panties, the panties heavily stained with blood which had oozed from a deep gash in her stomach. She didn't look very old . . . in her mid-twenties at the most. Very gently, Morgan felt for a pulse in her neck. No sign of life, but the flesh was still warm. She hadn't been dead very long.

As he fumbled for his radio to call the station there was the slamming of the door and a clatter of running footsteps behind him. He spun round and dashed to the top of the stairs. Hughes had gone.

3

There were too many people packed into too small a space. The single bar electric fire screwed on the wall, the dials of its prepayment meter spinning madly, belted out its one kilowatt of heat making the room a sweat-smelling oven.

'Turn that bloody thing off before we all cook,' ordered Frost. He opened the window, but the blast of cold night air that was sucked in immediately turned the room into a fridge. He slammed it shut and looked again at the still figure on the bed.

Dr McKenzie, the police surgeon, overtired and overworked, had paid his flying visit on his way to a terminally ill patient and had officially pronounced her dead, probably within the hour. Confirming death was all he was paid to do – let Drysdale, the snotty-nosed Home Office pathologist, who was paid ten times as much for far less work, determine the cause of death. There was little love lost between Dr McKenzie and Drysdale.

It was a tiny cubicle of a room. The original rooms had been subdivided with plasterboard partitions to pack in as many short-stay tenants as possible. There was just room for the bare essentials: a single divan, a plastic-coated chipboard bedside cabinet supporting a phone, also with a prepayment meter, and a narrow simulated pine wardrobe.

Morgan, whose shamefaced, mumbled apologies had been cut short by Frost, had been sent off with a couple of uniforms to look for the runaway Hughes.

And as if there weren't enough people in the tiny room, Liz flaming Maud had put in an appearance. Frost forced a smile, but could have done without her. She smiled back, but inwardly she was seething. No-one had bothered to tell her about the murdered prostitute. She had only found out by accident when she realized everyone else was missing. She was looking after Inspector Allen's cases, one of which was Linda Roberts, the tortured and murdered prostitute. This new killing could well be by the same man, so this should be her investigation, not Frost's, and as soon as she could drag him away to have a word in private she would demand he hand it over to her. In the meantime she was full of contempt for DC Morgan. 'It's beyond belief! A key witness – probably a prime suspect – and he just lets him run off.'

Frost wasn't too concerned. 'Hughes can't get far. We've got his car and we know his address. He's probably just round the corner spewing his guts up.'

'That's not the damn point!' snapped Liz. 'The man's bloody useless.'

'He's better than nothing,' said Frost, who had suddenly found an unexpected soft spot for Morgan now that the DC had finished the long and tiresome outstanding crime statistical return for him. Let Morgan do all the paperwork and he could be as bloody inefficient as he liked.

Frost gave a grunt of annoyance as he was jostled to one side by Harding from Forensic who was chalking around some splashes of blood on the floor by the bedside cabinet. No sooner had he moved than he was jostled again as the photographer moved in to do his stuff. There were too many people in too small a space and he could have done without Liz Maud breathing down his neck.

He squeezed against the wall and again looked through the red and black plastic handbag from the bedside cabinet. It contained close on £300 in crumpled five and ten pound notes, a lipstick, a powder compact, and three packs of condoms. He kept diving his fingers down the various compartments hoping to find some kind of identification but there was nothing. They had no idea who the dead girl was. He shuffled past Harding and bent over the bed to stare down at the pale face. 'Who are you, love?' he asked as his eyes travelled from the blood round her swollen nose and mouth, down to the gouts and thin snail trails of blood which patterned her bare stomach and stained the white panties.

Once again he checked her hands which were just starting to feel cold to the touch. No cuts or marks which would indicate she had tried to defend herself against her attacker's knife. Her long, scarlet-painted nails were unbroken, but her wrists showed bruising where she had been gripped tightly by her assailant. He needed the bloody knife and a team was out searching for it in rubbish bins, drains, gutters, hedges . . . Her killer would not want to be found with it on him, and would have dumped it at the first opportunity. Frost had also radioed through to the station asking them to give Hughes's car a thorough going-over. A bloodstained knife in the glove compartment would do wonders to narrow the field of suspects!

He looked up hopefully as Jordan and Simms came back. They had been sent knocking on doors in the building to ask if anyone had seen or heard anything, or perhaps knew the name of the dead woman. 'No joy,' reported Simms. 'Too late for most toms and the rest must have scarpered when they heard us arrive.'

'With all this activity you'll probably find most of

the girls will steer clear of the place until it dies down,' added Jordan. 'They only rent these rooms by the week and they're not going to get much trade with the fuzz crawling all over the place.'

'I'm sure the landlords keep meticulous records,' said Frost. 'I want names and addresses of all their tenants. We must know who this poor cow is.' His radio paged him.

'Wells calling Inspector Frost.'

'Yes?'

'That drunk – Harry Hughes. I sent a car round to the address he gave us. They've never heard of him.'

Frost hissed annoyance. 'The bastard! Get ownership details for his motor.'

'I've already checked. The registered owner sold it for cash last week . . . never took the buyer's name and the car hasn't been re-registered.'

'Shit!' hissed Frost. 'Let's hope we can pick him up before he makes it home.' He dropped the radio back in his pocket and revised his good opinion of Taffy bloody Morgan.

The phone on the bedside cabinet suddenly rang. No-one moved, then Harding reached out for it, but was stopped by Frost who crooked a finger to Liz. 'You answer it. You're Lolita. If it's a client, get him round here. He might know her name.'

Liz picked up the phone. 'Lolita,' she announced in what she hoped was a sexy voice. 'Yes, I'm free at the moment. Why not come over . . . we could take our time . . . Good, I'll be waiting.' She replaced the receiver and nodded. 'He's a regular. He'll be here in five minutes.'

Frost ordered all police cars to be moved from the street in case they scared the man off. They waited. Frost, an unlit cigarette dangling from his lips, lolled against the bedside cabinet, looking down at the dead girl on the bed. 'How old do you reckon she is?' he mused. 'Twenty – twenty-one? Three hundred quid in her handbag for one night's work and I've been slogging my guts out for three hours trying to fiddle a fiver on my car expenses. I'm in the wrong profession.'

Liz Maud, at the window, was staring down into the windswept street. The punter should have been here by now. 'I'm not sure that I fooled him.'

'You fooled him,' Frost assured her. 'After hearing that sexy voice he won't be able to get his dick out fast enough – it made me feel the same.'

She twitched a polite smile. A room with a blooded corpse on the bed wasn't the place for tasteless jokes. The street was silent and deserted. No sound of footsteps or a car. Then she stiffened. A shadow crept from around the corner. A man, walking briskly, making for the door of the flats. 'It's him!' Frost joined her at the window. 'What did I tell you . . . Look at the dirty sod, he's nearly running. Blimey, it's Mullett! Everyone hide!'

Only Collier took him seriously. The rest were too well versed in the inspector's dubious sense of humour to do anything but grin.

Footsteps tripping up the stairs. Liz stood by the bed, blocking the body from view. Simms and Jordan were on either side of the door, ready to grab. A tentative knock.

'Come in,' husked Liz.

The door creaked open and a man smartly dressed in a dark suit and matching overcoat bounded eagerly into the room, stopping dead in his tracks when he saw Liz. 'You're not . . .' he began, spinning round in alarm as the door slammed shut behind him and Jordan and Simms barred the way out. 'What the hell . . . ?'

Frost stepped forward and flashed his dog-eared warrant card. 'Police, sir. I'm afraid it's not going to be the erotic experience you were anticipating.' But the man, the blood draining from his face, wasn't listening. He was staring over Frost's shoulder. He could see the girl. 'Oh my God . . . !'

There was now no room to move so Frost took the man's arm to lead him outside to the landing. The man backed out, unable to tear his eyes away from the body. 'Is she . . . ?' He couldn't bring himself to say 'dead'.

Frost nodded. 'I'm afraid so. How well did you know her?'

'Know her?' The man waved his hands in protest. 'I don't know her. This is all a mistake, officer. I was looking for somewhere else. I've come to the wrong place.' He tried to move to the stairs, but Frost's grip on his arm tightened almost to the point of pain.

'Don't sod us about, sir. You phoned – you're a regular. What was her name?'

'Name? They don't tell you their real name any more than I tell them mine.' He fumbled in his pocket. 'She gave me this.'

A cheaply printed business card, green ink on grey cardboard. 'Lolita for Discreet and Lingering Naughty Fun – Denton 224435.'

Frost took the card. 'Lingering naughty fun? What's that – sado-masochism?'

The man flushed brick red. 'No, it damn well isn't, just . . .' He fluttered his hands vaguely, '. . . fun.'

'The poor cow didn't have much fun tonight,' said Frost. 'Any idea who killed her?'

'Of course not,' spluttered the man. 'Why on earth are you asking me?'

'Because at the moment, sir, you're all we've got. Did she mention any punters she was worried about?'

'I didn't visit her to discuss her life history, officer. I'm sorry. I can't help you. I want to go.'

Frost's grip on his arm remained firm. 'We can't

always have what we want, sir. Fill me in on some background. How did you first get to know her?'

'I happened to be driving past King Street and saw her plying for hire with the other girls. She was a new face and didn't look quite so raddled as most of the others so I thought I'd give her a go. We came back here and afterwards she gave me her card: said I should phone her the next time.'

'How many next times were there?'

'Five . . . six . . . I didn't keep count.'

Frost squeezed some life into his scar with his free hand. It was bitterly cold on the landing with the front door wide open. He gave the man his hard stare and noticed that he seemed to be avoiding his gaze. 'I think you know something you're not telling us, sir.'

'This is ridiculous. I don't know anything.'

'Tell you what, sir, let's go back to the station. If we wait long enough you might remember something important.'

'Look, officer . . . I can't get involved . . . I'm married. If my wife found out . . .'

Frost gave him a broad grin. 'That's a good idea, sir. What about if I drive you home, we wake up your wife and I question you in front of her. It might jog your memory.'

The man looked both frightened and angry. 'You bastard!'

Frost beamed happily back. 'Funny – people often say that to me, sir. I don't know why. So you have something to tell me?'

'I'm not making a statement. I'm just telling you something. I was here two nights ago. As I was getting dressed the phone rang. She answered it, all sort of sexy at first, then her face went white. Whoever was phoning had frightened the shit out of her. She was shaking like a leaf. She said, "Why don't you

55

leave me alone?'' – or something like that – then banged the phone down. I asked what it was about and she said it was nothing.'

'And you've no idea who the call was from?'

'No. Please can I go now?'

There was little point in detaining him further. Frost took the man's name and address then let him go. As he bolted thankfully down the stairs and out into the street, a gleaming black Rolls-Royce pulled up outside. The Home Office pathologist, Drysdale, a thin, austere figure, in a long black overcoat, looking like an undertaker. He was followed by his female secretary, a fading blonde who was always at his elbow taking notes, seemingly unfazed by the horrors he would delve into, but nervous of the winks and leers she all too often got from that awful Inspector Frost. She remembered the time she was bending to pick something up when a finger was jabbed in her rear and a raucous voice cackled, 'How's that for centre?' She blushed at the memory of it as she scudded up the stairs behind her master. 'What have you got for me this time?' sniffed Drysdale.

'A nice warm dead tom,' Frost told him, opening the door and ushering them both into the packed hothouse of a room.

Drysdale's nose wrinkled. 'I can't work in these conditions. Get everyone outside, please.'

Frost ordered everyone, except Liz, who looked as if she intended staying put anyway, to wait outside. Drysdale, staring fixedly at the figure on the bed, removed his overcoat and, without looking, held it out and let it go in the secure knowledge that his secretary would leap forward to catch it and fold it neatly before it had a chance to hit the floor.

His initial examination was brief. He bent over, his nose almost touching the blooded stomach as he examined the knife wounds. He then transferred his attention to the face and neck. 'She was on the bed when you found her?'

Frost nodded.

'She wasn't killed on the bed. She was standing when she was stabbed.' He pointed. 'See how the blood initially flowed downwards . . . but then changes direction as she was laid on her back?'

Frost gave a curt nod. He had worked all this out for himself.

Drysdale took a pad of cotton wool from his bag and carefully cleaned away a small area of blood from the stomach. 'Lots of blood. The wounds are deep, but relatively superficial.' He turned his attention to the hands, examining them as Frost had done. 'No cuts that would suggest she tried to defend herself. Bruising from manual pressure on the wrists.' Lastly he lifted the head from the pillow and moved back the long, black hair, revealing extensive bruising on each side of the neck. He opened the mouth and shone a small torch inside, then nodded. 'Death caused by manual strangulation.' Behind him, the blonde secretary's pen flew over her shorthand note-book, taking down her master's findings.

'You're bang on form tonight, doc,' said Frost approvingly. 'You haven't missed a thing Dr McKenzie spotted.'

Drysdale's lips tightened. He and the lowly Dr McKenzie were sworn enemies ever since the doctor disputed, and eventually overturned, part of his evidence at a local coroner's court. 'If the good doctor spotted it, it must be screamingly obvious.' He studied the face. 'Bruising round the eye, probably the result of a blow from a fist.' He lifted the head from the pillow again and slipped his hand underneath so he could explore the back of the scalp. 'Minor contusions,' he murmured to his secretary, 'and . . .' he withdrew his hand and looked at his fingertips, '. . . a small amount of bleeding.' He looked up at Frost. 'Did the good Dr McKenzie spot that?'

'No,' said Frost, wiping the triumphant smirk from Drysdale's face by adding, 'He didn't – but I did!' He showed the pathologist some small red smudges, ringed with Harding's blue chalk on the wall above the splodge of blood on the thin carpeting. 'I reckon she was standing here. As he strangled her she jerked her head back and banged it on the wall . . .'

Drysdale sniffed his grudging agreement. He liked to be the one with the theories. 'Do we know her name?'

'Not yet, doc.' Frost flashed the green business card. 'You don't indulge in naughty lingering fun by any chance?'

Drysdale flushed angrily. 'No, I don't.' He snapped his fingers for his secretary to pass him a mercury thermometer and took the room temperature. A second finger snap produced a clinical thermometer which he slipped under the armpit of the dead girl. He studied the reading and did a mental calculation. 'She's been dead about an hour. Ninety minutes at the most.'

Frost nodded his agreement. 'You're probably right, doc . . . The bloke who was enjoying her favours about an hour ago was pretty certain she was still alive.'

Drysdale signalled his secretary that he wanted his overcoat, holding out his arms as she helped him on with it. 'I've finished for now. You can remove the body when you like. I'll perform the autopsy tomorrow morning. Eight o'clock.' He stared significantly at Frost who was always rolling up at post-mortems anything up to half an hour late. 'It would be a welcome change if you were there on time.' With a curt nod to Liz, he took his leave.

As he left, the others filed back in. The phone

58

shrilled. Frost held up a hand for silence and again signalled for Liz to answer it. 'If it's another punter, get him in. We've got to find out who she is.'

Liz picked up the phone. 'Lolita . . .' As she listened, her expression changed. She frantically beckoned Frost over, holding the receiver away from her ear so he could listen in, but as he reached her the caller hung up, leaving Liz scowling at the buzz of the dialling tone. 'Damn.' She jiggled the rest so she could dial 1471.

'A punter?' asked Frost.

She shook her head. 'No. A man. He said, "That was just a taste, Lolita . . . next time it will be something really serious . . ."' The pay phone wouldn't let her dial 1471 until she inserted a pound coin. She obtained the caller's number, then got through to the exchange for the caller's location. 'Damn,' she said again, hanging up. The call came from a public phone box in King Street.

Without much hope, Frost sent a car round in case the caller might still be there. 'And I want this line tapped and all incoming calls monitored and recorded.' Back to Liz. 'Would you recognize the voice again?'

She pursed her lips in thought. 'I might, I'm not sure. He sounded a nasty piece of work.' Now would be a good time to tell Frost she wanted to take over the case before he got too involved. 'Could I have a word – in private?'

'Sure.' They went outside to the landing, pressing against the wall as the two undertaker's men brought a black-painted coffin up the stairs for the removal of the body to the mortuary. 'What can I do for you, love?'

From inside the room came the crackle of heavy duty plastic being unfolded and then the hiss of the long zip on the body bag. Liz closed the door. 'A

59

prostitute killed by a punter . . . could be the same man who killed Linda Roberts, which is one of my cases. I should be leading this investigation.'

Frost had doubts that the two cases were connected – tonight's tom hadn't been tortured – but if Liz took over, she would have to attend the crack of dawn autopsy and he could have a few hours' lie-in. 'It's yours, love,' he told her. 'I never fight for more work . . .'

'Mind your backs, please!' called the big, red-faced undertaker cheerfully. They moved to one side so the coffin could be man-handled down the stairs and out through the front door. As they watched, the uniformed officer on duty at the front door called up to them: 'Urgent message for Inspector Maud. Would you contact the station. Something to do with that armed robbery.'

PC Lambert in Control had taken the call. A near hysterical woman, almost incoherent, just sobbing and sobbing. He had to squeeze the details out of her drop by drop. 'Whatever the trouble we can help you, madam. Can you tell me your name?'

'My name? What does my name matter? They shot him. They stole our car. He's bleeding to death.'

'Shot? Who's been shot?' Lambert clicked his fingers urgently to gain Sergeant Wells' attention.

'My husband. There's blood everywhere.'

'Where are you?' He signalled for Wells to listen in on the other earpiece.

'They shot him . . . They stole our car . . .' She again broke down into uncontrollable sobbing.

Lambert tried to calm her. 'We can help you, madam, but we must know where you are.'

'The public call box . . . corner of Forest Road . . .'

'Is that where your husband is?'

'No – but I can take you to him.'

Wells put down the earpiece and dialled for an ambulance.

'Wait there, madam,' said Lambert. 'Don't leave the phone box . . . an ambulance is on its way.' He hung up and radioed the message to Liz Maud.

As Detective Inspector Maud drove towards Denton Woods, an area car, siren blaring, roared past in the opposite direction clearing the way for a following ambulance which had already picked up the victim and his wife. She swore softly. If she hadn't seen them she would have wasted precious time searching for them in the woods. She squealed the car into a tight U turn and tagged on behind the area car. Damn, damn, damn . . . She had played this all wrong. She should have asked Frost to take over the armed robbery so she could concentrate on the murder case. She'd put this in hand as soon as she got back to the station.

The grim shape of the Victorian Denton General Hospital loomed up ahead and the ambulance turned off down an 'Ambulances Only' lane, while the area car, Liz following closely, drove to a parking area near the main entrance. She skidded to a stop behind them and confronted them, eyes blazing, before they had a chance to get out of their car. 'Next time you damn well let me know you've left the scene with the victim,' she snapped.

The two men, PCs Baker and Howe, looked at each other in puzzlement. 'We told the station,' said Howe. 'Sergeant Wells said he would let you know.'

Wells! Bloody Wells, up to his tricks again. Her radio buzzed. This would be him, belatedly passing on the message, hoping that by now she was floundering in the woods. 'Yes?' she snapped.

'Acting Inspector Maud—' began Wells.

61

She cut him short. 'Sorry to disappoint you, Sergeant, but it didn't work.' She clicked off, still seething.

'They'll be in Casualty,' Howe told her, leading the way down the long echoing corridor.

'Fill me in,' she said.

'Mr and Mrs Redwood – both in their seventies. They were driving back from a friend's house and as they went through Forest Lane they saw a man lying at the side of the road, another man bending over him waving to flag them down. They stopped, thinking the man was injured. Redwood switched off the engine and got out. The next thing he knew there's a shotgun stuck up his nose and they were demanding his car keys. Like a silly sod, Redwood makes a run for it, so this bloke calmly shoots him in the legs, grabs the keys, turfs out the old dear and they both drive off leaving the old boy bleeding and the old girl screaming.'

'Was this before or after the armed robbery?' asked Liz.

'Before. They nicked the car to do the job.'

Liz frowned. 'Why nick it? What happened to their own car?'

Howe shrugged. 'No idea. Perhaps it broke down.'

'Then it's got to be in the woods, somewhere near where they ambushed the couple . . . Did you look?'

'No – our main concern was getting the old boy to the hospital.'

'Well, he's here now . . . Get back there and look. I'll take over here.'

They turned back to the main entrance as she followed the signs to 'Accident and Emergency' where, even at that late hour, there were several people, some the obvious victims of pub fights, waiting for attention. She thought she recognized a couple of them from the coachload of drunken football supporters at the station earlier.

'They've taken Mr Redwood straight up to the theatre,' the staff nurse told her. 'That's his wife over there.' She nodded towards an elderly woman in a thick grey woollen coat who was strangling a handkerchief to death with gloved hands. The old lady looked up anxiously as Liz went over, thinking it might be the nurse with news of her husband. Liz sat on the bench beside her.

'Can you tell me what happened?'

The story came out a few disjointed words at a time. She had little to add to what she had already told the two policemen. 'They shot him – in cold blood – they shot him . . .'

Liz nodded in sympathy. 'Can you describe them?'

'It all happened so quickly . . . They were medium height . . . in their mid-twenties, I think . . . dark clothes . . . zip-up jackets. The one with the gun had this black ski mask thing hiding his face and the other one wore a blue baseball cap, the peak pulled down. He had a wispy beard, and he wore an ear-ring, a silver stud thing in his right ear. When the other one shot my husband, he laughed, he thought it was a great joke.'

'When they spoke, what did they sound like?'

'Just ordinary. I think they were local . . . they didn't say much, just "Give us the keys." '

Liz persisted with her questioning, but got little more from the woman except that she doubted if she would recognize either of them again. A tired-looking doctor, making a great effort to stifle his yawns, approached them. 'We've sent your husband up to Nightingale Ward for the night, Mrs Redwood. His injuries are minor, but he's in a state of shock. Hopefully he can go home tomorrow.'

'His leg?'

'We've got all the pellets out and cleaned him up. No permanent damage.' He pointed to the staff nurse. 'The nurse will take you to the ward.'

'Is he in a fit state to answer questions?' asked Liz.

The doctor shook his head. 'He's still groggy from the anaesthetic . . . Best wait until the morning.'

She smiled her thanks. This suited her. She wanted to get back to the more important murder inquiry. Frost could take over the questioning of Redwood in the morning. She radioed the description of the two men to Control, then made her way back to her car. She was almost at the exit doors when a red-faced and panting young nurse caught up with her. 'Inspector. The old gentleman who was shot in the petrol station. He wants to speak to you. Says it's important.'

Damn and double damn. Liz hesitated, trying to think of a reason to get out of seeing him. The longer she delayed getting back to the murder investigation, the more Frost would be getting his heels dug in too far to give it up. This was her case. A successful murder inquiry would give her chance of promotion the boost it needed.

'Inspector . . . ?' said the nurse, waiting for her reply.

Liz sighed and forced a smile. 'Would you take me to him, please.'

With the body and Liz Maud out of the way they were able to move furniture about and give the room a thorough search. This produced two major finds. A bloodstained flick-knife was found under the divan bed, probably kicked there during the struggle. 'Get it checked for prints,' said Frost, who then remembered the green business card in his pocket. He passed it over to Detective Sergeant Hanlon. 'If we haven't found out who the poor cow is by the morning, Arthur, show this to the local print shops. They might come up with a name.'

Hanlon wasn't too sure. 'You can run these off on a home computer now, Jack. She probably printed it herself.'

'Try anyway,' said Frost.

And then Simms, who was dragging the wardrobe away from the wall, yelled with excitement. 'Something here, Inspector.' Wedged between the wardrobe and the wall was a wallet. Frost took it carefully by the edges and flicked through the contents. Banknotes to the value of some £400, credit cards and credit card receipts and a diary full of telephone numbers. Frost beamed. 'Our drunken friend's missing wallet,' he announced. 'And he told us a porky about his name . . . it's Gladstone . . . Robert Gladstone and he lives in Denton.' He radioed for Morgan to go and pick him up.

One of the search parties radioed in to report they had had no luck in finding the missing knife. 'Ah!' said Frost. 'Might be a good idea to let them know we've already found it.' There was little more he could do on the spot, so he left them to get on with it and drove back to the station.

Gladstone, now sobered up, looked uneasily at Frost. He was wearing a white, one-piece overall provided for him while his own clothes were away for forensic examination. 'Look . . . I don't want to get involved in this. You've got no right '

'Shut up!' said Frost cheerfully, dropping into the chair opposite and sticking a cigarette into his mouth. 'Do you want to confess now, or shall we waste time beating you up and claiming you fell down the stairs while drunk?'

Gladstone stared warily at Frost, not certain

whether to take this seriously or not. 'I don't have to put up with this. I'm the victim here.'

Frost dragged the cigarette from his mouth, eyes opened wide in mock amazement. 'You're the victim? I thought the poor cow on the bed was the victim!' He nodded for Morgan to start up the tape machine to record the interview.

'I came to you to report a crime.'

'You reported the wrong one, though, didn't you? I suppose it slipped your mind to tell us you'd killed her.'

'Killed her! That's bloody stupid. If I killed her, why did I take that dozy Welsh cop back to her place?'

'You killed her, then you panicked and drove off, then you realized she'd nicked your wallet . . . You didn't have the guts to go back in case you were spotted, or in case some other punter had already found the body and called the police.'

'That's bloody ridiculous!'

'If we found a body and your wallet, we wouldn't have wasted time looking for anyone else to pin it on, would we? You know how we like to jump to conclusions.'

'You're jumping to conclusions now. I told you what happened.'

'Then tell me again. It might sound less like a pack of lies the second time round.' Frost dribbled smoke which rolled across the table between them like a creeping barrage and put on his look of absolute disbelief as the man told his story.

'I'm driving down King Street eyeing the talent when I spots this one, leaning against the phone box. I hadn't seen her before and I fancied a bit of fresh meat so I beckons her over. I said, "How much?" she says, "Forty quid" and I said, "You'd better be bleeding good for that, love," and she answers, "Try me." She hops in my motor car and directs me to her place. I thought I was on to a winner. She was doing all her stuff, squeezing the old thigh and what-not in the car, but as soon as I pulled up outside her gaff, she seemed to change.'

'How do you mean?

He shrugged. 'It was as if something had upset her. She just lost interest in me.'

'Perhaps she'd just felt the size of your dick?' suggested Frost.

'Bloody funny! Anyway, I follow her up the stairs, she strips off and we gets down to it.'

'And . . . ?'

'She was rubbish – just lay there like a bleeding wet fish studying the cracks in the ceiling.'

'And you complained?'

'You bet I did. I told her she was crap and if I paid her what she was worth she'd get sod all. I offered twenty which was bleeding generous. She told me to stick it up my arse and pay the agreed price.'

'Just love talk, then. Was that when you knifed her?'

Gladstone glared at Frost. 'I only stuck one thing in her and it wasn't a bleeding knife.'

A tentative tap at the door. Wearily, Frost pushed himself up. No-one would interrupt the questioning of a murder suspect unless it was important. He opened the door. Bill Wells beckoned him outside. 'Forensic have matched the prints on the knife, Jack. They're the tom's . . . no other prints.'

'Shit!' He scratched his chin in thought. 'Her prints . . . which means it was probably her knife. She must have cut herself in the struggle. Has the lab checked for blood on Gladstone's clothes yet?'

'They're still working on it. I'll let you know as soon as I hear. Oh, and Mr Mullett wants to see you.'

'Bloody hell! I thought the sod had gone home. What did he say about his motor?'

'Nothing I could repeat.'

Frost nodded and returned to the interview room. 'Right . . . so she came at you with a knife . . . then what?'

'Knife? Of course she didn't come at me with a knife. She came at me with her bleeding long fingernails. I didn't mind them digging in my back, but when she tried to scratch me eyes out . . .'

'Was that when you strangled her?'

'Strangled her? I never touched her!'

Frost leant across the table. 'Show me your hands.'

Frowning, Gladstone put his hands, palms upwards, on the table. Frost turned the right hand over and tapped the knuckles. They were grazed with a dribble of blood and slightly swollen. 'You punched her . . . she had a black eye. Don't bother denying it, we can get Forensic to match skin samples.'

'All right, so I hit her – once – and in self-defence . . . I didn't want my eyeballs stuck on the ends of her painted bleeding fingernails. I finished getting dressed and got the hell out of there.'

'Slow down,' urged Frost. 'You've missed out the bit about wrapping your hands round her neck and squeezing the life out of the poor cow.'

'The poor cow was alive, well and effing and blinding as I left. I drove off, realized the bitch had nicked my wallet, so . . . back I go . . .'

'Is this when you strangled her?'

'How many more bleeding times . . . I didn't even get back in . . . The cow had locked the door on me.'

'The door wasn't locked when I took you back there,' said Morgan.

'Of course it wasn't, you Welsh twit – she had to open it to let the killer in . . . unless he was already in there. Come to think of it, I did hear a man's voice.'

'And you've only just remembered it,' cut in Frost. 'Do me a bloody favour!'

Gladstone leant back in the chair and folded his

arms defiantly. 'All right. If you're not going to believe anything I say, I'm not saying another word. I want a solicitor.'

'Your prerogative,' said Frost. He watched Gladstone being led back to a cell, then yawned and stretched his arms wearily. He wondered if there would be time to watch the videoed fight in the rest room before the duty solicitor arrived and he wished Liz Maud would hurry back so she could take over this case.

'You won't forget Mr Mullett wants to see you,' reminded Morgan.

'It's one treat after another,' said Frost, pushing himself up, but before he could do so, Bill Wells came in. 'Good news, Jack.'

'Mullett's gone home?'

'Not quite as good as that. Forensic phoned. Traces of blood on Gladstone's jacket which match the blood from the knife wound.'

Frost expelled a stream of cigarette smoke in a happy sigh of relief. 'We've got him then. That's the clincher we need. He can lie and deny it as much as he flaming well likes, but there's only one way he could have got her blood on his jacket . . .' His voice tailed off as he became aware that Morgan was wriggling uncomfortably in the chair next to him. 'What's the matter, Taffy – do you want to do a wee?'

'No, guv . . .' He was squeezing his hands and staring at the ground in embarrassment, hoping Bill Wells would leave. 'Something I should have mentioned earlier,' he mumbled.

Sensing something tasty, Bill Wells kicked the door shut and leaned forward with interest.

'Go ahead, Taff,' urged Frost. 'We're all friends here. What have you done – had it off with Mrs Mullett?'

'Nothing like that, guv. It's about Gladstone. When I took him back to the flat . . .'

'Yes?' prompted Frost.

'When I went back to the flat with him, he was up the stairs and in the room before I could stop him. By the time I got there he was shaking her and demanding to know where his wallet was.'

Frost's jaw sagged. 'Are you telling me you let him touch the body?'

'To be fair, guv, I didn't know there was going to be a body.'

'So any blood on his jacket could well have got there then?'

Morgan nodded miserably. 'I thought I'd better mention it.'

'Flaming heck,' said Wells, dropping into the vacant chair. 'I've heard some stupid things in my time—'

'Yes,' cut in Frost, 'mainly about me. Your phone's ringing, Bill.'

Wells strained his ears. 'I can't hear it.'

'Whether it's ringing or not – go and answer it!'

Reluctantly, Wells left, taking his time, hoping to hear more, but Frost waited patiently until the sergeant was out of earshot.

'A bit of a balls-up, Taff, to put it mildly?'

Morgan nodded his dejected agreement.

'We all make balls-ups, son. I've been known to make the odd one myself, but when it's a murder inquiry you don't keep it a bloody secret.'

'I know, guv . . . I'm sorry, guv . . .'

The DC was the picture of misery. No point in nagging him any more, the damage was done. Frost chewed at his knuckles, trying to think of a way to salvage the situation. 'The thing is this, Taff. Are we dealing with a clever bastard who deliberately got in there first so there would be a reason for the blood on his jacket? He doesn't strike me as that clever, but you

70

never can tell by appearances. Mullett doesn't look a complete twat, but he is.' He stared up at the ceiling. 'I think we've got to let him go.'

'Let him go?' echoed Morgan.

'We've got nothing to hold him on. When his solicitor turns up he'll tear our case to shreds.'

'I'm sorry guv. It's all my fault.'

'No. In a way, you've helped, Taffy. You've made me look at it from another angle. If he was that bloody clever, why would he run away? Why would he give us a fake name and address?' He stood up. 'I don't think he did it. We let him go. We can always pull him in again if we're hard up for another suspect.' He yawned. 'What a bleeding night; false gen about the missing kid, the pillow burglar strikes again, an armed robbery and a dead tom. If it wasn't for Mullett's car being smashed it would be a complete wash-out.' He snapped his fingers. 'Mullett! Let's see what he wants.'

Mullett was in the car-park examining what those drunken hooligans had done to his Rover. The wing was crumpled, the rear light smashed. It was in no state to be driven to County tomorrow. He'd be a laughing stock. He would have to borrow his wife's Honda. Ah, at last! Frost shuffling out of the station and coming over to him. The same scruffy mac, that same tired scarf. Hadn't the man anything else to wear? But that wasn't the main thing on his mind. He wanted to find out about the prostitute killing. He had the awful thought the victim could have been the harridan who approached him when he was stopped at the traffic lights. There weren't many blue Rovers in Denton. What if someone had seen her approach him? Headlines about kerb-crawling top policeman kept flashing in his mind.

'Nasty,' said Frost, nodding at the damage.

'Yes,' agreed Mullett through clenched teeth. That stupid Sergeant Wells. He was commanding a Division of incompetents.

'It must be hard to say no to a drink at these County meetings,' muttered Frost, bending to take a closer look himself. 'Your best bet is to say it was parked and some drunken sod ran into it.'

'That's exactly what did happen,' snapped Mullett.

'Good for you!' nodded Frost approvingly. 'I almost believe you myself and I can always see through a lie.' He straightened up, fingering the car expenses form in his pocket, anxious to gauge the opportune time to present it to Mullett for his signature. 'You wanted to see me, Super?'

'Ah . . . yes.' Mullett tried to sound disinterested. 'This prostitute killing. Was she young . . . old . . . ?'

'Early twenties,' said Frost. 'Dark-haired, medium height. Why – do you think you know her? We're trying to trace her regulars.'

'No, no . . .' said Mullett hastily, relieved that she didn't sound at all like the same one. 'Of course I don't know her. I want this case cleared up quickly, Frost. We now have a second dead prostitute. We don't want panic because there's a serial killer on the loose.'

'We don't know it's the same bloke,' said Frost. 'The victims are toms but there seems no other connection.'

'I understand you've handed the case over to Acting Inspector Maud? You didn't think of clearing it with me first?'

'I didn't believe it necessary. The first dead tom was investigated by Inspector Allen and she's taken over from him.'

Mullett waved a dismissive hand. 'I know all about that, but we're talking serial murder. What are they going to say at County tomorrow when they learn that a woman – I mean an acting inspector is in charge of such an important case? No. I want you to take it over.'

'She can handle it,' insisted Frost.

'Allow me to be the judge of that,' snapped Mullett. 'She's an inexperienced woman officer.'

'Who's got to gain experience.'

'But not at our expense, Frost. If this blows up in our face it will be my head on the chopping block. She can work under you if you like, but you are in charge.'

Frost looked up as a grey Nissan bumped its way into the car-park. 'There she is, Super. Shall I call her over so you can tell her yourself?'

'No,' said Mullett hastily. 'Better if it comes from you. It will underline that you're in charge . . .' He tugged open the door of his Rover. 'Got to go . . . early start tomorrow.'

'Hold it, Super.' Frost grabbed the car door, preventing it from closing. 'Before you go, would you OK my car expenses?'

Mullett stared in annoyance at the claim form with its wad of scruffy petrol receipts attached. For some reason Frost never seemed to patronize petrol stations who provided a printed receipt. He fingered through them doubtfully.

'Got a minute, Liz?' called Frost, beckoning her over. Mullett snatched the pen from Frost's hand and scribbled his signature. 'Keep me posted,' he muttered as he slammed the car door and drove off.

She took the news badly, staring tight-lipped at Frost as if it was all his fault. 'I presume you'll be covering the post-mortem tomorrow then?' she asked icily, before spinning on her heel and marching to her office.

'Unless you'd like—' said Frost, his sentence cut off as the doors slammed behind her. 'I'll take that as a no,' he muttered. Shit. What a lousy bloody night. He looked at his watch. 3.15 in the morning. In five hours he would be watching Drysdale slice the dead tom up. But sod it. That was tomorrow. Mullett had gone. He had the station to himself. Nothing he could do about the dead tom until the morning. An Indian takeaway, a handful of Mullett's fags from the hospitality box and the recording of the big fight on the telly in the rest room. Things could be worse.

4

'I'm sorry, guv,' mumbled Morgan. 'I'm truly sorry. I don't know how it happened.'

'It happened, you Welsh nit,' snarled Frost, 'because you recorded the wrong flaming channel. We're all sitting there like a load of prats, expecting the big fight, and what are we watching? The flaming singing nuns in *The Sound of bloody Music*.'

'Sorry, guv,' said Morgan again.

'Sorry, guv! That's your catch phrase. I can forgive you letting that drunk maul the corpse last night, but sodding up the recording of the big fight . . .'

Morgan hung his head in shame.

'Chance to redeem youself. Go and get me a mug of tea and a bacon sandwich and bring it to the murder incident room. If you turn up with cocoa and a fairy cake, you're sacked.' Frost yawned. He'd had a rotten night. After the fiasco of the big fight video, he'd staggered off to bed just after four, but sleep had stubbornly eluded him. He just lay there, smoking, sucking hard on the cigarette from time to time so he could check the crawl of time on his wrist-watch in its red glow. When he finally drifted off to sleep he had dreams of the autopsy, but the body being hacked about by Drysdale was not the prostitute; it was Vicky Stuart, the little girl with the gap in her teeth, who suddenly sat up from the autopsy table and screamed, waking him in a cold sweat. And just as he was drifting off again, the flaming alarm clock shook him awake at 7.45, just in time to tumble out of bed, splash his face with water, a quick shave, then off to the mortuary to watch Drysdale slice open the unknown tom on an empty stomach.

Drysdale, methodical, waspish and impassive, was able to tell him little he didn't know already. Death due to manual strangulation and the stab wound probably self-inflicted as her attacker tried to wrest the knife from her.

Frost was puzzled that there were no traces of the assailant's skin under the long, unbroken fingernails. 'Surely she would have tried to scratch the bastard's eyes out, doc?'

Drysdale lifted the head and indicated the swellings at the back of the skull. 'Her head was banged several times against the wall with considerable force. This could have caused concussion at which point she would have been incapable of defending herself.' He pointed to the livid yellow patch near the left eye. 'She was punched.'

'We've got the bloke who gave her the black eyes, doc, but we don't think he was her killer.' His stomach rumbled noisily. 'I need to get some stomach contents myself, doc . . . a bacon sandwich – so unless there's anything else you can tell me?'

There was nothing else. 'A name would be a convenience,' said Drysdale.

'As soon as we find out who she is, you'll be the first to know,' Frost assured him. Flaming hell. Bad enough it was a murder inquiry without having to waste manpower trying to find the victim's name.

'Did you see the big fight on the telly last night?' the mortuary attendant asked as he made his way out.

'No, I bleeding well didn't!' snapped Frost.

*   *   *

76

He sat on the corner of the desk in the murder incident room warming his hands round the mug of tea Morgan had brought him. He chewed the last morsel of the bacon sandwich, wiped his hand down the front of his jacket, then nodded at the group of six men who formed his murder squad. Manpower was in short supply since Mullett had generously agreed to loan eight uniforms and a DC to County to help in their drugs bust operation. 'Anyone seen Detective Inspector Maud?' he asked. All heads shook. 'Ah well, we'll carry on without her.' He lit up a cigarette. 'We have one dead tom. Anyone found out who she is yet?' He looked up hopefully, but again heads were firmly shaken.

'I chatted up a couple of the girls last night,' said Jordan. 'One of them had a room in the same block. She said the dead girl hadn't been there very long, a few weeks at the most. They hadn't spoken, so she didn't know anything about her.'

'Very bleeding helpful. Have we checked the landlord?'

Detective Sergeant Hanlon raised a hand. 'They're a limited company registered in the Cayman Islands. That block in Clayton Street is handled over here by local agents but they don't open until ten. I'm on my way there as soon as this briefing is over.'

Frost nodded. 'We want her name and home address – I presume they take up references.'

'Odds are they don't bother,' said Hanlon. 'As long as the girls can pay a month's rent in advance, plus a hefty deposit, they're satisfied.'

'Then find out how she paid them – cheque, credit card or greasy fivers red hot from the sweaty palms of her clientele.'

'I'll check,' said Hanlon.

'OK,' said Frost, standing up. 'Let's just run over what we do know. We know she had a row with this drunk who welted her one in the eye. He finds his wallet's been pinched and comes to us. While he's away, someone else calls and kills her.'

'Gladstone could have killed her himself,' put in Jordan. 'I don't think we should have let him go.'

'He could have done it, son, but I don't think he did. Anyway, we know where he lives in case we run short of suspects. Let's proceed on the assumption it was someone else – and someone who followed hard on Gladstone's heels because she hadn't had time to get dressed.'

'Couldn't she have got dressed, gone out and picked up her killer then got undressed for him?' asked Hanlon.

'Gladstone had given her a black eye,' said Frost. 'If she went out again to tout for trade, she'd have slapped some make-up over it; but she didn't. So, if she didn't go out to pick him up, he came to her. He knew where she worked . . . he'd been there before.'

'Any fingerprints?' asked Simms.

'Fingerprints going back to the year dot,' said Frost. 'Every flaming client she's ever had, but we're checking them all out. Mullett went as white as a sheet when I told him.'

'Is there any connection with this one and the murdered tom Inspector Allen was working on?' Jordan asked.

Frost patted the file on the desk. 'Linda Roberts was tied to a bed by her wrists and ankles, gagged, then tortured, her stomach burnt with a lighted cigarette.' He pulled the cigarette from his mouth and sizzled it to death in his mug. 'For good measure she was raped and suffocated. Last night's tom was killed standing against a wall, strangled and no sign of torture. So unless he was fussy about stubbing out his fags on a bloodstained stomach, I don't think there's a connection, but we'll keep our options open.'

He turned to the full-face photograph of the dead woman which had been pinned to the wall. 'So what do we know about her? She hadn't been on the game long, by all accounts. We don't know if she's a local girl or not. Let's get her photograph circulated to the media . . . someone must recognize her. In the meantime, where does she live? Why hasn't someone reported her missing?'

'She could have lived where we found her, guv,' said Morgan. 'She had a bed, a phone, heat . . .'

'. . . a sink and a toilet,' continued Frost, 'which gave the punters two places to pee down; but no fridge, oven, pantry, crockery. This poor cow had to eat. She lived elsewhere and she works late, so how does she get home?'

'She could live within walking distance,' offered Jordan.

'Then why rent a flat? Why not take her clients to her house?'

'Perhaps her family would object.'

'So what does her family think she's doing, working late at night, coming home with her handbag stuffed with tenners? A slight possibility she lives within walking distance, but what if she doesn't?'

'She's got a car?' said Morgan.

Frost jabbed a finger at the DC. 'That's what I reckon, Taffy. So where is it? It's going to be parked near the knocking shop. There were cars nose to tail last night. This morning most of the owners will have driven off to work. I want someone to go and check all cars still standing and find out who owns them.' He snapped his fingers as another thought struck him. 'She might have come by cab. Check with all the local cab firms. Did they drop her off there last night – if so, where did they pick her up?'

Bill Wells came into the incident room. 'Got a woman for you in the lobby, Inspector.'

'She'll have to wait,' grunted Frost. 'I never have intercourse immediately after a bacon sandwich.'

Wells grinned. 'You'll want to see this one. She's a tom . . . and her flatmate has gone missing.'

Frost's eyes lit up. 'Hold it, everyone. We might be getting a name.'

The pungent smell of the perfume she was wearing fought a losing battle with the pine disinfectant that had been sloshed down on the interview room floor after the ravages of the night before. She was in her late thirties, but without make-up looked a lot older. Straw-blond hair, skin darkly tanned, and fingers that matched Frost's for nicotine staining. She was sucking heavily on a cigarette as he entered. He sat opposite her and put the file with the dead prostitute's photograph inside on the table in front of him. He smiled. 'Your flatmate's gone missing? Since when?'

'I don't know.' She snatched the cigarette from her mouth and flicked ash all over the floor. 'I've been away for two weeks' holiday in Spain with my boyfriend. I came back last night expecting to find her in the flat. No sign of her.'

'What does your flatmate do for a living?'

She glared at him, smoke streaming from her nostrils like an angry dragon. 'You bloody well know what she does . . . same as me . . . we're on the game. She's had some weird clients in her time. I reckon one of them's done her in.'

'Where did she take her clients?'

'A room in those flats in Clayton Street. We shared it.'

'I see.' Frost tried to keep his face impassive. He opened up the folder and took out the photograph. 'Is this your friend?' he asked gently.

She looked at it and shook her head. 'No.'

Frost frowned. 'Are you sure?'

'I ought to know what she bleeding looks like, didn't I? That's one of the other girls . . . down on the second floor, I think.'

'You know her?' said Frost excitedly. 'What's her name?'

'I don't know her bleeding name. I've passed her on the stairs a couple of times. She hasn't been there long. Look – sod her whoever she is, it's my flatmate I'm worried about.' She opened her handbag and took out a photograph of a fat, blowsy, ginger-haired woman in her fifties.

'Flaming heck,' exclaimed Frost, recognizing the woman immediately. 'It's big bleeding Bertha – ten ton of tit and tongue.' Bertha had been arrested quite a few times for soliciting, drunk and disorderly and for assaulting a police officer.

'A bit of bleeding respect,' snapped the woman. 'She helps pay your flaming wages. She's missing. Something's happened to her.'

'She could have gone away for a few days – perhaps she wanted a holiday too.'

'No bloody way. We've got a dog – little Chummy. Bertha idolizes it. When I got back to the flat last night, there's dog's mess all over the floor and the poor thing was starving, no water, no food, nothing. Bertha would never have left it to starve. That dog was like a kid to her.'

Frost scratched his chin. This wasn't looking too good. 'You said she had some weird clients?'

'Yes. She's no glamour puss, she has to grab what she can get. Some of the rubbish she brought back to the flat! I'm not fussy, but I wouldn't go within a mile of them. Some wouldn't take their boots off in bed and there were others you wished they'd bleeding well kept them on.'

'Are her belongings still in the flat?'

'Yes. All her clothes, her bank book . . .'

'Credit cards? Cash?'

'She always kept them with her – in her handbag.'

'Any idea what she would have been wearing?'

'Her red dress and her long black fur coat.'

'Have you checked your room in Clayton Street?'

'Not yet.'

'We'll do that,' said Frost, taking details. He stood up. 'We'll do what we can. If she turns up in the meantime, let us know.'

She lit up a fresh cigarette for the street and shook her head with concern. 'I really am worried about her.'

Frost nodded. He was worried too.

He escorted her out and went back to Wells in the lobby. He showed the sergeant the photograph. 'She's gone missing.'

Wells studied it. 'Best thing that could have happened to her.'

Frost grinned. 'Her flatmate thinks she's been done in and I've got one of my nasty feelings that says she might be right. Circulate details and get someone to check her place of business in Clayton Street; there might be a body there we missed.' He looked up at the wall clock. Time was racing by and so much still to be done. 'Any idea where Liz Maud is?'

'She crept in late then went straight in to see Mullett,' Wells told him.

Mullett made a great show of pushing the pile of papers to one side to let Liz know she was tearing him away from much more important matters, then put on his 'tired, overworked, but my staff come first' expression. 'You wanted to see me, Sergeant . . . er, Inspector?' He knew what it was about, of course. These damned women always claiming sex discrimination. WPCs were fine for searching female prisoners but promote them, give them a bit of authority, and

82

the minute something happened they didn't like they started screaming 'sex discrimination'.

'The murdered prostitute . . .' began Liz.

Mullett frowned and pretended to consult a note on his desk. 'Ah yes. The one in Clayton Street. Inspector Frost is handling that, I believe.' He consulted his Rolex. 'I hope this won't take long. I want to look in on his briefing meeting.'

'It should be my case,' insisted Liz. 'It could be the same killer as the prostitute murder Inspector Allen was handling – a case I've taken over from him.'

Mullett expressed surprise. 'Mr Frost didn't think they were connected.'

'Well, I do.'

He took off his glasses and made great play of polishing them as he gave Liz his warm, friendly, open smile. 'Teamwork, Inspector. That's the keyword, teamwork. No cowboys, no Indians, no generals, no privates – all one big team.' These were the words the Chief Constable had used in yesterday's meeting at which Mullett had nodded his fawning agreement. He was surprised that Liz didn't seem to be doing the same. 'You and Frost will make an excellent team.'

'But it will be his case, not mine.'

'Someone's got to be in charge,' said Mullett, 'and he is, er . . .'

'A man?'

'A more experienced officer.'

'So he's the general and I'm the private? I see.' She stood up abruptly. 'I see.'

'Thanks for being so understanding,' said Mullett. 'I knew you'd understand.'

'Yes,' hissed Liz, breathing fire at him. 'I understand perfectly.'

The door closed behind her as Mullett sank back in his chair and raised his eyes. 'Women!' he protested to the ceiling.

*   *   *

Frost pinned the enlargement of Bertha's photograph next to the photograph of the dead woman from the night before. 'Some of you may recognize her. Big Bertha – Bertha Jenkins. She's gone missing. It may not tie in with last night's dead tom, but they both plied for hire from the same building in Clayton Street.' He filled them in on the details. 'Two dead prostitutes and now one missing, so I'm worried . . .' He paused. All heads turned as the door opened and Police Superintendent Mullett, shiny and gleaming in his 'going to County' best uniform, marched in. Everyone sprang respectfully to their feet. Mullett signalled for them to be seated, noting with annoyance that Frost had made no effort to raise himself from the corner of the desk.

'If I could have a few words, Inspector?'

'Right,' barked Frost. 'Super's going to say a few words. Try and look as if you're paying attention.'

Mullett gave a tight smile. 'I want this one cleared up as soon as possible. Crimes involving women of the street get maximum attention from the press and this, in turn, stirs up cries from the respectable members of the community demanding we clean up the red light area. Even at this early hour I have received numerous phone calls complaining about kerb-crawling . . . predatory motorists looking for women, not watching where they are going, causing accidents.'

Frost looked up. 'The Super smashed his car up last night.'

'It happened in the station car-park,' snapped Mullett, ignoring the sniggers.

'I didn't know the details,' said Frost.

Mullett's angry glower bounced harmlessly off Frost's expression of utter innocence. 'Now that we're adopting this excellent team work initiative of County's I'm looking for improved results. Our unsolved crime figures are appalling and I want them brought down. The fewer unsolved crimes, the better the figures. So the best of luck and let's hope for some good news when I report to County.' With a curt nod to Frost, he marched briskly out.

As the door closed behind the Divisional Commander, Frost got to his feet. 'The Super has put his finger on it as usual. The more unsolved crimes we have, the worse our unsolved crime figures – so what's the answer?'

'Fiddle the unsolved crime figures?' suggested Morgan.

'I've already done that,' said Frost, 'and they're still bad, so let's try the hard way. You all know what to do, so go out and do it.'

He swilled down the cold dregs of his tea, drowned his cigarette end in the mug and ambled back to his office to rake half-heartedly through the pile of paper in his in-tray. Lots of memos from Mullett demanding all sorts of answers, which were shuffled down to the bottom of the pile. A letter handwritten in green ink caught his attention. He plucked it up and held it disdainfully at arm's length between thumb and forefinger as he read it.

'What's that, guv?' Morgan had followed him in.

'One of our local nutters who reckons he's got second sight. He's telling us where to find Vicky.' Frost nodded to the 'Missing Girl' poster on the wall. 'Listen – "The missing girl will be found on grass, near trees under a blue sky." That narrows it down, doesn't it?' He screwed up the letter before hurling it in the general direction of his waste-paper bin. The search for Vicky Stuart had come to a dead end. They had searched everywhere, dragged the canal and the river, pleaded for information over the media, followed up hundreds of sightings; the girl had been seen with long distance lorry drivers, with a black-bearded man in

France, with a convoy of New Age travellers . . . All had proved negative. And now this flaming soothsayer wanted to get in on the act. He looked across at Morgan who was sitting at his desk flicking through the phone directory. 'Aren't you supposed to be out working?'

The DC held a hand to his jaw. 'Sorry, guv – got a tooth giving me gyp. Do you know the name of a good dentist?'

'There are no good dentists,' said Frost. 'They're all sadistic bastards. Tie a bit of string to it with a brick on the end and drop it out of the window.'

The office door crashed open and slammed shut and there was Liz Maud, snorting fire. She jabbed a finger at Frost. 'You told Mr Mullett you didn't think the two prostitute murders were connected.'

'Yes, love,' nodded Frost ruefully, 'and if I had known the sod was going to put me on the case, I'd have lied. I didn't want to get up at the crack of dawn and see Drysdale filleting that poor cow.'

'You knew I wanted that case. By rights it should be mine.'

'We'll work together on it,' said Frost. 'If I sod it up, I'll take the blame. If we crack it, you can take the credit.'

She gave a grudging nod. Unlike her, she knew the inspector didn't want to rise any higher in the force.

Morgan finished a phone call and called over to Frost: 'Is it all right if I take a bit of time off to visit the dentist, guv?'

'Sure,' nodded Frost. 'Take all the time you like – as long as you do it in your lunch hour.' Back to Liz. 'How's your armed robbery going?'

She suddenly felt a wave of nausea ripple through her stomach and sat down heavily in the spare chair.

'You all right, love?' asked Frost.

'Just a stomach upset,' she muttered. She'd been

putting it off, dreading the result, but as soon as she got back to the flat she would use the pregnancy testing kit. 'The armed robbery? I haven't got very far yet. A description of the two men, but no sign of the car they hijacked. The old boy who tackled the gunman demanded to see me last night to tell me nothing we didn't know. I'm on my way now to the hospital to talk to the husband.' She shot an accusing glance at Morgan. 'You were supposed to be checking the background of the cashier.'

'Was just about to do it as you came in, ma'am,' said Morgan, scuttling out of the office.

Frost grinned to himself. Morgan was picking up his own bad habits.

Police Sergeant Bill Wells squinted up at the wall clock, then pushed open the doors to the stairs leading up to the canteen for a tentative sniff. He frowned. He couldn't smell frying bacon. If they'd run out of cooked breakfasts again . . . PC Collier was due down to relieve him any second. He should have made Collier wait and gone up first himself but flaming Mullett kept phoning, demanding all sorts of stupid information for his meeting at County. Damn. Collier or no Collier, he was going up for his breakfast. It wouldn't hurt for the lobby to stay unmanned for a couple of minutes.

He screwed his face up in annoyance as the sound of someone clearing their throat and a gentle tapping on the desk demanded his attention. A little fat man in a checked suit, clutching a plastic carrier bag. Not another dead cat, he pleaded. People were always bringing dead cats into the station. 'Found this in my front garden, officer.'

'Yes, sir?' he grunted, ready to grab the bag, stuff it under the desk and belt upstairs.

'Can I speak to someone?' asked the man.

Aren't I bloody someone, mutered Wells under his breath. 'What about, sir?'

The man pushed the carrier bag under Wells' nose. 'I found this in my garden.'

Wells peered warily inside, remembering the woman with a similar carrier bag who had brought evidence of a burglar defecating on her carpet for DNA testing. If this was the same, he'd made certain Liz Maud had to handle it. But this was different. Grinning up at him from the bottom of the bag was a human skull.

Frost raised his head from the folder when Wells burst in demanding to know where Wonder Woman had crept off to.

'The hospital,' Frost told him. 'She'll be back after lunch.'

'Then you've drawn the short straw,' said Wells, passing over the carrier bag. 'Bloke found this in his back garden.'

Frost looked inside. 'Bloody hell!' He pushed the bag away. 'If it isn't claimed within three weeks, tell him he can keep it.' He went back to the folder. 'Give it to Morgan, it will be good experience.'

'He's out doing a job for Wonder Woman. It's got to be you. There's no-one else available.'

'Sod it!' groaned Frost. 'Why do I always get landed with the long-dead?' He followed the sergeant out to the lobby and nodded curtly to the little fat man. 'Found it in your garden?'

The man nodded. 'I was pulling down an old shed. We're selling the house and my wife thought the shed was an eyesore and would bring the price down. When I broke up the concrete base I found this.'

'How long had the shed been there?'

'Donkey's years. It was there when we moved in and that was thirty years ago.'

Frost fished out the skull from the bag and looked

at it, hoping it would give him inspiration. He was struggling to find reasons to send Fatty away and forget the whole thing. 'Probably built your house on an old burial ground – they did that, you know.'

The man shook his head. 'It was marsh land. They had to drain it before they could build. You don't have graveyards in marsh land.'

You're too bleeding clever for your own good, thought Frost. Aloud he said: 'That's all you found – just the skull?'

'That's all I brought. There's lots of other bones there as well. I thought it best not to disturb them.'

Frost nodded gloomily. 'We'll get someone down there to have a look.' He waited for the man to go, then turned to Wells. 'I want two uniforms with shovels.' As the sergeant was making the arrangements he put the skull on the counter and stuck a lighted cigarette between its yellowed teeth.

'Very funny!' sniffed Wells. 'Now get the bleeding thing out of here.'

Frost put the cigarette back in his own mouth. 'How old do remains have to be before we don't have to bother to investigate them?'

'Seventy years.' Wells turned his attention to PC Collier who had returned back late from the canteen. 'Any breakfasts left?'

Collier shook his head. 'You might get a bacon sandwich if you hurry, Sarge.'

Wells hurried. He would tear Collier off a strip when he got back.

Frost took one last look at the skull before dropping it back in the carrier bag. 'You'd better be over seventy years old,' he told it, 'or you've ruined my bleeding day.'

The area car pulled up outside the semi-detached house with the 'For Sale' board stuck firmly in the lawn by the front gate. PCs Collier and Jordan got out, picks and shovels over their shoulders, looking like two of the seven dwarfs returning home after a stint in the diamond mine. A grumpy-looking Frost followed them up the garden path. The front door opened before they were half-way and the fat man scanned the street anxiously before urging them in. Behind him, arms folded, stood his wife, a dragon of a woman, her lavender-dyed hair complementing the smell of lavender furniture polish which hit them like a baseball bat. She didn't look very happy. 'That's right!' she barked at her husband. 'Let everyone in the bloody street know we've got the police coming.'

'I didn't know they'd come in a police car, did I?' protested the fat man.

'What did you expect them to come in – a corporation dust cart?' She switched her attention to Frost and Co. 'Wipe your feet and shut the door – quick.'

Her eyes glowered at them as they marched down the hall which had been lined with old newspapers to protect the carpet from police hobnails, through the kitchen, and into the back garden.

The broken concrete was stacked neatly alongside the components of the dismantled wooden shed. Poking through the compact earth was something that looked suspiciously like a human shoulder bone. 'All right,' sighed Frost, moving well out of the way. 'Get digging.'

From the row of houses overlooking the garden many lace curtains twitched. Uniformed policemen digging up a garden was of consuming interest.

'I hope you're satisfied,' nagged the woman to her husband. 'Now everyone in the flaming street knows!'

'What was I supposed to do?' pleaded the man.

'Like I said – dig another hole and bury the lot.'

Best bit of bloody advice you ever had, thought Frost.

'There might have been other skeletons there for all I knew,' protested the husband.

'*Might?* With our flaming luck you can bank on it. How are we going to sell the place now?' Her head jerked as she glowered up at the twitching curtains and open windows. 'Had your bloody eyeful, have you?' she bellowed.

This had the effect of increasing the number of spectators as other people rushed to their windows to see what the noise was all about. Frost was finding it chilly, just standing and watching. 'I suppose there's no chance of a cup of tea?' he asked as she spun round to return to the house.

'You're bloody right – there's no chance,' she said, slamming the door. Her husband gave an apologetic smile and hurried in after her. They could hear her strident voice berating him non-stop as they worked. 'I bet she's fetching his pipe and slippers,' said Frost.

Liz Maud had stopped off at her flat on the way back from the hospital. The old boy hadn't been very helpful, simply confirming what little his wife had already told them. The smell of cooking from the hospital kitchen had brought on the nausea and she was sick in the car-park. There was no putting it off any longer. She opened up the pregnancy testing kit and read the instructions.

Collier and Jordan had shifted much of the covering earth and were now down on their knees, brushing dirt away carefully so as not to disturb the position of the bones. 'I think we've uncovered it all now, Inspector,' called Jordan.

Frost mooched over then looked down glumly. There appeared to be a complete skeleton, minus the head, lying full length. He tossed the skull to Jordan so he could put it in position. 'Great Plague victim,' he pronounced firmly.

'A bit later than that, I think,' said Collier.

'Fell out of a Zeppelin then. Eighty years old if it's a day.'

The back door opened and Dr McKenzie, the duty police surgeon, toddled out. Frost gave him a cheerful wave and hissed for Collier to nip out and move the area car if the doctor had parked his own in front. McKenzie had been known to put his own car accidentally into reverse when driving off, especially when too many grateful patients had given him a drop of something to keep out the cold. His florid complexion, slightly unsteady gait and a strong smell of whisky suggested the cold had been well and truly kept out this morning. 'What have you got for me, Inspector?' he asked as he accepted one of Frost's cigarettes.

'Stone Age skeleton,' said Frost, showing him the bones. 'Too ancient to bother you with really, but we've got to go by the book.'

The doctor hunkered down. 'Stone Age?' he mused.

'At least,' Frost assured him.

'It's a male and he's been dead for some time.'

Frost nodded. 'Trampled on by a dinosaur, I reckon, doc. So he's been dead at least a hundred years?'

McKenzie shook his head. 'Not as long as that.'

'Seventy-one at least?'

'You can't tell by just looking. You'll have to get them over to Denton Hospital. One of their consultants is an expert on bones; he'll be able to tell you.'

'Need we bother with all that?' pleaded Frost. 'Can't we tie it up now?'

McKenzie said nothing. He was gently prodding the back of the skull with a stubby finger. 'The skull's fractured.'

'And that's what killed him?'

The doctor put the skull back in position and rubbed the dirt from his fingers. 'No way of knowing, Jack – he could have been disembowelled and pumped full of arsenic first for all I know. The consultant at the hospital might help you there.'

Frost pulled a face. 'Let's be practical, doc. I've got a dead tom and a missing kid to worry about. I can't waste time sodding around with the Piltdown Man. I know I can't pin you down, but just say, in your honest opinion, bearing in mind that you're smoking one of my fags, that he's been buried for seventy years at least. I might even find a bottle of whisky in the car . . .'

McKenzie scratched his cheek thoughtfully, but suddenly squatted down again and began scratching away some caked earth from around the wrist. He frowned, scraped away some more, then stood up so Frost could see. 'If I remember rightly, Inspector Frost, Stone Age men told the time by the sun.'

'Shit!' said Frost.

Encircling the brown arm bone was a wrist-watch on a stainless steel strap.

'Am I still on for the whisky?' asked McKenzie.

'Like hell you are,' snapped Frost. 'Go and ask the lady of the house for a cup of tea.' He radioed the station for SOCO and someone from Forensic, then hurled his cigarette on the pile of bones and drove back to the station.

'Shit!' said Liz. The plastic rod was showing a blue band. She checked the instructions just in case she had misread them. She hadn't. She was pregnant.

5

He was back on the edge of the desk in the murder incident room listening glumly to the string of negative reports from his team. After a day of knocking on doors, making inquiries, they were still unable to put a name to the dead girl. She had paid the first quarter's rent in cash, so the letting agents didn't bother taking up references. The name she had given them was Jane Smith but there was no Jane Smith at the address she provided, which turned out to be a newsagent's. Registration numbers of cars still parked in the vicinity of Clayton Street had turned up nothing that would help: the only registered women owners were in their sixties. The few prostitutes who had staggered from bed to answer the hammering at their doors knew little of the dead girl except she was fairly new on the game and didn't seem to have a pimp and kept encroaching on other girls' territories.

Frost's eyes gleamed up at this last piece of information. 'Follow that through,' he told Hanlon. 'If she encroached on another girl's patch, a pimp might have tried some heavy stuff to warn her off and it went too far.' His eyes travelled round the room. His team all looked tired; the tiredness that comes from working bloody hard and getting nowhere. 'I'm afraid you're all having to go out again tonight when the girls are all out working. Some of those who didn't answer the

94

door this morning might know something.' He yawned. 'Until then, I suggest we all go home and get some kip.'

He stifled another yawn as he watched them file out. He could do with a spot of kip himself. The phone rang and the WPC in the corner answered it. 'Forensic, Inspector,' she called. 'Got some news for you on that skeleton.'

'Can it wait?' he asked, winding his scarf round his neck and edging towards the door.

'They say no.'

'Tell them I said "sod them" and I'll look in on my way home.' As he walked out to his car, shivering in the cold, he wondered where Liz Maud, his partner in the investigation, had got to.

Liz was back in her flat, finishing a phone conversation with the abortion clinic in London – a clinic well away from the prying ears and eyes of Denton Division. They would admit her tomorrow afternoon for an operation to be carried out the following day. All being well, they assured her, she should be back at work within a week. She gave them her credit card details and made the appointment.

Frost mooched into the Forensic lab, all white tiles and stainless steel, ignoring scowls from Harding, the senior technician, who was showing disapproval of the cigarette dangling from the inspector's lips. Frost grunted at the array of bones laid out on the table in front of them to form a human skeleton.

'It's complete,' said Harding proudly.

'Glad we've got the full set,' said Frost without enthusiasm. The grinning skull, cleaned of dirt, showed yellow fangs. Frost puffed smoke into the nose cavity and watched it emerge in swirls from the eye sockets.

'I'd prefer it if you didn't do that,' sniffed Harding.

Frost pinched out the cigarette and dropped it into his mac pocket. 'Right. Just tell me his name, address, inside leg measurement and who killed him, and I'll be on my way.'

A thin smile from Harding. 'We can't tell you that, Inspector, but we can tell you quite a bit about him.' He picked up part of the arm bone and showed Frost where it had been sawn neatly through. 'The consultant at Denton Hospital did that for his tests. In his opinion we have the skeleton of a man in his early thirties.' As Frost shrugged disinterest, Harding replaced the bone carefully in position, then pointed to the brown-stained leg bone where a crack showed near the ankle. 'See that fracture? He broke his ankle a few weeks before the time of death.'

'Hold on,' said Frost, squinting closely at the cracked section. 'How do you make that out?'

Harding smiled, glad of a chance to explain. 'Broken bones try to heal themselves. They gradually knit together again, but the knitting processs stops at death. The consultant says the amount of healing there indicates a few weeks only.'

Frost pointed to the skull. 'What about the fracture?'

'Definitely made at the time of death and it's probably what led to his death, although the fracture alone might not have been fatal had he received prompt medical treatment.'

'Could it have been an accident – say his bad leg made him fall downstairs and fracture his skull?'

'The consultant doubts if anything other than a blow from the good old blunt instrument could have caused an injury like that.'

'Did he say how long the poor sod had been dead? I know he can't be precise, but within a minute or so?'

'Definitely less than the seventy you'd like it to be,

Inspector. Between forty and fifty years, he reckons. And that's borne out by this.' Harding picked up a small plastic bag with the wrist-watch inside. 'We managed to trace the maker. They first made this particular model forty-five years ago.'

Frost took another look at the skull. 'Anyone checked his choppers?'

'All his own teeth and in quite good condition apart from a couple of fillings. That doesn't help much and I doubt if we'll find any dentist who still keeps patients' records from so long ago.'

Frost frowned at the skeleton. 'He's not making it easy for us to identify him.'

'He's being particularly unhelpful,' agreed Harding. 'We sifted all the earth from around the burial site and found nothing. Vegetable matter such as cotton would rot away after being in the ground for so long, but some trace of clothing should be left – buttons, buckles, zips, metal eyelets. There was nothing, absolutely nothing.'

'Which means?'

'Unless he was undressed after death, it suggests he was stark naked when he was killed – apart from the wrist-watch.'

Frost kneaded some life back into his scar. It was always freezing cold in the Forensic lab, just like the hospital morgue. He stared up at the ceiling for inspiration. 'Starkers, except for his watch? The only time I'm starkers, except for my watch, is when I'm having it away but want to keep an eye on the time so I don't miss the football results on the telly.' He watched Harding put the watch back in the drawer. 'Thanks for sod all.'

Harding smiled the smug smile of a man who had something up his sleeve. 'There's something else, Inspector.' He pulled out something from under the lab bench. A polythene bag containing something encrusted in rust. Frost took the bag. Inside, heavily corroded, were the rusty remains of a kitchen knife, its handle long-since crumbled away, the metal spike which had run through the handle ending in a metal ring so the knife could be hung on a hook. 'We found it underneath the skeleton,' said Harding.

Frost stared at the long-bladed knife. It would have been a wicked weapon when new. 'Are you saying he was stabbed?'

Harding shook his head. 'There's no way of tying the knife to the body, I'm afraid. It was under the skeleton and could have been buried long before.'

Frost gave a snort. 'Thanks for even more sod all,' he said. 'That helps a flaming lot.' As he made for the door he paused. 'Are you sure he's dead?'

Harding frowned. 'What do you mean?'

'The bastard's just pinched one of my fags,' said Frost, pointing to the skull which now had a lighted cigarette in its mouth.

'It's still not funny,' snapped Harding, coldly.

But Frost was laughing to himself all the way back to his car.

Quarter past ten and he was back at the station with the feeling it was going to be another long, hard night. He had filled everyone in on the details known about the skeleton, but stressed they weren't to spend any time on it. 'We've got the killing of more recent meat to sort out first.' He looked up as the door creaked open and Morgan, hoping to sneak in unobserved, began to tiptoe across to a vacant desk. 'I'd like to apologise to DC Morgan,' said Frost, 'for not waiting fifteen bleeding minutes before he condescended to join us.'

Morgan gave a sheepish grin. 'Sorry, guv . . . damned alarm clock . . .'

'Yes, if you switch them off and go back to sleep

98

they're no bleeding good, are they?' He noticed the DC rubbing his jaw. 'How did you get on with the dentist?'

Morgan rattled a little white box. 'Gave me some painkillers, guv. Said he couldn't touch it until the swelling had gone down.'

'That's what the nurse said to me,' Frost told him, 'but I think she was talking about my dick.' He heaved himself off the corner of the desk. 'You all know what to do. Chat up the ladies of the night, spurn their tempting offers and see if they can name that tom!'

Back in his office he was surprised to see Liz Maud waiting for him.

'Quick word, Inspector.'

'Sure.' He waved her to a chair. 'How's the armed robbery going?'

'I'm getting nowhere . . . but I'm afraid I'm going to have to hand my cases over to you.'

His eyebrows shot up. 'Oh?'

'I've got to go to London for some medical treatment.'

He looked concerned. 'Nothing serious, I hope?'

She shook her head. 'No . . . a minor operation . . . I'll be back in a couple of days.'

'Good.' It wasn't flaming good. They were already short-staffed and now all her cases were going to be dumped on him. He waited. It didn't look as if she was going into details, but he could make a guess and it wouldn't be for ingrowing toenails.

'I'll be off tomorrow afternoon and probably back next Friday.'

'Well, don't come back until you're properly fit. I'll try not to sod your cases up too much.'

She smiled. 'I'm sure you won't.'

'What's the problem with the armed robbery?'

'They had to have swapped cars somewhere near

99

where they shot the old boy . . . but we can't find either car.'

Frost scratched his chin. 'They might not have gone to the woods for their own car. They could have walked. They might even live near the woods.'

'Possible,' she shrugged, 'but if they lived locally, they would have dumped the old boy's car somewhere in Denton . . . So why haven't we found it?'

'Because we're bleeding inefficient,' Frost told her. 'And we're working on a shoe-string thanks to Mullett's generosity in giving County all our spare manpower. We haven't got the bodies to go up and down every side street and alley.'

She nodded. 'I suppose so.'

He found a pencil stub and turned over one of Mullett's memos so he could write on the back. 'Tell me about your cases.'

Station Sergeant Bill Wells took an instant dislike to the man the minute he barged through the doors. But then he felt this way with most members of the public who came crashing in with their petty grievances, expecting instant attention. This one, a lout in his late twenties with close-cropped hair and a scowling face, was snapping his fingers for Wells to attend to him. 'Yes?' grunted Wells. He wasn't going to waste a 'sir' on this rubbish.

'My car's been stolen.'

'Stolen car?' Wells tugged a form from a stack and pushed it across. 'Fill in the details.'

'You fill in your own flaming forms. I know who's stolen it and I want her arrested.' He pushed the form back.

'And who do you think has stolen it?' asked Wells.

'I don't *think*, I flaming *know*! It's my girlfriend . . . my ex-flaming-girlfriend now. She's run off and pinched my motor.'

100

'You're saying she took it without your permission?'

The man rolled his eyes up to the ceiling. 'That's what stealing means, doesn't it? Would I be wasting my time with flaming wooden tops if I had given her permission?'

Wells gritted his teeth to keep his temper. Let's hope she's driven the flaming thing over a cliff, he said to himself. The man took a cigarette from a packet and stuck it in his mouth. Wells waited until he had it well lit before pointing to the 'No Smoking' sign. 'If you don't mind,' he said, hoping Frost wouldn't spoil it by slouching in with a cigarette going full blast. Scowling, the man ground the cigarette under foot. Wells smiled sweetly. 'Give me the details – as briefly as possible. We're very busy.'

'We both work nights. I usually drive her to work and pick her up in the morning. I didn't go to work yesterday as I went up to London to see the big match.'

Wells jabbed a finger. 'I remember you now. You were here last night with those other yobbos in the coach. Was it you throwing up in the bloody corner?'

'No, it wasn't me throwing up and yes, I was here. Anyway, as I wouldn't be able to drive her, I told her to phone her work and say she was sick or something.'

'Why couldn't she drive herself?'

'Because she hasn't passed her driving test. If she had an accident or anything, the insurers wouldn't pay out. When I got back in this morning, no sign of her and more important, no sign of my car.'

'So what did you do?'

'What the hell could I do? I went to bed. I woke up about four this afternoon; still no sign of her. I waited until ten o'clock when she should be at the hospital and phoned them.'

'The hospital?' queried Wells.

'She's a nurse, does the night shift at Denton

General – at least, that's what she told me. When I phoned them today they said they'd never heard of her.'

Wells rubbed a hand over his face. This was getting beyond him. 'Never heard of her? Was she an agency nurse?'

'I don't know – what difference would that make?'

'Some of these part-time agency nurses give false names to avoid having to pay income tax. She might have used a different name.'

'According to Denton General, the only nurses working nights in her ward were two West Indians and a nun . . .' He tugged a photograph from his pocket and stuck it under Wells' nose. 'Does she look like a bleeding nun?'

Wells squinted at a photograph of an attractive girl in a very low-cut dress, leaning forward to show yards of cleavage. The cleavage was so attractive, it took him a while to look at her face. He stared. 'Just give me a moment, sir.' He used the phone in Control, out of earshot of the man, and buzzed Inspector Frost. 'You'd better get out here right away, Jack.' He looked again at the photograph. She definitely wasn't a nun . . . she was the murdered tom.

Frost tapped a cigarette on the packet and lit up. He was leaning against the wall of the interview room, watching the man closely as Liz interviewed him.

'What the hell's going on?' asked the man. 'The wooden top outside says you're all terribly busy, now I get two detective inspectors falling all over me about a stolen car.'

Liz made an attempt at a reassuring smile. 'Just a couple of questions.' She glanced at the form on the table. 'You are Victor John Lewis, 2a Fleming Street, Denton?'

'Bang on, darling. I haven't changed my bleeding name and address since I filled that form in five minutes ago.'

Liz pointed to the photograph. 'And this is Mary Jane Adams, your girlfriend?'

'Yes.'

'You live together?'

'Yes.'

'How long have you been together?'

'Six months. What the hell has this to do with getting my car back?'

'Bear with us. Where do you work?'

'At the all-night petrol station in Felton.'

'When did you see Mary last?'

'Just after five o'clock yesterday afternoon when I left to pick up the coach.'

'When you woke up this afternoon and she wasn't back, weren't you worried?'

'Of course I was worried – she'd walked out on me before, but this time she took my bloody motor. When you find her, I want the cow charged.'

Liz shot a glance at Frost in case he wanted to ask some more questions before they told him about the girl. Frost moved into the chair next to Liz. 'I'm afraid we've got some bad news for you, Mr Lewis.'

The mortuary attendant parked his chewing gum on the underside of the table, put on his doleful expression and led them through to the refrigerated section. He pulled open the long drawer, twitched back the sheet and stood respectfully in the background. The face, washed clean of make-up, looked like that of a young schoolgirl. Lewis stared, then his face screwed up in pain as he turned away. He nodded to Frost. 'Yes . . . that's Mary.'

Lewis was knuckling tears from his eyes on the way back, but apart from a few sympathetic grunts, Frost said nothing, his mind on other things. He wasn't being callous. He had driven grieving relatives back from the morgue so many times, it was almost a routine. He couldn't get involved in their grief, otherwise he would be grieving every bloody day and his job would become unbearable.

Back at the station Frost sat Lewis in the main interview room with a mug of strong tea while he nipped out to gather up the reports Morgan had been making for him. He flicked through them. 'Another job for you, Taffy boy. Lewis says he used to drop her off and pick her up from outside the hospital at the end of her shift. If she was plying her trade in Clayton Street, how did she get there? It's too far to walk. Check with the local cab firms.'

'What for, guv?' asked Morgan.

'Lewis could be lying. He might have known she was on the game and dropped her off outside the flat at Clayton Street. If he dropped her off outside the hospital and then she called a cab that would suggest he had no idea she was a tom which would sod up my theory.'

He collected Liz on his way back to the interview room. 'Could Lewis be the bloke you heard on the phone last night?'

She shook her head. 'No. He's nothing like him.' She frowned. 'You don't suspect Lewis, do you?'

Frost shrugged. 'I've got to suspect someone, and he's all we've got at the moment.'

Lewis sat hunched at the table, sucking at a cigarette, the mug of tea cold, scummy and untouched. He raised his head as Frost and Liz came in. 'A prostitute! I still can't believe it.'

'I know,' said Frost, sounding truly sorry. 'And to make things worse we've got to ask you some searching questions.'

Lewis sniffed back a tear and nodded. 'Ask what

104

you like. As long as it helps you catch the bastard who did it.'

Frost shuffled the reports on the table in front of him. 'We've been making a few inquiries about Mary, Mr Lewis. The nearest she got to being a nurse was working in the canteen at Denton General.'

Lewis stared, unable to take this in.

'Four months ago she got the sack,' continued Frost. 'She'd been putting the takings in her pocket instead of in the till.'

Lewis buried his head in his hands. 'You think you know someone and she turns out to be a prostitute, a liar and a thief.' He looked up. 'We were going to get married . . .'

Frost waited as Lewis lit up another cigarette. 'I know this has all come as a nasty shock, Mr Lewis, but just to eliminate you from our inquiries, could we have an account of your movements last night?'

The man wiped a hand over his face. 'As I said, I left the flat just after five and picked up the coach for Wembley – a crowd of us were going from the club. We saw the match and got tanked up. On the way back we stop at this off-licence place. There was a bit of a punch-up – some of the lads had tried to nip out without paying. We're off in the coach swilling down booze to get rid of the evidence. It all gets a bit hazy from there. I remember some cops picking us up and taking us to the nick. Then they bunged us back in the coach, but someone managed to hot-wire it and we got away. We all ended up in a pub somewhere near the motorway.'

'What pub?' asked Frost.

Lewis shook his head. 'No idea . . . it's all a blur.'

'How long were you there?'

'Couple of hours, I think.'

'How did you get back to the flat?'

'One of the blokes had parked his car there. He

drove a crowd of us back. Don't ask me who it was.'

'You got back and Mary wasn't there?'

'Too right – and neither was my flaming car. I could have murdered the cow.' His face contorted as the import of the words hit him. 'God, what am I saying?'

'It's all right,' soothed Frost. 'Then what?'

'I flopped on the bed fully dressed and didn't wake up until about four in the afternoon with a splitting headache. Mary wasn't in bed with me.'

'So what did you do?'

'I still wasn't worried . . . I thought she'd sodded off somewhere to teach me a lesson. She knew I needed the car to take us both to work so I was sure she'd be back before then. I must have fallen asleep in the chair. I woke up just before ten. No Mary and no motor. I phoned the hospital, and they hadn't heard of her! And now I know why!'

'There was a threatening phone call while we were at her place in Clayton Street,' said Frost. 'Any idea who it might have been?'

'No, but there were a couple of queer phone calls at the flat. She'd been edgy for some time and jumped a mile each time the phone rang – always dashed to answer it before I did. I was beginning to suspect there was another bloke.'

'Who did she say it was?'

'She tried to pretend it was someone from work playing a joke, but she didn't sound as if she thought it was funny.'

'And you just let it go at that?'

'You didn't push things with Mary if she didn't want them pushed – not if you didn't want a screaming row.'

'She had a temper?'

'We both had, I suppose. The rows were awful, but it was fun making up.' He stared into space as if a specific memory had hit him then gave a brief, sad smile and shook his head. 'There were lots of good times.'

'I'm sure there were,' nodded Frost. There were even good times in his own marriage that the many bad days couldn't entirely wipe out. 'Just for the purpose of elimination, Mr Lewis, we'd like to have the clothes you were wearing last night.'

He frowned. 'My clothes?'

'The killer would have got blood on his clothes. I know you'd want us to be thorough.'

'They're at home. I'll bring them in.'

Frost stood up. 'I'll save you the trouble. Let's go and collect them.' Then he sat down with a thud. What a stupid sod he was. An important detail and he'd forgotten to ask. And there it was, staring up at him from the table. The form Lewis had filled in giving details of his missing car. A dark brown 1988 Toyota Corolla. The vandalized car with the slashed tyres outside the apartment building in Clayton Street was a Corolla. He quickly checked registration numbers. Lewis was shown as the registered owner. He berated himself. Stupid fool. Why hadn't he made the connection before? A tap at the door. Morgan beckoned him out.

'I've checked with the cab firms, guv. Denton Minis had a fairly regular pick-up from outside 10 Clayton Street to Denton General Hospital . . . a woman. Sounds like our tom.'

'Yes,' agreed Frost dolefully, 'and it sounds like I'm losing my only bleeding suspect.'

A poky little bed-sit with a small bathroom and a kitchen. The black and orange studio couch which also served as a twin bed was rammed up tight against the sash window and on shelves fixed to the opposite wall a cheap hi-fi unit sat next to a fourteen-inch remote control colour TV. Alongside the studio couch stood a small dark-wood cabinet on which there was a phone and a china ashtray overflowing with cigarette stubs, some only half smoked and mashed to hell. 'Do you both smoke?' Frost asked.

'Only me.' Lewis took the ashtray and emptied it into a bin, blowing the overspill from the cabinet top. 'Mary hated all the muck of fag ends – said the smell gave her a headache.' He lit up another cigarette and started filling up the ashtray again.

Frost went over to two pine effect single wardrobes, one on either side of the door leading to the bathroom. He opened the door to one. Woman's clothes: coats, dresses, shoes. A handbag dangled from one of the hooks. He clicked it open: make-up and tissues. He hooked it back and closed the door. 'Did she usually take a handbag with her when she went out?'

'Yes. A red one, keys, credit cards and things.'

There had been no sign of a handbag at the Clayton Street flat, thought Frost. So where was it? He cursed his stupidity. The car. It was probably in the car. As soon as he'd finished with Lewis he'd give the motor a going-over.

'If we could have the clothes you were wearing last night,' he reminded.

'Sure – won't be a tick.' As Lewis went into the kitchen and rummaged in the laundry basket, Frost poked around, opening and closing drawers, looking for inspiration that didn't come. Lewis gave him the clothes in a plastic bag. 'Thanks,' said Frost. 'If you think of anything that might help, you will let us know?'

Lewis nodded, then flopped down on the studio couch, sniffing back tears. 'I just can't believe she's not coming back.'

'I know, I know,' cooed Frost soothingly. To himself he said, You killed her, you bastard, you bleeding killed her. But how was he going to prove it?

*   *   *

'You still suspect him, guv?' asked Morgan as Frost climbed back in the car.

'When you've only got one suspect,' grunted Frost, 'you don't let little things like watertight alibis stand in the way. Check with the other people on that coach. Let's make certain he was with them when the girl was killed.'

The brown Toyota was in a sorry state: headlights smashed, tyres slashed, bodywork crumpled as if hit with a sledge hammer. The driver's window had been shattered. Frost squeezed his arm through and opened the door, then shone his torch inside. Even the seats had been slashed. Frost brushed away the crystals of glass and slid onto the driver's seat He dug down deep into the glove compartment. 'Hey presto!' He pulled out a purse containing loose change and some credit cards. Also, a Nationwide Building Society deposit account pass book. The account had been opened three months earlier and there were regular entries, almost daily. The balance stood at over £6,000. 'The wages of sin!' muttered Frost to Morgan. 'Check if she made a will and Lewis is the sole beneficiary.'

'Girls of her age don't make wills, guv,' said Morgan. 'They don't expect to die.'

'Check anyway.' He rapped his forehead with his knuckled hand. Something was worrying him. The car keys. Where the hell were the car keys? 'First thing tomorrow, Taffy, you turn that flat upside down. The car keys have got to be there somewhere – she didn't hot wire the bleeding thing.' He called the station to get the car collected for forensic examination and was just slipping the radio back in his pocket when it squawked his name. 'Control to Inspector Frost.'

'Yes?'

'Can you get over to Denton Hospital right away, Inspector, liaise with DI Maud.'

109

'Why?'

'Young girl just been admitted . . . badly beaten up. She's a prostitute.'

'On my way,' said Frost.

Liz Maud was waiting for them by the entrance and led them up to the admission ward. 'Could be a tie-in with last night. She's been beaten up pretty badly – bruising, cracked ribs.'

'So what happened?'

'A lorry driver spotted her lying by the side of the road near Denton Woods. He thought she'd been the victim of a hit and run and phoned for an ambulance. The doctor says she's been punched and kicked.'

'Do we know who she is?'

'She won't say a blind word to me. Her handbag's full of condoms and the name on her credit card is Cherry Hall . . . In here.'

They followed her through a darkened ward and then into a side room where a heavily bandaged figure lay still on the bed. The bandaging covered most of the head and all that could be seen of her face was a pair of grey eyes stabbing them with hostility.

Frost flopped down in the chair by the bed. 'You look like Queen bleeding Nefertiti,' he told her. She didn't answer. He unhooked the chart from the foot of the bed and studied it, shaking his head in mock concern. 'It says, "Condition very serious, but co-operate with the police and you'll live." '

'I'm in pain,' hissed the girl. 'I want to be left alone.'

'Greta Garbo wanted to be left alone,' said Frost, 'and now she's dead!' He checked to see there was no nurse in sight and stuck a cigarette in his mouth. 'Come on, love. Tell me what happened and I'll go, cubs' honour.'

'Nothing to tell. I'm at Denton Terrace, freezing

cold, not much trade about, when this bloke pulls up. I didn't like the look of him, but he wasn't going to get trampled in the rush, so we agrees a price and I get in his car. He drives off to somewhere near the woods and parks. I'm starting to unbutton my dress when the bastard belts me one . . . That's it. I don't remember any more.'

'He just beat you up – for no reason?'

'Yes.'

'That wasn't very sociable. You didn't make any disparaging remarks about his appendage or anything?'

'I never saw his appendage, only his bleeding fist and there was nothing wrong with the size of that.'

'Describe him.'

The bandaged head shook. 'I don't remember.'

'Come on,' urged Frost. 'You remembered enough to say you didn't like the look of him.'

'Middle age, medium height, medium build, dark clothes.'

'Clean-shaven?'

'Yes.'

'We've got him then,' said Frost. 'There can't be more than twenty million blokes with that description.' He puffed smoke up to the ceiling. 'What sort of car?'

'Just a car. I know nothing about cars.'

'Old, new, big, small, diesel, petrol, steam-driven?'

'Medium sized . . . fairly old.'

'Colour?'

'Darkish.'

Frost flicked ash on the floor. 'You're sodding me about, aren't you, love? You could describe him perfectly if you wanted to.'

'I've told you all I can remember.'

'How old are you?'

'Seventeen.'

'Been on the game long?'

'Couple of months.'

'Got a pimp?'

'No.'

'I thought not. You say this bloke picked you up at Denton Terrace? That's where Harry Grafton's girls flash their knickers. I bet they didn't like a young piece of stuff like you encroaching on their turf?'

'It's a free country.'

'I reckon they warned you off, but you gave them the two-fingered salute, so Harry sent one of his persuaders to teach you a lesson. Right?'

'I'm saying nothing.'

'He smashed you up, love – are you going to let him get away with it? He could have killed you!'

She just lay stiff and still, willing him to go.

Frost sighed. 'If you want the bastard to get away with it, that's your prerogative. Like you said, it's a free country.' He pinched the cigarette out and dropped it in his pocket. Liz and Morgan followed him out.

The night sister was at her desk behind a newly delivered large bunch of flowers. She looked up at the inspector. 'Did Cherry tell you who did it?'

'Sudden loss of memory,' Frost told her.

'Whoever did it wants locking up. I hardly recognized her when she was brought in.'

Frost stopped in his tracks and walked back. 'You know her?'

The nurse nodded. 'She used to work here . . . in the staff canteen.'

Frost exchanged glances with Liz. 'When was this?'

'About four months or so ago. She didn't stay long.' The nurse rose from her chair and picked up the bunch of flowers. 'Perhaps these will cheer her up.'

Frost held up a hand. 'Hold on . . . Someone's sent her flowers?' He checked the card on the bouquet of red and pink carnations. 'To Miss Cherry Hall, Nightingale Ward . . . To Pastures New . . . Bon Voyage . . .' 'Who the hell would have known she was here – let alone get the right ward?'

'People can always phone the switchboard and ask,' the nurse told them. 'They have an updated list of admissions.'

Frost's eyes lit up. 'Do you tape all calls?'

'Yes,' said the nurse. 'In case people claim we've given the wrong information.'

Frost sent Liz to go down to the switchboard to check, then he picked up the bunch of flowers and waited in the corridor. He was on his second cigarette when the clatter of shoes on parquet flooring signalled Liz's return. She was panting and had to wait a while to catch her breath. 'The stairs in this place . . .'

Frost nodded. He knew all about the stairs. His wife had been up on the fourth floor. 'You've got something?'

One last gasp before she was ready to talk. 'Yes. A man phoned about half an hour ago. Asked how Cherry Hall was and what ward she was in. They told him and he hung up.'

'And . . . ? I can see from your face there's more.'

She fluttered a hand telling him to be patient. 'I listened to the tape of the call . . . It was the same man who phoned last night.'

Frost expelled a mouthful of smoke, then picked up the flowers. 'Right. Let's pay her another visit . . .'

She was still lying motionless, eyes tightly closed, pretending she was asleep and hadn't heard them return. He squeaked the chair noisily and thudded down in it. 'The bloke who beat you up sent you some flowers. Wasn't that nice of him?'

She didn't answer.

He shook her violently by the shoulder. 'OK, Fanny, we stop playing games now.'

She shrugged off his hand. 'I've nothing to say. Now get out!'

'Do you know a girl called Mary Adams?'

She stiffened. 'We used to work here together . . . so what?'

'Your friend who sent the flowers. We think he called on Mary last night.'

'Oh?' She feigned indifference.

'He won't be sending her any flowers though . . . the poor cow couldn't smell them if he did. She's dead!'

The eyes widened. 'Dead? Mary dead?'

'He strangled her, the same bloke who beat you up, so you are now going to tell me who he is.'

'I want my clothes. I'm getting out of here.' She struggled to get up, but Frost pushed her down.

'You're not going anywhere, love, you're a key witness. And to help you not go anywhere, we'll have a nice policeman sitting by your bed, twenty-four hours a day.' That'll bring the pains on with Mullett, he thought.

She lay back, eyes fluttering. 'He said he'd kill me if I went to the police.'

'He won't be able to kill you if we've got him locked up. Tell me about you and Mary Adams.'

'We used to work here in the canteen . . . long bleeding hours, starvation wages. They tried to make out we were nicking from the till and we got the push. Mary didn't want to let her boyfriend know – they were saving up for a house. She told me she was going on the game, said it would be easy money. So we both had a go. I used to share a place with her in Clayton Street where we could take the punters, but we weren't earning enough to pay the rent, so Mary said we should go to Denton Row and get the kerb-crawlers. The other girls didn't like it and we started getting threatening phone calls. I stayed away for a couple of weeks, but I wasn't earning, so I went back. And this . . .' a bandaged hand indicated her bandaged face, '. . . was what happened. He said I was to leave Denton and if I went to the police I'd end up in the bottom of the canal with conger eels for customers.'

'And who was it who beat you up?'

'One of Harry Grafton's bully boys. I don't know his name.'

'Describe him.'

'Big . . . heavy build . . . wonky nose . . . looked as if it had been broken.'

Frost's eyes gleamed. He turned to Liz. 'I know him. Mickey Harris, one of Harry's pit bulls . . . used to be a wrestler.' He stood up, sliding the chair back against the wall.

'You won't tell him I grassed?' the girl pleaded.

'You won't come into it, love,' smiled Frost. 'Beating you up is small beer . . . We're after him for murder.'

6

They went to pick up Mickey Harris without Liz
Maud who had a pile of paperwork to clear before her
trip to London. Morgan's lustful eyes watched her as
she pushed through the swing doors. 'For a detective
inspector, she's got a nice little bottom on her, guv,'
he commented as they drove off.

'Can't you get your mind on higher things?' grunted
Frost, who was thinking exactly the same. 'Turn left
here . . .'

Mickey Harris's house was in darkness and the
space outside where his car should have been parked
was empty. Frost pounded and kicked at the front
door and the noise echoed in a house that was
obviously unoccupied. He climbed back in the car.
'We'll pick him up first thing in the morning.' He
yawned. 'Back to the station, Taff.'

They never made it to the station. As they turned
into the Market Square the radio called him. It was
Bill Wells. 'Just had a call from a motorist, Inspector.
Reckons he's found a woman's body.'

'Bum-holes!' moaned Frost. 'I could have done
without this. Where?'

'In the undergrowth by the old Denton Road, near
the Denton turn-off.'

'That's near the old service station where we were
looking for the kid. What was he doing there?'

116

'He stopped off for a pee – said he nearly wee'd all over her. He sounded shattered . . . said she was naked with blood all over her.'

'I was all eager when you reached the naked bit,' grunted Frost. 'I've gone off her now. Is the motorist waiting for us?'

'No. He said he didn't want to get involved. He reported it, then rang off. Jordan and Simms are at the location waiting for you. Oh, and Wonder Woman's on her way over there as well.'

'The more the merrier,' said Frost. 'We're on our way.' He turned to Morgan. 'A chance to see your favourite bum again, Taffy. Turn right at the top here . . .'

The metal sign in front of the deserted petrol station was still clanging madly as the night wind sawed across the forecourt. Jordan and Simms climbed out of the area car and waited, coat collars turned up against the bitter cold, as Frost and Morgan pulled up.

Frost shivered and wound his scarf tighter as he surveyed the desolate area of scrubland dotted with skeletal bushes which were bending in the wind. 'The quicker we find her, the quicker we can get a nice marquee erected and keep warm.' He looked up and down the length of the old road. A lot of ground to be covered, but there were short cuts. 'If the bloke who found her stopped for a pee, we can assume he didn't want to walk far with a full bladder. He'd pick the nearest bushes to the road. Jordan, Simms, you take that side of the road, the Welsh Rarebit and me will take this. And mind where you tread; it's not only widdles that motorists do behind bushes.'

The wind was cutting through him like a rusty saw and he wished he was wearing something more substantial than his paper-thin mac. He cupped his hands round the glowing tip of his cigarette to steal some warmth. 'You take that end,' he told Morgan. 'I'll start from the old petrol station.'

He trudged through the long, wet grass which soon made his trouser legs sodden. In the distance was the glow of sodium lamps and constant throb of traffic from the new road. There were no lights along this section of the old road and they had to use torches. Frost's torch kept flickering and promising to die on him. He should have replaced the battery long ago. He swore bitterly as hidden bramble thorns scratched blood from his icy cold hands as he searched under bushes. He had the awful feeling this whole thing was someone's idea of a joke – give the fuzz something to do instead of handing out parking tickets to blameless motorists.

'Over here, Inspector!' Jordan was calling urgently from across the road, the beam from his torch soaring skywards like a searchlight, homing them over. Frost squelched across the road, Morgan hard on his heels.

Jordan's torch flashed down on the body, which was silvery white in the moonlight. Behind a clump of bushes, half hidden in the long, wet grass, lay a girl in her early twenties, sightless eyes staring up into the night sky, the mascara on her lashes running down her cheeks. She was naked. There were angry red and charred burn marks on her stomach.

Simms stared at the face. 'I know her, Inspector. I don't know her name, but she's one of the toms who hang out around the Tenwood area.'

Frost reached out a hand and steered Jordan's torch beam on to the girl's arms and legs. There were deep blooded grooves etched into her wrists and ankles where she had been tied down and where she had strained to get free. He touched the flesh. Stone cold and hard. She had been dead for some time. As he was radioing through for a full forensic team and a pathologist, another car pulled up and Liz Maud dashed over to them.

'Can I see her?'

Frost stepped back. Liz knelt by the body and studied the burn marks on the stomach, comparing them with the photograph of the earlier victim, Linda Roberts. 'Identical,' she muttered.

Frost nodded. He didn't need a photograph to tell him that.

'There's no dispute about it now,' insisted Liz. 'The same killer as Linda Roberts. This is my case.' She stared at him, her eyes hungry and pleading.

'You can have it with pleasure,' Frost told her, 'but you'd better clear it with Mullett first. Have a word with him in the morning.'

'I'll phone him now.' She hurried back to her car and dialled the Divisional Commander on her mobile. Mullett wouldn't be pleased being woken up at three in the morning, but this case was important to her. A successful murder investigation would clinch her promotion to inspector. She'd cancel her appointment at the clinic, even if it meant losing the hefty deposit. 'Come on, come on,' she muttered impatiently as the ringing tone droned on and on in her ear.

At last a sleepy voice answered. 'Mullett.'

'DI Maud, sir. Sorry to bother you, but it is import-ant . . .' She quickly explained. A second prostitute murdered, identical to the Linda Roberts case – her case. She wanted to take charge; it was her right . . .

She could sense the ice crackling down the line as Mullett's annoyance grew.

'This could, and should, have waited until the morning,' he snapped.

'I'm sorry, sir, but I thought it was important—'

He didn't let her finish. 'It is not important, and the answer to your ill-timed request is no.'

The ice now crackled from her direction. 'Might I be permitted to ask why, sir?'

'I was going to tell you in the morning. Inspector Allen is returning to Denton the week after next so you will be reverting to your normal rank. There is absolutely no point in Frost handing over to you, then in ten days' time you handing back to Mr Allen. Inspector Frost must handle it.'

'But, sir—'

Again Mullett didn't let her finish. Didn't the damn woman have any consideration? 'That's enough, Inspector. And if you hope to get on in the force, you will never phone me at this hour again with routine matters.' A click and the dialling tone. She switched off and stared at the dead phone, wanting to relieve her feelings by hurling it through the car window. The bastard. Ten days. With luck she could have had this tied up in ten days. She felt like bursting into tears, but wouldn't give anyone the satisfaction. She rammed a cigarette in her mouth, then spun the car around and drove back to Denton.

The bright blue marquee protecting the body from the elements flapped and whip-cracked in the wind. Frost, hands thrust deep in his mac pocket, a cigarette drooping from his mouth, watched as Harding and the forensic team poked about in the grass. He felt redundant and wished the pathologist would hurry up and arrive so he could get back to the warmth of the station.

'Inspector!' PC Simms had returned. He had been sent out with a photograph, knocking on doors of known prostitutes to see if any of them could name the dead girl. 'One of them recognized her. Her name is Angela Masters – new kid on the block.'

'When was she last seen alive?'

'Two nights ago. The other toms were surprised

she wasn't on her regular beat. They thought she was ill.'

'The poor cow was bloody ill all right,' muttered Frost. He shivered and rubbed his hands together. Come on, bloody Drysdale. There was nothing the pathologist could tell him about the body that he couldn't see for himself and the post-mortem wouldn't be until the next day, preferably not at the crack of dawn like last time.

Headlights painted the sides of the marquee orange and the purr of an expensive car engine could just about be heard above the scream of the wind. The pathologist had arrived.

Drysdale, followed by his faithful blonde secretary, squeezed through the flap of the marquee, his expression souring at the sight of the loutish Inspector Frost. He should have guessed it would be him. Frost's cases always seemed to involve bodies in appalling weather conditions in the middle of the night. He nodded curtly. Frost stamped his cigarette out and waved a hand to the body. 'All yours, doc.'

Drysdale's lips tightened at the 'doc'. 'Another prostitute?'

'Yes, doc, and we've got a name this time so you can put a tag on her toe.'

The pathologist bent over the body and nodded his recognition. 'We had one like this a couple of months ago – one of Inspector Allen's cases, if I recall.' He knelt on the plastic sheet covering the grass and peered at the burns and wounds on the stomach. 'Exactly the same.' He stared hard at the face. 'She'd been gagged – you can see where the cord bit into her mouth.'

'Yes,' agreed Frost. 'The bastard who did this didn't want her screams to disturb the fun of his cigarette stubbing.'

Drysdale snapped his fingers as an order to his

secretary to provide him with surgical gloves, which he slipped on for a brief internal examination. 'Sexual activity took place shortly before death . . . From the bruising around the thighs I'd say she resisted it.'

'I wouldn't expect her to welcome the bastard with open legs,' said Frost. 'DNA sample?'

Drysdale shook his head. 'I don't think so. He seems to have used a condom.' He straightened up. 'Can we turn her over, please?'

Frost nodded to the two uniformed men to do this. The girl's white back and buttocks were marked with a criss-cross pattern of blooded weals and cuts and mottled with yellowing bruises.

'Buttocks and back beaten with a thin cane . . . exactly like the other girl. As before, I'd say you're looking for some kind of sexual pervert.'

'Well, that lets the vicar off the hook,' grunted Frost. 'Cause and time of death?'

'Cause – suffocation, like the other one, probably a pillow held over the face. Time of death?' He shrugged. 'Twenty-four to forty-eight hours.' He peeled off the surgical gloves and dropped them into the plastic bag his secretary was holding out. 'I'll do the post-mortem tomorrow – eleven o'clock. You can move the body when you like.' With a jerk of his head for his secretary to follow, he marched back to the Rolls-Royce.

Frost stuck a cigarette in his mouth and watched as the body was lifted into a cheap coffin by the two undertaker's men, one of whom shuddered as they lifted her.

'Someone's given her a right going-over.'

'She wouldn't answer our questions,' grunted Frost.

Morgan ambled over. 'Who would treat a woman like that, guv?'

'A bastard who likes inflicting pain,' said Frost. 'She might have been willing, up to a point – let herself be

122

tied up, but then it went too far. He was enjoying himself too much to stop.' He looked at his watch. Three thirty in the morning. 'Let's get back to the station.'

He pinned up the photograph of Angela Masters alongside the others on the wall of the murder incident room and waited while Morgan handed out copies. 'I'm sorry it's so late. If that bleeding motorist could have controlled his bladder, she might have been found at a more convenient time. I'm briefing you now so you can go off home for some kip then go straight out tomorrow morning knocking up toms. We need to know if they've had any kinky clients who wanted to tie them up and welt them with a cane. If so, we want details. When did they last see Angela Masters? Did anyone see her go off with a punter?' He turned to the pin-board. 'She was killed, beaten and used to stub out fags in exactly the same way as Linda Roberts, eight weeks ago. Inspector Allen questioned all the toms about Linda without any luck, and we're probably going to have the same flaming luck, but that won't stop us from asking all over again. Warn the girls they should only go with customers they know. This bloke did it once, he liked it and did it again. We're no longer looking for a punter who went too far. We're now looking for a serial killer.' He nodded to Arthur Hanlon who was waving a hand. 'Yes, Arthur? Not going to confess, are you?'

Hanlon grinned. 'The girl who was killed in Clayton Street – do you think there's any connection?'

Frost shook his head. 'No, Arthur. We're pinning that one on Mickey Harris. Mickey likes using women as a punch bag. He hits them with his fists and he doesn't tie them up first.' He turned back to the pin-board and pointed to Big Bertha. 'We've now got to start worrying about Bertha. If a tom goes missing, from now on, we fear the worst, so ask around, find out when was the last time anyone saw her, who was she with. You know the drill.' He looked at the other two photographs on the wall; the skull dug up under the shed and the gap-toothed Vicky Stuart. Two cases that would have to be pushed into the background until they caught the tom killer. 'Right, off you go.'

As they filed out, he jabbed a finger at Morgan. 'You be here at nine tomorrow so we can pick up Mickey Harris. He's been known to put cops out of action when they try to arrest him and you can be spared more than anyone else.'

9.10 a.m. Morgan was late. Frost chomped tastelessly at the fatty bacon sandwich, dropping crumbs all over the lead story as he skimmed through the *Denton Echo*. HOUSE OF HORROR REVEALS ITS GRISLY SECRETS, screamed the headline. The news about the dead prostitute had arrived after the paper had gone to press, so they were making a meal of a lesser story. The phone rang. 'Young lady to see you, Inspector,' said Bill Wells. 'I've put her in No. 1 interview room.' Before Frost could ask who it was, Wells had rung off. Damn. He hoped this wouldn't take long; there was more than enough to get through as it was.

No sign of Wells in the lobby, but the swing doors banged open and Morgan, just finishing knotting his tie, charged in and looked shamefacedly at Frost. 'Sorry I'm late, guv, but—'

'I'll hear your lies in a minute, Taffy – we've got a young lady to see first.' He pushed open the door of the interview room, Morgan following quickly, running a comb through untidy hair as he did so. Shit! Sitting there, grim-faced, handbag clasped to her chest, was old mother bloody Beatty. 'I'm being stalked,' she said.

'Oh,' said Frost, trying to sound concerned. 'Give

124

the details to the sergeant outside and we'll look into it.' He backed to the door.

'No,' she snapped. 'The sergeant said I was to talk to you.'

With a resigned sigh, Frost slumped down in the chair opposite her. 'Describe him.'

She leant forward. 'That's just the point,' she said earnestly. 'He never looks the same. Sometimes he's thin and clean-shaven, sometimes he's fat with a moustache.'

'Sounds like Laurel and Hardy,' said Frost.

She glared. 'This is not funny, Inspector. He was outside my house last night, walking up and down the street, staring up at my window, hoping to see me undressing. I feel his eyes on me as I go to the shops. I turn, but there's no-one there. He's too clever for that.'

'Right,' said Frost, nodding gravely, 'I think I know who it is.' He stood up. 'Leave this to us. He won't trouble you again.'

She didn't look too convinced as he ushered her out. 'That bastard Wells!' he snarled.

'You said you know who he is?' said Morgan.

'Yes, I do, Taff. He's a figment of her bleeding imagination. See her getting undressed? I'd pay a hundred pounds not to.' He opened the door a crack to make certain she had left. 'Come on. Let's go and arrest Mickey Harris.'

Still no car parked outside and the milk on the step hadn't been taken in. Just to make sure Frost hammered at the door and gave it a couple of kicks, then crouched down and peered through the letter box at the morning paper with its HOUSE OF HORROR headlines lying on the mat.

'Where now, guv?' asked Morgan, hoping the inspector would say 'Back to the station' so he could calm his rumbling stomach with a canteen breakfast. But Frost had other ideas.

'We're going to call on super-ponce Harry Grafton. He's the one who tells Mickey which toms to beat up.'

The wages of sin had definitely paid off for Harry Grafton. Denton Grange was a large brick gabled house in mock Tudor, set well back behind a small spinney which sheltered it from the vulgar gaze of people driving along the main road – probably on their way to one of Harry's prostitutes. They passed a 'Warning!! – Guard Dogs' sign and coasted through the spinney and on to the main entrance. Four expensive cars were parked in front of the house. The doors of a mock Tudor garage were open and a heavily built man, carefully polishing an already gleaming silver grey Rolls-Royce, looked up as Frost's Ford juddered to an exhaust-coughing halt. He put down his chamois leather and walked over to them. 'If you haven't got an appointment, piss off.'

'I've got something better than an appointment, Jeeves,' said Frost. 'I've got this.' He flashed his warrant card. 'Kindly inform your master the fuzz want to see him.'

The man scowled at the card, then led them inside the house to an oak-panelled hall. 'Wait,' he grunted as he disappeared down the passage.

'Did he say "Feel free to look around"?' asked Frost. 'Let's see how the rich pimps live.' He pushed open a door which led into a large room with bay windows overlooking a lawn and a covered swimming pool. The room held the rich smells of expensive leather, wool and cigar smoke. Their feet sank ankle deep into thick-piled carpeting on which stood a five-seater settee in pale blue hide and four matching armchairs. Frost sniffed in the heady aromas. 'The smell of opulence, Taff,' he said, dropping down into

126

one of the armchairs, his eyes taking in the forty-two-inch wide-screen digital TV set with surround sound, the massive corner bar, complete with beer pumps, then up to the ceiling which was painted a midnight blue and decorated with silver stars. 'All it wants is a slop bucket and a spittoon,' he decided, 'and it would be a proper home from home. I wonder how many dicks had to work overtime to pay for this little lot.'

The door clicked open and Harry Grafton came in, a swarthy-skinned man in his mid-forties, dark hair balding, a thin black moustache and cold eyes which failed to match the oily smile. He wore a scarlet dressing-gown and could barely close his mouth over the fat cigar between his lips. The car polisher was at his side.

'Inspector Frost. An unexpected pleasure.' He clicked his fingers and pointed to a cassette recorder on a side table which his sidekick switched to record. 'I hope you don't mind, gentlemen. I like to have all conversations recorded, in case there is any dispute as to what has been said.'

'A wise precaution, Harry,' nodded Frost. 'It stops me from lying my bloody head off. We want to see Mickey Harris.'

Grafton pulled the cigar from his mouth and studied the glowing end. 'Mickey? Why?'

'Grievous bodily harm. He beat up a tom last night.'

Grafton smiled as if the idea were preposterous. 'And what makes you think it was Mickey?'

'She fingered him.'

Harry Grafton frowned, then clicked the smile back on. 'She was mistaken, Inspector. Mickey was here all night, never went out.'

Frost shook his head and tutted. 'God can hear you telling these lies, Harry.'

Grafton walked over to the cassette recorder and

127

pressed the pause button. 'Off the record, Inspector, I do look after a few girls. It's hard enough for them to make a living at the best of times without these young amateurs muscling in on their territory. There's not enough trade to go round, so sometimes we have to give them a little slap on the wrist and suggest they would be better opening up shop elsewhere.'

'This was more than a little slap, Harry. Mickey put this seventeen-year-old kid in hospital. Broken nose, cracked ribs – she was coughing up bits of blood and teeth when I saw her. Put me right off my black pudding for breakfast.'

It was Grafton's turn to do the head-shaking and tut-tutting act as he released the pause button on the recorder. 'Disgraceful, Inspector. The animals who do that should be put inside – but it wasn't Mickey. As I said, he was here all night. I have witnesses.'

'Who?'

'Myself and six of my employees.'

'Quantity, but not quality, Harry. A rich pimp and six of his hired thugs.'

'As against the evidence of a single prostitute.' He smiled smugly. 'I think we both know which of us the courts would believe. But to show my good faith, even though I am not involved in this in any way and just to ensure my good name should not be smirched, I will personally see that the unfortunate girl is well compensated.'

'I'm sure you could buy her off, Harry, but there was another girl Mickey had a go at.'

'Oh?'

'Mary Adams. Had a place in Clayton Street.'

A brief flicker of recognition instantly suppressed as Grafton again studied the glowing end of the cigar and shook his head vaguely. 'Name means nothing to me. When was this supposed to have taken place?'

'The night before last.'

128

Grafton smiled. 'Then again it couldn't have been Mickey. He was here all that night as well.' He turned to the car polisher. 'Isn't that right, Richard?'

Richard nodded his vigorous agreement. 'Dead right, Mr Grafton.'

'Mickey didn't stop at slapping her wrist, Harry. He killed the poor cow.'

The cigar drooped as Harry's mouth gaped open. 'Killed . . . ?'

'We're talking murder, Harry, and we've got Mickey well and truly in the frame. Before we start discussing perjury and perverting the course of justice, do you still want to give him an alibi?'

Grafton's finger crashed down on the stop key of the recorder. He rewound the tape then waited while it erased before turning back to Frost. 'I know nothing about any killings. I don't want anything to do with this.'

'So Mickey wasn't with you the two nights in question?'

'No.'

'Is he here?'

Grafton jerked his head to his sidekick. 'Fetch him.'

As the man sidled out, Grafton snatched the cigar from his mouth and squashed it out in an ashtray shaped like a naked, recumbent woman. Frost winced. It reminded him of the cigarette burns on the dead girl's stomach. Footsteps outside and the sidekick returned with Mickey Harris, a thickset brute of a man in his forties with a boxer's flattened nose and thick ears. He scowled at Frost before turning to Grafton. 'You wanted me, Mr Grafton?'

'The fuzz want you for questioning,' snapped Grafton, underlining his instructions with a jab of his finger. 'Keep your mouth shut, don't say a bleeding word, don't even pass the bloody time of day until our lawyer gets there. Right?' Without waiting for

Mickey's reply, he turned on his heels and stomped out of the room.

Frost took Harris by the arm. 'Come on, Mickey. We're going walkies.'

Frost thumbed through his in-tray as he impatiently waited for the brief to turn up. Harris wouldn't say a dicky bird until the solicitor arrived. He tugged out a report from Forensic. They hadn't found any traces of blood on the clothes and shoes from Lewis, the boyfriend of Mary Adams, so Mickey Harris was now his one and only prime suspect and somehow he couldn't see Mickey as a strangler. But he was all he had. A groan from Morgan attracted his attention. 'What's up, Taffy? You on heat again?'

'No, guv, it's this damn abscess.' He rubbed his cheek and winced.

'You know what they say, Taff – abscess makes the heart grow fonder.' Morgan quivered a wan smile. He didn't think that half as funny as Frost who was coughing and spluttering with laughter at his own joke.

A tap at the door and Liz Maud entered carrying a couple of case files.

'I thought you'd be away by now?' said Frost.

'I've got to clear it with Mr Mullett first,' she told him, 'and he's not in yet.' She dropped the files on his desk. 'Could you baby-sit these for me until I get back? The only active investigation is the armed robbery.'

Frost flipped the file open. 'You've found the get-away car, then?'

She sat in the vacant chair. 'Wesley Division found it down a back street in the town. Blood all over the floor by the driver's seat which matches blood from the mini-mart and splashes of white paint everywhere.'

Frost scratched his chin. 'Wesley? That's over twenty miles away.'

'Yes. Wesley are checking on known villains in their Division.'

'But why come all the way from Wesley to rob a tuppenny-ha'penny mini-mart in Denton? There must have been plenty of fatter targets closer to home.'

She blinked. That aspect hadn't occurred to her. 'Maybe the cashier was in on it and they thought it would be easy.'

'You checked out the cashier?'

Liz nodded. 'We found nothing on her – but that doesn't mean to say she's clean.'

Bill Wells poked his head round the door. 'Mickey Harris's brief has arrived, Jack.' He gave Liz a curt nod. 'And Mr Mullett has just come in, Sergeant – sorry, I'm ten days premature – I meant Inspector.'

Frost dropped down into the old, familiar chair which seemed to mould itself round him and watched Kirkstone, the sleek and plump solicitor, dust his chair carefully with a handkerchief before allowing his £600 suit to touch it. Kirkstone grunted as Frost intoned the preliminaries and watched in a bored fashion as Morgan started the cassette recorder. Frost slid across a photograph of the seventeen-year-old Cherry Hall. 'Recognize her, Mickey?'

Mickey gave it the briefest of glances before shaking his head. 'No.'

'You don't know who she is? You don't know her name?'

Mickey glanced at the lawyer, who nodded he should answer. 'Correct.'

'She's a prostitute who'd been plying for hire on Harry Grafton's sacred turf. Did Harry ask you to warn her off?'

Another check with the lawyer. 'No.'

'Come off it, Mickey. Harry told you to warn her off but you were having such fun beating up a seventeen-year-old girl, breaking her ribs, knocking out her teeth, you just couldn't stop. Is that what happened, Mickey?'

Kirkstone gave a little cough and a slimy smile. 'As my client doesn't know the young lady and has never met her, there is no way he could have hit her.'

'Good point,' agreed Frost. 'But if he didn't know her and didn't beat her up, why did he phone the hospital to ask how the poor cow was?' As Mickey opened his mouth to answer, Frost's hand came up to stop him. 'Before you deny it, Mickey, you should know that the hospital tapes all calls and you came over loud and clear.'

'A word with my client,' said the lawyer. Frost leant back and smoked as Harris and Kirkstone huddled together murmuring inaudibly, until the lawyer indicated that Mickey was ready to answer.

'All right, Inspector. I didn't tell the truth because I was embarrassed. I was a client of hers a couple of nights ago. Someone told me she had been beaten up, so I phoned the hospital to enquire about her. I even sent her a bunch of flowers.'

'An act of kindness,' smirked the lawyer.

'You make me feel a swine for ever doubting you,' said Frost. He took the photograph back and swapped it for one of Mary Adams. 'Recognize this one, Mick?'

Mickey stared at the photograph then shot a quick glance to the lawyer who, with a barely perceptible shake of the head, told him to say no.

'No.'

'Her name is Mary Adams, trade name Lolita. She operated from a flat in Clayton Street. Ever been there?'

'Never.'

'When business was slack she used to go after the crumpet hunters in Denton Parade and King Street, an area on which Harry Grafton felt he had monopoly trading rights. Harry told you to warn her off, didn't he – to rough her up a bit?'

'No. And if she says I did, she's lying.'

'Yes – she's lying . . . in the bleeding morgue, Mickey. You went too far this time. She's dead.'

'Dead?' Mickey blinked with indignation. 'That's rubbish. I never touched her. I never went near her.' He turned to the lawyer for support but Kirkstone appeared to be busying himself writing copious notes on a sheet of A4 paper. Mickey was on his own with the murder charge.

'You like to phone them up after you pay them a visit, don't you, Mickey? You thought you'd phoned this girl, but she couldn't answer the phone as she was dead. You actually spoke to one of my women officers. You boasted about beating Mary up.'

Mickey's head was being violently shaken from side to side. 'No. It's bloody lies.'

'You phoned her, Mickey. We've got you on tape.' Frost was picking his words carefully in case of future legal arguments. He only had Mickey on tape for the hospital call. 'Couple more photographs you might recognize.' These were of the other two prostitutes, the ones who were tied and tortured. The solicitor leant over to look at them and shuddered, moving his chair slightly, distancing himself even more from his client. Mickey was staring aghast. 'Oh no – you're not pinning all your bloody unsolved crimes on me. All right, I beat up the kid in hospital, but I never laid a finger on Mary Adams.'

'But you phoned her, Mickey. You told her next time it would be really serious.'

Mickey stared at Frost, his eyes blinking rapidly, but before he could answer, the solicitor intervened.

'If my client had killed this woman, Inspector, why would he phone her up with further threats?'

'He phoned,' said Frost, 'to see if she was still alive.'

'No!' shouted Mickey. 'I phoned to tell her about her bloody car.'

'Her car?' echoed Frost, wondering what the hell this was about.

'I'd phoned a few times warning her to stay off of Harry's patch, but she took no notice. I was going in to give her a going-over but she wasn't in, so I decided to do her car in instead. I slashed the tyres and gave it a few welts with a sledge hammer. It was a warning. If that didn't work, next time it would be her; that's what I was phoning about.'

'Naturally,' smarmed Kirkstone, 'my client will pay for any damage he inadvertently did to the car.'

'You smashed her car,' said Frost, 'and then you went up to the flat to tell her what you had done. She went for you with a knife and you killed her.'

'Like I said, she wasn't in – out tomming on Mr Grafton's patch, I reckoned. I left it a couple of hours, then I phoned her and that's the honest, bloody truth!'

Kirkstone leant back in his chair and flashed Frost an ingratiating smile. 'Might I ask how this young lady was killed, Inspector? It's probably slipped your mind that you neglected to tell us.'

Frost groaned inwardly. It hadn't slipped his mind. This was the weaker part of his case against Mickey. 'She was strangled.'

'Strangled?' exclaimed Kirkstone in mock surprise. 'You're saying she wasn't beaten to death?'

'No,' grunted Frost.

'And these other two unfortunate women – did they show any signs of being punched . . . beaten with fists?'

'No,' admitted Frost grudgingly.

'So their injuries are not at all consistent with those of the young girl in hospital?'

'Correct,' muttered Frost.

'I take it there is nothing to connect my client with the two deaths?'

Frost nodded gloomily. The bastard had him on the ropes.

'So we can dismiss that allegation entirely. The only connection he has with the death in Clayton Street is the phone call which he admits to making and for which he has given a satisfactory explanation.'

'He's given an explanation,' said Frost, clutching at what little bit of straw was left, 'but it may not be the true one. I want the clothes he was wearing that night for forensic examination.'

'I was wearing the clothes I've got on now,' said Mickey, starting to take off his jacket. 'I take it you're not interested in my underpants and socks?'

'Definitely bloody not,' shuddered Frost. He was wasting his time with Mickey. He knew it. The man had nothing to do with the killings, but let Forensic have a sniff round the clothes, you never knew your luck. He shoved the photographs back in the folder and stood up. 'Give my colleague a statement, and your clothes, and you'll be released on police bail.'

Kirkstone patted his papers into shape and dropped them in the leather briefcase. 'I'll get your other suit sent in,' he told Harris. 'Don't sign the statement until you have read it out to me over the phone.' He followed Frost out. 'You haven't got the shadow of a case, Inspector.'

'We've definitely got him for the poor cow he put in hospital,' said Frost.

Kirkstone smiled. 'I wouldn't be at all surprised if the young lady dropped the charge, Inspector.'

'How much is Harry going to pay to buy her off?' asked Frost.

Another smile from Kirkstone. 'I shall pretend I didn't hear that.' With a curt nod he took his leave, humming happily as he strode down the corridor.

'Oily bastard!' snarled Frost at the departing figure.

Police Superintendent Mullett suppressed a yawn and stared down at the waspish memo County had sent him, returning Frost's outstanding crime figures with the carping comment, underlined in red ink, that until this was corrected the All Divisions Quarterly Statistical Summary was delayed and the Chief Constable would want to know why. Mullett's lips tightened. A Division was judged by its paperwork and yet again Frost had let him down. A tap at the door. He sighed. Even the man's knocking had a slovenly air to it. He began to say 'Come in' but was forestalled as Frost slouched in and dropped unbidden into the visitor's chair, a cigarette with a length of ash threatening to fall any minute, drooping from his mouth. 'You wanted to see me, Super?'

'Yes.' Mullett hastily slid the ashtray across but was just too late to stop the cylinder of ash from dropping on the carpet. He winced as Frost scuffed it into the pile with his shoe. 'I've had this from County.' He pushed the memo and the return across.

Frost give it a disinterested sniff. 'Those silly sods in County seem to think their bleeding figures are more important than solving crimes.'

'Head Office judge us on our paperwork, Frost. And in any case, your crime-solving figures are nothing to boast about.'

Frost shrugged. 'Never thought I boasted about them. What's their beef?'

'Their beef, Frost, is that your return omits quite a few of your own unsolved cases, but includes cases already shown on Inspector Maud's return.'

Shit, thought Frost. Morgan must have got the files mixed up. He scooped up the return and stood up. 'I'll do it when I get time.'

'You'll get it done today,' snapped Mullett, 'and I still haven't finished.' The way Frost kept looking pointedly at his watch and raising his eyebrows to the ceiling was starting to irritate. He tried unsuccessfully to stifle another yawn.

'Out on the tiles last night, Super?' asked Frost.

'No, I wasn't. I was woken in the early hours by that wretched Inspector Maud wanting to be put in charge of the prostitute killing and then I couldn't get back to sleep again. And then she had the damn cheek to come in here this morning demanding to be allowed a few days off. She knows how busy and short-staffed we are. Said she had to have an urgent minor operation at a private clinic, but wouldn't tell me what it was about, said it was personal woman's stuff. Do you know what it's about?'

Frost shook his head. 'Perhaps she's having her breasts enlarged,' he suggested.

Mullett sat back and frowned. 'Surely they're large enough already?'

'You'd know more about that than me, Super,' muttered Frost. 'I haven't really studied them like you.'

Mullett flushed a deep red. 'I haven't studied them. Some things you can't help noticing. Anyway, she's off for a few days, which leaves us even more short-handed.'

'Get some of our men back from County then.'

'No. I want County to see that we can manage no matter how short-staffed we are. We'll all have to be that much more efficient. She'll be back next week and Inspector Allen will be returning soon after that. We can hold out until then.'

Frost stood up and moved to the door. 'As long as you don't mind the overtime bill going up.'

'No way,' said Mullett firmly, remembering what the Chief Constable had said at the meeting. 'That is the easy way out.'

But he was talking to a closed door.

7

Frost added up the column of figures again to check Morgan's addition but made it yet a different total. He admitted defeat and signed the form anyway. 'Are you sure it's right this time?' he asked, tossing the crime return back to Morgan.

'Positive, guv,' replied Morgan. But he was always positive, completely undeterred by his record of past mistakes. He rubbed his jaw and winced. 'This flaming tooth doesn't half hurt.'

'It'll hurt a damn sight more when the bastard pulls it out,' said Frost, who hated dentists. The day wasn't going too well. The post-mortem hadn't turned up anything they didn't already know and Morgan's search of the flat in Clayton Street had failed to find the missing car key.

Arthur Hanlon came in and flopped wearily into a vacant chair. 'You wanted me to check on the clothes Lewis was wearing at the match, Jack. I've traced a few of the people he travelled with on the coach, but they were so drunk that night half of them don't remember what the score was, let alone what anyone was wearing. I also traced the bloke who gave them lifts back home. He confirms he dropped Lewis off at the flat, but doesn't remember what time.'

'Great,' said Frost. 'Everyone's so flaming helpful!'

'And this won't please you either.' Hanlon handed

Frost a fax from Forensic. 'The only blood on Mickey Harris's clothes came from the tom he put in hospital – nothing to tie him in with the dead Mary Adams.'

'Bloody Forensic!' muttered Frost, as if it was all their fault. He relit a dog-end and took a couple of drags. 'But I didn't expect them to find anything on Harris. This isn't his style. It's the boyfriend, Lewis, Arthur, I'm sure of it.'

'But his story checks out,' protested Hanlon. 'And Forensic found nothing on his clothes.'

'That's because the sod gave us the wrong clothes,' said Frost. He found the Forensic report and showed it to the DS. 'Look, traces of lubricating oil and automotive grease on jeans.'

'That's what you'd expect, Jack. He works in a petrol station.'

'He was going out that night with his mates, Arthur. He'd put clean flaming jeans on, not his working clothes.' The cigarette tasted foul, so he mashed it out and lit up another. As he flicked through the Forensic report he noticed something he had missed. A note stating that the attached envelope contained items found in the pocket of the jeans. What envelope? He found it in his in-tray and ripped it open, hoping to find something that would help. A couple of cinema tickets, a service till receipt for £10 withdrawn from Benningtons Bank in the High Street and a supermarket receipt for two hundred cigarettes. Disappointed, he was stuffing them back in the envelope when a thought hit him. 'He smoked a lot, didn't he?'

'What do you mean?' asked Hanlon.

'The ashtray in his flat, next to the bed. It was piled up with fag ends – about forty or more, I reckon.'

'So?'

'So when did he smoke them?'

Hanlon blinked. He didn't know what Frost was going on about. 'Does it matter?'

'Yes, it does flaming matter. When?'

Hanlon shrugged. 'Before he left for the match?'

'No. He left first. The girlfriend had a few hours to go before she had to leave, so she tidied up the place – he told us.'

'So?'

'She didn't smoke, Arthur,' explained Frost patiently. 'She hated mess. She wouldn't have left an ashtray piled high with fag ends. She'd have emptied it.'

'When he got back then, in the early hours?'

'But he told us he was dead beat and flopped straight into bed. It would have taken about two to three hours to have smoked all those fags even if you stuck them up your nose as well.'

Hanlon looked puzzled. 'I don't see where this is leading us.'

'Try this out for size, Arthur. He kills his girlfriend. When he gets back to the flat his mind's in a bloody turmoil; what the hell has he done? He can't sleep, so he lies on the bed and smokes himself sick. Some of those dog-ends had hardly been touched, a couple of drags and he stubbed them out.'

'Just because you lay in bed smoking, it doesn't mean you've killed your girlfriend.'

'Only if you're trying to be fair and logical, Arthur, which I am not. He did it, I bloody know it.' Frost snapped his fingers. 'Wait a minute!' He pulled the receipt for the cigarettes from the envelope, checked the date on his desk calendar then grinned triumphantly. 'At ten o'clock yesterday morning, Arthur, when he was supposed to be fast asleep in his little bed, he was at the supermarket buying two hundred fags . . . and he told us he didn't wake up until the afternoon.'

'All right . . . so he couldn't sleep and wanted a smoke.'

'You're missing the flaming point, Arthur. If he's awake at ten, he knows the bloody girl isn't back from the hospital where she's supposed to be working, and when he went out for the fags, he would have seen his car wasn't there, which means the story he told us was a load of flaming cobblers.'

'He might have thought she was doing the shopping – you don't have to go to bed the minute you get in from work.'

'Whose bloody side are you on, Arthur? I want this case out of the way. It's got nothing to do with the serial killings of the other toms and we're wasting too much time on it. Go and bring Lewis in. Don't arrest him, say I want to see him, but don't tell him what about . . . let's get him worried. Uncertainty, Arthur, nothing puts the wind up people more than baked beans and uncertainty . . .' He grinned to himself. It wasn't going to be such a bad day after all.

But the minute he walked into the interview room the nagging doubts began to fester. He had missed something, something right under his nose, but he didn't know what the hell it was. These bloody warning bells of his gave the warning without specifying the damn danger.

He sat in the chair and put the folder with the till receipt in front of him while Morgan fiddled with the cassette recorder. His mind was racing. He didn't have the bare bones of a sustainable case against Lewis. All he had was a gut feeling, and one lousy till receipt for cigarettes. If the case came to court without a confession, there was no way of proving that Lewis had gone out that morning and bought the cigarettes – the till receipt could have been issued to anyone.

142

What he needed was a confession, without it he was sunk. If Lewis insisted he was wearing his work jeans that night, there was no way of disproving it. And the car keys – why were they missing?

A tap at the door and Sergeant Hanlon came in with Lewis who was not looking the bundle of twitching nerves that Frost was hoping for.

'Have you caught the bastard?' asked Lewis, sitting in the chair opposite Frost.

'Not yet,' said Frost. 'But we know who he is, and with your help we'll nail him.'

'Anything,' said Lewis. 'Anything at all.' He dug in his pockets for his cigarettes, but Frost got in first, offering his packet and taking one himself. 'Thanks.' Lewis struck a match and held it out to light Frost's cigarette. Frost took his time, noting with satisfaction that the hand holding the match was trembling slightly. He steadied it with his own. We're getting to you, you bastard, he thought.

From the file on the table he took the typed copy of Lewis's statement. 'I realize it's upsetting asking you to go over this yet again but I want to make certain we've got our facts straight.' A quick glance at the first page. 'The last time you saw Mary alive was when you left for the match about five?'

Lewis nodded.

'When you got back in the early hours, you had no reason to think anything was wrong?'

'No – everything was as it should be!'

'You'd had an eventful night so you flopped into bed, went out like a light into a deep, untroubled sleep?'

'That's right.'

'You didn't wake up until late afternoon and that was the first time you realized she was missing?'

'Yes.'

Frost nodded, as if satisfied. And he was satisfied.

Things were going to plan. Lewis was digging his own grave with his mouth. 'Good. That checks with everything you've told us.' He smiled. 'People tell us lies, but we always find them out.' Lewis twitched a nervous smile back not certain how to take this. Now's the time to hit the bastard with the till receipt, thought Frost. He slowly opened the folder, keeping his eyes fixed firmly on the man's face to watch his reaction when he confronted him with proof of his lying.

Frost never reached the till receipt. He suddenly found himself staring goggle-eyed at the calendar on the wall. The date. The bloody date! That was what the little bell in his head had been warning him about. The wall calendar told him it was the 8th. The calendar in his office had said the 7th. Taffy Morgan had forgotten to change the flaming date which meant that the till receipt was for the morning before the murder, not the morning after and had nothing to do with the case. His one lonely trump card had been shot fairly and squarely right up the fundamental orifice. He now had absolutely sod all.

He kept his face impassive as his mind whirled, trying to think of some way to retrieve the situation. He examined the till receipt and gave an Academy Award-winning satisfied nod as if it was of the greatest importance, then placed it face down on the table. He took some more papers from the file, including the useless Forensic report, and positioned them, also face down, alongside the receipt. Let the sod think I've got a full house, he thought, instead of a busted bloody flush. Lewis's eyes were following every move Frost made. Right, this was going to be one hell of a bluff. He didn't even have one card to play. He took a deep breath.

'This is the position. We've got witnesses, we've got discrepancies in statements, we've got conclusive forensic evidence. We now know who killed your girlfriend, Mr Lewis. There's only one thing we need to know, and that's where you can help us.'

'Anything,' said Lewis, eagerly. 'Anything.'

Frost took a cigarette from his packet and slowly tapped it on the table. This was the moment. This was make or break. He lit up, then smiled his most charming and disingenuous smile. His voice sounded fatherly and full of compassion.

'Why did you do it, son?'

He held his breath and waited. Lewis scowled at him, eyes full of hate, his mouth opening and shutting as if his anger was too strong to allow him to speak. Frost's heart plummeted. I've blown it, he thought. I've bloody blown it. He stared down at the table, his mind in overdrive. A strange sound. A sound that, at first, he couldn't place. He looked up. Lewis's shoulders were shaking. He was laughing, laughing away to himself as if at some secret joke, perhaps at the absurdity of the accusation. Frost blinked. It wasn't laughter. Lewis was crying, his body shaking as uncontrollable tears gushed down a face screwed up in agony. He covered his eyes with his hands and his sobbing was almost pitiful to hear. The other two detectives were staring, just dumbstruck.

Frost got in quickly. 'You killed her, son, didn't you?' His voice was gentle.

'An accident.' The words were barely audible.

'Tell us about it. Get it off your chest – you'll feel better afterwards.' Frost sounded like a member of the Spanish Inquisition begging a heretic to confess so the torture could stop and he could be burnt at the stake. But Lewis was now only too willing and the words poured out almost as fast as the tears.

'Things were getting dodgy between us for some time. I thought she was seeing someone else. There were these mysterious phone calls, stuff locked away in her drawer which I wasn't allowed to see. Coming

145

back from the match that night, some of the boys had a go at the bloke in the off-licence and the cops hauled us into the nick. On the way there we diverted through King Street where all the tarts hang out and everyone in the coach started to yell and whistle and make obscene remarks at this prostitute, all slit skirt and big tits, picking up a drunk. I couldn't believe it. It was her . . . Mary . . . my bleeding girlfriend . . . the so-called bloody nurse . . .'

He scrubbed his face with his hands as if trying to wipe out the recollection.

'Go on, son,' prompted Frost.

'It was now all making sense. A couple of weeks ago I went to get some change from her purse and there was this key tagged "10 Clayton Street". When I asked her about it she said she'd found it in the street and hadn't got round to returning it. I told her that was where all the whores hung out, and she was all wide-eyed and innocent. "I never knew that," she said, all bleeding butter won't melt stuff. The cow. Going with all sorts of trash, and I was sleeping with her!' He raised his head. 'You wouldn't have a cigarette?'

Frost pushed the packet over and waited as Lewis took deep drags.

'I couldn't wait to get my hands on her. Your lot had us all in the nick, but there were too many of us. Suddenly the fuzz all sloped off because there was a fight or something, so I nipped down a corridor when no-one was looking and ended up in the car-park. I legged it round to Clayton Street and the first thing I see is my car, my Toyota, smashed to buggery. That was the last straw. I did my nut. I charged up the stairs and crashed into the flat, yelling and screaming at her. She grabbed for a knife to keep me off. We struggled. I got the knife away from her and kicked it under the bed. I don't remember exactly what

146

happened then, but I must have had my hands round her neck as I banged her head against the wall. Suddenly she went all bloody limp and slithered to the ground and I sobered up fast. I thought God, what have I done? I carried her to the bed and tried the mirror trick, but she wasn't breathing. Then the bloody phone rang and I panicked. I snatched the car keys, hoping I could drive away and get home before anyone saw me, but the windscreen was shattered – it was undrivable. I wandered down back streets and I bumped into some of the blokes from the coach, staggering from pub to pub. I tagged on with them and they assumed I'd been with them all the time – they were too drunk to know otherwise. I got a lift home. You know the rest.'

Frost nodded. 'The clothes you gave us for testing? They weren't the ones you were wearing, were they?'

'No. I bagged them up and put them out with the rubbish. It was collected this morning.'

'We'll find it,' Frost told him. 'Searching through rubbish bags at the council tip is what my Welsh colleague was born for. He certainly wasn't born for altering the bleeding calendar . . .'

'Well done,' said Mullett grudgingly. 'A case tied up quickly with the minimum of manpower. It can be done, you see, if you put your mind to it.' Frost jerked a two-fingered gesture of acknowledgement under the desk, unseen by Mullett who was hurrying back to his office, anxious to let County know that Denton Division, under his leadership, had done it again.

Frost yawned. Too many nights with insufficient sleep were catching up on him. There was nothing that couldn't wait a couple of hours so he'd nip back home and get his head down before the next crisis.

But the next crisis was waiting for him in the lobby.

*　　*　　*

Bill Wells, filling in his overtime claim form on the front desk, grunted with annoyance at the interruption as a woman in her mid-thirties, uncombed straw-blond hair, a cigarette dangling from her lips, barged through the swing doors and dumped a plastic carrier bag on the floor in front of the desk.

'Can I help you, madam?'

'You'd bloody better. My little girl's gone missing.'

Wells kept his expression fixed. Here was one of those 'I pay my rates so you'd better bloody jump to it' brigade. He pulled the cap from his pen. 'If you could let me have some details.'

'Details? Sod the bloody details. I want you out there looking for her.'

Wells sighed. Just his luck to get this loud-mouthed bitch. Collier, who should have been here, was out with DC Morgan scavenging the local rubbish tip on a job for Jack Frost. 'Let's try and keep it calm, shall we, madam?'

'Calm?' she shrieked. 'Calm? Some bleeding pervert's got my kid and you want me to keep calm.'

'The quicker I get the details down, the quicker we can start looking for her. Your name please, madam . . . ?' Ever since Vicky Stuart went missing nine weeks ago they had had a stream of agitated mothers panicking because their kids were late back from school. Wells looked up at the wall clock. Ten past five . . . school had been out less than two hours. The mothers were always insistent their kids had never been home late before, but when the kid eventually turned up, they'd been round a friend's house and had done it time and time again. '. . . and your address, please.'

'Mary Brewer, 2 Rosebank Road, Denton.'

'And the little girl – how old is she?'

'Jenny. She's only seven.'

'Is there a Mr Brewer?'

148

'No, there flaming well isn't. It's going to be pitch dark soon and you're asking these stupid questions.'

'And when did you see Jenny last?'

'When she came home from school for her dinner. I haven't seen her since.'

'What school?'

'Denton Junior.'

Wells stiffened. Denton Junior. The same school Vicky Stuart attended. 'Have you checked with her friends? She might be round one of their houses.'

'What – all bleeding night? Don't be stupid. She went missing yesterday.'

Wells blinked in astonishment. 'Yesterday? Your daughter's been missing since yesterday and you've only just got around to reporting it?'

The woman glowered back at him. 'Don't adopt that attitude to me. I couldn't report it any flaming earlier. I thought she was staying with her Nan, but she wasn't.'

Frost bustled through the door on the way to his car. He gave a brisk nod to Wells.

'Inspector!' Wells wasn't going to be stuck with this woman.

'It will have to wait, Sergeant. I'm off home.' He pushed open the swing door.

'Missing seven-year-old . . . Denton Junior School . . .' barked Wells.

Frost froze. The door swung back. He slowly turned round and walked back to the desk. 'How long has she been missing?'

It was the woman who answered. 'All bloody night. Don't tell me I've got to go over it all again.' The cigarette in her mouth quivered with annoyance.

Frost's shoulders slumped. God, he could have done without this. 'You'd better come with me,' he told her, unbuttoning his mac. 'Send us in a couple of cups of tea,' he called over his shoulder as he pushed through the door to No. 1 interview room and nodded her into the chair so recently vacated by Lewis. This was like seeing the same film over and over again. Lewis's cigarette butts were still piled in the ashtray.

Mrs Brewer drummed nicotined fingers impatiently on the table, watching Frost settle himself down, arranging his cigarettes and matches in front of him. Who was this scruff they had foisted off on her? They said he was an inspector, but he certainly didn't look like one.

'Right, Mrs Brewer,' said Frost, ready at last. 'Let's have the details.'

'How many more flaming times? I've already given them to that silly sod out there.'

'And now you're going to give them to this silly sod in here so he can tell the other silly sods who'll be out half the night looking for your daughter.' She was getting on his nerves. 'The last time you saw Jenny was yesterday around midday when she came home from school for her dinner?'

'Yes.' She added her cigarette end to the pile in the ashtray, then rummaged in her handbag for another. Frost didn't feel disposed to offer her one of his so waited until she lit up before opening his own packet.

'And you haven't seen her since?'

'If that was the last time I saw her, it's bloody obvious I haven't seen her since.'

'Call me old-fashioned,' said Frost, boiling over inside, 'but I would have started panicking twenty-four hours ago, not now.'

'Stuff your holier than thou sneers,' she snarled. 'I'm a bloody caring mother. That kid wants for nothing. I didn't panic yesterday because I thought I knew where she was. She was supposed to be spending the night round her Nan's.'

'Why?'

'My boyfriend was coming round. He doesn't like kids. It was only for one bloody night.'

'Where does your mother live?'

'21 Old Street.'

He scribbled the address down. 'And Jenny never turned up at your mother's?'

'Would I be bloody here if she had?'

Frost took a couple of deep breaths to control his rising temper. 'So why didn't her Nan get on to you when Jenny didn't turn up yesterday?'

'Because I hadn't told her the kid was coming . . . she's not on the phone. Jenny just calls there and her Nan looks after her.'

'Old Street is right over the other side of town. Are you telling me you'd send a seven-year-old over there without any warning? Supposing your mother was out?'

'She never goes out . . . and if she did, Jenny would simply come straight back. She's always got coppers for the bus.'

Frost nodded his thanks as Wells banged down two mugs of tea. He passed one across. 'So how did you know Jenny never turned up at your mother's?'

'I bumped into her at the supermarket about half an hour ago. As soon as I knew Jenny hadn't been there, I didn't sod about, I came straight round here.'

Frost stirred his tea with his pencil. 'Has Jenny ever gone missing before?'

'A couple of times . . . she just wandered off, went to the pictures or something. But never overnight – she knows she'd get a bleeding good hiding if she did.'

Frost took a sip at the lukewarm tea and shuddered. Bill Wells hadn't brought the Earl Grey out for this woman. He pushed the mug away. 'We'll need a photograph.'

She opened her handbag and handed over a tiny dog-eared colour print of a solemn-looking child.

'She looks bloody young for seven,' he said.

'It's over a year old, but it's the most recent one I've got.'

Frost regarded it doubtfully. Kids changed a hell of a lot in a year. 'The school takes photographs every term. Haven't you got one of them?'

She shook her head, showering ash all over the table. 'I didn't bother.'

'I see,' grunted Frost. 'We'll have to get one from the school. What was she wearing?'

'Greeny blue dress, black shoes and a blue anorak.'

'Right.' He scribbled this down. 'I'll get things moving this end. You go back home and wait, I'll be round to see you later. If Jenny does turn up, let us know right away.'

She buried her cigarette end under the pile of corpses in the ashtray and heaved up the carrier bag which was full of shopping. 'Any chance of a lift home?'

'None at all,' said Frost.

Joan Boscombe, headmistress of Denton Junior School, was slipping on her coat when Taffy Morgan arrived. He'd returned in triumph to Frost's office with the bloodstained clothes Lewis had dumped, and was sent straight out again to find out what he could from the school. The teacher wasn't pleased to see him. It had been a busy day and all she wanted to do now was go home and unwind. 'If this could wait until the morning—' she began.

'Sorry, teacher, but it can't,' said Taffy, showing her his warrant card and eyeing her up and down. She looked very young to be a headmistress . . . an air of authority combined with an air of vulnerability. Very sexy, he thought. 'It's about Jenny Brewer.'

'Jenny?' She dropped down in her chair. 'She wasn't at school today. Nothing's happened to her, I hope?'

152

'We hope so too,' said Taffy. 'The thing is, she never returned home after school yesterday.'

The headmistress went white. 'Oh my God, not another girl.' The memory of Vicky still pained.

'We don't know it's anything serious yet,' said Taffy. 'When was she last at school?'

The pages of a register were turned. 'Yesterday afternoon . . . I remember seeing her leave.' She unbuttoned her coat. It was hot in the office. Taffy's eyes bulged. A lovely figure for a teacher. You can smack my bottom any time you like, miss, he thought.

'We need an up-to-date photograph. The mother doesn't seem to have one.'

Her lips tightened and she sniffed disapproval. 'The mother!' She swung round to a filing cabinet and pulled out a file. 'This was taken just before Christmas.'

A postcard-sized colour print showing an older version of Jenny looking serious and pale, and there was what appeared to be a bruise on her right cheek. Taffy jabbed a finger. 'What caused that?'

'She *said* she fell.'

'But you didn't believe her?'

'Jenny seemed to fall a bit too often for my liking. There had been other bruises on her arms and legs but Jenny always insisted she had fallen. We alerted Social Services. They were supposed to be keeping an eye on the situation, but . . .' She shrugged hopelessly. 'The mother is a fluent liar. They couldn't prove anything.'

'Who's been hitting her . . . the mother?'

'I don't know . . . but she seems to go in for violent boyfriends. I've heard some of the other mothers talking.'

'Do you think the mother cares for Jenny?'

'I think she tolerates her. Jenny needs love and

affection and she certainly doesn't get it in that house. She's a very streetwise child for her age.'

Streetwise! thought Taffy. It was often best for kids not to be streetwise and think they could handle danger instead of running away from it. 'Did she have any close friends?'

'None that I know of. I'll ask around and let you know.'

'Thank you. We'll need to keep the photograph.' He slipped it in his pocket. Then he noticed her perfume. A heavy sexy unscholastic aroma. He wondered if she had a boyfriend. I bet she's a goer, he thought.

She stood up. 'Should we warn the parents?'

He shook his head. 'Not at this stage. There could be a simple explanation and we don't want to cause unnecessary panic.' He opened the door for her. 'Oh, one last thing – could you confirm she was wearing a greeny blue dress and a blue anorak yesterday?'

She frowned. 'No. She was in red – a red woollen dress.'

Morgan's turn to frown. 'Are you sure? We had a different description.'

'Positive. She usually wears the same old tatty things, this was new. She was flaunting herself in it.'

Taffy scribbled this down. He couldn't wait to get back to Frost to tell him. He hesitated. The perfume was working him up. 'Could I – er – give you a lift back to your place, miss?'

She smiled and shook her head. 'No, thank you. My partner will be meeting me.'

So the partner was to be the beneficiary of that perfume. Lucky bastard, thought Morgan, making for his car.

The girl's mother had slapped make-up on and done something with her hair. Her eyes, half closed against

154

the smoke from her cigarette, narrowed when she saw it was Frost at the door. 'You found her yet?'

'Not yet,' said Frost. 'A couple more questions.'

She led him through to the living-room where an older version of herself, a woman in her late sixties, sat at a table, sipping a cup of tea. 'My mother,' she explained. 'Jenny's Nan.'

Frost nodded a greeting and sat at the table. 'Jenny never turned up round your place then, Mrs Brewer?'

'I never knew she was supposed to be coming.' She scowled up at her daughter. 'Why didn't you let me know?'

Her daughter shrugged dismissively. 'Why should I? I knew you wouldn't mind.'

'Of course I wouldn't mind. I just want to be told. If you'd told me she was supposed to be coming I'd have been round to the police last night.'

'So it's all my fault now, is it?'

'Yes, it flaming is. It certainly isn't mine.'

'I don't give a sod whose fault it is,' said Frost wearily. 'We just want to find her. It's dark, it's bloody cold and she's been gone too long.' He jabbed a finger at Mary Brewer. 'A couple of questions.'

She raised her eyes to the ceiling. 'More bleeding questions!'

'Yes, more bleeding questions,' snapped Frost. 'You told me Jenny was wearing greeny blue dress when she went to school yesterday. The school tell us she was wearing a red woollen dress.'

She tugged the cigarette from her mouth so she could cough better. 'A red dress?' she spluttered. 'The silly sods don't know what they're talking about. She hasn't got a red dress.'

'The poor little mite has only got one dress,' put in the Nan. 'When did you last buy her anything new?'

'She don't go without, and if she had a red dress I'd be the first to know.'

155

'Was she wearing the blue dress when she came home for her lunch yesterday?' asked Frost.

'I suppose so.'

Frost stared up at her. 'What do you mean, you suppose so?'

'I wasn't here when she came in for lunch. I was at Bingo.'

'You told me the last time you saw her was yesterday lunchtime.'

'I didn't actually see her. I left her money for chips. When I came back the money was gone, so I knew she'd been home.'

'But you are sure she was wearing the blue dress when she went off to school yesterday morning?'

'She must have done, it's the only dress she's got. I've been trying to save up for something new, but money's tight.'

'Not tight when it comes to bloody Bingo,' said the Nan.

Frost knuckled the weariness from his eyes. 'Must have done?' he echoed. 'You saw what she was wearing, surely?'

'I didn't actually see her. I was still in bed. She gets her own breakfast.'

Frost stared in disbelief. 'She gets her own breakfast? A seven-year-old kid gets her own breakfast while her mother pigs it in bed?'

She folded her arms defiantly. 'You're here to find my kid, not give me a moral bleeding lecture.'

'Just for the record,' said Frost, 'when did you last see your daughter?'

'Night before last. She watched telly, then went up to bed.'

'As recently as that?' shrilled the Nan in mock disbelief. 'It's a wonder you'd still recognize her. Why did you pack her off to my place yesterday? I suppose that lousy boyfriend was coming round again.' She

156

turned to Frost. 'That bastard was always hitting that kid – the times she's come round to me, crying her eyes out.'

Frost turned to the mother. 'His name and address?'

'No,' she shrieked. 'He doesn't want to get involved.'

'Well, he bloody well is involved,' yelled Frost back. 'Name and address, please.'

'Dennis Hadleigh, Flat 2, Peabody Estate.'

'And what does he do, apart from hitting seven-year-old kids?'

'He's a lorry driver.'

Frost scribbled the details down on the back of his cigarette packet and stood up. 'I want to search the house.'

'Search the house?' Her voice went up an octave. 'Do you think I've done her in?'

'She could have got herself locked in a cupboard, or something,' explained Frost. 'It has happened.'

'Don't you think I'd know if she was in the house?'

'You don't know where she is half the time,' sniffed the Nan. 'You and that bastard could be having it away while Jenny was dying in the loft.'

Hands on hips, the woman glared down at her mother. 'I've just about had enough of your innuendoes, mother,' she snarled. 'Either you keep your mouth shut or you get out of my house.'

Shutting his ears to the in-fighting, Frost went to the front door and called in the rest of the team who were waiting in cars outside and got them to search the house and the small back garden. Jerking his head for Morgan to follow, he returned to the two women. 'Which is Jenny's room?'

It was at the top of the stairs. They squeezed past Jordan who was heaving Simms up through a trap door into the loft. A small room, still decorated with

Little Bo-Peep nursery paper. There was a single bed, neatly made with folded pyjamas on the pillow, a pink-painted chest of drawers on which stood a twelve-inch black and white television set and, on the other side of the bed, a white Melamine wardrobe.

Frost lit up a cigarette and parted the curtains to the sash window to look down on the small back yard where a uniformed officer, his torch cutting through the darkness, was prodding amongst the long, uncut grass. He shuddered at the feeling he had had so many times before. A cold, empty room. The room of a child who was not coming back.

Morgan pulled out the bed to make certain there was nothing underneath, then opened up the wardrobe where a few items of child's clothing swung from hangers. On the floor of the wardrobe were some down-at-heel shoes and a pile of well-read children's books.

Frost went through the chest of drawers. More clothes, all neatly folded, balled pairs of socks, handkerchiefs, knickers, everything he would expect to find. A nagging buzzing at the back of his brain was telling him he was missing something, but he couldn't think what it was.

Morgan had dragged the wardrobe away from the wall. 'Guv, look at this.' Hidden behind the wardrobe were some expensive children's annuals. They looked brand new. 'Get Fanny up here,' he told Morgan.

The woman came up and leant, arms folded, against the door frame. 'Found her in the wardrobe, have you?'

Touching them only by the edges, Frost held up the books. 'Did you buy her these?'

She fanned away cigarette smoke and squinted at them. 'No, I didn't. Where did they come from?'

'Stuck behind the wardrobe.'

'The little moo – she must have nicked them.'

158

'Perhaps,' said Frost, laying the books carefully on the bed. He snapped his fingers, suddenly realizing what it was that had been worrying him. He flung open the wardrobe door and waved a hand at the hangers. 'You said she usually wore this greeny blue dress . . . Is it any of these?'

She stared at the row of coats and cardigans and sniffed disdainfully. 'Do they look like flaming blue dresses?'

'When she came back from school the day before yesterday, was she wearing the blue dress then?'

'Of course she was.'

'You actually saw her with it on?'

'Yes. Why are you asking?'

'Because it's not here,' said Frost, 'that's why.' She didn't understand what the hell he was talking about, but sod her. 'Where would she have put it if it wanted washing?'

'In the linen basket next to the washing machine.'

'Go with her and see if it's there,' Frost told Morgan. He sat on the bed and waited, but he guessed what the answer would be. He looked round the room, bed made, pyjamas folded . . . The poor kid must have done all that herself, certainly not that slut of a mother. A thudding up the stairs as Morgan returned.

'Not there, guv.'

Frost yelled out to his team. 'Look out for a kiddy's blue dress . . . If you find any items of kid's clothing, I want to see them.'

He sat on the bed in the cold, scarf tight round his neck, and smoked some more, getting up to flick the ash out of the window, not wanting to mess up the kid's neat and tidy little room.

At last, dirty and dishevelled, the team filed in. 'The kid's not here, and no sign of any clothes,' announced Jordan.

Frost nodded. He expected nothing else. 'Someone's got her, and I've a nasty feeling in my water it's the same bastard who got Vicky.' He jerked a thumb at the books on the bed. 'Put them in an evidence bag. I want them checked for prints. She might have nicked them, but on the other hand some nice kind dirty bastard of a man might have given them to her as a little present . . . "and don't tell your mum, love . . ."' If she left for school wearing a blue dress and turned up in a red one, she must have stopped off on the way to change clothes, perhaps at the house of the nice kind man who gave her the books.' He felt himself go cold as he said it. 'My gut feeling is she's dead, but let's hope my track record holds and I'm wrong. Let's get a search going. It's freezing out there, so the sooner we start, the better.'

He clicked on his mobile phone and called the station. 'I want every available man in on this search, Bill – off-duty men as well.'

'Have you cleared it with Mullett?' asked Wells.

'I'll clear it with him,' said Frost. 'And get the underwater team to stand by. We'll start dragging the canal tomorrow.'

The search was already under way as he drove back to the station. He could see the beams of torches cutting through the dark of Denton Woods. 'Shouldn't we start dragging the canal tonight?' Morgan asked.

'If she's in the canal, she's dead,' said Frost bluntly. 'I'm never in a hurry to find a kid's dead body.' He turned the heater up. It was cold in the car, but a damn sight colder out in the open. If the kid was out there . . . in the dark . . .

As they drove past King Street he noticed there were very few toms out. Not the cold that was keeping them in. They had heard about the body found the previous night. Too many bloody cases, too few men and too little time.

'Guv . . .' Morgan was dragging him from his reverie. 'Radio, guv.'

It was Bill Wells. 'Jack . . . Just had a phone call. A man reckons his eleven-year-old son has gone missing. The kid goes to the same school as the two missing girls!'

Shit, thought Frost. It never rains but it bleeding buckets down. He took the address. 'We're on our way . . .'

8

The door was opened by WPC June Purdy, a bouncy little brunette in her mid-twenties. Frost was glad Morgan wasn't with him. The DC would have been panting all over her like a dog on heat. He wouldn't mind doing a bit of panting himself, but this wasn't the time. 'Fill me in, love,' he asked.

'Eleven-year-old Tony Scotney. Went to school today as usual, never came home for his tea, and they haven't seen him since.' She was not one to waste words.

Frost rammed a cigarette in his mouth. 'Why didn't they report it earlier?'

'They suspected he'd sneaked off to the cinema straight from school . . . he's done it before, apparently.'

She led Frost into the living-room where the father, dark-haired, early forties, a permanent frown creasing his forehead, was pacing up and down. The mother, a few years younger, sat huddled up in an armchair, biting her lip to stop the tears and drumming her fingers incessantly.

'For God's sake, stop that,' snapped her husband. He looked up anxiously as Frost came in. 'Any news?'

'We're still looking,' said Frost. He hadn't organized a separate search, but the teams searching for the girl had been alerted. 'We need a photograph.'

Silently, the mother handed over a photograph taken at the school around the same time as that of the missing Jenny Brewer. A boy, dark-haired like his father with a hint of devilment in his eyes. He stuffed it in his pocket. No-one was inviting him to sit, so he plonked himself down in a chair near the fire and loosened his scarf. 'I understand Tony's done this sort of thing before?'

'He's never stayed out this late,' said the woman.

'The little sod,' shouted his father. 'I'll wring his bloody neck.' He stopped as worry overcame anger, then took his wife's hand and patted it gently.

'When did you last see Tony?' asked Frost.

The mother answered him. 'Lunchtime. He wanted to see the new Walt Disney at the Regal, but he was rude to me, so I said no. He started shouting at me and stamped off.'

'You've checked with his friends?'

'The first thing I did,' said the father. 'He left them after school and told them he was going to see the film.'

'Would he have had the money to go?'

The mother shook her head. 'I wouldn't give it to him. In the past he would have taken it from my purse when I wasn't looking, but now I don't give him the chance . . . I always keep it with me.'

'You're sure there was nothing missing from your purse today?'

'Positive. There were only notes in it and they're still all there.'

'You checked with the cinema?'

'Of course I did,' snapped the father. 'Went with the manager and we looked everywhere . . . he wasn't there.' He stared at the floor and shook his head. 'The little sod. If he's doing this just to teach us a lesson, I'll . . .' He left the sentence hanging and sprang to his feet, glaring at Frost. 'Questions, questions, questions.

You won't find him with bloody questions. I'm going out to look for him.' He barged out and they heard the front door slam.

'I'm sorry he's so rude,' said his wife. 'He's worried sick.'

Frost nodded sympathetically. He was bloody worried too. Two kids missing the same day. A paedophile gang operating in Denton? God, he hoped not. He shuddered at the thought, but kept his voice casual, trying to think of words to reassure her. 'We deal with missing children all the time, Mrs Scotney. The parents worry themselves sick, then nine times out of ten the kid comes swaggering back, as bold as brass.'

'But why would he stay out so late?'

'Perhaps he's afraid of what his father might do to him?' suggested Frost.

She shook her head and sniffed back her tears. 'His father's all talk . . . he threatens, but doesn't do anything. I sometimes think it would be better if—' The phone cut her short. With a gasp of hope, she snatched it up. 'Yes . . . ?' Her face fell. 'No, mother, still no news . . . Please stay off the line.' She hung up. Her shoulders shook. She was crying.

Frost squeezed her shoulder. 'Don't worry, love. Tony's going to be all right, just you wait and see.' Empty words. How the hell did he know? But she knuckled away her tears and smiled bravely as if she believed him.

He pulled the WPC to one side and lowered his voice. 'Stay with her, and while you're here, give the place a thorough going-over. The little sod could well be hiding somewhere just to pay them back.'

He let himself out. A heavy clammy mist was forming. Just the thing for a night bloody search. As he climbed in the car and turned up the heat, his radio buzzed. Bill Wells from the station. 'Didn't want to

164

call you while you were in the house, Jack, in case the parents overheard. We think we've found the boy.'

Frost's stomach tightened into a hard knot. The sergeant's tone made it clear this was bad news. 'You *think* we've found him?'

'Kid answering his description taken to Denton Hospital. Victim of a hit and run . . .'

'Shit! Where did it happen?'

'The slip road running along Denton Woods.'

'Denton Woods? What the hell was he doing there?'

'No idea. We had a call from a motorist, wouldn't give his name. He told us where to find him. Said the kid ran straight out in front of his car, didn't give him a chance.'

'And how is the boy?'

'He's in intensive care, Jack. They don't expect him to pull through.' Wells paused. 'Someone's got to break the news to the parents.'

Frost looked back at the house. He didn't want to go back in there with this sort of news. 'A road accident? Traffic should do it.'

'With the search for the girl, we're thin on the ground, Jack – and you are on the spot.'

'Yes. Always in the right place at the wrong bleeding time.'

'Then you'll do it?'

'Yes, anything for a laugh.'

He took one last drag on his cigarette, pitched it out into the darkness, then went back to the house and jammed his thumb in the doorbell.

PC Jordan bumped the area car along the pot-holed short cut which would take them out of the woods and back on to the main road. He and Simms should have had their meal break half an hour ago but this hit and run accident had held them up. The mist was thickening and visibility shrinking fast. Simms had his head stuck out of the side window to ensure they didn't end up in the ditch running alongside the lane. Suddenly he pulled in his head. 'Stop the car!'

Jordan braked. 'What is it?'

'A car, no lights, parked among the bushes.'

Jordan groaned. 'Top bleeding marks for observation.' His stomach was rumbling, begging for food. 'All right, but let's make it quick. I'm starving.'

They climbed out and walked back to a dark grey BMW, not more than a year old. The doors were locked and no sign of the driver. Simms felt the bonnet. 'It's not been here long.'

'Joy-rider?' suggested Jordan.

'Joy-riders don't lock the bleeding thing up when they leave it. Better check it out.' While Jordan radioed Control Simms shone his torch inside. A mobile phone on the passenger seat next to a briefcase, nothing else.

'Not reported stolen,' said Jordan, giving the tyres a perfunctory kick. 'Can we go and get something to eat now?'

'The owner probably doesn't know it's missing yet,' said Simms. 'You don't abandon an expensive motor like this in the middle of the woods.'

'Perhaps it broke down?'

'He's got a mobile phone. He'd phone for assistance and wait in the warm.' He lifted his hand for silence. 'Did you hear that?'

From behind some bushes, a groan then the sound of someone being violently sick.

'Just what I wanted to give me an appetite for my supper,' moaned Jordan.

They waited by the BMW until a short, pasty-faced man in his early thirties, wearing a sheepskin-lined leather jacket, staggered from the bushes, wiping his mouth with a handkerchief and dabbing sweat from his forehead. He started when he saw the two

166

policemen, but managed to force a weak grin. 'I've been sick,' he explained.

'So we heard,' said Simms, holding out a hand. 'Driving licence, please, sir.'

The licence confirmed that the man was Patrick Thomas Morris, the registered owner of the car. Hoping that was the end of it, Jordan edged back to the area car, but Simms hadn't finished. His nose twitched. 'Have you been drinking, sir?'

The man looked even more unhappy. 'Drinking? No – a beer . . . just one beer . . .'

'I'm sure you're right, sir,' said Simms, 'but I'm sure you want us to check.' He fetched a breathalyser. Jordan watched anxiously while Morris blew into the mouthpiece. Let it be negative, he pleaded silently. I want my flaming supper. He suppressed a groan as the crystals changed colour.

Simms showed it to the man. 'More than one beer, sir – you must have miscounted. I'm afraid you will have to accompany us back to the station.'

'No – please.' The man was clasping his hands together beseechingly. 'I only had one beer while I was driving, I swear. But I then felt sick, so I stopped and took a sip of brandy to settle my stomach.' He pulled a flask from his hip pocket to show them. 'I wasn't going to drive any more. I was going to sleep it off in the car, I swear.'

Simms shot a questioning glance to Jordan who shrugged, indicating, I'm hungry – let the poor sod go.

Simms chewed it over, then nodded. What the hell. If they drove him back to the station he'd probably be sick all over the back of the area car and by the look of his greenish face there was a lot more to come up before the night was out. 'It's your lucky night, sir—' he began, but stopped in mid-sentence. Jordan, on his way back to the area car, was beckoning him over urgently. 'What's up?'

Jordan pointed. The front nearside wing of the BMW was dented and the headlamp glass shattered. 'Shit!' hissed Simms. They returned to the man, who was trying to appear unconcerned. 'Spot of damage to the front of your motor, sir. Haven't been in an accident, have you?'

'What, that?' The man attempted a weak laugh. 'Did that this morning – hit the gatepost when I drove out of the garage.'

'And been driving around all night with only one headlamp?' tutted Simms. 'That's a very serious offence.' His voice hardened. 'You didn't do it when you hit the boy, by any chance?'

'Boy? What boy?' Sweat was beading his forehead.

'The boy in intensive care. The boy you hit and sent flying . . . or are you too bloody drunk to remember?'

The man dabbed his face with his handkerchief again. 'I don't know what you're talking about, officer. I haven't hit anyone.'

'I think,' said Simms, taking his arm and steering him into the area car, 'we'd better take a little drive down to the station.'

The interview room was warm, almost too warm, but a welcome change for PC Collier who had been out pounding the beat in the cold. The man was pacing nervously up and down, from time to time mopping sweat from his face with a none-too-clean handkerchief. 'How much longer?' he demanded.

'The inspector should be here soon.'

'You've been saying that for the past half-hour. This is all a mistake. Do you think I could hit someone and not know it? I want a solicitor.'

'Ask the inspector when he comes in,' said Collier.

The door crashed open as an untidy individual backed in carrying a mug of tea on which was balanced a greasy-looking sandwich. He plopped down in a chair and beckoned the man to sit opposite him. 'Frost,' he announced. 'Detective Inspector Frost. Sorry to have kept you waiting.' He looked at the arrest report and took a bite at the sandwich. 'Mr Patrick Morris, is it?'

'Yes . . . and I want to protest. This is all a terrible mistake.'

'I'm sure it is,' agreed Frost, 'but don't worry. I've asked our Forensic boys to see if the blood on your car's headlamp is the same group as your gatepost.'

The man stared at Frost, his face scarlet with rage. 'You bastard!' he spat.

'Sticks and stones,' reproved Frost gently.

Morris fluttered an apologetic hand. 'I'm sorry, I'm sorry.' His head sank down. 'I wasn't even going fast; just pootling along. The kid came straight at me. He didn't give me a chance.'

'He was sober, you were drunk,' said Frost.

Morris pushed himself up to shout at Frost. 'I was not drunk.'

'And I'm not bloody deaf,' said Frost, wiping his mouth after a swig of tea. 'Please sit down.'

Morris sat. 'I'm sorry . . . I'm sorry.' He leant over to Frost. 'I'm an oil company representative in line for promotion. One drink-driving offence and I lose my job. Do you think I'd risk that? I was not drunk. I was stone cold bloody sober. I had the brandy afterwards.'

'Drunk or sober, you knocked an eleven-year-old kid down and you didn't stop.'

'I couldn't afford to get involved; my job—'

'Sod your bloody job. The kid's in intensive care. You could have done something to help him.'

'The man in the other car came running over. I left it to him.'

Frost's head snapped up. 'What other car?'

'An old banger – a blue Vauxhall Astra. It was parked up on the verge. When I hit the boy the Astra driver dashed over to him. There was nothing I could do to help so I phoned for an ambulance on my mobile.'

'Yes,' snapped Frost, 'a great humanitarian gesture. Remind me to nominate you for the Nobel Prize.' He dropped the crust from his sandwich into the mug of tea and pushed it away. 'Describe the man.'

'Middle-aged – forty-five to fifty. Darkish hair, going bald.'

'Clean-shaven?'

'Yes, I think so. It all—'

'I know – it all happened so fast,' said Frost, finishing the sentence for him. 'Build?'

'Average.'

'Clothes?'

'A suit. A dark suit, I think.'

'A suit!' exclaimed Frost. 'Well, that saves us looking for a man in a dress.'

'If I could tell you more, I would,' snarled Morris. 'It's in my own interest that you find him. He'll confirm I wasn't speeding and the kid didn't give me a chance.'

'Then you'd better hope we do find him,' said Frost, 'because at the moment I don't rate your chances at all.' His cigarette end joined the sandwich crust in the mug of cold tea. He stood up and nodded at Collier. 'The constable will take your statement.'

Bill Wells was hovering outside the interview room, waiting for him. 'Initial report from Forensic, Jack. Glass from the headlamp definitely matches up with the glass found at the scene.'

'They always confirm what you know already,' grunted Frost. 'He's admitted knocking the kid down.'

'And Traffic reckon the skid marks where he braked indicate he wasn't doing more than thirty mph at the most.'

170

'Knickers!' said Frost. 'I was hoping to throw the book at the bastard.'

His phone was ringing when he got back to the office. WPC June Purdy from the hospital. 'The boy died ten minutes ago, Inspector.'

He threw his head back and swore at the ceiling. 'Shit! Do the parents know?'

'They were with him when he died.'

He felt ashamed that his relief that he would not have to break the news to the parents almost outweighed his sadness at an eleven-year-old boy's death. 'Are they still there?'

'Yes.'

'I know it's difficult, love, but ask them if they know anyone who drives a blue Vauxhall Astra; a man in his late forties, going bald – someone who might give their son a lift. Phone me back right away.'

'Was he the hit and run driver?'

'No. He's a possible witness. We've got the hit and run man but it doesn't appear as if the kid gave him much of a chance. Baldy might be the bloke who drove the boy to the woods and I've got a nasty feeling about the bastard. You don't take an eleven-year-old to Denton Woods in the middle of the night to pick mushrooms.'

She phoned back in five minutes. The parents knew no-one of that description.

'Too much to hope it would be that easy,' sighed Frost. 'Get back here, love, and bring the boy's clothes so Forensic can tell us sod all about them.'

He sat at a desk in the murder incident room, moodily smoking as he replaced the boy's bloodstained clothing in the evidence bag. A smaller bag held items taken from the boy's pockets. He shook them out on the desk: a comb, eight pence in copper coins, a handkerchief and the torn half of a cinema ticket. Open in front of him was the file on the first missing girl, eight-year-old Vicky Stuart. Looking through its many pages of typescript he had spotted that a couple of witnesses reported seeing a blue car cruising past the school on the afternoon Vicky went missing, but the car hadn't been traced. He drummed his fingers on the desk top. There were millions of flaming blue cars and the fact that the Vauxhall Astra was blue probably didn't mean a damn thing, but he had one of his feelings . . .

He checked his watch. Ten minutes past midnight. Mullett had only authorized overtime for the search parties until midnight so they should be returning soon. The mist was pressing a greasy kiss against the window. He hoped it would clear by the morning when the search would be resumed.

A tramping of tired feet announced the return of the first of the search parties as they headed up the stairs to the canteen. He gave them a few moments to get settled, then followed them up. They all looked tired and dejected. No need to ask if they had found the girl. He made his way over to a table where Detective Sergeant Arthur Hanlon sat with five off-duty police officers, all cold and miserable, gratefully warming frozen hands round mugs of scalding tea. 'Where's Taffy Morgan?' Frost asked, dragging a chair over to join them.

'He's where I'm soon going to be,' replied Hanlon, 'fast asleep in a nice warm bed.'

Frost gave a knowing smile. 'You do tell fibs, Arthur. You're not going to bed for hours yet. I've got another job for all of you.' A mass groan. He grinned and pushed his cigarettes around. 'I know – I'm a rotten bastard and I could be wasting everybody's time, but there's the slimmest of chances this might lead us to the girl.' He turned his head as Jordan and

Simms, finishing their meal break, walked past. 'The boy died,' he told them.

Jordan shook his head sadly. 'Poor little sod.' He buttoned up his greatcoat. Another cold six hours before their shift ended.

'Is that the hit and run?' asked Hanlon.

'Yes,' nodded Frost. 'Only the driver didn't run very far – we've got him. He reckons the kid came flying out of a parked blue Vauxhall Astra straight into his path. He's a nasty, slimy bastard, but I'm ashamed to say I believe him, which is why you've got to do a bit more work.'

They looked at each other, wondering where this was leading. He expelled a mouthful of smoke and watched it whirl lazily up to the ceiling. 'We've got a kid, in a blue Astra, with a strange man in the middle of the bloody woods at night. Why? And why did the kid come flying out of the car like a bat out of hell?'

'You're suggesting the bloke was a child molester?' asked Hanlon.

'This is how I see it, Arthur. The bloke offers to drive the kid home, but instead takes him to the woods. Just as he starts his stuff, the kid manages to scramble out, but runs straight into the other car.'

'What has this got to do with the girl?' asked Howe, one of the off-duty PCs.

'Probably sod all,' conceded Frost, 'but the day Vicky Stuart went missing, two of the witnesses mentioned a blue car cruising past the school as the kids came out. The Astra was blue.'

'And you think it's the same man?' exclaimed Hanlon. 'Just because it's a blue car? It's a bloody long shot, Jack.'

'Maybe, Arthur, but it's all we've got . . . before this we had sod all.' He produced the cinema ticket. 'This was in the kid's jacket pocket – a ticket for tonight's

173

performance of the Disney. It's an adult's ticket. Does that suggest anything?'

A sea of blank looks.

'The boy would have got in at the child's rate, so this isn't his ticket. Try this out for size. He's hanging about outside the cinema when some nice kind balding gentleman says, "Going to see the film, sonny?" "I haven't got any money, kind balding gent," replies the boy, so the man offers to pay for him. In they go. The bloke buys one adult ticket and one child's ticket. Comes the interval. The kid hadn't been home for his tea, so he's hungry. "Go and buy a hot dog," says the nice man in the dirty mac. The hot dogs are in the foyer and you've got to have your ticket to get back in again, so the man gives him a ticket . . . the wrong one as it happens, but that doesn't matter.'

They looked at each other and grudgingly nodded. 'It fits, Jack,' said Hanlon, 'but you're making a lot of assumptions.'

Frost pulled a wad of photographs of the dead boy from his pocket and handed them around. 'Then see if we can get some hard evidence. One of you go to the cinema – they're doing an all-night horror programme so they'll still be open. Does anyone remember this kid coming in with a man in his forties, balding dark hair, dark suit. The programme finished at 8.25, but they didn't get to the woods until around ten. My guess is that the nice man took the kid out for a meal. So some of you surf the fast food joints. I want another couple of you to sift through computer records of middle-aged child molesters, baldies preferred, but many of them might not have started going bald when we arested them. Drag them out of bed, find out where they were tonight and see what car they own. Lastly, I want someone to go through the computer for blue Astras, at least five years old, owned by people in the Denton area.'

'How do we know he's local?' protested Evans.

'He's got to be,' said Frost. 'He hangs about the local school, he goes to the local cinema and he knows where to park in Denton Woods. When you get the list of Astra owners, check it against our child molesters. If you can say "Snap" we throw the book at the sod whether he's guilty or not.'

'And this is all on official overtime?' asked Evans, remembering Mullett's strictures that he didn't object to people doing overtime so long as they didn't always expect to be paid for it.

'Money's your bloody God!' said Frost. 'Yes . . . all on official overtime, but don't drag it out.'

He left them to get themselves organized, then went down to the lobby to tell Bill Wells what he had arranged. 'Book them all in for extended overtime, Bill.'

'You know Mullett's got to authorize it,' Wells reminded him. 'He went berserk last time you sent our overtime expenses sky high.'

'He'll be in bed,' said Frost, doubtfully. 'He might even be having it away.' He dialled the number. 'Still, if it's with his wife he'll be glad of the interruption.'

Mullett wasn't glad of the interruption. The phone had woken him from a deep sleep. 'Authorize overtime? On the flimsiest of evidence? You don't even know for certain that the boy was ever in the blue car, just that there was one in the vicinity.'

'Which didn't wait for the ambulance,' Frost reminded him.

'There could be all sorts of reasons for that,' replied Mullett, who couldn't think of any. 'I'm sorry, Frost, I'm not authorizing overtime.'

'Fair enough, Super,' said Frost. 'But if it is the same blue car, this bastard could be holding the missing girl. I know the budget has to take precedence over a human life—'

175

'Ten hours,' cut in Mullett hastily, 'and not a second over.'

'Per man?' asked Frost hopefully.

'In total, Frost, in total, and you'd better come up with something to justify it.'

'Well?' asked Bill Wells as Frost put the phone down.

'He said we could have all the men we wanted for as long as we liked,' Frost replied.

He sat in his office, fighting tiredness, answering the phone as the negative reports came in. 'Sorry, Inspector,' reported Evans, the last on the list. 'No-one remembers anything.'

'Call it a day,' yawned Frost.

He took a stroll to the computer room, where Howe and Collier were wading their way through armfuls of computer print-outs. 'No joy yet, Inspector.'

'Keep trying,' he grunted. Flaming heck, Mullett would have kittens when he saw the overtime bill especially for a nil result.

Back to his office with the nagging feeling that even if they found the man he would have nothing to do with the missing girl. A quick flip through his in-tray. More news to add to the gloom. The beaten-up tom had decided not to press charges. She'd been paid off and Mickey Harris would walk scot-free. This was not going to be a night to remember.

A quick squint through grime-encrusted windows out to the car-park. The swirling mist was thickening. Cars were murky outlines and the sodium lamps reduced to dirty orange smears. It looked cold and miserable which was just how he felt . . .

Another yawn. Sod it, he was so tired he could hardly think straight. Nothing more he could do here. He dragged his scarf from the peg and wound it round his neck. At the doorway he paused, waiting, hoping the phone might ring and he'd be told they had found the driver and the girl. Silence. He clicked off the light, shut the door behind him, and made for his car.

The car heater was playing its usual tricks and kept blasting cold air. He was frozen by the time he reached his house where the central heating had switched itself off at midnight so the place was as icy and unwelcoming as the morgue. Shivering, he scooped up the post from the door mat; two bills and three circulars, one marked in red 'This is not a circular'. He chucked them on the hall table and dumped his mac on top. He could go a cup of something hot, but was too dead beat to make it.

He thudded up the stairs and clicked on the electric blanket. The phone rang the second his head touched the pillow.

The phone was downstairs, in the hall. He'd wanted one by the bed but when his wife was alive she wouldn't hear of it; said the ringing would wake her up and she wouldn't be able to get back to sleep again. He kept promising himself he'd get an extension, but hadn't got round to it. What was it this time? Another bloody killing? Another dead tom? He threw aside the bedclothes, gritted his teeth against the shock of the cold lino to his bare feet and went down to the phone.

He didn't recognize the voice and at first couldn't make out what the man was saying. 'Who is this?'

'PC Bearsley of Traffic. Sorry to phone you at home, Inspector, but we have a problem.'

'Traffic? Why the hell are you calling me for a traffic problem?' His teeth began to chatter. It was freezing in the hall.

'I can't talk about it over the phone, Inspector. Please get here quickly – corner of Saxby Street and Avon Drive.'

'It had better be bloody urgent.'

'It is, Inspector,' Bearsley assured him, 'it is.'

Frost was still shivering as he drove but kept the window down so the cold air would stop him falling asleep at the wheel. Why was he doing this? Dragged out of bed at five past four in the morning just because some damn traffic cop thinks it's urgent.

As he turned the car into Saxby Street he passed a metallic green Nissan, its paint scraped and a wing crumpled. A yellow and red striped traffic car was waiting, its lights out. Two worried-looking traffic policemen came over to meet him. Bearsley introduced himself. 'Glad you got here so quickly, Inspector.' And then Frost saw the crashed Ford Sierra which had driven straight into a wall at the end of the cul-de-sac. 'The driver must have put his foot down, not realizing it was a blind alley,' said Bearsley, headlight glass scrunching underfoot as they approached the vehicle. 'It's a miracle he wasn't killed.'

'Have you called an ambulance?' asked Frost, wondering why he was being involved.

'If we did, it would make it official and you might want to avoid that.' Bearsley shone his torch through the driver's window so Frost could see inside.

Frost bent and squinted. 'Flaming bloody hell!'

Lolling in the driving seat, a bleary-eyed Taffy Morgan, blood trickling from his forehead, gave Frost a shamefaced smile as the inspector yanked open the door. The interior of the car stank of whisky and vomit which was all over the DC's jacket. 'Bit of a prang with the car, guv,' slurred Morgan.

'You stupid bastard!' hissed Frost.

Morgan looked ready to burst into tears. His face crumpled. 'One whisky, guv, that's all I had, one little whisky.'

'One? You've spewed up five doubles down your

flaming jacket.' He checked that the two traffic officers were out of earshot. 'I don't know how I'm going to get you out of this, Taffy.' He jerked a thumb back to the rear window. 'Have you seen what you've done to that poor sod's brand new Nissan?'

Morgan creaked his head painfully round, focusing with difficulty. 'How did that happen?'

Frost examined the wound on the DC's forehead. Lots of blood but not too deep. 'Do you need to go to hospital?'

Morgan touched his forehead and seemed surprised to see red on his fingers. 'Bit of sticking plaster, that's all.' He wiped his fingers on a clean part of his jacket. 'What's going to happen, guv?'

'If there was any justice, Taffy, you'd be charged, imprisoned, castrated and kicked out of the force. Lucky for you there's no bleeding justice.' He thought for a moment. 'I'll see what I can do.'

He went back to the two traffic policemen. 'How did you find him?'

'He was weaving all over the road. When we slammed on the siren he put his foot down and swung the car into Saxby Street. The next thing we heard was the scraping of metal and then this bloody crash.'

'Did any member of the public see what happened?'

'I doubt it. If it had been reported, the station would have contacted us, and they haven't.'

'And you haven't radioed details to the station?'

'No. We thought we'd let you know first.'

Frost grunted his thanks. 'Good. Now forget all about it. Drive off and continue your patrol.'

They looked at each other doubtfully. 'I don't think we would get away with it, Inspector. Someone could have seen him; someone could be looking out of their window at us now.'

Frost did a quick scan of the nearby houses. All

were in darkness. 'You didn't drag me out of bed just so I could watch you arrest the poor sod, did you? Do what I say – forget it. Any comeback and I'll take the full blame. You'll be in the clear.'

They looked questioningly at each other then gave a reluctant nod, knowing that if Frost said he would take the blame, then that's what would happen. 'All right, Inspector.'

Frost grinned happily. 'Thanks, lads. And if ever you murder your mother-in-law give me a bell – I owe you one.'

'But what about his wrecked car?' asked Bearsley. 'And there's a couple of thousand quid's worth of damage to that Nissan. How do we explain that away?'

'You know what I think happened here?' said Frost. 'I reckon a flaming joy-rider nicked Morgan's motor and caused all this damage. I'll report it the minute I get home.'

'A joy-rider?' exclaimed Wells incredulously, answering Frost's phone call. 'At this time of the morning?'

'His watch must have stopped,' said Frost. 'Morgan was round my place. We heard a car starting up and when we looked out of the window, this bloke was driving it off. We nipped down and tried to follow him, but he lost us in the fog.'

'Bloody convenient,' sniffed Wells. 'And what was Morgan doing round your place at four o'clock in the morning?'

'We were discussing ways to bring down the outstanding crime figures.'

'Now I know you're lying,' said Wells. 'All right, I'll report it as stolen. Any idea where we should start looking for it?'

'Just a shot in the dark, but try Saxby Street,' said Frost. 'And whoever finds it, tell them not to sit in the driving seat . . . the bloke I saw nicking the motor looked as if he was going to be sick all over it.'

'Charming,' muttered Wells. He lowered his voice. 'That Welsh bastard isn't worth it, Jack. Why are you sticking your neck out?'

'Because if I got into that sort of trouble I'd hope my mates would lie their flaming heads off for me – it's one of the few perks of the job.'

He hung up and yawned, rubbing sore and gritty eyes. Morgan had been left, snoring noisily in the back of his car outside. Let him sleep it off until morning. Morning! He was due to brief the search parties at eight, so with luck he might snatch three hours' sleep. One last look at the phone, daring it to ring. Half-way up the stairs it defied his dare, and rang and rang and rang . . .

He fumbled the receiver to his ear and stifled a yawn. 'Frost.' He braced himself for the worst. You didn't get good news phoned through in the wee small bleeding hours. But he was wrong.

'Inspector!' An excited PC Collier. 'We might have something on that car. Guess who owns a dark blue ten-year-old Astra?'

'Say it's Mr Mullett and you've made my night,' said Frost.

'Better than that,' crowed Collier. 'Bernie Green.'

'Not *the* Bernie Green?' said Frost, flipping through the record cards of his memory. 'Never heard of him.'

'Not in your league, Inspector. A small-time flasher. He's done time for assaulting kids – nothing serious, touching them up in the cinema, things like that . . . and he's going bald!'

'Eureka!' exclaimed Frost, his tiredness suddenly vanishing.

'We've still got quite a few names to check. He might not be the one.'

'Even if he isn't the right one, he'll bloody do for me,' said Frost. 'What's his address?'

'56B Gorge Street, Denton.'

He scribbled it on the wallpaper. 'I'm on my way. Meet me outside his house.'

Gorge Street was crammed with parked cars and he had to double park alongside the area car as Collier and Howe came over to meet him.

'Which house?'

Collier pointed to a dilapidated building with steps leading down to a basement area. 'Down there. "B" stands for basement.'

'I thought it stood for bum-holes,' muttered Frost. They peered down the stone steps to the area where mist swirled around overflowing dustbins, soggy cardboard boxes and other junk. 'These bastards never live in rose-covered cottages, do they?' sniffed Frost. 'Is there a back way?'

'A yard of sorts and a broken-down brick wall,' Howe reported. 'We did a recce as soon as we got here.'

'Get round there,' Frost told Collier. 'He might make a run for it.' He pushed open the rickety iron gate to the steps, the rusty screech setting his teeth on edge and, with Howe following, descended the steps. A single sash window was almost opaque with the grime of ages and his torch beam bounced off the glass when he tried to see inside. He found his penknife and tried to manipulate the sash lock.

'What are you doing?' Howe whispered.

'I want to get inside,' whispered Frost. 'If he's got the kid in there, we need to get to her before he does. I don't want a bloody knife to her throat and the demand for a fast car and Concorde to Buenos Aires.' Sweat poured as he worked away with the penknife, but he had to admit defeat. The window was held tight in the iron grip of multiple layers of ancient paint. 'I think I'm going to have to accidentally smash the glass,' he said, looking round for something suitable. 'Don't want to wake the bastard though.'

'Guv!'

Frost froze and looked up. Morgan – bleeding Morgan – was swaying unsteadily at the top of the steps, peering blearily down. 'What are you doing, guv?'

Frost groaned and hissed for silence just as Morgan managed to kick a milk bottle and send it crashing down the stone steps.

'Have another go,' snarled Frost. 'I don't think the people in the next street heard you.'

'Sorry, guv,' said Morgan, then a yell as he missed his footing and went crashing down the steps.

A light came on from an upstairs window. 'What's going on down there?'

'Police,' called Frost, shining his torch on Howe so the man could see his uniform. Howe was groaning inwardly. Why did events with Frost all too often turn into farce? As the man's head withdrew another light came on – this time from the basement window.

'Shit,' said Frost, 'we've woken the sod up!' Not much element of surprise now. He hammered on the door. 'Open up – police!' He kicked the door and yelled again. 'Open up or we'll break the door down.' This proved easier said than done. The door was locked and heavily bolted and Howe's shoulder was getting numbed and bruised from charging at it in the confined space of the area. Frost's radio crackled. PC Collier. 'I've got him, Inspector. He was trying to climb over the back wall.'

Morgan was dumped back in the car. Frost and Howe hurried round to the rear entrance to find a triumphant Collier holding the handcuffed arm of red and white striped pyjamaed, bare-footed Bernie Green.

'Hello, Bernie,' said Frost. 'We were passing so we thought we'd drop in.' Green, teeth chattering, didn't answer. 'Get him in the house,' Frost told Collier.

He took a quick look round the yard which held an outside toilet and a brick-built coal bunker, and waited while Howe's torch explored the interiors. No sign of the girl. They followed Collier and Green down the stairs to the basement flat, a miserable room, cold and damp from the mist which had crept down from the open door. The single room held a bed, a table, two chairs and, in the corner, a tiny cooker and a sink. Nowhere to hide a body. Frost switched on an ancient electric fire which glowed dimly, but did little to raise the temperature. Green was still shivering violently, so Frost snatched the eiderdown from the bed and wrapped it round him. 'Don't want you dying of cold before we beat a confession out of you, Bernie,' he said.

Green looked up at the inspector, his face a picture of misery. 'I never touched him, Mr Frost. I swear to God I never laid a finger on him.'

Frost said nothing. He held his hands out to the electric fire and gave the man his disbelieving stare.

'How is he, Mr Frost?' asked Green at last.

'He's dead,' said Frost bluntly.

'Dead? Oh God.' He buried his face in his crooked arm, his shoulders shaking. 'I never did anything.'

'That's right,' nodded Frost. 'You did sod all – you just left him to die in the middle of the road.' He shuddered. The cold and damp and squalidness of the miserable little room were getting to him. 'Take him down to the station. This place is giving me the creeps.'

9

'I swear on a stack of bibles I never touched him, Mr Frost . . . He suddenly ran out of the car – for no reason.'

Frost dribbled smoke from his nose and looked contemptuously at Bernie Green who cowered in the chair opposite him, a blanket over his pyjamas. 'Don't lie to me, Bernie,' snapped Frost. 'I'm not in the mood. I'm tired, I've had a lousy day and I don't give a sod whether I keep my job in the force or not, so I might ask this nice constable to step outside for a moment while you accidentally smash your face against all four of these walls.'

Howe gave a warning cough to remind Frost the interview was being taped.

But Frost's outburst had the required effect. Bernie's tongue flickered over dry lips. 'I was *going* to do something – I never do things against their will. I offered him money if he'd let me do something. That's when he ran out. I swear I never laid a finger on him.' He pointed to his case file on the table. 'You check my file . . . I always ask them first . . . I always get their consent.'

Frost flipped through the file, fingering its pages by their edges as if they were too dirty to touch. 'Yes, but most of the poor little mites were below the age of consent, Bernie.' He showed him a page. 'This little girl of six, for example. I don't suppose she had any idea what you wanted in exchange for the bag of jelly babies.'

'I was punished for that, Mr Frost . . . that's all over and done with. But the boy tonight was eleven. All he had to say was no and I wouldn't have touched him. I'd have driven him home. He had no need to go running out of the car like that.'

'He was shit scared, Bernie. You take him to the woods in the middle of the night, you demand sexual bloody favours from a kid. He must have been terrified.'

Green stared down at the floor. 'I'm sorry. I just can't help myself sometimes . . .'

'And what about the two little girls from Denton Junior? Couldn't you help yourself with them either?'

The man raised his head and frowned. 'What two little girls?'

Frost flicked two photographs across the table. 'Vicky Stuart and Jenny Brewer.'

Green stared open-mouthed, then shrank back. 'Oh no, you're not pinning them on me.'

'Where are they, Bernie?'

'I don't know. I want a lawyer.'

'You'll want an armed bodyguard if we set you free and let the boy's father know where you live.'

Again Howe gave a warning cough. A confession obtained as the result of threats would be thrown out of court. Frost ignored him. He knew he was skating on the thinnest of ice, but finding the girl alive was more important to him than a conviction. 'For the last time, where are they, Bernie?'

Green leapt to his feet, the blanket falling to the floor. 'I don't know anything about them,' he shouted.

Frost waved him back to the chair. 'I'm not deaf, Bernie, you can lie to me quietly if you want to.' He gave his benign smile. 'Are they still alive?'

'I don't know anything about them.'

'Did you take them to the woods in your car, like the boy? Are they buried in the woods?'

'I don't know.'

'Your car was seen outside the school, Bernie.' To be fair, a car the same colour as yours, he thought, but who's being fair? 'Where did you take them?'

'I didn't take them anywhere.'

'Did you take them back to your luxurious apartment, Bernie, to that smelly little basement flat? We can check, you know. We can go over every inch of the place.'

A look of relief flickered across Green's face. 'You can do what you like . . . you won't find anything.'

'And every inch of your car. If we find so much as a flake of skin, a hair even, from either of those two girls . . .'

Bernie jerked back as if he had been struck. 'A hair?'

'That's all we need for DNA tests, Bernie.' He smiled sweetly. 'Not a problem, is it?'

Green buried his face in his hands. 'Hold on, Inspector . . . give me time to think . . .'

Frost blew smoke up to the ceiling, then nodded happily at Howe. The confession was coming.

After a few seconds Green sat up and pushed the photograph of Vicky Stuart away. 'I know nothing about her, Mr Frost, but this one . . .' He tapped the photograph of Jenny Brewer. 'I know something about her.'

Frost turned Vicky's photo face down. 'Then tell us about Jenny.'

'I want to do a deal. I'm out on parole on condition I don't go near schools or approach kids. If I do, I have to go back and serve out my sentence. I don't want to go back to prison, Mr Frost.'

187

'You're already going back to nick for sodding about with the boy,' said Frost, 'so you've got damn all to lose. Tell us what you know and I promise you I'll do what I can.' Which will be sod all, he told himself.

Green pointed to the photograph. 'I might have given her a lift.'

Frost's eyebrows soared. '*Might?* What do you mean, might?'

'All right. I did give her a lift so it's possible you might find one of her hairs in my car but it won't mean anything. I just gave her a lift, that's all it was, a lift . . .'

'And when was this?'

'Couple of days ago . . . the day she went missing. I was sort of driving past the school just as the kids were coming out and I sees this little girl in red trotting along, all on her own. It was peeing with rain and she had no mac so I asked if she wanted a lift. She said would I take her to Argylle Street.'

'Argylle Street?'

'Yes, a few blocks away from the school. I drove her there. She told me she was going to have her photograph taken. I said, "I've got some nice pictures at home, would you like to see them?" She said no and got out and ran across the road to this house. I watched her ring the bell, a bloke answered and she went in.'

'What was the house number?'

'I don't know, but it was the one on the corner.'

'You actually saw her go inside?'

'Yes. I waited ten minutes or so in case she came out, but she didn't, so I drove back home.'

'You knew the kid had gone missing, you knew we were looking for her, so why didn't you come forward with this earlier?'

'How could I?' implored Green. 'I wasn't supposed

188

to approach kids. I'd have gone straight back in the nick.'

Frost stood up. 'Right, Bernie. As you've got your pyjamas on, you can retire to a nice warm cell and have a kip. We'll check your story out and God help you if you've been lying.'

He had done it so many times before, he could almost do it in his sleep: walk to the front door, jab the bell push, pound the door with the flat of the hand and yell, 'Open up – police!', then turn and stare down the street, not consciously seeing, but taking everything in. Argylle Street. Another street choked with parked cars, plus two double parked police cars. His radio paged him. 'I'm in position, Inspector.' Collier had been sent to the rear of the house to block any escape route.

Again Frost thumbed the bell push, letting it ring and ring and ring.

At last an upstairs light came on. A sash window was raised and a head poked out. 'Who is it?'

'Police,' yelled Frost. 'Open up.'

'Police? Oh my God!' The window slammed shut. Frost waited, shivering as the damp night mist bit through his clothes. Sounds of doors slamming and lights coming on in various parts of the house, but the front door remained closed. 'He's taking his flaming time.' He was about to radio through to Collier to warn him to be prepared for a dash to freedom when there was a clicking of locks and the front door opened to reveal a rotund little man in his mid-forties, fully dressed and zipping up a driving jacket. He seemed nervy and agitated. 'Oh dear, how bad is she? Did they say?'

Completely wrong-footed, Frost spluttered, 'I'm sorry, sir . . . how bad is who?'

'My mother. The hospital said if her condition

189

worsened . . . I'm not on the phone you see . . .' Then
he saw the two police cars. 'What has happened . . .
It's serious, isn't it . . . Mother's dead?'

'We're not here about your mother,' said Frost.
'Perhaps we could come in. It's freezing out here.'

'Yes, of course, of course.' Shaking his head in
puzzlement he ushered Frost, PCs Simms and Jordan
following, into a small room furnished with two
easy chairs, a table and a sideboard on which stood a
small colour TV set. He clicked on the log effect
electric fire, then turned to face Frost, showing him
his trembling hands. 'Look at me. I'm shaking. Every
time there's a knock at the door I fear the worst.' He
dropped down in an armchair, unzipped the driving
coat and checked his watch. 'It must be something
terrible if you've come here at this time of the morning. You want to break it gently, don't you? Then say
it, she's dead, isn't she?' He was biting hard on his
lower lip.

'Like I said, we're not here about your mother,
sir,' Frost told him, his eyes travelling round the
room. 'We're here on an entirely different matter.' He
nodded for Jordan to take up the questioning, leaving
himself free to have a potter around.

Used to Frost's ways, Jordan stepped forward.
'I'm PC Jordan, sir, and this is Detective Inspector
Frost who is in charge of the investigation into the
disappearance of two missing children, Vicky Stuart
and Jenny Brewer.'

The man's face showed concern. 'Those poor
children. What their mothers must be going through
. . .'

'Could we know your name, sir?'

'Weaver – Charles Edward Weaver, but I don't see
how this concerns me.'

'We've had reports, Mr Weaver,' continued Jordan,
'that one of the girls was seen entering your house on

190

the afternoon she went missing.' He showed the photograph of Jenny Brewer. 'This little girl, sir.'

Weaver took the photograph in a hand that shook. He studied it, then looked up at Jordan in dismay. 'I didn't know it was her.'

Frost, who was edging towards the sideboard for a surreptitious rummage through its drawers, stopped in his tracks. 'What do you mean?'

Weaver wriggled in his chair to face Frost. 'Your informant is partly correct, Inspector. That little girl came to my house. She knocked and said something about wanting me to take her photo.'

'Why would she ask that, sir?' said Jordan.

The man transferred his attention to the constable. 'She must have seen me out and about with my camera – photography's my hobby. I pretended my camera was broken and she went away. She never came in.'

'Why did you tell her your camera was broken?'

Weaver gave a sad smile. 'A single man alone in the house with a young child? You know how neighbours talk.'

I hope they bloody talk when we chat them up, thought Frost, easing open one of the sideboard drawers. 'And you are positive she didn't come inside the house? You didn't close the front door behind her even for a second?'

'Definitely not, officer. It was all over in seconds. She went skipping off . . . It was pouring with rain. There was a blue car outside. I got the impression she might have gone off in that.' His face furrowed in sadness. 'And she was the one who is missing? Poor little mite. A lovely girl.'

Weaver sounded sincere and genuinely upset, but Frost was feeling that buzz, that almost sexual thrill of excitement that was whispering to him that this was their man. Weaver, with his tubby avuncular figure,

191

was someone kids would trust implicitly. And what was this the sod had in his sideboard? Frost carefully moved his hand to the drawer and began tugging out the wad of photographs he could feel inside.

'As you will appreciate, sir,' said Jordan, noticing what Frost was up to and desperately trying to hold Weaver's attention, 'we have to follow up all leads. Our information is that the girl did go inside your house . . .' He held up a hand to stifle Weaver's protest. 'I accept your assurance, sir, but we have to check. We'd like to do a thorough search.'

Weaver couldn't be more co-operative. 'Of course, Constable. Search where you like.' He turned to Frost who quickly snatched his hand away before Weaver could see what he was up to. The photographs were of birds and animals and local views which bitterly disappointed Frost who hoped for pornographic poses of nude children. 'We appreciate your co-operation, sir,' he told Weaver, closing the drawer with a shove from his rump as he moved forward. 'I knew it wouldn't be necessary to get a warrant.' He poked a cigarette in his mouth, but before he could light up, Weaver fluttered a hand.

'I'd be obliged if you didn't smoke.' He patted his chest. 'Asthma. It affects my breathing.' He produced an inhaler from beside his chair and applied it to his nose.

Frost returned the cigarette to its packet. 'We'll get on with the search, then.'

The rest of the team were called in and ordered to tear the place apart. But as sure as he was that Weaver was their man, he was equally sure they wouldn't find anything in the house. The bastard was too flaming smug, too bloody helpful, running after them, showing them around, pointing out things they might have missed.

He went with Simms up the stairs, Weaver leading

the way and flinging open the first door they came to.
'My bedroom . . .' A single bed, a wardrobe and a
dressing-table. Nowhere anything could be hidden.
Frost opened the wardrobe door for something to do.
Men's suits, shirts, shoes . . . 'She's not here,' he
grunted.

'Or anywhere, Inspector. But feel free to search
where you wish.'

We're wasting our time, thought Frost. The sod's
enjoying himself too much.

They passed the bathroom where Collier, kneeling on the floor, was carefully unscrewing the bath
panels.

Weaver frowned. 'I do hope he's going to replace
those.'

'Of course he will,' Frost assured him. 'You won't
know we've ever taken them out.' Some hopes – they
had no time for such niceties. The panels would be
rammed back if he was lucky and the screws left for
Weaver to replace.

The second bedroom was tiny, a single bed
squashed up against a wall and a small wardrobe.
Weaver looked sad. 'Mother's room,' he told them.
With a wicked grin he nodded towards a commode
alongside the bed. 'You can look in there if you like,
but I don't remember when I last emptied it.' Frost
chanced it. It could have been full of pornographic
photographs . . . but it was empty.

A dragging sound from below sent Weaver running
downstairs to see what they were up to, leaving Frost
and Simms alone in mother's room.

'What do you reckon, Inspector?' asked Simms.

'I reckon he enticed the kid into the house and he
killed her,' answered Frost. 'I've got no proof, but I
just know it.'

A call from downstairs sent them both to the
kitchen. 'We've got a locked door, here,' said Jordan.

Weaver came scurrying in. 'That's my dark room. I'd be obliged if you took my word for the fact there is no-one in there.'

'Your word is good enough for me, Mr Weaver,' lied Frost cheerfully, 'but my superiors are mistrusting bastards and they'd have my guts for garters if I didn't take a peek.' He held out his hand. 'So if you've got the key . . .'

Weaver produced a key from his pocket and unlocked the door. 'Please be careful – there's a lot of sensitive material in there.' He pressed the switch and a red, low-wattage bulb glowed dimly. Frost squeezed in. It was a pantry converted to a dark room and there was hardly any space to move. A narrow bench on which stood an enlarger and numerous developing trays. In the corner a tiny sink had been fitted with a cold water tap. Just above Frost's head was a shelf carrying bottles and tins of photographic chemicals and stacks of boxes of photographic paper. He lifted the lid to a couple of the boxes, but that was all they contained, photographic paper. Too much to hope that the pornographic pictures would be in so obvious a hiding place.

He switched off the light, forced a smile and emerged. 'As you say, Mr Weaver, nothing there.' He looked hopeful as the rest of the search team returned, but all shook their heads. They too had found nothing.

'Everything as it should be, Mr Weaver. Sorry we've wasted your time.'

Weaver gave an understanding smile. 'You had your job to do, Inspector.'

'How long has your mother been in hospital?'

'Nearly three months . . . she couldn't swallow, but they've operated.' He obviously didn't want to go into any more details.

'I wish her well,' said Frost.

194

Back in the car with the sleeping Morgan making bubbling snoring sounds from the back seat, Frost lit up the cigarette he had been denied in the house and chewed things over. The old lady had been in hospital for nearly three months. An empty house, mother out of the way, the ideal opportunity to get up to all sorts of tricks just at the time Vicky Stuart went missing. He looked back at the house. The lights were still on, then a curtain twitched from an upstairs window. The sod was checking up to make certain they were leaving. He revved the engine and drove off, followed by the other two cars. Once round the corner he stopped and flagged the others down while he radioed through to the station. 'I want a twenty-four-hour surveillance on Weaver, starting from now.'

'Twenty-four-hour surveillance?' echoed Wells. 'That's going to make the overtime budget look sick. You've cleared it with Mr Mullett?'

'Yes,' lied Frost. He'd do it first thing in the morning. Mullett might not be in the agreeing mood if he was dragged out of bed yet again and he couldn't risk the sod saying no.

'All right,' sighed Wells, 'I'll get it organized. Tell Collier he's on the first four-hour shift.'

He was tired but his brain was whirling, spinning out ideas and possibilities, making it impossible to sleep. He made himself a cup of instant coffee and switched on the television and found himself watching a black and white early western where a very youthful John Wayne was beating a baddie to a pulp with punches that missed by yards. He closed his eyes, just for a minute. The next thing he knew was being jolted awake by the phone in the hall screaming at him. John Wayne, his white cowboy hat still in place, was massaging his knuckles and looking down at

195

his opponent. He could only have been asleep for seconds. He staggered out to the phone.

It was Collier. 'I'm following Weaver,' he reported. 'He got into a car a couple of minutes ago. He was carrying something.'

Frost was now fully awake. 'What was he carrying?'

'I couldn't see. The fog's thickening and I had to park well down the street so he wouldn't see me.'

'What make of car?'

'A green Metro . . . I couldn't get the registration number.'

'Where are you now?'

'Bath Road. I'm going to need some back-up.'

'I'll get back-up,' Frost told him. 'Whatever you do, don't lose him.'

Grabbing his coat, he phoned the station. 'We need back-up. Weaver's on the move.'

'All I've got is Jordan and Simms in the area car,' said Wells, 'and they're at Tomlin Street flats . . . the pillow case bandit has struck again.'

'Sod the pillow case bandit, he can wait. Get them over here . . . now!'

The fog was getting denser and the windscreen wipers on Collier's car were working overtime smearing the glass. Fog helped conceal him from Weaver, but made the Metro very difficult to follow. He could just make out the dirty red smears of the car's rear lights which would disappear abruptly as the Metro went through a patch of really thick fog. Suddenly the red flickered and vanished again and this time didn't come back. There was a junction ahead. Weaver had turned off on to the main road. Collier accelerated, looking left and right and seeing nothing. Which way had he gone? Damn. He'd lost him. He turned left, hoping against hope that this was correct. On and on through swirling mist, getting more and more anxious, and seeing nothing ahead. He should have turned right. He picked up the radio to tell Frost he had lost him when his heart quickened. Dimly, some way ahead, two red lights. The Metro. It had to be the Metro. The lights veered to the left. Collier spun the wheel to follow, feeling the tyres bump and judder over an unmade road. Where was he? He couldn't see a bloody thing. He had completely lost his bearings in the fog and was frantically trying to work out his location so he could report to Frost. He wound down the window to see better and suddenly heard the sound of water splashing down into water. The canal! Of course . . . he was on a little-used track which led to the canal. What was Weaver doing here?

Head outside the car, he could see a bit better. The splodges of red ahead were getting bigger – they weren't moving. Weaver had stopped. Collier swung his car over to the grass verge and switched off his lights. He radioed Frost and told him what was happening. 'Get out and see what he's doing,' ordered Frost.

Collier climbed out, shivering as the damp insinuated its way through his greatcoat. The mist was clinging tenaciously to the canal making visibility almost nil and he had to inch blindly towards Weaver's car, keeping well away from the edge of the tow path. He could hear the water, but couldn't see it. A car door opened and slammed shut. Weaver was getting out. A pause, then a splash. Something heavy thrown into the canal. Collier strained his eyes and could just make out the outline of a man, staring down into the water. It was Weaver, who turned and went back to his car. Collier hurried back to his own vehicle and radioed Frost. 'He's chucked something in the canal.'

'Did you see what it was?'

'No, quite a splash though. Hold on.' Collier could

hear an engine starting up. 'I think he's driving off. Do I follow?'

'Yes.' But Frost instantly changed his mind. 'No. Stay there.' The boot, thought Frost despairingly. The bloody boot. He could have had the kid's body in the boot and we never searched the flaming car. The bugger sat there wearing a driving coat and we never thought to search his bloody motor!

Headlights from the Metro flared in the windscreen as Weaver drove past. 'He just passed me.'

'Let him go. Get down to the canal and try and find out what he chucked in – it might be the kid. I'll get some more bodies and we'll join you.' He radioed through to the station for the underwater emergency team.

'Has Mullett agreed this?' queried Wells.

'Sod Mullett, the kid could be drowning. Just do it, Bill, I'll square things with Mullett. And I need more men – all you can spare. The canal's going to be a sod to search in this weather.'

'They're all off duty, Jack. It'll mean extra overtime. Mr Mullett said—'

'Just bloody do it, Bill. I'll take the can – and tell all patrols to look out for Weaver's green Metro. I want to know where it goes.'

'Registration number?'

'I don't know, but there can't be many green Metros about at this hour of the morning.' He wound his scarf round his neck, steeled himself for the dash out into the cold and headed for his car.

The worsening visibility caused him to miss the turn-off and he had to waste valuable minutes back-tracking and trying again. Bumping down the unmade road leading to the tow path he could just make out the flashing blue light of an area car which had got there before him. A burble of voices led him to some four or five men all thick-coated against the cold, poking and prodding the canal water with long sticks. Two cars were parked on the tow path, their headlamps trying weakly to push through the mist and give the searchers some light. Thick fog, like dirty clumps of cotton wool, rolled along the surface of the canal making it near impossible to make out where the tow path ended and the water began.

Frost grabbed Collier's arm. 'How's it going?'

'Not too well, Inspector. I never saw where he dropped it, I only heard the splash, and he might have dropped it near the bank or thrown it right in the centre. It's far too deep for anyone to wade in at this point.' He shook his head in self-reproach. 'I should have got closer. If it was the girl and she was alive when she went in, she'll be long dead by now.'

'We can only do our bloody best, son,' slashed Frost. 'We're not miracle men.' The whining growl of approaching vehicles. The underwater search team. 'About bloody time,' muttered Frost.

Within minutes floodlights were erected and a portable generator was chugging away. The team began donning frogmen suits as the duffel-coated sergeant in charge got his instructions from Frost. 'What are we looking for, Inspector?'

'A man who we suspect has abducted a seven-year-old kid has chucked something in the canal. It could be the kid.'

'When and where was it dumped?'

Frost shrugged. 'In this general area somewhere. The officer heard the splash, but didn't see anything. This was about an hour ago.'

The sergeant stared down into the smoking murk of the canal. 'No-one's going to live an hour in that.' He left the inspector and went over to his team. Frost called his own men over and ordered them to start a systematic search along the bank now that the area was floodlit. He mooched up and down, smoking cigaettes that tasted foul and occasionally kicking at a clump of grass to relieve his feelings.

His radio called him. Charlie Alpha, the other area car, had spotted Weaver and had followed him back to his house.

'He's inside now, Inspector.'

'Stay and watch,' ordered Frost.

'We're supposed to be on patrol. How long do we wait?'

'All flaming night if necessary. If he makes a move outside, follow him and let me know.'

From the canal came the creak of oars, then a soft splash as the frogmen plunged in. The duffel-coated sergeant joined Frost. 'This little lot is going to cost a bomb,' he said. 'I hope your super's prepared for it.'

Frost gave a non-committal grunt. God, he dreaded telling Mullett tomorrow. It would be all his fault, especially if it came to sod all.

A splash as a frogman's arm came up and waved frantically. 'He's found something,' said the sergeant, moving forward.

Frost's heart thudded madly. Was it the girl? He almost wanted it to be the girl so the exercise wouldn't be in vain and Mullett wouldn't be able to give him a bollocking in the morning. He shook his head, ashamed of himself. Don't let it be the kid, please . . . let it be junk, rags, that bloody commode . . . I want the kid to be alive.

It was a small suitcase, tied securely with cord. The metal catches were shiny so it hadn't been in the water long. It was far too small to hold a child's body. They rowed it over to Frost and everyone crowded round to watch as he cut the cord and forced open the catches with his penknife. Inside was a black bin liner, folded over and sealed with plastic tape. Frost ripped it open, taking out first a house brick which had been included to make certain the case sank and then a large wad of brown manila envelopes held together with elastic bands. He pulled out one of the envelopes and opened it. Photographs. Lots of photographs, some black and white, some colour, all of children – small children – mostly in the nude, all obscene. Frost nodded significantly then turned to Collier. 'You only heard one splash?'

Collier nodded.

'Shall we stop looking?' asked the sergeant.

'No.' Frost shook his head. 'These bastards tend to use the same hiding place. He could have dumped the girl earlier. Give it a good going-over.' He straightened up and stuffed the envelopes and the bin liner back in the case. 'I'm going back to the station to check these and see if we recognize any of the kids. If Vicky or Jenny are in there, we've got him.'

The photographs were spread out before him on his desk when Bill Wells came in to report that the search had yielded nothing.

'Send them all home,' said Frost, pushing his packet of cigarettes over. 'Not a lot of joy with the photographs. No-one I recognize and none of them are our missing kids. We'll circulate them in case other Divisions can come up with something.'

Wells picked one up and studied it. A naked girl on a bed, legs spread-eagled. She couldn't have been more than nine. 'You reckon Weaver took this?'

Frost shrugged. 'He took some of them, but these sods share their goodies around. We'll get some fingerprints off them so we can prove he handled them.' He yawned and rubbed his eyes. 'I'm too bloody tired to pull him in for questioning now. First thing tomorrow.' He checked his watch. Twenty past six. 'I mean first thing today . . . we get a search warrant, arrest him, and go over his place brick by

201

brick.' He pushed the photographs back in the envelopes and heaved himself up. 'I'm off home for some kip.'

'You've got to be back by eight to brief the search party,' Wells reminded him.

Frost slumped down again. 'Sod it. Right. I'll kip down in the office. Give us a shout at half past seven – tea, toast, and the full English breakfast.'

'And what morning papers would you like?' asked Wells sarcastically.

'The *Financial Times* and the *Beano*,' replied Frost.

Police Superintendent Mullett spun the wheel and coasted his repaired Rover past the lines of vans and cars of the search party and slid neatly into his allotted parking space. He was pleased to note that the overnight mist had cleared considerably, having had visions of a fog-bound search party, sitting in the canteen drinking tea, waiting for the weather to improve while the cost of the exercise mounted and mounted. Many months to go before the end of the financial year and already his overtime budget was getting dangerously close to its permitted figure. Frost was notoriously poor with his paperwork, so Mullett would have to remind him not to round times up to the nearest hour or half-hour just to make the calculations easier. With so many men, even a few minutes would multiply out to quite a large sum.

He nodded a brisk greeting to Station Sergeant Wells who was bringing the incident books up to date. 'Good morning, Sergeant. Where's the search party?' He had decided he would give the troops a few well-chosen words of encouragement before they went out, dropping very heavy hints that time was money and everything had to be paid for.

Wells, dead tired, stumbled to his feet. 'Morning, sir. They're in the briefing room.'

Mullett frowned. The man looked half asleep. He was a disgrace. What sort of an image was this to present to the public? 'You're looking very jaded this morning, Sergeant?'

'Sorry, sir. I've been on duty all night and I've had to extend my shift – there's no-one to relieve me.' He gave a brave, modest little smile, waiting for a few words of sympathetic praise from his Divisional Commander. He waited in vain.

'No relief? Then you should organize things better,' Mullett told him. 'And even if you feel tired, try not to show it. The public don't want to know your problems.'

'Yes, sir . . . sorry, sir,' mumbled Wells, boiling with barely suppressed rage. It was Mullett's fault there was no-one to relieve him. Half the force had been seconded to County for this flaming drugs operation.

Mullett consulted his wrist-watch. 'Cup of coffee in half an hour,' he called over his shoulder as he made his way up the corridor.

He strode into the briefing room, pleased at the way all leapt respectfully to their feet. He waved them down, his mouth smiling while his eyes travelled the room working out how much of a dent this little lot would make to his planned budget for the year. There were some faces he didn't recognize – men and women from other Divisions who had been drafted in. He found himself an empty seat near the front and checked his watch. Ten past eight. He frowned. Frost, who should have started the briefing at eight o'clock sharp, had not yet made an appearance and a roomful of people on full pay were just sitting and waiting. He turned his head. 'Does anyone know where Inspector Frost—'

Before he could finish his sentence the door banged open and Frost, carrying a bacon roll perched on top of a mug of tea, bounced in. Mullett screwed his face

203

up in annoyance. The man was a mess – unshaven, clothes crumpled and he hadn't even bothered to run a comb through his hair. What an example to show other Divisions. As Frost passed Mullett he flicked a hand. 'Don't bother to get up, Super.'

Mullett, who hadn't the slightest intention of getting to his feet, didn't join in the general laughter, but glowered and pointedly studied his watch.

Frost dumped his bacon roll on the desk and took a swig at the tea. He beamed at the assembly. 'This bloke is crossing the desert when he sees this naked tart buried up to her neck in the sand . . .'

Mullett raised his eyes to the ceiling and groaned. This was neither the time nor the place for one of Frost's dubious jokes.

'Stark flaming naked. Just her head showing. She says, "Please help me. I wouldn't submit to the Sultan's sexual demands so he did this to me. Please dig me out." "If I do," says the bloke, "what's in it for me?" She says, "About four pounds of wet sand." ' Frost led the laughter. No-one laughed louder at his jokes than he did himself. Mullett, who didn't understand it, forced a smile to show he was one of the lads.

When the laughter subsided, Frost took another swig of tea and now looked serious. 'Right, that's probably the last laugh you're going to have today.' He turned to the wall board. 'We're looking for this kid.' He tapped the large photograph. 'Jenny Brewer, seven years old, left school two days ago, hasn't been seen since. It's bleeding cold out there and if she's still alive, the sooner we find her the better, but my gut feeling is that if we find her, we find a body, so it's not going to be a bag of laughs. The good news is we have a suspect who might be able to save us all a lot of time by telling us what he's done with her.' He switched his gaze to the window. 'The mist has cleared up quite a bit now, but according to the

204

clever sods in the Met Office, it's going to get thicker and thicker, so unless Mr Mullett wants to hold things up with some encouraging words . . .' He turned, eyebrows raised in query, to the Divisional Commander who flushed, forced a smile, mentally conveying his 'Time is Money' speech to the waste bin, and shook his head. 'OK,' said Frost, 'then off you go, and good luck.'

Mullett stood up and beckoned him over. 'My office, Frost, now!'

Mullett repositioned his blotting pad to dead centre, then pulled the in-tray towards him. There seemed to be an awful lot of overtime claim forms for him to sign. He was tugging the cap from his Parker pen when there was a half-hearted knock at the door and in slouched Frost who flopped into a chair before being asked. 'Please sit down,' said Mullett in his witheringly sarcastic tone which was completely lost on Frost.

'Thanks, Super. You wanted to see me?' He looked at his watch. 'If you could make it snappy, I've got a suspect to pull.'

'I'll take as long as it takes,' snapped Mullett. He jabbed a finger. 'Look at you! A disgrace. When you walked into that briefing meeting I didn't know where to put my face. Those clothes look as if they've been slept in.'

'Top marks for observation, Super,' said Frost. 'They have been slept in. I was up until six this morning following a lead on the girl. I had to kip down in the office.'

'That wouldn't have stopped you from shaving,' barked Mullett.

Frost rubbed his chin. Damn. He'd forgotten to shave. 'Bloody electric razor conked out. I'll borrow one as soon as I get back to the office.' He began

205

to ease himself out of the chair. 'So if that's all, Super . . . ?'

Mullett flapped a hand to wave him back. 'That is not all, Inspector.' He began totalling up the hours on the overtime claims when he noticed the thick wad of more overtime forms underneath. His mouth sagged open. 'What are these?' He waved the offending forms at Frost. 'Eight off-duty men called in last night, four hours' overtime *each*? I authorized ten hours total.'

'Oh, sorry about that, Super,' began Frost. 'I was going to tell you about that—'

'You don't *tell* me about overtime, Frost,' cut in Mullett. 'You ask . . .' His voice tailed off. He had now spotted the indent for the underwater search team. 'What is this? What is this?' His voice had risen an octave. 'Do you know how much they charge per hour . . . ?' he spluttered.

'No – but it will be on the invoice,' said Frost, trying to be helpful. He filled Mullett in on the events of the night before, dragging a couple of the photographs they had found and passing them over. As he finished, Mullett stared at him in goggle-eyed disbelief, his Parker pen a blur as it sped over his blotter, doing sums to work out the total expenditure then staring aghast at the final figure. 'How am I going to clear this with County? Even I haven't the authority to sanction an operation of this size.' He took off his glasses and pinched the bridge of his nose. 'I hold you responsible, Frost. I won't accept any of the blame.'

'Then I'll take all the bloody blame for a change,' snapped Frost. 'You don't count costs when a kid's life is at stake.'

'But a child's life wasn't at stake, was it? One splash and you jump to conclusions. All you got was some lewd photographs which would still have been there in the morning and could have been retrieved without any overtime . . .'

'Last night I didn't have the benefit of your flaming hindsight,' said Frost angrily.

'Don't adopt that tone with me, Frost,' snarled a red-faced Mullett, equally angry. 'The only thing that might get you off the hook is a result.'

'I'll get you a result,' said Frost, standing up. 'I'm bringing Weaver in, then I'm getting Forensic to go over his place inch by inch.'

'And if you find nothing? What have you got? All this unauthorized expenditure for a few pornographic photographs.'

'We'll nail him,' said Frost, moving to the door and trying to convince himself. 'And if we're lucky we'll nail him for both kids . . . two for the price of one. How's that for a bargain?'

He closed the door firmly behind him. It was a good exit line, but could he possibly pull it off?

10

The search warrant was waiting for him on his desk. He stuffed it in his pocket and was giving his chin a quick going-over with the electric razor when the door creaked open and a death-warmed-up DC Morgan staggered in, unshaven, eyes red-rimmed, clothing soiled and crumpled and reeking of stale spirits and vomit. 'Good morning, vicar,' said Frost.

A sickly grin from Morgan. He flopped into a chair, wincing at the pain from his throbbing head.

'So what happened last night?' Frost asked.

The act of furrowing his brow in an effort to remember made Morgan wince again. 'It's all a bit vague, guv. There was this young lady and we had a drink . . .'

'Another bit of crumpet?' said Frost. 'You can't leave them alone, can you?'

'It's difficult to say no when they waggle it under your nose, guv.' He winced yet again as his fingers touched his forehead and found the gash. 'I remember getting into the car and driving off, but it gets a bit hazy after that.' He listened, looking more and more shamefaced as Frost quickly filled him in.

'It must have been those painkillers from the dentist . . . they make you drowsy.'

'Only if you're well pissed to start with,' said Frost, pulling on his mac. 'Get off home and clean yourself up before Mullett sees you. He's already given me a bollocking for looking like a tramp and I'm Beau Brummell compared to you. Stay away from the station. Report to Sergeant Hanlon and join the search for the missing kid.'

'Right, guv . . . sorry, guv . . . owe you one, guv.' He sidled out as PC Jordan came in.

'Was that a tramp or Taffy Morgan?' he asked.

'Both,' grunted Frost. 'SOCO and Forensic ready?'

'In the van and waiting.'

'Right,' said Frost. 'Let's pay our respects to Mr Weaver.'

'A search warrant?' blinked Weaver, staring at the document Frost had thrust into his hand. He had been roused from his bed by their hammerings and was still tying the cord round a grey dressing-gown. 'But this isn't neessary, Inspector. I told you yesterday, you can search where you like.'

'You are too kind, sir. I wish all citizens were as decent and co-operative as you.' Frost jerked a thumb to his team. 'Start with the upstairs rooms.'

Weaver watched in dismay as Forensic and Rawlings, the Scenes of Crime Officer, thundered up the stairs. 'It's a mess up there, I'm afraid.'

'Don't worry yourself,' beamed Frost amiably 'It'll be a lot more of a bleeding mess when they've finished.' He took Weaver by the arm and led him to the small kitchen where PC Jordan was opening and shutting drawers. 'We can talk in here, sir.' He noticed a bag of boiled sweets on the table. Sherbet limes. He hadn't had sherbet limes since he was a kid. 'Are these yours, sir?'

'Yes,' snapped Weaver, snatching the bag from him. 'They're mine. I don't use them to lure young children in here, if that's what you're implying.'

'I wasn't implying any such thing, sir,' said Frost. 'I

209

was hoping you'd offer me one.' He pushed Weaver into a chair then pulled a wad of photographs from his pocket and began to deal them out on the table, like a hand of cards. As each photograph was laid down, Weaver flinched. 'I believe these are yours, sir?'

Weaver shrank away as if he wanted nothing to do with them. 'Not mine, Inspector – definitely not mine.'

Frost looked across to Jordan in mock exasperation. 'We've boobed again, Constable. These aren't the gentleman's photographs.' He turned back to Weaver. 'I can't apologize enough, sir, so if you'll just explain why your fingerprints are all over them and how it was you were seen dumping them in the canal last night, we'll say no more about it.' He folded his arms and waited.

Weaver had gone the colour of chalk. He hung his head and mumbled to the table top. 'All right, Inspector. Yes, they are mine. To my deep shame I get pleasure from studying photographs of children . . .'

'Naked children,' corrected Frost.

'Yes. It sounds bad, but it's harmless. I just like to look at photographs, that's all. After you called here yesterday I was concerned you would find them and get the wrong idea, so I decided to get rid of them.'

'Did you take any of them yourself, sir?'

A quick shake of the head. 'Oh dear me, no. I bought them.'

'From a man in a pub you'd never seen before?'

Weaver gave a thin smile. 'Something like that. I paid cash. I don't know his name.'

Frost nodded as if he accepted this. 'Fair enough, sir. But something puzzles me. If I liked to dribble over photographs of bare young flesh, like you, I don't think I'd turn away a seven-year-old girl who knocks at my door and begs to be photographed. I'd have her stripped off and my Box Brownie out before you could say "Cheese".'

Weaver flushed angrily. 'You can believe what you like, Inspector, but I told you exactly what happened. She never came into the house.' The sound of nails wrenched from wood coming from above made him start. 'What is that?'

'That's the floorboards coming up – in case you forgot to tell us about the body.'

Weaver smiled. 'You can tear the place apart, Inspector. There is no body here.'

'It doesn't have to be a body,' Frost told him. 'We'll settle for a single hair, a shred of clothing. DNA can do the rest.'

The mention of DNA had the same effect on Weaver as it had on Bernie Green. He began twitching in agitation. 'DNA?'

'One hair, that's all they need, sir – they'll be disappointed if they find a body. They get paid extra for doing DNA tests.'

Weaver pulled the dressing-gown tighter around him. He was shaking, but not from the cold. 'There's something I should tell you.'

'My ear-hole is at your disposal, sir.' Frost sat in the chair opposite him and pulled out a cigarette, but remembering Weaver's asthma, reluctantly shoved it back in the packet.

'I'm afraid I didn't quite tell you the truth . . .' He paused. Frost said nothing. He knew when to keep his mouth shut. Weaver's tongue moistened dry lips. 'I did let her in. It was foolish of me, but she seemed such a sweet little girl. I did take her photograph – fully clothed, of course – and then she left. Even though it was innocent and harmless, when I learnt she was missing, I panicked and threw the photographs away.'

'And the film?'

211

'I threw that away as well.'

Frost stared hard at him. Weaver wouldn't meet his gaze. 'And what about the other little girl, Vicky Stuart?'

'I know nothing about her. I've never seen her. It was just Jenny, I swear it.'

'Inspector!' PC Simms was calling from the top of the stairs. 'Would you come up and have a look at this, please.'

Frost thudded up the stairs. Simms, in Weaver's bedroom, had pulled the wardrobe away from the wall. Sellotaped to the back was a large manila envelope. Frost felt it. There seemed to be photographs inside. He yelled for Weaver to be brought up. 'Any idea what this contains, sir?'

Weaver collapsed on the bed and buried his face in his hands. Frost removed the envelope and shook out the contents. A series of black and white photographs of a young girl, some semi-clothed, others in the nude. The girl was Jenny Brewer.

Frost rammed the photographs in Weaver's face. 'You couldn't bear to part with them, could you? All right, you bastard, where is she? What have you done to her?'

Weaver flinched and sniffed back tears. 'I've done nothing with her. She was alive when she left here.'

'You're lying,' snarled Frost. 'You lie until you're found out, and then you lie some more to cover up your lies. Where is she?'

Weaver shook his head, knuckling his eyes.

'Charles Edward Weaver,' intoned Frost, 'I'm arresting you on suspicion of being involved in the disappearance of Jenny Brewer . . .' He tailed off. He never could remember the words of the new caution and had to step back so Simms could finish it off for him.

'This is a nightmare,' blubbed Weaver. 'I'm innocent.'

'Take the innocent bastard away,' said Frost.

The cleaners had given the interview room a flick over. Its permanent smell of sweat, old socks and stale cigarette smoke was now tinged with pine disinfectant. Frost squeaked a chair across the brown lino and plonked himself down opposite Weaver. As he waited while Simms set up the cassette recorder, he rammed a cigarette in his mouth and lit up without thinking. One puff before Weaver was coughing, spluttering and flapping his hand to clear away the smoke. 'Please, Inspector – my asthma.'

Frost pinched out the cigarette and dropped it back in the packet. 'Sorry. Tell me about Jenny.'

'She saw me in the street with my camera and wanted her photograph taken . . .'

'When was this?'

'A few weeks ago. I told her no, but she kept knocking at my door. In the end, I let her in.'

'Why?'

'She looked so pitiful. I felt sorry for her. I didn't intend taking those photographs. It just happened.'

'She just happened to strip off and you just happened to have your camera handy?'

Weaver bowed his head and didn't answer.

'Did she do it for free?'

'I gave her sweets. I bought her little gifts, annuals, toys . . .'

'Clothes?'

'A red dress. She kept it at my place.'

'Why?'

'Jenny didn't want her mother to know.'

'And you didn't want her mother to know what you were doing with her daughter. So you paid the kid? You bought her presents to entice her to come?'

Weaver stared at the wall behind Frost and shrugged. 'If you want to put it that way.'

'Where is the red dress?'

'I burnt it.'

'What time did Jenny arrive on the day she disappeared?'

'A little after four. She came straight from school.'

'What time did she leave?'

'About a quarter to five. She said she had to get round to her grandmother's house. It was raining, so I gave her a pound for the bus fare.'

'How did she leave – the front way . . . the back way?'

'The back way. She said she didn't want any of her school friends to see her.'

'And you didn't want the neighbours to see her either.'

Weaver gave a wry smile. 'You know how neighbours talk.'

'With good bloody reason in this case. Let's pretend you're telling the truth. What do you reckon happened to her after she left you?'

Weaver spread his hands. 'I don't know, but if I were you, I'd start questioning her mother's boyfriend. Jenny told me he used to hit her. I saw bruises.'

Frost brought out the photo of the first missing girl. 'I'm showing the suspect a photograph of Vicky Stuart,' he told the tape. 'Tell me about Vicky.'

Weaver sighed. 'How many more times . . . I have never, ever in my life seen or spoken to that child. Jenny was the only one and I never so much as laid a finger on her.'

'Call me a sentimental old fool, if you like,' said Frost, 'but I think you're a bleeding liar. I think you know damn well where they are.'

Weaver shook his head as if in sorrow. 'I'm sorry

you don't believe me, Inspector. I can only tell the truth and the truth is I don't know anything about them other than what I have told you.'

Frost's lip curled contemptuously. 'Are they dead? Is that why you won't tell us where they are?' He jerked his head round angrily as someone knocked at the door of the interview room. The red light was on and he was interviewing a murder suspect. He flicked a finger for Simms to see who it was.

It was Sergeant Bill Wells who waved Simms aside and beckoned urgently to Frost to come outside. 'The hospital phoned, Jack. Weaver's mother has taken a turn for the worse. They think he should get over there right away.'

Frost found a dog-end in his pocket and took a couple of quick drags before grinding it underfoot. 'The bleeding woman picks her moments to go critical.' He went back in. 'Bit of bad news for you, Mr Weaver, I'm afraid.'

No other cars were available, so Frost had to drive him to the hospital, deliberately taking a route which led past Denton Woods, slowing down as they passed lines of men and women painstakingly searching for the missing Jenny Brewer. 'Tell us where she is,' he pleaded.

Weaver, staring out of the window, sighed. 'If I could, I would. I just don't know.'

'Her mother is desperate.'

'Her mother is a cow and the boyfriend used to beat her up. You should be questioning them, not wasting your time with me.'

The car crawled past another group, breaths smoking in the cold air, as they pushed through waist-high grass and bramble.

'There was a funeral in our street last week,' said Frost. 'Little boy of three, run over by a bus. The

215

wreath from his mum and dad was in the shape of a kiddy's scooter – his favourite toy. It broke my heart.'

'It would have broken mine as well,' said Weaver, dabbing his eyes with a handkerchief. 'I'm terribly sentimental about things like that.'

Crocodile tears, thought Frost gloomily. How the hell do I get through to the sod? Weaver lay back in his seat, looking relaxed, but as they approached the hospital Frost sensed the man was tightening up, looking slightly uneasy. 'Anything wrong, Mr Weaver?'

'Wrong? No, of course not. Just worried about my mother.'

The denial was a little too strong. Weaver was uneasy about the hospital. The kid was somewhere in the hospital's sprawling grounds. He'd tell Hanlon to make the search of the grounds a priority.

Once through the main entrance Frost had a job keeping up with Weaver as he hurried to his mother's ward. They climbed stairs, passed ward after ward, then a sharp turn to the right. 'This is it,' Weaver announced. He trotted in, only to stop abruptly and turn to Frost in dismay. A complete stranger, another woman, was in his mother's bed. The old girl's croaked, thought Frost gloomily, but a nurse tripped across to explain that the old lady had been moved to a side ward where she would be more comfortable.

The nurse took them to a small, single-bedded room where an old woman, her face as white as the hospital sheets, lay with her eyes closed, mumbling to herself. 'Visitors for you, Mrs Weaver,' said the nurse breezily. The old woman made no sign that she had heard. 'Stay as long as you like,' smiled the nurse to Weaver. Frost stiffened. *Déjà vu*! Those words . . . This room . . . It was the same bloody room. He knew every inch of it: that same zigzag crack in the ceiling over the bed, the peeling white paint on the skirting

216

board. This was the room where they had put his wife so her dying wouldn't disturb the rest of the ward and where she could be quickly wheeled across the corridor to the big lift down to the mortuary without upsetting the other patients. 'Stay as long as you like, Mr Frost.' This was the room where he had sat, staring at the blank walls day after day, night after night, waiting for her to die. The walls seemed to be closing in on him. He felt suffocated and wanted to get out.

Weaver, seated in the chair by the bed, was talking quietly to his mother whose eyes had fluttered open. He took her hand, the parchment skin showing a map of thin blue veins, and gently stroked it. 'It's me, mother – Charles.' If she knew he was there she gave no sign. Her mouth opened and closed a few times as if she was trying to say something, then the eyes fluttered shut . . . just the way Frost's wife's eyes would flutter shut.

Frost backed away to the door. 'I'll leave you to it for a while,' he whispered, almost feeling sorry for the poor sod. Outside he sucked in fresh air, then wandered off to a side passage where he could smoke without the nurses seeing him, staring, eyes half closed against the smoke, through the fourth-floor window to the surrounding countryside. At this height he was above the mist and could see clumps of it in the hollows clinging to the ground and then, suddenly emerging from it, a line of searchers looking for the girl. He switched his gaze down to the hospital grounds. To his left stood the old nurses' home, now empty, ready to be demolished. Lots of sheds and outbuildings, plenty of places to hide a seven-year-old girl's body. Weaver would often visit the hospital when it was dark.

He pulled out his phone to call Hanlon, remembering in time that mobiles weren't allowed within the hospital as they could interfere with medical equipment. He took the lift to the ground floor, then walked outside, dialling Hanlon's number.

'We've already done the hospital grounds, Jack,' Hanlon told him.

'I want them done thoroughly.'

'They were done thoroughly,' protested Hanlon.

'Do them again,' Frost ordered. 'This is where the kid is . . . I know it.'

'I don't want to pull men off other areas at this stage, Jack, areas we haven't searched yet.'

'All right.' He pinched out the cigarette and dropped it back in his pocket. 'But as soon as you've got a team free, I want them here. Pander my whim, Arthur, I've got one of my nasty feelings.'

Back again to the fourth floor where he peeked in on Weaver who was still sitting by the bed talking to her in a low, gentle tone. 'I've got your room waiting all ready for when you come home, mother . . . and Aunt Maisie sends her love . . .' The old woman's eyes remained closed and she wasn't hearing him.

Frost looked at his watch, surprised to see they had only been here for ten minutes. Time was crawling, just as it did when he visited his wife. He went out for another cigarette, then remembered he was supposed to be covering the armed robbery case for Liz Maud while she was away so wandered up to the fifth floor to talk to the old boy who had tackled the robber and got shot in the legs for his trouble.

'He left this morning,' the nurse told him. 'Discharged himself.' Frost made a mental note to find time to see him at his home. A slight chance he might remember a bit more about the gunman.

He gave Weaver another half-hour, then drove him back to the station. The man seemed withdrawn, but looked up and pushed a smile. 'I think my mother looked a bit better today. Now they've moved her to that private room she'll get better in leaps and bounds, I know she will.'

Frost gave a non-committal grunt. 'We're going to search the hospital grounds,' he announced. 'We reckon that's where you've put the girl.' He pretended to be looking straight ahead, but watched Weaver out of the corner of his eye. The man didn't seem at all worried.

'I hope you find her, Inspector. And I hope you find her alive and well, then you can stop wasting your time on me and get after the real culprit.'

Frost felt the slightest flicker of doubt as to Weaver's guilt, but his gut feeling shook this off. The sod was as guilty as sin. He drove through the red light area, realizing that until they found the girl, they didn't have the resources to do much, if anything, about the serial killer. Sod Mullett and his generosity in giving away half the bloody station staff to County.

Sergeant Bill Wells slammed shut the door to Weaver's cell then chalked the time on the small blackboard outside. 'You can't hold him much longer without charging him, Jack,' he told Frost.

Frost nodded gloomily. 'We need a body. I can't charge him with murder unless we find the kid.' He followed Wells back to the front desk where the internal phone was ringing. Wells answered it. 'Mr Mullett is getting edgy at the build-up of overtime, Jack. Wants an itemized breakdown of the possible total sum involved on a day by day basis.'

'I'll have a bleeding breakdown if he doesn't get off my back,' said Frost, edging towards the door. 'Tell him I've just gone out, and I may be some little time.' The outside phone rang. He waited as Wells answered it in case it was one of the search teams.

'It's that old boy who was injured in the armed raid,

Jack. Says he's received some money in the post . . . reckons it's from the bloke who shot him.'

'Right,' said Frost, glad of a legitimate excuse to go out. 'I might not be back until after Mr Mullett's gone home . . .'

The old boy, Herbert Daniels, his leg heavily bandaged and reeking of hospital antiseptic, opened the front door as far as the security chain would permit and stared at Frost's warrant card. 'You're not the woman policeman.'

'You're too bleeding observant,' said Frost. 'Can I come in?'

He followed Daniels into a tiny living-room where a huge coal fire roared away. The room was like a tropical greenhouse and Frost was soon unwinding his scarf and shucking off his mac. He pulled a chair further away from the fire and sat down. 'Understand you've had some money, Mr Daniels?'

Daniels handed Frost a padded envelope. 'Came yesterday morning.' Inside was a wad of used bank-notes, some speckled with white paint. 'Five hundred quid in there,' Daniels told him. 'I counted it – and there's a message.'

A folded sheet of paper with handwritten block capitals read: 'SORRY. WE DIDN'T MEAN ANYONE TO GET HURT.'

'Sorry!' snorted Daniels. 'They shoot your bloody leg off and say sorry . . . hanging and bleeding flogging, that's what they want.'

'But preferably not in that order,' murmured Frost. He was studying the address on the envelope, also handwritten in capitals, 'HERBERT GEORGE DANIELS, 2 CLOSE COURT, DENTON'. He looked across at the old boy who was carefully arranging his injured leg on a stool. 'How long have you lived in Denton, Mr Daniels?'

'Just over a month. Came here from Leeds when my wife died. I wish I hadn't now – nutcases with bloody guns. Wouldn't have happened in my day – we had the death penalty then.'

'Do you have any friends in Denton?'

'Years ago, but they're all dead now.'

'Relatives?'

'My son's in Australia, there's no-one else.'

'I see.' Frost chewed on his knuckle. 'Have you joined any organizations or clubs since you've been in Denton?'

'The Denton Senior Citizens' Club. I go there a couple of days a week for a game of draughts and me dinner.'

'Do you know anyone there?'

'An old boy called Maggs, that's all. I play draughts with him . . . Why?'

Frost tapped the envelope. 'Whoever sent this money knew your middle name and your address. You're not yet in the phone book or on the voting register, so how did they get it?'

Daniels shrugged. 'I expect they got it from somewhere.'

'Yes, I expect they did,' said Frost. 'I hadn't thought of that.' His trouser legs were scorching from the heat of the fire so he moved the chair even further back, then fumbled for a cigarette, but decided against it. Only two left in the packet and the old sod might expect to be offered one. 'You haven't joined any other clubs, have you – clubs you'd rather not talk about?'

The old man scowled at him angrily. 'What the hell do you mean?'

'Strip clubs . . . blue film clubs?'

'That's a flaming insult.'

'Whoever sent the money must have got your full name and address from somewhere, Mr Daniels, and a strip club would be the sort of place they might frequent.'

'Well, it ain't the bloody place I frequent.'

Daniels couldn't tell Frost any more about the gunman than the brief description he had already given, so the inspector took his leave.

After the sauna bath atmosphere of the old man's room, the freezing cold air outside hit him like a plunge in icy water. He hurried to the car and tried unsuccessfully to get the heater to work. The interior still held the smell of stale spirits and vomit after his previous night's escapade with Morgan but there was no way he was going to open the window to let fresh air in. He wound his scarf tighter and was half-way back to the station when he stopped. A thought had struck him. He wondered if the other old boy – the one who was shot and had his car pinched – had also received money from the robbers. He was keeping quiet about it if he had. He radioed the station for the name and address. 'And get someone to check the membership lists of all the strip clubs and so on to see if Daniels is on them.' The old boy may have denied it, but best to make certain. He swung the car round and made for the other shotgun victim's house.

Mrs Redwood, thin and frail and in her seventies, peered nervously at the warrant card.

'Inspector Frost? Where's that nice young lady?'

'She's off sick. Just a quickie. Have you had any money sent to you in the post?'

She blinked. 'Money? No – why?'

'The gentleman who was shot had some money sent to him by the gunman.'

'Well, they didn't send us any and we wouldn't have kept it if they did. It wasn't their money, it was stolen.'

'If you do receive anything, please let us know. How's your husband?'

'In pain, but recovering. Did you want to see him?'

'No thanks,' said Frost hurriedly. He'd had enough of old boys with their legs bandaged for one day.

PC Collier was waiting for him in his office. He had drawn a blank with the various Denton clubs he had phoned. Frost plonked in the chair and scratched his chin. 'So where did they get his name and address from?'

'The milkman? The newsagent?' suggested Collier.

A firm headshake from Frost. 'The milkman or the newsagent don't bother taking down your middle name.' He drummed his fingers on the desk then pulled the note sent to Daniels from his pocket and read it aloud. ' "We didn't mean anyone to get hurt." It doesn't add up.'

'I don't follow,' said Collier.

'They say they didn't mean anyone to get hurt, yet they shoot the other old sod in the legs and pinch his car. They meant to hurt him all right, but didn't send him any money.'

'Probably don't know his address,' said Collier.

'If they found Daniels' address, they could find *his* bloody address.' Frost stared up at the ceiling. Something was nagging away at the back of his brain . . . He dug deeply into his memory, then snapped his fingers. 'Cordwell – the bloke who owns the mini-mart, didn't he prosecute some old age pensioner recently – caught her shoplifting? There was a stink about it in the paper.'

'That's right,' nodded Collier. 'Old dear got fined £200 . . . Not her first offence.'

'I think her name was Maggs, son. Check it for me. It's important.'

As he waited for Collier, he rummaged through his

in-tray, discarding all memos he didn't have time or the patience to deal with – mostly memos from Mullett starting with 'May I remind you . . .' or 'When may I expect . . . ?' That chore done, he stared out of the window. Barely three o'clock and already starting to get dark with a thick mist descending again. The search parties wouldn't be able to work for much longer. Had Hanlon searched the hospital grounds again yet? He looked up as Collier returned.

'You're right, Inspector. Mrs Ruby Maggs.'

Frost interlaced his fingers behind his head and leaned back in his chair, beaming with delight. 'And Maggs is the old boy Daniels plays draughts with at the geriatrics' club. He'd know Daniels' address and he'd have a lovely grudge to bear against Cordwell who owns the mini-mart.'

'You're not suggesting Maggs was the bloke with the shotgun?' asked Collier. 'The man whose car they pinched said he was a lot younger.'

'Maggs could have a son, or a grandson, and got them to do it for him.' Once Frost had a theory he was reluctant to let it go. He snatched his scarf from the peg. He was feeling pleased with himself. Great to have this all tied up for Liz Maud when she returned. 'Come on, son, let's go.'

It took some time for Maggs to open the door. His laboured breathing and cries of 'I'm coming, I'm coming' seemed to go on for ever as he creaked his way up the passage. The front door opened to reveal a man in his late seventies, gasping for breath and leaning heavily on a stick. He was surprised to see Frost. 'I thought you were the District Nurse.'

'People often mistake me,' said Frost. He showed his warrant card. 'A couple of words, if you don't mind.'

Mrs Maggs, looking even frailer than her husband, was huddled in a chair by the fire. 'Police?' she gasped in alarm, holding a heavily veined hand to her mouth. 'We're sending the money off for the fine today. I'm sorry it's taken so long, but—'

'It's nothing to do with that, Mrs Maggs,' cut in Frost. 'It's about that robbery at the mini-mart.'

Husband and wife looked at each other. 'We read about that, didn't we, dear?' she said.

'Yes,' agreed Maggs. 'Gave me the biggest laugh I've had for ages. That sod Cordwell deserved to be robbed.' He held his wife's hand and squeezed it tight. 'Pity they didn't take more.'

'It was a friend of yours who was shot, Mr Maggs,' Frost told him. 'Mr Daniels.'

Maggs frowned. 'Who's Daniels?'

'Your draughts-playing friend.'

'Oh – you mean Bert? I never knew his second name. Oh dear. I never knew it was him.' He shook his head in dismay. 'How is he?'

'Not too badly hurt.' Frost heaved himself out of the chair. This was a waste of time. Maggs seemed genuine in not knowing Daniels' full name. Another theory flushed down the pan. 'I won't bother you any more, Mr Maggs.' And then he saw it. Behind the clock on the mantelpiece, a large brown envelope, the name and address handwritten in block capitals. He leaned over and pulled it out. Yes, identical to the one received by Daniels. It was empty.

Grunting with pain, Maggs rose and snatched it from him. 'That's personal!'

'Where's the money?' asked Frost.

Mrs Maggs, visibly distressed, was staring open-mouthed at her husband whose hand was shaking vigorously, bidding her to keep quiet. 'What money?'

'Was there a note with it?'

'We know nothing about no note. This is private, none of your business.'

Frost looked at them both. The man defiant, the

woman close to tears. No point in bullying them into an admission. It was obvious they too had been sent part of the robbery money and he now had a bloody good idea who had sent it. He buttoned up his mac. 'All right, Mr Maggs. I might need to talk to you again . . . but in the meantime, don't spend any of the money you didn't receive.'

Collier drove him to the Redwoods' house where Mrs Redwood seemed surprised to see him back so soon. 'A couple of points I should have cleared earlier, Mrs Redwood. Can I come in?'

Her husband, wearing a dressing-gown over pyjamas, sat in the living-room, his bandaged leg up on a stool. Frost declined the offer of a cup of tea. He smiled sympathetically. 'How are you feeling, Mr Redwood?'

His wife answered for him. 'He's still in a lot of pain but he's healing slowly.'

'Good,' said Frost.

Redwood eased his leg to a more comfortable position. 'Are you any closer to catching the swines that did it?'

'Very close,' Frost told him. 'In fact, we hope to make an arrest today – which is why I'm here.' He was studying the old man's face and noticed the slight start his words had produced.

'That's good news, Inspector,' said the wife, putting an arm round the old man's shoulders.

'How's Mr Daniels?' asked Redwood.

'Not too bad,' said Frost. 'Good job you had the gun pointing down.'

The man's head snapped up. 'Me?'

'Did I say "you"?' said Frost, sounding surprised he could make such a stupid mistake. 'I meant the armed robber.' He shook his head in annoyance with himself. 'I've so many things running through my mind, I get confused. They sent him money, did you know?'

'You told my wife earlier.'

'Did they send you any?'

'No – and if they did I wouldn't have accepted it.'

'Mr Daniels is not going to accept it either. They also sent a wad of money to a bloke called Maggs. He goes to your Senior Citizens' Club, doesn't he?'

'The name rings a vague bell.' Redwood was no longer looking up at Frost.

Frost scratched his chin. 'I wonder why they didn't send you any? You suffered more than Daniels . . . they nicked your car as well.'

Redwood shrugged and shook his head. 'No idea.'

Frost dragged a chair over and sat next to the old man, giving him one of his disarming smiles. 'You couldn't post it to yourself, I suppose. What did you do with the rest of the money?'

Redwood dropped his gaze. 'I don't know what you're talking about,' he mumbled.

But his wife could stand the strain no longer. 'For God's sake tell him . . . he knows anyway.' She broke down and sobbed.

Redwood took her hand and held it tightly, then raised his eyes to Frost. 'It all went wrong,' he told the inspector. 'Fire the gun up in the ceiling to frighten the life out of them, grab the money and run. It should have been all over in seconds. But Daniels had to act the bloody hero and grabs for the gun. I never meant the damn thing to go off . . . he got half the pellets in his leg, I got the rest in mine.'

'How did you know the security cameras weren't working that night?'

Redwood gawped, wide-eyed with dismay. 'Not working? You mean you didn't have our car on video?'

'We had sod all on video. Are you saying you didn't know it was out of action?'

227

'I didn't even know they had security cameras until we were driving away and my wife spotted them.' He gave an apologetic smile. 'I suppose we're not really cut out for this sort of thing.'

'I've known it done better,' said Frost. 'What have you done with the money?'

'We sent it anonymously to charities. We didn't want it.'

Frost frowned. 'Then why the hell did you pinch it in the first place?'

'That damn man Cordwell who runs the supermarket chain, he's raking in millions and he takes people like poor old Mrs Maggs to court for stealing a couple of packets of biscuits. There was another old dear a few months ago. Rather than face the disgrace of going to court, she took an overdose. We were angry. We wanted to make him pay.'

'Cordwell wouldn't have felt a bloody thing,' said Frost, 'and he would have got all the money back from his insurance company anyway. Bastards like him always win. What happened after you drove away?'

'It was all panic. Connie told me we were on that damn security camera . . . paint from the carrier bag all over the seat, shotgun pellets in my leg and I was terrified I might have killed Mr Daniels.' His face screwed up at the pain of the recollection. 'It was Connie's idea that we made up the story about the car being hijacked and the man shooting at me. She left me in the woods while she went off to hide the car, then she phoned the police.'

'You say you sent the bulk of the money off to charities?'

'Yes. Connie parcelled it up and sent it anonymously.'

Frost pulled out a pen. 'Which charities?'

They looked at each other. 'Will it make any

difference to what sentence we get if I tell you?' asked the man.

Frost shrugged. 'Probably not.'

'Then let them keep it. I suppose you'll take the money back from old Maggs?'

'He denies receiving it,' said Frost, 'and if you deny sending him any, there's not much we can do.'

'Then I didn't send him any.'

'Fair enough,' nodded Frost. 'Then the charities got it all.' He stood up. 'I've got to take you in.' He sounded almost apologetic.

Redwood's arm tightened around his wife, who looked ready to collapse. 'What will happen to us?'

'You'll give us a statement, then you'll be charged, then you'll probably be released on police bail pending the court hearing.'

The man blinked in dismay. 'We won't go to prison, will we?'

'It was armed robbery,' said Frost. 'If only you hadn't used that loaded bleeding gun you might have got off with a caution.'

'We thought it would make it more realistic.'

'Well it certainly took me in,' grunted Frost, 'especially when you nearly shot that poor sod's leg off.' His voice softened. 'I don't know what sort of sentence you'll get, but play up your motive and keep limping on that bad leg and wincing. The judge might think you've suffered enough.' He was helping the man on with his coat when he remembered what he should have asked earlier. 'Where's the shotgun?'

'Locked away in the cupboard under the stairs,' Redwood told him. 'Shall I go and fetch it?'

'No,' said Frost hastily. He didn't want the old boy to return with the gun and demand a fast car and a plane. 'I'll get one of our firearms blokes round to pick it up.'

Redwood raised his chin so his wife could wind a

long woollen scarf round his neck. 'The key's in the bureau with the shotgun licence.'

'Shotgun licence?' echoed Frost.

'A police shotgun licence. I suppose that's how you got on to us in the first place?'

'Yes,' lied Frost. 'It was the first thing I thought of.'

'Another case solved then, Jack?' beamed Police Sergeant Wells.

'I can solve other people's cases, but can't solve my own.' He pulled a face. 'A couple of geriatric Bonnie and Clydes trying to do Cordwell one in the eye. If there was any justice the poor sods should have got away with it.' He scribbled a note and attached it to the case file. 'Liz Maud can have the credit when she comes back. I don't mind solving her cases, but I'm damned if I'm going to do her paperwork.'

'That cow solves more cases when she's away then when she's here,' sniffed Wells.

Frost stared out of the window. It was getting dark and the mist was thickening. 'I think I'll go and see how the search parties are doing.'

11

Detective Sergeant Arthur Hanlon followed the silent
line of men and women as they moved slowly forward,
poking and prodding. He checked his watch. It was
almost too dark to see the dial. Nearly five o'clock,
time to call the search off until the morning. A police
whistle shrilled, echoed by other, fainter, whistles in
the distance. Wearily, the searchers, miserable and
dispirited, straightened up and made for their transport. A long, cold, fruitless search.

Hanlon nodded as they trudged past him to the
parked cars. His back hurt from continually stooping.
He was cold, his trouser legs were sodden from wet
grass, his clothes clammy where moisture had dripped
and trickled from overhanging branches. He ached all
over and he was hungry. He looked around. Where
was Jack Frost? The inspector had come down to
check on progress and had then wandered over to the
hospital buildings to join the few men Hanlon had
been able to spare to search them yet again. A waste of
time, but the inspector was insistent.

He needed to talk to Frost to find out if he should
send the search teams straight out in the morning or
wait for a briefing. Mullett was getting very fidgety
about overtime being paid to men with cups of tea in
their hands, laughing at Frost's dirty jokes, instead of
getting down to the nitty-gritty of searching. And had

Frost dismissed the men doing the hospital grounds search? Mullett had insisted that no overtime was to be paid for after five o'clock. Hanlon rubbed his hands together to restore the circulation, then climbed in his car and headed for the hospital grounds to find Frost.

The numbing wind cut right through him, but at least it was driving away the mist. He turned up his coat collar as he plodded over the thick carpet of wet, fallen leaves along the little-used paths at the back of the hospital. There was Frost's car, the radio chattering away aimlessly with no-one to listen to it. Somewhere in the distance someone had lit a bonfire and the wind carried the smell of burning leaves. Then another smell. Cigarette smoke. Frost was near, but he couldn't see him in the dark.

'Jack?'

A grunt in reply. Hanlon squeezed through some bushes and there was Frost, cigarette drooping, slumped against the crumbling brick wall of a derelict hospital shed. Hanlon looked around anxiously. No sign of the other men so he hoped Frost had sent them home.

'I've called off the search for tonight, Jack. We'll meet up again at the station first light tomorrow.'

Frost took the cigarette from his mouth. 'Cancel it.'

Hanlon blinked, not sure he had heard correctly. 'Cancel it?' he echoed. He stared at the inspector as the glow from the cigarette lit up his face, a face grey with fatigue, looking older than his years. 'Why, Jack? We can still find her.'

Frost stared into the distant dark, squinting against the smoke from his cigarette. 'I've found her, Arthur,' he said quietly. He jerked a thumb at the shed.

Hanlon's face creased into a puzzled frown. 'She can't be there, Jack. We searched it thoroughly this morning, and this afternoon.'

232

'Then you couldn't have been thorough enough,' snapped Frost, 'because she's in there.'

Hanlon moved away to look, but Frost caught his sleeve. 'Don't be in such a bloody hurry to see her, Arthur. She's dead. The bastard has raped and strangled her . . . he's nearly torn her apart.'

He snatched the cigarette from his mouth and hurled it savagely into the darkness, then pulled out the packet and offered it. Hanlon, who rarely smoked, took one. 'We'll need the police surgeon, Forensic—' he began.

'I've called them,' said Frost, clicking his cigarette lighter. They lit up and smoked, saying nothing. Car headlights sheared through the darkness. 'That will be them now.'

Harding, with two of his staff from Forensic, homed in on Frost's shouts. 'Where is she?' Frost led them to the shed door.

'I thought this had been searched earlier?' said Harding.

'We must have missed her,' muttered Frost, switching on his torch and pulling back a length of sacking that had once held fertilizer. He moved back so Harding could see.

Harding bent over the tiny body. The girl, wearing a green dress, lay on her side, the body slightly curved as if she had been carried in someone's arms before being dumped on the floor. In the corner of the shed, apparently just thrown in, was a child's blue anorak. The girl's eyes were open and marks of bruising were evident around her neck.

Harding briefly lifted the skirt then, with a look of disgust, straightened up. 'She's been raped!'

'Tell me something I don't know,' grunted Frost.

'Has the pathologist seen her yet?' Harding asked.

'No, so try not to move her. You know what a fussy sod he is.'

Headlights hurled their shadows against the far wall. The rest of the Forensic team had arrived. Frost took Harding's arm and lowered his voice. 'I've got the sod who did this, but not enough proof to make it stick. Find me evidence to nail the bastard, and if you can't find anything, bloody plant it!'

A nervous twitch of a smile from Harding who was never sure when Frost was joking. 'If there's anything here, Inspector, we'll find it, I promise you.' He called the rest of his team over as Frost went outside to wait for the pathologist.

He was speeding down the Bath Road on his way back to the station, a thousand thoughts swirling, like the mist, round his brain. Then he noticed the speedometer . . . he was doing over eighty. That's right, kill yourself, you silly sod. He slowed down to a fairly respectable sixty. He was nearly at the station when he realized he hadn't broken the news to Jenny's mother. Shit! He slammed on the brakes and squealed into a U turn. This was the part of the job he hated.

'Dead?' She broke down and he was holding her tight, saying nothing as her body shook and hot, scalding tears splashed down her face. How many times had he held mothers like this, telling them of the death of their kids? Too many times! What a bloody job!

'I never treated her right,' she sobbed, 'but I loved her. I really loved her.'

Frost nodded, patting the back of her head soothingly, still saying nothing. Pity you didn't love the poor cow more when she was alive, he thought. Aloud he murmured, as if it would make her feel better: 'We've got the bastard, love . . . we've got the bastard who did it.'

*   *   *

Ignoring the incessant ringing of the phones, Bill Wells stamped his feet to get the blood flowing, then felt the radiator in the lobby to make sure it was working properly. It was going full blast but didn't seem to be warming the place up very much. He clapped his hands over the papers on his desk to keep them in place as the lobby door crashed open and Frost, maroon scarf streaming behind him, hurtled in. 'Mr Mullett wants to see you, Inspector,' called Wells.

'Hard luck,' said Frost over his shoulder as he dashed past. 'I want Weaver in the interview room – now!'

Wells jerked a thumb to the constantly ringing phones. 'The press won't leave us alone. They're screaming for a statement.'

'They can bloody scream. Get Weaver.' And the swing doors slammed shut behind him.

Wells returned to the desk. Ignoring the outside lines, he picked up the internal phone. It was Mullett. 'Yes, sir, he's just this minute come back. Yes, I did tell him. I'm sure he will be with you soon.' He held the phone away from his ear as Mullett bleated his annoyance. 'Yes, sir, I'll tell him.' He banged the phone down and yelled for Collier to fetch Weaver from the cell, then turned his attention to the other phones. 'Yes. I can confirm we have found a body of a young girl. Sorry . . . no further comment at this stage . . .'

Weaver blinked at the light as Collier ushered him into the interview room, smoothing back his hair and rubbing his face as if he had just been wakened from a sound sleep. He gave Frost his 'always willing to help' smile. Frost stared at him, nose wrinkled with contempt as he flicked a finger to the chair. 'Sit!'

Weaver sat, looking hurt at the inspector's tone.

'You're interested in photographs, aren't you?'

235

asked Frost, snatching a photograph from the file on the table and thrusting it in Weaver's face. It was the Forensic coloured Polaroid photograph of the dead Jenny Brewer, eyes bulging, blood trickling from her nose and mouth.

Weaver flinched and pushed Frost's hands away. He closed his eyes and refused to look.

'Recognize her?' demanded Frost, barely in control of himself. 'That's how we found her. Were her eyes open in terror like that when you raped the poor little cow? Seven years old, you bastard – seven years old.'

The colour seeped from Weaver's face. He slid his chair back from the table as if trying to get as far from the photograph as possible. 'You're trying to incriminate me,' he shrilled. 'You want a suspect, so you're framing me.'

'Did you give her one of your green sweets first? "Here little girl, have a sweetie while nice Uncle Charlie rapes you then chokes the bloody life out of you"?'

Weaver started sobbing, then leapt to his feet, sending the chair crashing back to the wall. 'You framed me. You planted the body . . . you . . .' Then his eyes opened wide and his hand went to his throat, tearing open his collar. He was making deep wheezing noises as he desperately tried to suck in air. Frost sprang up and flung the door open. 'Bill! Get his bloody inhaler.' He looked helplessly at Collier, hoping the constable would know what to do as Weaver sank to his knees, fighting for breath. After what seemed ages, Wells returned with the inhaler. 'Get him a doctor,' said Frost, 'and bloody quick.' He snapped a glance at Collier. 'Interview terminated at 8.20.'

'8.24,' corrected Collier.

'What bloody difference?' snarled Frost as he stamped out.

*　　*　　*

Mullett waylaid him as he slouched back to the office. He was not going to let Frost get away this time. 'You've found Jenny Brewer? Why am I always the last to know?'

'Sorry,' mumbled Frost. 'I was on my way to see you now.'

'And she was found in a place that was supposed to have been thoroughly searched earlier?'

'Yes.' He was in no mood for a bollocking and had to suppress the urge to barge Mullett out of the way and get back to his office.

'So most of today's search, which involved sixty men and women, many on overtime, was a complete and utter waste of time?'

'No. We found her.'

'But if she had been found the first time that shed was searched we could have called off the teams hours ago. Have you any idea what this little lot has cost?'

'No,' answered Frost. 'Funnily enough, that was the last thing on my mind. All I was stupidly thinking of was trying to find the poor little cow.'

Mullett glowered. 'Don't try to be clever with me, Frost. We all wanted that, but everything has to be paid for. Who was supposed to have searched that shed?'

'No idea,' replied Frost, 'but I'm going to find out.' He did know, but wanted to talk to the man before dropping him in it with Mullett.

'I want his name the minute you find out. I'm throwing the book at him, Frost.' He spun on his heels, then realized he hadn't involved Frost in this foul-up. He jabbed an accusing finger. 'You were in charge, Frost. It was your responsibility to check and double-check. Your usual sloppiness had no place here.'

He turned and stamped back to his office, sped on his way by a two-fingered gesture.

Frost slumped in his chair and stared at his

in-tray which was stacked high with reports from the officers interviewing prostitutes in connection with the serial killings. As he flipped through them, WPC Polly Fletcher, sandy hair, freckles and a snub nose, came in with another wad of paper. She had been manning the phones in the murder incident room and had taken messages from toms reporting clients who liked to indulge in rough sex play. Frost smiled at her. She looked so flaming desirable. Flipping heck, he thought, if I was twenty years younger and not so bloody tired, I'd show her what rough sex play means. He took the reports and glanced through them. 'Anything helpful here, Polly?'

She shook her head. 'Descriptions are all pretty vague and none of them seem really violent. A couple of possibles which I've marked.' She bent over to show him where she had circled some details. As she did so a wisp of sandy hair brushed his cheek and he could smell the perfumed soap she had been using on that freckled skin. Suddenly he didn't feel tired any more. 'Ta, Polly.' He watched as she walked out, her little bottom wiggling delightfully. Thank God Morgan wasn't here . . . he'd be chewing up the furniture. And that reminded him. Where the hell was Morgan? A quick cigarette as he waited for the doctor to see Weaver so he could continue the questioning. Fortunately, one was already on the premises attending to a drunk with a cut head, so it shouldn't take long.

Bill Wells came in. 'The doctor's seen him, Jack. Only a mild attack, nothing to worry about.'

Frost gathered up the files. 'Wheel him into the interview room.'

Wells shook his head. 'He's refusing to say another word until he sees his solicitor.'

Frost hurled the files down on his desk in disgust. 'How long will that take?'

238

'We're trying to track him down. His office is closed and we're getting no reply from his home number.'

'Get on to his staff. He might be on a flaming round the world cruise for all we know. Tell them it's urgent. I need to find out what Weaver's done with the other kid.'

'All in hand,' Wells assured him. He paused at the door. 'Is it true Taffy Morgan was supposed to have searched that shed where the kid's body was found?'

Frost nodded.

'He should be chucked out of the force . . . He's rubbish.'

'So am I,' grunted Frost, 'but I'm still here.' He pretended to busy himself with papers until the sergeant had left. He didn't want to talk about Taffy until the man had had a chance to defend himself.

The phone gave a little cough. He snatched it up on the first ring. Harding from Forensic. 'Preliminary findings on the shed and the girl, Inspector.'

Frost cradled the phone on his shoulder as he reached for a pen. 'Let's have it.'

'Still more tests to carry out, but things don't look too hopeful. Fibres and odds and ends on the kid's clothing and hair. I expect we can prove some of these came from Weaver's house, but I understand he admits she's been there?'

'She was raped. The DNA should put the finger on him.'

'It looks as if he used a condom, Inspector.'

Frost sighed a stream of smoke. 'Safe bleeding sex has got a lot to answer for. It can't be all bad, you must have some good news?'

'We might have. Does your suspect smoke?'

'No – he's a paragon of bleeding virtues: doesn't drink, doesn't smoke and always uses a condom when he rapes seven-year-old kids.'

'Then forget the good news – we found a fairly fresh cigarette end near the body.'

'Send it down. I'll smoke it later. Anything else to brighten up my day?'

'No, but we'll keep trying.'

Frost banged down the phone. If Forensic couldn't help, he'd have to try to wring a confession out of Weaver. He rang Wells. 'Found that solicitor yet?'

'Give us a chance, Jack. It's only a couple of minutes since we last spoke.'

As he put the phone down, the outside line rang. The pathologist's secretary. 'Mr Drysdale could do the autopsy on the girl now, Inspector, if you could get over here.'

'On my way,' said Frost.

Frost stood well back from the pool of light that splashed down on to the autopsy table. He didn't want to see what Drysdale was doing to the poor kid, he just wanted to know the result, hoping the pathologist would find something that would link the crime positively to Weaver. Every now and then Drysdale would move back so the man from Forensic could take photographs.

'Extensive tearing and bruising around the vaginal area,' Drysdale intoned flatly. He lifted one of the child's arms and examined the wrist. 'Traces of adhesive . . . probably from sticky tape of some kind.'

Frost nodded. That was one of the first things he had spotted. The wrists would have been bound together to stop the kid struggling during the assault. He felt a surge of despair. This bloody mortuary was becoming a second home – so many nasty murder cases, so many days and nights watching Drysdale methodically cutting and slicing.

'Fading bruises on the arms, legs and buttocks,'

continued Drysdale. 'Made at least a week before death.'

'Yes,' Frost told him. 'When the poor cow wasn't being raped, the mother's boyfriend used to hit her.' Drysdale grunted. That sort of background was of no interest to him. 'More signs of adhesive around the mouth . . . Hello!' Frost's head snapped up. Drysdale was teasing something from the child's mouth, something sodden and grey, which he dropped into a kidney bowl, then prodded with the tweezers. 'Bathroom tissue of some kind. Looks as if he used a ball of it as a gag.'

Frost joined him to examine the mess in the stainless steel bowl. 'Toilet paper! He used toilet paper!' He tugged out his mobile phone and, watched by a frowning Drysdale, got through to Control. 'Send someone over to Weaver's house right away. I want the toilet roll from his bog bagged and sent over to Forensic . . . and search the place for condoms. If they find any, let me know right away.' He turned back to Drysdale who was again teasing away at the mouth, extracting more tissue. 'Get it all out, doc – every piece. Try not to tear it.'

Drysdale glowered. 'I don't need you to tell me how to do my job, Inspector.' He dumped another sodden wad into the kidney bowl. 'She could have choked on this.'

'Did she?' asked Frost.

'No. She died of manual strangulation.'

'She was a feisty little kid, doc. She'd have put up one hell of a fight. Could she have scratched him? Anything under her nails?'

In answer Drysdale lifted a waxen arm and pointed to the fingers. The nails were bitten down to the quick. 'She couldn't have scratched him if she wanted to.'

'I bet the poor little cow wanted to,' said Frost

bitterly. Nothing at all yet to link Weaver to the crime. 'I need something, doc, I really do.' He turned his head away as Drysdale's scalpel slashed across the tiny stomach.

'She ate two boiled sweets about half an hour before she died.' The pathologist held up a small glass jar in which little bits of green floated. 'Lime drops, or something.'

'He admits to giving her sweets,' Frost told him.

'Nevertheless, it might be an entirely different brand. Someone else might have abducted her after she left your suspect's house.'

'She left his house in a bloody bin liner,' said Frost. 'I'm not out to prove the bastard innocent. I want proof of his guilt.'

'Dead some forty-eight to sixty hours,' said Drysdale.

'Last seen alive two days ago, doc.'

'Nearer forty-eight hours, then. Ample evidence of sexual penetration, but no trace of semen, suggesting a condom was used or ejaculation did not take place.'

Frost switched off. He didn't want to hear this part. Poor little cow, mouth stuffed with toilet tissue to stifle her pleading screams, hands taped behind her back so she couldn't fight off dear old Uncle Charlie who had given her the nice green sweets. He tore himself away from his thoughts and found himself staring at the pale face. 'She was a pretty little kid,' he said.

Drysdale looked up from his cutting and gave the face a quick glance. 'Yes. I suppose she was . . .'

As soon as the autopsy was over, Frost hurried out to his car and radioed through to the station to find out if Weaver's solicitor had been traced yet. 'He's on his way, Inspector. Be about an hour.'

'And Morgan?'

'Hasn't turned up yet. By the way, toilet paper from

242

Weaver's house has been sent over to Forensic. No sign of any condoms.'

'Right.' He clicked off. An hour to kill. He didn't feel like going back to the station with Mullett lurking about so he detoured to the Forensic lab to find out if they had any joy matching up the toilet paper.

'It will be another twenty-four hours,' protested Harding, who was overseeing the work of one of his white-coated assistants.

'I haven't got twenty-four hours. I want to know now.' He knew he was being unreasonable.

Harding showed him the toilet roll taken from Weaver's bathroom. 'All we can say at the moment is that this, and the substance taken from the girl's mouth, appear to be of the same type and colour and from the same manufacturer.'

Frost sighed with relief. 'Well, that's something. I'd be up the flaming creek if they were different.'

'The trouble is, Inspector, this is one of the top-selling brands . . . millions are sold every week. You've probably got the same type in your bathroom.'

Frost shook his head. 'I use Mullett's memos . . . they give me more satisfaction.'

A technician, who was squinting down a micro-scope in the far corner, beckoned Harding over. They held a murmured conversation and, from the look on Harding's face when he returned, Frost knew he wasn't going to like this.

'I'm afraid the probability is that the samples are from two entirely different rolls.'

'It doesn't take twenty-four hours when it's bad bleeding news, does it?' moaned Frost bitterly. 'How can you be so sure?'

'We were trying a long shot. If the sheets in the girl's mouth had been torn from the roll in Weaver's bathroom, there was a faint chance we could match up

243

the perforations. We'd have to be damn lucky, of course.'

'And he'd have to be bloody constipated. She went missing two days ago.'

'I said it was a long shot. Anyway, no joy. The paper in the girl's mouth came from a brand new roll.'

'How the hell do you know that?'

'The manufacturers always seal down the end of the roll to stop it flapping open.' He held up a new roll. 'You can see the ridge on this one here.'

Frost nodded gloomily. 'Everything you wanted to know about bog paper, but were afraid to ask. And the roll from Weaver's house?'

'At least three-quarters used. Either Weaver got through a hell of a lot of toilet paper in a very short time, or he had a brand new roll handy and he used that. Find the brand new roll and there's a good chance we can match the perforations.'

Out with the mobile to call Control. 'Get another team over to Weaver's place. Go through drawers, cupboards, cases, the lot. We've looking for another toilet roll. If they have no luck, forage his rubbish bins. Use as many men as you like, but find it.' Back to Harding. 'Anything else?'

'Nothing that helps. We can prove she was in Weaver's house, but he's admitted that already, so it doesn't help much.'

He sat and smoked and fidgeted, watching Harding's slow, methodical examination of the clothing. He couldn't stand people being methodical, it was so alien to his own method of working. Sod it. He couldn't sit around doing nothing. He pinched out the cigarette that was annoying Harding and decided he would look in on Weaver's place to see how the search for the elusive toilet roll was progressing.

Two police cars were parked outside and lights

blazed from every window. Frost thumbed the door-bell. 'Could you spare a few moments to discuss the meaning of the scriptures?' he asked Jordan who opened the door to him. Grinning, the PC led him into the house. 'We've found it,' he announced triumphantly.

Through to the kitchen where a twelve-pack of supermarket toilet rolls lay on the table. 'Ta-ra!' fanfared Jordan.

Frost's face fell. He did a quick check, just in case, then shook his head. 'Sorry, son, these are no good. I'm after an almost new roll with just a couple of sheets torn from it.' He explained briefly, annoyed with himself that he hadn't made it clear earlier.

He wandered from room to room, watching as drawers were wrenched open and the contents tipped out, cupboard doors opened and slammed shut. Lots of noise, much activity, but achieving nothing. He went back to the kitchen and took a peek in the bread bin. The half-used loaf inside was growing thick green mould like a decomposing body. He shut the lid quickly.

Jordan joined him. 'We've looked in all possible places, Inspector. Shall we try the loft?'

'He wouldn't be such a twat as to hide it,' answered Frost. 'If he realized it might be important, he'd have destroyed it, but look anyway.'

He was beginning to feel depressed again. They had practically nothing on Weaver that would stand up in court. The last-minute stroke of luck that at times came to his rescue was having one of its many off-days. He jabbed a finger at Jordan. 'Have we searched the dustbin?'

'Yes, but the council emptied them yesterday – it was almost empty.'

Simms returned, brushing dust and cobwebs from his uniform. 'Nothing in the loft,' he reported.

The other two PCs, Evans and Howe, joined them. They too had found nothing. Frost sent his cigarettes on the rounds and they all sat and smoked as he chewed things over in his mind.

'If it's that important,' suggested Simms, 'I suppose we could do a search of the rubbish sacks down at the council depot?'

'If he realized how important it was,' said Frost, 'he'd have destroyed the damn thing. If he didn't realize, then he wouldn't have binned an almost new bog roll with plenty of wiping space left.' He stood up. 'Finish your fags. Don't rush, you're on overtime – then call it a day.'

Back to the car and a radio call to the station. 'Is Perry Mason there yet?'

'The solicitor phoned, Jack,' said Wells. 'He's stuck on the motorway behind a lorry that's shed its load. He'll be at least a couple of hours.'

'Another couple of hours?' echoed Frost. 'Sod it, we can't wait. Tell Weaver he's got to come up with a brief who can turn up in fifteen minutes, otherwise he'll have to make do with the duty solicitor.'

'We can't force him to do that, Jack.'

'But he might not know that. Try it on.' Frost waited patiently for Wells to radio back.

'He won't wear it, Jack.'

'Then sod him . . . burn his bloody toast for breakfast.' He had no sooner replaced the handset when his mobile phone rang and a voice he didn't recognize asked, 'Inspector Frost?'

'That depends who's calling,' he replied guardedly.

'We haven't met – Detective Chief Inspector Preston, Belton Division.' Belton was the neighbouring Division to Denton.

'What can I do for you?' asked Frost, hoping there was nothing.

'It's what I can do for you, Inspector. You reported

Bertha Jenkins, a big fat tom, missing. I think we've found her.'

George Owen, Station Sergeant, Belton Division, clicked on his polite smile. 'Can I help you, sir?'

'Chief Inspector Preston, please.'

'Oh – you'll be Inspector Frost. Mr Preston told me to expect you.' Preston had said: 'If a scruffy bastard in a dirty mac turns up, it'll be Jack Frost from Denton. 'Mr Preston is at the incident site. I'll try to contact him.' He popped into the Control room leaving Frost to mooch around the lobby, reading the tattered police notices about the Colorado Beetle and Foot and Mouth Disease. Suddenly he was staring at a familiar face. Vicky Stuart, smiling her gapped-tooth grin . . . 'Missing Girl'. He turned away. What had that bastard Weaver done with this poor little cow? He looked at his watch, anxious to get back to Denton before Weaver's brief arrived.

The station sergeant returned. 'Mr Preston says can you make your own way to the site? He's got no-one available to bring you.' He gave Frost directions, adding, 'You can't miss it.'

He missed it, finding himself floundering down country lanes that led nowhere and the fog thickening. Eventually he managed to get back to the main road and spotted the turn-off guarded by a young constable who seemed glad to have a car to stop. 'You can't go down here, sir.' He wouldn't believe Frost was an inspector until he had studied the dog-eared warrant card. 'Just round the bend, sir,' he directed, fumbling for his radio to let the chief inspector know.

It was a dark, bumpy, rutted dirt road, overhung with dripping trees, but as he turned the bend everything sprang into life with floodlights, cars double parked, radios chattering, men crawling over the grass verge and a small tent-like structure glowing orange from the lights within.

Heads turned as he approached the taped-off area to the tent which was well back from the road. One or two of the old hands recognized him and waved. The younger men wondered who the scruff was.

Detective Chief Inspector Preston, thin, balding and unsmiling, greeted him with a curt nod. 'We could have done without this. It's your damn crime with the victim dumped in our Division.'

'Stick her in the car and I'll take her back to Denton,' grunted Frost, hating the man on sight. 'Where is she?'

'Where do you think? We didn't put the tent up to go camping.' He ducked through the flapped entrance and Frost followed.

She lay on her back, eyes open, like the others. Naked, her heavy sagging breasts sprawled over the rolls of fat on her stomach, a stomach disfigured with weals, bruises and burns. Dyed red hair, now blackened by wet grass, cushioned the head. Frost stared down at her. 'That's her,' he said. 'That's Big Bertha.' He knelt on the polythene sheeting spread alongside the body and lifted a cold, heavy, wet hand. Deep marks were grooved into the raw blooded wrist. 'The poor bitch has had a right going-over,' he muttered.

'Suffocated, probably with a pillow,' said Preston. 'The doctor reckons she's been dead a couple of days at least.'

Frost straightened up and rubbed his hands together to get the chill of death out of them. 'Who found her?'

'A motorist cut through to relieve himself and spotted her.'

'Our last one was found by a motorist having a pee,' said Frost. 'He wouldn't give his name.'

'Ours ditto,' said Preston.

Frost consulted his watch. The solicitor should be well on his way by now. He lifted the flap and measured the distance to the road with his eyes. 'If she was lugged all this way, whoever dumped her must have been a strong bastard.'

'She was probably dragged,' said Preston.

Frost dropped down on his knees again and lifted the body slightly, ignoring Preston's alarmed protests that Drysdale wouldn't like it. 'If he'd dragged her there would be abrasions.' He pointed. There weren't any.

'Needn't have been one strong man – could have been two men,' suggested Preston, annoyed that he hadn't spotted the absence of abrasions.

'Or the seven bleeding dwarfs,' snapped Frost. 'We've got to get this bastard and bloody quick – he's got the taste for it.'

A slamming of car doors and the murmur of voices sent Preston dashing over to the tent flap. He peeked out and signalled urgently to Frost. 'It's Drysdale,' he hissed. 'If he thinks we've moved the body . . .'

'Don't panic,' said Frost, lowering the body back to its original position. 'All we've got to do is look innocent and lie.'

Drysdale, followed by his blonde secretary, pushed through the tent flap, his warm smile of greeting to Preston freezing when he saw Frost standing behind him. 'Twice in one day, Inspector,' he sniffed.

'Some days you can't believe your luck,' said Frost. He checked his watch again. 'Sorry to disappoint you, doc, but I must love you and leave you. I've a suspect to interview back at Denton.'

Preston took Frost to one side. 'We need to co-operate on this – pool our resources, share our information.'

'I'll send over what we've got,' said Frost. 'It amounts to sod all: no descriptions, no leads, nothing, but it might help. I'm pinning my hopes on catching the sod in the act.' With a brief nod he ducked through the flap on his way back to his car.

Bill Wells looked up as Frost marched over. 'Solicitor's here. I've put him in No. 2 interview room. He doesn't like being kept waiting.'

'He kept me waiting long enough,' said Frost. He unbuttoned his mac and loosened his scarf. 'Any sign of the flaming Welsh wizard?'

Wells shook his head. 'He never came back here, Jack. I even sent someone round to his digs, but no-one in. I reckon he's on the nest somewhere.'

'He probably thinks having it away is more fun than having his goolies chewed off by me,' said Frost. 'If he does condescend to make an appearance, I want him.' He pushed through the swing doors and made his way to the interview room.

Fosswick, the solicitor, had been to an official function and was still wearing evening dress under his thick black overcoat. He was annoyed at being dragged away and even more annoyed, after hurrying through that damned fog, to be dumped in a drab, cold interview room and told to wait. A scruffy little man who matched the scruffy little room came in and introduced himself as Detective Inspector Frost.

The solicitor acknowledged him mournfully. He was hoping for someone far more senior and impressive to make his evening less of a waste of time. 'I don't know why you've dragged me down here, Inspector. We rarely do criminal work and I hardly know the man. We dealt with the purchase of his house about three years ago, and that's about it.'

'It's not me dragging you down here, sir, it's your client. We're holding him for questioning in connection with the abduction, rape and murder of a seven-year-old girl.'

The solicitor's face was expressionless. 'I see. And what makes you think my client is involved in this?'

Fosswick listened intently as Frost outlined the details, a growing expression of concern and distaste on his face. This was not the sort of case he wanted to be involved in. He pulled out a gold fountain pen and made a few notes, telling himself that he would pass the details on to someone else first thing in the morning, someone more used to dealing with such sordidness. 'You haven't actually charged him yet?'

'No, sir, but it is our intention to do so.'

Fosswick replaced the cap on his pen. 'I'd now like a few words with my client.'

'I'll go and get him for you.' Frost opened the door, then closed it again. 'The other little girl might still be alive, sir.' He held up a photograph of Vicky. 'If you could persuade your client to tell us where she is . . .'

Fosswick scowled. 'I am not here to do your job for you, Inspector. My first duty is to Mr Weaver.' He looked at the photograph and his expression softened. 'However, I'll see what I can do.'

Not such a bad old bastard after all, thought Frost as he made his way to the cell area.

The shrill, urgent ringing of a bell sliced through his thoughts. The alarm from the cell area, usually rung when an officer was being assaulted or a prisoner was taken sick. At first he took no notice. Probably the drunk causing trouble. The uniformed boys were quite capable of handling crises like that. He was aware of the sound of running feet and voices raised in panic and the other prisoners banging their cell doors and shouting. Over it all Bill Wells calling, 'Cut him down, quick . . .' then, yelling up the corridor, 'Get an ambulance.'

Frost raced down to the holding area. The door to

Weaver's cell was wide open. Two uniformed men were bending over a figure on the floor, one pummelling the chest, the other giving the kiss of life with Wells looking anxiously on.

Frost stared down at Weaver, skin blue, neck strangely elongated. 'Bloody hell! What happened?'

'He's topped himself,' said Wells, sounding furious as if this was personally directed against him. 'The silly sod has hanged himself.' He pushed past Frost and yelled again down the corridor. 'Where's that bloody ambulance?'

One of the PCs stood up. 'No hurry for the ambulance, Sarge. He's dead.'

12

'No-one can blame me for this,' bleated Wells, making his case to anyone who would listen. 'I checked him a few minutes ago and he was all right.' The banging and kicking of doors from the other cells reached a crescendo. 'Shut up!' he yelled, to little effect.

'How could he hang himself?' asked Frost, kneeling by the body and feeling yet again for a pulse, hoping against hope that Weaver was still alive. Wells pointed. On the floor lay a coil of white nylon cord, the knotted noose at the end cut where they had removed it from Weaver's neck.

'Where the hell did he get the rope from?' Wells demanded. 'I searched him when you brought him in this morning, Jack – you can testify to that?'

'Yes,' grunted Frost, bending and picking up the cord which had a beige plastic tassel at the end. It looked familiar. He frowned. Where had he seen it before? Then he remembered. Shit! The hospital. The cord on the venetian blind in the mother's room. When he left Weaver alone, the sod must have cut off a length – there were scissors on the trolley by the bed. Bloody hell! Mullett's going to have a field day over this.

Frost ordered the uniformed men out of the cell and sat down on the bunk bed. 'What a bloody mess!'

Wells sank down beside him and stared down at

the body, shaking his head in disbelief. 'It's all bloody Mullett's fault, sending half our manpower away to help other Divisions. We should have a proper custody officer. I'm having to do two jobs. I haven't got time to do them both properly.' He looked imploringly at Frost. 'There's going to be an investigation, Jack. They'll be looking for scapegoats so let's get our stories straight. I searched him – you saw me.'

Frost lit up a cigarette. 'Don't worry, Bill. If there's any blame going, I'll cop the lot.' He expelled a lungful of smoke. 'When did you last look in on him?'

'About a quarter of an hour ago.'

'He's been dead more than a flaming quarter of an hour.'

'Half an hour ago then,' snapped Wells, hysterically. 'All the jobs I have to do, I can't be expected to remember exactly when.'

'You entered it in the log?'

'I haven't had time. Those flaming phones have been ring, ring, ringing non-stop.'

'Then do it now.' He flicked ash on the floor, just missing the body.

'He left a note,' said Wells. 'He says he didn't do it.'

'A note?' Frost's head snapped up. This was the first he had heard of a suicide note. 'Where?'

Wells pointed. 'Taped to the inside of the cell door.'

Frost slammed the door shut and there it was, stuck to the door with a strip of surgical tape, scrawled on the back of one of Weaver's mother's old hospital charts. Weaver had planned this all out in advance as he sat in that room, squeezing the hand of his dying mother. Leaving it stuck on the door, Frost leant over to read it:

Dearest Mother:
I didn't do it. They are making me out to be some kind of perverted monster. That Inspector Frost is

254

framing me. He's bullying me to confess to something I didn't do. I am innocent, but I can't stand the shame.

Goodbye mum. See you in heaven.

Charlie

'In heaven!' snorted Frost. 'In bloody hell more like it. He'll be able to complain to Mullett personally when the time comes.'

'I don't think anyone else has seen it,' confided Wells. 'We could get rid of it.'

'I might fake evidence,' said Frost, 'but I don't throw it away. Leave it.' He stood up and wearily wiped his face with his hands. 'Let's break the sad news to Hornrim Harry.'

Mullett, lips tight with anger, stared coldly at Frost. 'You left him, unattended, in a room with scissors and cord, a man you suspected of being a child killer? You left him?'

'Yes,' said Frost.

'Surely, even anyone with the minimum of common sense—'

'Yes,' snapped Frost, biting off the end of Mullett's pointless reprimand. 'I was wrong. I know I was wrong. I felt sorry for the poor sod. His mother was dying.'

'He claims he is innocent.'

'So did Crippen. Every murderer I've arrested has claimed to be innocent, it's par for the course.'

Mullett waved this to one side. 'I've listened to the tapes of your last interview. As he says, you bullied him. He was weeping.'

'I bet that poor kid was weeping when he raped her.'

Mullett glared. This was not how he expected people to accept reprimands. 'A bungled, incompetent, mishandled investigation, with tragic consequences.'

'Nothing was bungled,' snapped Frost. 'If the silly bastard hadn't topped himself it would have been an ongoing investigation. If we found he didn't do it – and it's a bloody big "if" – we would have let him go.'

'If, if, if!' countered Mullett. 'A death in custody and an innocent man. The press will be down on us like a ton of bricks.'

'Innocent my arse!' exploded Frost. 'He killed that kid and dumped the body.'

Mullett flushed angrily. 'I've said all I intend to say for the moment, Frost. There will be an investigation of this death in custody and I am going to put in a strong recommendation that you be suspended from duty.'

'Thank you very much,' said Frost, scraping the chair across the carpet as he stood up. 'For a moment I was terrified you'd be on my side.'

He left Mullett glowering at the slammed door.

Police Sergeant Wells wriggled uncomfortably and ran a finger round the tight collar of the brand new shirt which was chewing into his neck. His new shoes were pinching his feet, but the scuffed, old ones would have looked incongruous against his best, newly pressed, uniform.

Barely half-past eight the next morning, but already Mullett had arrived with Chief Superintendent Bailey and Chief Inspector Hopley, the two senior officers from County. They had swept past the front desk and straight into Mullett's office, not bothering to acknowledge his presence. A grim-looking lot of bastards, he thought, like the prison governor and the hangman on their way to wake some poor sod up on his final morning.

The internal phone buzzed and he was ordered to bring in three coffees. Pre-warned by Mullett not to use chipped enamel mugs – as if he flaming well would – he put the china cups on their matching saucers and carried them into the old log cabin. The conversation stopped dead and all eyes followed him as he lifted the tray over and set it on the desk at the precise spot indicated by Mullett's finger.

He backed out as if leaving royalty.

'You are Sergeant Wells?' barked Chief Superintendent Bailey, thickset and beetle-browed, breaking the silence. 'The custody segeant?'

'Yes, sir,' replied Wells eagerly, glad of the chance to get his story in early. 'I checked him regularly. I went by the book—'

Bailey's hand chopped him short. 'Later, Sergeant, later – we're having coffee.'

Mullett, deeming a glower was called for, glowered Wells out of the room. He beat a hasty retreat and dashed down the corridor to Frost's office to make his report.

Frost leant back in his chair and surveyed the new uniform in amazement. 'Very smart, Bill . . . are you on a promise tonight?' He, himself, had made no effort to dress up for the inquiry, the same shiny suit and greasy tie.

'The inquiry, Jack. I'd have thought you might have tarted yourself up.'

Frost brushed ash from the front of his jacket. 'If they're going to hang you, they don't give a toss if you're wearing a smart suit or not.'

Wells moved some files and sat in the spare chair. 'Bailey and Hopley are here. They look a right pair of bastards.'

'Everyone from County are bastards,' murmured Frost.

'We've got to get our stories straight, Jack,' said Wells for the hundredth time. 'I searched him – you saw me – and I checked that cell regularly.'

'Every other second,' nodded Frost. 'Don't worry,

it's my blood they're after, not yours. Just tell them the truth – it'll throw them off their guard.'

Both heads turned as the office door creaked open and Morgan, looking much the worse for wear, lumbered in, rubbing his eyes and yawning.

'Look what the cat's sicked up!' said Frost.

A sheepish grin from Morgan. 'Sorry I'm late, guv.' A painful nod to Wells as he tottered over to his desk and shook a couple of paracetamol tablets into his hand. He swallowed them dry.

'Where the hell were you yesterday afternoon?' demanded the inspector.

Morgan frowned. Frost knew where he was. 'With the search party, guv.'

'After that? We were all looking for you.'

'I felt rough, guv, shagged out after flogging my guts out looking for that little girl. I didn't go back to the station. I went straight to my digs, took some pain-killers, then went to bed.'

'I phoned you. I sent someone round to your place,' put in Wells. 'They nearly kicked the door in. No-one answered.'

'Ah!' Morgan looked shamefaced. 'I felt a bit better after a while, so I went out. Spent the night at a friend's place.'

'A female?' asked Frost.

'Er . . . yes.' He rubbed a hand across his forehead. 'I think we overdid the drink.'

'I think you overdid the other as well,' snapped Frost. He lit up. 'So you flogged your guts out looking for the girl?'

'Yes, guv.'

Frost riffled through the pile of roneoed forms filled in by the search parties. 'You searched that old garden shed in the hospital grounds?'

The DC's brow creased as he tried to remember. 'Did I, guv?'

Frost waved the form at him. 'You've ticked it to say you did.'

'If I ticked it, then I searched it.' He frowned. 'What's the problem?'

'The problem,' Frost told him, 'is that the shed you thoroughly searched is where we found the girl.'

Morgan blinked, wincing as he firmly shook his head. 'No, guv, that's not possible.'

Frost glared. 'Yes, guv, it is bloody possible, because that's where I found her.'

'Then Weaver must have put it there after I searched.'

'That was clever of him, seeing as how he was in our custody all day.'

'Then someone else dumped it for him.'

'Just to oblige him? The man's a loner, he's got no friends. Don't let's beat about the bush. You ticked it off, but you didn't search it.'

Morgan loosened his tie and flapped the front of his shirt to cool himself. 'We are talking about the same place, guv – little shed, fertilizer sacks, a sort of shelf thing on the wall?'

'Yes.'

'I searched it, guv,' insisted Morgan. 'She wasn't there.'

'And what about when you searched it the second time?'

Morgan now looked embarrassed. 'A second time, guv?'

'You were told to go back and search again.' Frost waved the form. 'You've ticked it to say you did.'

Morgan's head sank. 'There was no point in searching it a second time, guv. It was a tiny place, no room to hide anything. She wasn't there.'

A derisive snort from Wells, who had been listening intently.

Morgan flushed. 'Look, guv, I may be all sorts of a shit, but if I'm looking for a kid, then I flaming well look. I lifted the sacks, each one. She wasn't there, I swear it.'

Frost looked hard at him, smoke dribbling from his nose. 'Weaver topped himself last night, left a note saying he didn't do it and I had hounded him to death.'

The DC leant back in the chair, mouth sagging, eyes wide open. 'Bloody hell!'

'And now the Gestapo are here from County to carry out an official inquiry. They'll be questioning you.' He pulled his desk drawer open and took out a tube of extra strong mints. 'Start sucking these . . . if they smell liquor on your breath . . .'

Morgan put one in his mouth. 'Look, guv. I searched that shed. The kid wasn't there, but if it would help you, I'll say that I bungled it and ticked off the wrong shed on the form.'

'You're positive you searched it?'

'Positive, guv.'

'Is there any way you could have missed her?'

'You saw the place, guv. No-one could have missed her.'

'Human dung!' moaned Frost. He mashed out his cigarette in his ashtray. 'This makes things a bit complicated.' His internal phone buzzed. He waved a hand for Morgan to answer it. The summons to Mullett's office.

Frost stood up and tugged a couple of the worst creases out of his jacket. 'Do you think it would look as if I were playing on their sympathy if I wore my George Medal?'

'Yes,' said Wells.

'Then I'll be subtle. I'll say, "I'm sorry my coat sleeve is wet, but I dropped my George Medal down the karzy and had to fish it out." '

'That should win the sympathy vote,' said Wells. He paused. 'Best of luck, Jack.'

'Thanks,' Frost replied. 'If I have to drop you in it to keep my job, you will understand, won't you?'

Wells tried to keep the smile on his face. He was never certain if Frost was joking or not.

The grim-faced trio sat in a row behind Mullett's mahogany desk like officers at a court martial. Frost almost expected to see a sword with the blade pointing towards him. He pulled a chair over and sat down.

'Please sit down,' said Mullett. He introduced the other two officers and let the chief superintendent take over the questioning.

Bailey, a big, hard-faced man, gave Frost his long, cold, intimidating Medusa stare, a stare which had reduced many a hardened suspect to a quivering wreck, all too ready to cough the lot. Frost, who could outstare anyone, flashed back his friendly smile. 'Morning.'

Bailey nodded to Chief Inspector Hopley, who took out a notebook and began to scribble notes. 'We could have done without this, Frost. We've had four deaths in custody already this year and now a fifth . . . And as it is someone who might well be innocent . . .'

'He was guilty,' cut in Frost.

Bailey stared again, then continued where he left off as if Frost hadn't spoken. '. . . this is the last thing the Chief Constable wants.' He pulled a pipe from his pocket, then a tobacco pouch. Slowly and deliberately he filled the pipe and lit up. Frost took the opportunity to have a cigarette himself.

Bailey waved the pipe at Mullett. 'You don't mind, I hope?'

'Of course not,' said Mullett, forcing a grin, his eyes watering from the pungent smoke that wafted across.

Bailey took the pipe from his mouth. 'It was put to us that you should be immediately suspended from duty.'

'Oh?' said Frost, looking at Mullett who quickly turned his head away and stared through the window.

'This damn George Medal of yours makes the whole thing high profile. The press would have a field day: "George Medal Hero Suspended", that sort of media rubbish.' He jabbed the pipe stem at Frost. 'And that is something the Chief Constable definitely does not want.'

Mullett firmly shook his head from side to side. 'Neither do I.'

'We want to use your medal to our advantage, not our disadvantage,' added Bailey, shooting a glance at Mullett who had abruptly to change gear and go into a vigorous nod. 'This is not an official inquiry – that will follow. This is simply a damage limitation exercise.' He held out a hand to Hopley who pushed the case files over. 'I've been looking at the files. This man Weaver admitted the girl had been to his house and admitted he took photographs of her?'

'After we'd found where he'd hidden them, yes.'

Bailey spread the photographs over the desk and pushed them around with his pipe stem. 'Nude photographs but nothing really pornographic.' He slipped them back in the folder. 'Weaver also tried to dispose of a quantity of hard porn photographs?'

'That's right,' nodded Frost.

'And that, really, is the sum total of your evidence against him – there was no forensic evidence on the body to link the girl's death to Weaver?'

'No, but what we had made him a prime suspect.'

Bailey gave a non-committal grunt. 'I've been listening to the tapes of your interviews. You bullied him, harassed him, reduced him to tears.'

Mullett put on his pained expression and slowly

shook his head to signify his disapproval at Frost's inexcusable behaviour.

'I would have done the same,' continued Bailey. 'A kid murdered and raped – I'd have smashed the bastard's head against the wall.'

Mullett blinked. He changed the headshake to a nod of approval, but wasn't too happy.

'But I'd have made sure the bastard didn't top himself,' Bailey went on. 'And if he left a note protesting his innocence, I'd have made damn sure it disappeared bloody quickly.'

Mullett's nod of approval was getting weaker. Bailey was known for his unorthodox methods and it was common knowledge that many of his convictions had been secured on fitted-up evidence.

Frost remained silent. He could see things were swinging his way.

'Then we come to you leaving Weaver alone at the hospital, giving him the opportunity to get enough rope to hang himself.'

'Inexcusable,' said Mullett.

Bailey's head slowly swivelled to Mullett. 'Very excusable, Superintendent. Weaver's mother was dying. We use Frost's compassion to counteract the charge of harassment.' He swung back to Frost. 'No chance she's died yet? It would help our case.'

'She's not co-operating,' said Frost. 'She's still alive.'

Bailey shrugged. 'Never mind, we must build our case on the materials we've got. So, out of compassion you let him see his dying mother for a few minutes on his own, but instead of gratitude, he took advantage of your kindness. You knew you were breaking the rules but you realized how he felt, having suffered a similar loss yourself.' With a grunt of satisfaction he jabbed a finger at Hopley. 'Note that down, Chief Inspector, that's a terrific angle.' He beamed at Mullett, whose responding beam was matching.

'There's the question of the finding of the girl's body,' Hopley reminded him.

'Yes,' nodded Bailey. 'That's a bastard. As I understand it, the girl's body was found in a place that had already been searched while Weaver was still in custody?'

'Yes,' agreed Frost, grimly.

'You've spoken to the officer involved?'

'Yes. He is adamant the girl wasn't there when he searched.'

'As far as this initial inquiry is concerned, we are going to be unaware of that fact. We expect the officer concerned to change his story. We leave that to you.'

Frost said nothing. If they thought his silence was acquiescence, that was their look-out.

Bailey slammed the file shut. 'Right. We can keep the lid on this for a while. We won't release the suicide note until the coroner's inquest. By then, I'm hoping you will have made an arrest.' He shook the dottle from his pipe into Mullett's clean, cut-glass ashtray. Frost added his cigarette end to the pile. 'The Chief Constable, apparently, doesn't want to lose you, Frost. You've done very well for the Division in the past . . . a history of excellent solved cases.'

'Thanks to teamwork,' put in Mullett.

'Of course; under the devoted leadership and guidance of your Divisional Commander.'

'I must have been away that day,' murmured Frost. He went to stand. 'If there's nothing else . . . ?'

'Wait,' said Bailey, ordering him back in the chair. 'Your recent clear-up rate isn't at all good – in fact it's bloody lousy. We want it improved. We're going to return some of the men your Divisional Commander kindly loaned us for the drugs bust operation, so you won't have the excuse of shortage of manpower. We want this killer of prostitutes apprehended before he carves up any more, and we want this child murder case cleared up, and damn quickly.'

'Right.' Frost stood up again.

'And if you can implicate Weaver in any way . . .'

'If he's guilty,' replied Frost, 'I'll implicate him.'

Wells tapped on the door and looked in on Frost, who was scribbling on a pad. Frost nodded him to a chair. 'Larry, Curly and Mo want me to do a report on your claim to have looked in on Weaver,' he murmured. 'How do you spell "lying bastard"?'

Wells grinned. He had already been let off lightly by the investigation. 'You've got a visitor. Sandy Lane from the *Denton Echo* – says it's important.'

'Did he look as if he had any fags?'

'He'd just opened a fresh packet.'

'Then show him in.'

Sandy Lane, chief reporter for the *Echo*, bounded in, his dark blue duffel coat flapping. 'It's brass monkey weather out there, Jack,' he said as he tossed a cigarette over to Frost before taking one himself.

'If you think I'm going to break the Official Secrets Act for one lousy fag, you can think again,' said Frost, accepting a light. 'I never do it for less than two.'

Lane grinned and settled down in the chair. 'Jenny Brewer,' he began. 'The dead kid . . .'

'Yes,' said Frost guardedly. 'What about her?'

'The whisper is that Weaver didn't do it.'

'It's still an ongoing investigation,' said Frost, 'and he's still my number one suspect . . . but that is off the record.'

Lane pulled a shorthand notebook from the duffel coat and flipped to a page scrawled with shorthand symbols. 'Does the name Henry Plummer mean anything to you?'

'Yes, he's a nutcase. He keeps getting on to us with

his vague prophecies. "You will find the body on something green, under something blue," so she could be anywhere in the world except the Sahara desert or the North Pole.'

'He says he's seen her body in a dream.'

'I saw a girl's body in a dream – she was in bed with me. I told her not to speak with her mouth full. Did I tell you the joke about the bloke getting married?'

'Never seen a blue one before, yes, Jack, four times. Plummer says he can describe things about the girl that never appeared in the papers.'

'Like what?'

'Look, Jack, I want a story out of this. If he does lead you to the body, I want an exclusive.'

'Like what?' repeated Frost.

'On her right wrist – he says she was wearing a bangle.'

Frost stiffened. Vicky Stuart had been wearing a bangle, a fact that had not been released to the press.

'Is it true?' asked Lane.

'No comment,' said Frost. 'Did he say what kind of bangle – gold, silver, lucky charms that didn't bring the poor little cow any luck?'

'Solid plastic, green and yellow sea shells.'

Frost slowly exhaled smoke. An exact description. Only a few people knew about it and the details had never been released. 'Where is this clever bastard?'

'In my office.'

'Then trot him over here.'

He paced the office impatiently, waiting for Lane to return. He spun round as the door opened, but it wasn't the reporter. It was Detective Sergeant Authur Hanlon who handed over a small brown manila envelope. 'This was in the post, Jack.'

Frost glanced at the handwritten address:

The Detective in Charge
The Jenny Brewer Investigation
Denton Police

There was something small and round inside. He ripped it open and pulled out a single folded sheet of cheap, lined notepaper. The message was in the same handwriting as the envelope:

You have made a mistake and arrested the wrong man. The body is in the shed at the back of the hospital. The button came from her dress.

He shook out a blue button which had a short length of black thread attached. A button was missing from Jenny's dress when they found her. The postmark stated the envelope had been posted at the main Denton post office, 3.15 p.m. the previous afternoon. He showed the note to Arthur Hanlon who skimmed through it.

'Whoever sent this, Jack, knew where the body was before we found it.'

'I love people who state the flaming obvious,' said Frost. 'Send the button over to Forensic and let's see if it matches the others – knowing my luck, it's bound to.' He shook his head. 'It doesn't make sense. If I'd done a murder I'd be over the bloody moon if the fuzz arrested someone else for it, I wouldn't try to clear him.'

'A murderer with a conscience?' suggested Hanlon.

'A murderer with a conscience doesn't rape seven-year-olds,' said Frost.

As Hanlon left, Bill Wells poked his head round the door. 'You in the mood for a bloke with second sight, Jack?'

'I'm in the mood for a sex-starved sixteen-year-old with a hundred fags to spare. I wouldn't kick her out if she only had fifty.'

'Then you're out of luck. It's Sandy Lane with that fortune-telling weirdo.'

'Wheel them in,' Frost told him. 'He reckons he can find Vicky Stuart for us.'

The tweed-suited man with Sandy Lane was in his late fifties, gaunt, and sporting a goatee beard. Frost took an instant dislike to him.

'You spurned my gifts in the past, Inspector,' said Plummer, looking cock-a-hoop, 'but at last you've come to your senses.' He declined Frost's offered cigarette. 'Alcohol and cigarettes deaden the mental powers, as I'm sure you've found out.' He produced a worn leather wallet from his jacket pocket and took out a newspaper cutting carrying a photograph of Vicky Stuart. 'This is the little girl I keep seeing, calling out to me in my dreams. You don't know where she is, do you, Inspector?'

'No,' grunted Frost, mentally adding, and neither do you, mate. This was going to be a complete and utter waste of time and he had so many other things to attend to. That bleeding skeleton for a start.

Plummer rubbed his hands briskly. 'I'd like a full-scale map of Denton, if you please.' Frost found him one and Plummer carefully unfolded it over the surface of Morgan's desk. He sat in Morgan's chair and took several deep breaths, slowly expelling air from his lungs. 'To purify the system,' he told the inspector.

Frost raised his eyebrows to Lane. He was getting fed up with this already. Plummer gave him a pitying smile. 'Patience, Inspector. These things can't be rushed.' He addressed Lane, who he considered a more receptive audience. 'Last night I had a dream, a vivid dream. A child was crying out.' He imitated a small child's voice: ' "Help me . . . please help me . . ." I saw her face clearly.' His finger stabbed the newspaper cutting. 'It was that child.' If he was expecting a favourable reaction from Frost, he didn't get one.

'When is the big film going to start?' Frost asked. 'I'm getting bored with the Mickey Mouse.'

Plummer, looking hurt, ignored him. 'I immediately sprang out of bed and felt something drawing me to this copy of the *Denton Echo*. I opened it, and there was this picture . . . the little girl from my dream. I concentrated on it and could feel hatred, pain, violence. There were trees, grass, leaves . . .' Again he looked at Frost.

'So all we've got to do is to find somewhere where there's trees, grass and leaves, and we've got her. Thank you very much.' Frost rose to his feet, bringing the meeting to a close.

Plummer stayed in his chair. 'You have no faith in me, have you, Inspector?' He smiled knowingly. 'But I will change that. Do you have any item here that would have been in the girl's possession? Something actually handled by her?'

Frost opened the file and took out the school photograph of the smiling, gap-toothed Vicky. She had brought it home from the school for her mother.

'Perfect, perfect,' breathed Plummer, placing the photograph on the map. He closed his eyes and swayed from side to side. 'I can feel her presence . . . she has control of my hand. She is saying, "I'm here, I'm here." ' Then his finger quivered and descended on to the map. 'There! This is where you will find her, Inspector.' He opened his eyes and beamed triumphantly up at Frost.

Frost leant over to see the spot indicated. A small section of Denton Woods, cut off by the new motorway. 'Marvellous,' snorted Frost. 'We've already searched there three times, twice with men, once with dogs. We found nothing.' He snatched the map from the desk and made a hash of refolding it. 'On your way – I've wasted enough time over this.'

'I'm prepared to go with him on my own,' said Sandy Lane. 'You'll look a right prat if we find her after you refused to come.'

'I never look anything other than a right prat,' said Frost. He unhooked his mac from the rack. 'All right, but make it quick.' Opening the door, he yelled down the corridor for Morgan. 'Get the car round, Taffy. We're going body-hunting . . .'

The long grass was sodden and their trouser legs were soon soaked to the knees with a cold clamminess the howling wind was doing its best to turn to ice. Plummer had led them off the main path and they were plunging into an overgrown area where trees creaked and groaned. Frost exchanged exasperated glances with Morgan. It was obvious that Plummer, looking more and more despairing, was hopelessly lost. Behind them, deadened by a fringe of trees, came the steady roar of motorway traffic. Sandy Lane, stumbling along behind them, was trying hard not to meet Frost's eye.

'Can we stop when we reach Edinburgh?' asked Frost sarcastically.

'I'm sorry,' flushed Plummer. 'This isn't an exact science, you know.'

'It was a bleeding exact science when you jabbed your finger on the map,' snapped Frost. 'We passed the place where we would definitely find her some ten minutes ago.'

'She's here, somewhere,' insisted Plummer. He stopped and slowly looked about him, shaking his head. 'No . . . I'm sorry . . . something's wrong. I just don't know.'

'My fault for agreeing to come with you,' grunted Frost who wasn't going to waste time on recriminations. 'Let's go home.'

They had driven barely half a mile with Plummer glumly staring out of the window when he suddenly yelled, 'Stop the car!'

Morgan, at the wheel, looked to Frost for instructions.

'What now?' asked Frost.

Plummer craned his neck, staring back at the way they had come and pointing excitedly to a clump of forlorn trees on the other side of the road. 'She's there!'

'She bloody well gets about a bit, doesn't she?' snorted Frost.

'She's there!' insisted Plummer. 'I'm positive. I can hear her calling, "I'm here . . . I'm here . . ." '

Frost sighed and nodded for Morgan to do a U turn and drive back to the indicated spot. 'Your last bloody chance,' he told Plummer.

They trudged along another winding, muddy path, then through more trouser-soaking grass, Plummer running ahead of them, excitedly, like a dog catching the scent of a rabbit, beard bristling, eyes glowing. He stopped and waited for them to catch up. 'The child is very near. I can feel the vibrations.'

'You'll feel the toe of my boot up your arse if this is another waste of time,' grunted Frost.

The path narrowed and bushes on either side were brushing against them. Plummer took another couple of steps, then abruptly stopped, his face contorting as if in extreme pain. 'I feel her suffering, her soul cries out in torment.'

'Go on, then,' urged Frost. 'We're right behind you.'

Plummer shook his head. 'No. I can't go any further.' He pointed. 'She's there, Inspector, behind those bushes.'

Frost barged him out of the way, briars snagging his mac as he squeezed through. His nostrils twitched. Something. Something unpleasant. Faintly at first, then it hit him hard. A smell he had experienced too often before. The sickly, rancid carrion odour of death and decay. 'Morgan, come here,' he barked. 'Sandy, you stay put with Plummer.'

With Morgan tagging close behind, he parted some brambles and stepped into a small clearing overgrown with sodden tall grass. Morgan bumped into him as he halted. 'Shit!' he hissed.

'What is it, guv?'

Frost pointed.

They stared down at a mess of sodden clothes and bloated flesh that was once an eight-year-old girl.

Morgan closed his eyes and looked away. 'I thought we'd searched this area, guv?'

'We did,' Frost told him. 'Three times. She must have been dumped here after we searched.'

'What's going on?' yelled Sandy Lane.

'Stay there,' ordered Frost. 'We're coming out.'

They gingerly retraced their steps, anxious not to disturb any evidence which might be lurking in the long grass.

'You've found her, haven't you?' asked Plummer, a smug smirk of triumph on his face.

Frost stared coldly. 'Yes, we've found her, and it hasn't made our day like it seems to have made yours.' He sent Morgan back to the car to mobilize the murder team, then stopped Sandy Lane who was tugging a mobile phone from his inside pocket.

'Hold it, Sandy.' He pulled the reporter to one side and lowered his voice. 'She hasn't been identified yet, so just say we've found a body, and don't send one of your tactful reporters round to the mother's house before I've been over to break the news; she's going to take this bloody badly. And lastly, don't mention Plummer's part in this.'

'Now hold on, Jack,' protested the reporter. 'We've paid good money for this exclusive. Plummer's red hot news.'

Frost glared incredulously. 'You've what?'

' "Clairvoyant Finds Body Of Missing Girl" – it's a dream story. We've paid £5,000 for the exclusive world rights.'

'You never told me this,' said Frost, angrily. 'I'd never have gone along with it had I known.'

'Then you would never have found her.'

'Listen, Sandy. I don't care how much you've paid that smug bastard, but he's too clever for his own good. He knew where she was and not through bloody second sight. He's got a lot of questions to answer.'

'You don't believe in second sight?'

'Not even at £5K a bleeding throw. That bastard *knew* she was there. He's just become my number one suspect.'

13

The pathologist emerged from the small temporary canvas tenting erected over the body which had the effect of containing the reek of decay, but Drysdale didn't appear to mind. 'Sexually assaulted and manually strangled, like the other girl,' he told Frost. 'Killed elsewhere, of course, and brought here some time after death.'

'How long has she been here?' Frost asked, hoping it was well after the time the area was thoroughly searched.

'Difficult to tell without knowing the previous storage conditions. At a guess I'd say some two to three weeks.'

'Storage conditions?'

'I suspect the body was kept in a deep freeze of some kind before being brought here.'

'A deep freeze?' echoed Frost. 'Bloody hell!' The freezer compartment to the fridge in Weaver's house was tiny and nowhere near big enough to store a body. He made a mental note to check Plummer's house and see what sort of a deep freeze he had.

'If she was killed shortly after she went missing,' continued Drysdale, 'then there would have been much more evidence of decay. I should be able to be more precise when I do the PM. I've a busy schedule, but I can fit it in today – two o'clock this afternoon, Denton Hospital mortuary.'

'I'll be there, doc,' said Frost.

No matter how many times Frost said it, Drysdale always winced at the 'doc'. He couldn't stand the man's coarse familiarity. As he left, Harding and the Forensic team, who had been waiting patiently, went inside the canvas shelter.

Frost's mobile phone bleeped. Mullett calling from the station. 'You've found the girl?'

'Yes. Raped and strangled like Jenny.'

'By the same man?'

'I bloody hope so. It's hard enough finding one killer, let alone two.'

'I understand you've arrested this man Plummer. Can I take it you now accept that Weaver was innocent?'

'No. I reckon Weaver and Plummer acted together. Plummer could have hidden Jenny's body while we had Weaver in custody, then sent that letter with the button.'

'Hmm,' grunted Mullett, sounding unconvinced. 'Try and speed things up. The news has leaked out that we're holding a suspect and we're being inundated with phone calls from the press. And something else. I've had an irate Chief Inspector Preston from Belton Division on the phone. You haven't sent over the files on the prostitute killing he asked for.'

'Damn,' said Frost. 'Funny how you forget things when some bastard strings himself up in his cell. I'll see to it as soon as I get back.'

'Make sure you do,' Mullett snapped. 'These things reflect on the Division. Have you told the girl's parents yet?'

'No,' said Frost, fingering the plastic bracelet found on the body. He was going to ask them to identify it as Vicky's. He didn't want them to have to see the body in its present state. 'I've got that treat to come.'

'After weeks of uncertainty, it might even come as a relief,' suggested Mullett.

'Yes,' said Frost bitterly. 'We might even have a few laughs about it.' He clicked off the phone and dropped it in his pocket. No point in putting it off any longer. He walked to his car and drove to the parents' house.

It was Vicky's mother who opened the door. She had seen his car pull up outside and couldn't wait to hear the good news that Vicky had been found and was alive and well. Then she stared and clutched her chest. His face told her everything. He looked at her and sadly shook his head. She forced herself to ask 'Vicky?'

Frost nodded.

'Dead?' She was already shaking her head, refusing to believe what he was going to tell her.

He nodded again. He always tried to be detached and not let these things affect him, but this time he found himself struggling to hold back the tears.

She put her arms round him and hugged him tight. 'You poor man,' she crooned, as if soothing a child. 'You tried so hard, you hoped for so much.' And she was comforting him.

In the living-room her husband sat with his arm around her, the tears they had both held back for so long now flowing freely. Over the mantelpiece, in the original of the police poster photograph, their dead daughter smiled down at them.

Frost took the green plastic bracelet from his pocket. 'Is this Vicky's?'

The mother took it, holding it in her open palm. 'Yes,' she nodded. 'It's . . .' She couldn't bring herself to say her daughter's name. She closed her hand tightly and pressed the bracelet against a tear-stained cheek.

'We need it back,' said Frost, gently. He had to prise open her palm to take it.

'Did she suffer?' asked the husband.

'No,' lied Frost, firmly. 'She didn't suffer.'

'And will you get the man who did it?'

'Yes,' said Frost. 'That I can promise you. We'll get him.'

Drysdale looked at the large clock on the tiled mortuary wall and frowned. Ten past two. He'd specifically told Frost two o'clock and couldn't start the autopsy until the inspector deigned to put in an appearance. There would be an official complaint about this.

A slamming of doors and the sound of raucous laughter. The pathologist's lips tightened. He didn't need to turn round when the mortuary doors opened and closed. 'You've kept me waiting, Inspector.'

'I've been breaking the news to the kid's parents,' said Frost, shuffling on one of the green autopsy gowns he always felt such a fool wearing. 'Not the sort of thing you can cut short.' DC Morgan, who had come in with Frost, had difficulty with his gown and smiled gratefully as Drysdale's secretary helped him find the sleeves.

'If you're ready, at last.' Drysdale pulled on a pair of surgical gloves and surveyed the body like a diner ready for his main course. Hovering at Drysdale's shoulder, the green-gowned SOCO man waited patiently, his camera at the ready. Overhead a large extractor fan whirled lazily, but didn't seem to be doing much to improve the fetid atmosphere.

Frost stared down at the tiled floor and let his mind wander. He'd give his flaming pension for a cigarette. He didn't want to watch the proceedings unless it was absolutely necessary. Morgan seemed to find it impossible to tear his eyes away from Drysdale's

277

blonde secretary. Whenever she met his gaze, she flushed, bent her head and scribbled furiously in her shorthand notebook.

'Ah . . . !'

Frost looked up. Drysdale, who had been probing the girl's mouth, had extracted a sodden mess of something. 'Toilet tissue . . . like the other girl . . . used as a gag.'

'The bugger was nothing if not consistent,' said Frost as the mess was dropped into a plastic jar held out by SOCO.

'And, like the other girl, she was raped before death but as before, he seems to have used a condom, so no chance of DNA identification.'

The pathologist reached for a scalpel to open up the stomach. Frost turned his head away. This was the part of post-mortems he really hated. Morgan, looking green, had lost interest in the secretary and was sitting in a chair at the back, dabbing his brow with a handkerchief.

'It would help if I had your attention, Inspector,' said Drysdale peevishly. Frost raised his head. The pathologist was dropping something into a sample jar. He held it up so Frost could see. Little lumps of something brown floating in a murky liquid. 'The last thing she ate very shortly before death . . . I think it is a sweet . . . a toffee or something.'

Frost nodded grimly. The bastard always gave them a sweet to suck while they were waiting to be raped and murdered.

Drysdale slashed, hacked and weighed as the extractor fan proved more and more ineffective, but nothing of further importance was found. At last he was finished and was washing his hands at the sink as the mortuary attendant did his best to sew the tiny body into something more presentable. 'About time they got some decent soap,' complained Drysdale, scrubbing away at his nails. 'My findings are as before, Inspector. Like the first girl, she was gagged, sexually abused, then manually strangled. The body then appears to have been stored in a sub-zero temperature, probably a domestic deep freeze. Date of death?' He shrugged. 'The unknown storage conditions mean I can only guess. I'd say nine, ten weeks.'

'Which is round about the time she disappeared,' said Frost. He sighed. 'Thanks, doc.' A jerk of his head to Morgan who had recovered enough to be chatting up the secretary. They discarded the green gowns and dropped them in the bin, then hurried out of the building to suck in lungfuls of clean, cold, untainted air before climbing into the car for a smoke.

'Post-mortems are part of the job I hate, guv,' said Morgan.

'It's not as much fun as frisking toms,' agreed Frost, sliding into the passenger seat.

Morgan switched on the ignition. 'That Drysdale's secretary, guv. I've got a thing about long-legged blondes. I wouldn't mind having her.'

'I reckon she's seen enough organs to last her a lifetime,' said Frost.

Back at the station he was barking out orders to the murder squad. 'I want Plummer's house searched. See if there's any porno pictures of kids, or anything at all that would tie him in with Weaver. And do Weaver's place over again, see if there's anything to tie him up with Plummer.' As he was leaving the incident room he remembered something else and spun round. 'Vicky had been eating toffees just before she was killed . . . so see if Plummer's got any bags of sweets.' No sooner out, than he was back again, telling the WPC who was manning the phones to photocopy the prostitute serial murder files and send them over to Belton Division right away. Then back yet again as he thought of something else. 'Bag up all the note-paper and envelopes you find at Plummer's place and send it over to Forensic. Let's see if they can match it with that anonymous letter with the button.'

As he scuttled back to his office, Bill Wells yelled that Plummer was demanding to know why he was being held.

'He's supposed to have bloody second sight, let him find out for himself. I'll talk to him in a minute.'

His in-tray was overflowing again – more state-ments taken from prostitutes about weirdo clients. Nothing that looked promising. The internal phone rang. Harding from Forensic.

'Vicky Stuart, Inspector. Did she have a pet dog?'

'No.' He shouldered the phone to his ear as he lit up a cigarette.

'Did Weaver?'

'No – why?'

'We've found hairs from a black dog on Vicky's clothing. Find the dog and we can match them.'

'I'll do some checking.' He hung up and wiggled the cigarette up and down as he thought. His hopes were raised, but the dog hairs could have come from any-where. He buzzed for Arthur Hanlon.

'Arthur, you questioned Vicky's school friends when she first went missing. She used to visit their houses. Did any of them have a dog with black fur?'

Hanlon thought for a moment. 'Two of them, Jack . . . a black and white spaniel and a black mongrel.'

Frost showed his disappointment, but at least it would eliminate the animal hairs as a possible clue to the killer.

'Go to the houses, get samples of the dogs' hairs and send them over to Forensic for testing.'

He took another long drag at the cigarette before pinching it out and yelling for Morgan to accompany him to the interview room for a cosy little chat with Plummer.

Plummer's beard was bristling with anger. 'I hope you are prepared for a substantial claim for false arrest. This is absolutely intolerable.'

Frost looked hurt. 'A few questions, Mr Plummer. I naturally assumed you'd be more than anxious to help us. After all, if it wasn't for you we might never have found her.'

Slightly mollified, Plummer sat down. 'If I can help you further . . .'

Frost smiled his gratitude and dragged the other chair to the table. He jerked a thumb at Morgan. 'My colleague, here, sir, doesn't understand one or two things about what has happened. He's a bit slow on the uptake, I'm afraid, on account of being Welsh. Perhaps you could enlighten him?'

'Of course,' Plummer turned enquiringly to Morgan who looked blank, not knowing what was expected of him.

'My colleague was puzzled how you could make a mistake with the map, Mr Plummer. You told us your psychic powers would enable you to pinpoint the body, but you were over a mile out.'

Plummer tugged at his beard and smiled. 'I'm afraid I don't know the answer to that, Inspector. I have no control over my gifts.'

'Quite, sir,' nodded Frost, 'the way some people have no control over their bladder.' He leant over as if sharing a confidence. 'You see, sir, my colleague tends to think the worst of people. He reckons the only way you could know where the body was, would be because you dumped it there in the first place.'

Plummer's eyes blazed. 'That is both insulting and ridiculous!'

Frost wagged a reproving finger at Morgan. 'See, you've upset the gentleman. I knew you would.'

'Sorry,' mumbled Morgan, playing up to the inspector.

Another smile at Plummer. 'I told him, sir, that if you had killed the kid and dumped her body, you would know where it was and wouldn't have to rely on the map.'

'Quite!' snapped Plummer.

'But do you know what he had the damn cheek to come back with?' asked Frost. 'He said you were probably a damn good body dumper, but a bloody poor map reader.'

Plummer's face reddened. 'Are you making an accusation, Inspector?'

Frost's air of friendliness switched off abruptly. 'You knew the body was there, didn't you? A bit hazy about directions because you probably dumped the kid when it was dark.'

'How dare you!' Plummer's fist crashed down on the table. 'I come here to help and you make these wild accusations—'

'If you didn't put her there, how did you know where to find her?'

'I have the gift of second sight.' He stood, eyes glazed, pointing a quivering finger as if he was receiving a divine revelation. 'You have recently suffered the loss of a loved one.'

'That's right,' snapped Frost. 'My hamster died yesterday. Now sit down and stop sodding us about.' He waited for the man to sit. 'My personal life, Mr Plummer, is an open book, you've only got to look through the newspapers.'

'I don't need to,' the man answered. 'My information comes from inside.'

'And that's where you'll flaming well end up,' fired back Frost. 'You killed Vicky Stuart and then hid her body.'

Plummer shoved his face close to Frost. 'How dare you,' he hissed. 'You've already harried one innocent man to his death, you are not doing the same with me. The first time I saw that poor child's body was when I led you there. I am answering no more questions without the presence of a solicitor.'

'Your privilege, sir.' Frost stood and patted his papers together. 'One last question – do you have a dog?'

Plummer's brow puckered. 'Yes – why?'

'Would my second sight be correct in saying that it is a black dog?'

'Yes . . .'

Frost smiled sweetly. 'We found dog hairs on the child's body. They can't be from your dog because you've told us you haven't been near the body before, but just to prove your innocence, I'm arranging for samples to be collected so that we can be sure they don't match.' He looked at Plummer with concern. The man's face had suddenly drained of colour. 'Are you all right, sir?'

Plummer flapped a limp hand. 'Perfectly all right, thank you.' But he didn't look it.

'Good,' said Frost. 'Let's see about getting you a solicitor.'

'Well?' asked Sergeant Wells as Frost swaggered across the lobby.

Frost smirked with satisfaction. 'As guilty as hell. Sluice out Weaver's old cell and check Plummer's pockets for rope.'

'What progress?' asked Mullett. Frost had been dashing in and out of the station, finding bodies, attending post-mortems, interviewing suspects, but hadn't bothered to keep his Divisional Commander informed. 'I can't hold the press off much longer.'

'I expect to charge Plummer this afternoon,' Frost told him. 'Just waiting for Forensic to report on the dog hairs.' He quickly brought the superintendent up to date.

'Good,' beamed Mullett. 'This case has taken up too many man-hours already. All of this will be in your today's progress report, of course?'

'Of course,' lied Frost emphatically. He hadn't the time to waste on this stupid paperwork.

'And I'm still waiting for your report for yesterday.'

'I was working on it when you called me in, Super,' replied Frost. 'All these flaming interruptions, I won't have time to do it now.'

But Mullett knew when not to listen. 'On my desk in half an hour please,' he said, clapping the phone to his ear and punching out the number for County.

Frost retrieved the progress report from the depths of his in-tray and gave it a cursory glance. It demanded full details of daily progress: man-hours, overtime, expenses . . . A footnote stated, 'If not enough room, use a second sheet.' 'There's plenty of room,' muttered Frost, scrawling 'Some progress made' right across the sheet and chucking it in his out-tray.

The phone rang. Forensic. 'We've got a positive match on those animal hair samples, Inspector.'

'And people say you're bloody useless,' said Frost. 'Terrific.' He gave the thumbs-up sign to Morgan as he reached for his pen. 'Shoot!'

'The dog hairs from the girl's clothing definitely match sample number three.'

Frost glanced at the Forensic Test Request form, left by Hanlon. He frowned. 'Wait a minute. You mean sample two – sample three came from one of Vicky's school friends' dogs.'

'That's right. That's the one that matched.'

'But what about sample two?'

'Nothing like it, entirely different.'

'You're not looking properly – I want a second flaming opinion.'

'We've checked and double-checked, Inspector, as we always do. The confirmation report is on its way.'

'I can hardly bleeding wait.' He banged the phone down with a snort of rage. 'They're useless,' he wailed. 'Never tell you what you want to know . . . only things that sod up your case.'

'So it's not Plummer's dog?' asked Morgan.

'You've got a rapier-sharp mind, Taffy. No, it came from the dog of one of her school friends.' He rammed a cigarette in his mouth with such force it bent double. 'Damn.'

'Never mind, guv. It may not be Plummer's dog, but it still doesn't let him off the hook.'

'We've found nothing in his house to tie him in with Weaver. No sweets, no photographs of nude kids, not a flaming thing we can use. We're going to have to let him go.'

The internal phone buzzed. Frost signalled for Morgan to answer it.

The DC listened, then quickly slapped a hand over the mouthpiece. 'Mr Mullett, guv. Wants to know if we've got the lab report on the dog hairs.'

'That flaming git always senses when things are going wrong,' moaned Frost. 'Tell him no – they're not in yet.' He repaired his cigarette with a bit of stamp edging and lit up. The other phone rang. Bill Wells to tell him that Plummer's solicitor had spent some time with him and they now wanted to see the inspector.

'Knickers!' moaned Frost. 'This is where I get sued

285

for wrongful arrest. A policeman's lot is not a happy one.'

Plummer's solicitor was a thin, sour-looking individual, who looked even sourer when Frost and Morgan came into the interview room. As they sat down, he unzipped his briefcase, took out a sheet of paper covered in neat handwriting and passed it across to Plummer who read it through then addressed the inspector. 'I imagine you now have the laboratory results on the dog's hairs?'

Frost nodded. He was about to take the test result from the folder when Plummer suddenly buried his head in his hands and began sobbing. The solicitor looked embarrassed and stared at the wall. Frost looked puzzled, but remained silent and waited. It was usually a good sign when they started blubbing.

At last Plummer sniffed back the tears and shook his head in self-reproach. 'I lied to you, Inspector. I had no idea my dog had gone anywhere near that poor child's body.'

Frost kept his face impassive. What the hell was the man babbling on about? 'Oh.'

'To my eternal shame, I was not telling the truth when I said I had never seen that poor child's body before today. On the advice of my solicitor I have prepared a written statement.' He slid the sheet of paper across the table to Frost. 'I knew the body was there. I saw it yesterday when I was out with my dog. The dog found it and started barking. When I saw her . . .' He shook his head to try and erase the memory. 'I was going to report my discovery right away, then I recalled how you had mocked and scorned my gifts in the past and decided to prove you wrong.'

'And to get five thousand quid from the papers for your exclusive story?'

The solicitor looked surprised. Plummer hadn't told him about this.

Plummer hung his head. 'I wouldn't have kept it, Inspector. My conscience wouldn't have let me.'

'Neither would the judge in the fraud case,' said Frost. He glanced down at Plummer's statement. 'So you found the body yesterday and you wasted twenty-four hours before you decided to tell the police?'

The solicitor thought this a good moment to intervene. 'Naturally my client withdraws any claims he may have against you for wrongful arrest.'

'Very generous of him,' sniffed Frost, basking in the unfamiliar role of the aggrieved party.

'My client further realizes that he could be accused of wasting police time and hampering an inquiry, but in view of his frankness, we hope you will take a more lenient view.'

'He was only frank because we found out he was a bleeding liar,' said Frost. 'But he's fortunate that we're too busy to sod about with minor crimes. We might need to question him further, but for the moment, he can go.'

Mullett was smouldering with rage at being let down yet again by Frost after he had told County that an arrest was imminent. 'So not a single thing to tie him in with Weaver: no pornographic pictures, nothing to suggest he is a paedophile and no matching notepad or envelopes?'

'You forgot the sweets,' said Frost. 'We didn't find them either.'

Mullett's lips tightened. 'So where exactly do we stand with the child killings now?'

'Nowhere.'

'Precisely.' Mullett took off his glasses and polished them carefully. 'It isn't good enough, Frost, it just isn't good enough.' He waved a sheet of figures. 'All the overtime, all the man-hours, and for what?'

'I think "for sod all" are the words you're searching for,' said Frost. Why must the man rant on and on about the bleeding obvious? 'I know it's cost us a lot of money to get nowhere. We didn't find the bodies earlier because they weren't there. One was stored with the fish fingers somewhere and God knows where the other one has been. We've checked and double-checked, followed up all leads—'

He was stopped in mid-flow as the phone rang and Mullett held up a hand for silence. 'It might be County,' he murmured, adjusting his tie in case it was. It wasn't County.

'Charles! Hello . . . Long time no speak . . .'

As Mullett listened, he frowned and reached for his Parker fountain pen. 'Who . . . ?' He scribbled a name down on his notepad and carefully ringed it round. 'As a matter of fact, Charles, we were just about to send for it, but you've beaten us to the punch. We look forward to receiving the file. How's Mildred? Good . . .' He hung up and stared grimly at Frost, drumming his fingers on the desk top. 'You say you've followed up every lead?'

'Yes,' said Frost guardedly, sensing that the sod knew something he didn't.

'That phone call, Frost, was my opposite number in Greyford Division – Superintendent Hilton.'

'Good old Charlie,' said Frost. 'Mildred all right?'

Mullett ignored this. 'He says he is sending us their file on Dennis Hadleigh – he was surprised we hadn't asked for it earlier.'

'Dennis Hadleigh?' asked Frost, his mind racing. Who the hell was Dennis Hadleigh? The name rang a bell, but . . . Then he remembered. Hadleigh was Mary Brewer's live-in boyfriend, the man who was supposed to have knocked Jenny about. 'What file? I never even knew he had a record.'

'You didn't know, Frost, because you didn't damn well check. I had to lie and pretend we knew all about it. For your information, Hadleigh used to live in Greyford. He was arrested two years ago for sexually abusing an under-aged girl, the eleven-year-old daughter of the woman he was then living with.'

'Oh!' said Frost weakly.

'You didn't check on the boyfriend?'

'I was going to, but as soon as Weaver entered the frame we didn't look any further.'

'A typically blinkered approach,' sniffed Mullett. 'You concentrate all your resources on the wrong man and let the real killer go free. Pick him up now. With luck we could clear this up by tonight.'

Luck, thought Frost, what's happened to my bleeding luck? He pushed himself wearily out of the chair. Mullett had got him this time. The flaming boyfriend. He'd never given him another thought. 'When should the file get here?'

'Later this evening, but don't wait for it. The arrest of the right person would make a welcome change.'

Frost grunted his agreement. He was so disheartened, he closed the door quietly, leaving Mullett, teeth gritted, waiting for the slam that never came.

Dennis Hadleigh was in his mid-twenties. He rippled with muscles and as he folded his arms to stare disdainfully at Frost, the sleeves of his jacket shot back to reveal a mass of tattoos. He scowled. 'Are you going to tell me what this is all about?'

'I think you know what this is about,' snapped Frost, poking a cigarette in his mouth and scratching a match across the table top.

'Pretend I don't,' said Hadleigh. 'Tell me.'

'You are kindly helping us with our inquiries into the death of Jenny Brewer.'

'You didn't have to drag me down here to get me to do that. I'm as anxious to catch the toe-rag who did it as you are. I take it he isn't the bloke who topped himself?'

Frost took a deep drag and balanced the cigarette on the matchbox. 'We thought we'd try looking a lot nearer home!' He flickered a smile. 'Why did you do it?'

Hadleigh gaped. 'You think I did it? You think I killed and raped a seven-year-old kid?'

'Why not? You like them young, don't you . . . young, choice, unsullied?'

Hadleigh bent across the table. 'Yes, as it happens I do like them young, choice and unsullied, but not that bloody young.'

'You've done it before, though, haven't you?' asked Frost.

The suspect leant back in his chair and nodded wryly. 'You mean Samantha – young, choice, unsullied Samantha?'

'Yes,' agreed Frost, trying to sound as if he had all the facts. He wished he had the bloody file in front of him. He hadn't the faintest idea what the girl's name was. 'Samantha, your girlfriend's daughter, just like Jenny.'

'Nothing like Jenny. Jenny was seven years old, for Pete's sake!'

'And Samantha was eleven.'

'A couple of weeks short of her twelfth birthday.'

'And one more candle on the cake made all the difference?'

Hadleigh gave a sour smile. 'You don't know the facts, do you?'

'We've got that treat to come,' Frost told him. 'Your file's on the way over. Suppose you fill us in

290

with all the hot, intimate details. Did you welt her the way you welted Jenny?'

The smile vanished. Hadleigh reached inside his jacket and pulled out a worn leather wallet which he thumbed through until he found a small coloured photograph. He flicked it across the table. 'That is Jenny. Her mother didn't give a toss about her. Jenny was no bleeding angel, but you couldn't help liking the kid. In spite of everything she always came up with a smile.'

'The poor little cow didn't have a smile on her face when I found her,' said Frost.

Hadleigh said nothing. He leafed through the wallet again and found another photograph which he slid over to Frost, face down. Frost flipped it over and could feel Morgan's hot breath on the back of his neck as he picked it up to study it. A long-haired blonde, stripped to the waist, hands cupping large prominent breasts as she lay back on a cushion and pouted at the camera.

'That,' said Hadleigh, jabbing a finger, 'is sweet, innocent, eleven-year-old Samantha. She took the photograph herself with an automatic camera. If that was offered to you on a plate, would you turn your nose up at it?'

Give me her bleeding address, thought Frost. Aloud he said: 'She was still under age.'

'Under age or not, she'd had it away with half the boys in her class. She couldn't get enough of it. Flaming hell, I'm only flesh and bleeding blood. She calls me up into her bedroom – says she couldn't get her telly to work. When I goes in, there she is, stark bloody naked. You may not believe this, but I did try to push her away – not very hard, but I tried.'

'So she overpowered you and had her way with you?'

Another wry grin. 'No such flaming luck. Her

mother came in before anything happened and yelled
"Rape" then she called the police and before I know
what's happened I was handcuffed and off to the
nick.'

'Then what?'

'Lucky for me Samantha didn't want any trouble.
She said I came into the room without knocking and
she was getting undressed. I was fully clothed, nothing
had happened, so the charge had to be dropped, much
to the disappointment of the Old Bill.'

Frost took a long, slow drag on his cigarette to give
himself time to think. It looked as if another promising
suspect was about to bite the dust. 'The night Jenny
went missing, where were you?'

'I was out with Mary – her mother – you know
that. That's why we both thought she was round her
Nan's.'

Frost passed the two photographs back to Hadleigh
after prising the one of Samantha from Morgan who
was staring at it goggle-eyed. 'Thanks for your help,
Mr Hadleigh. You can go now.'

Hadleigh replaced the photographs in his wallet.
'That's all?'

'For the time being. We might want to talk to you
again.' If only to have another look at the photograph,
he thought. Frost opened the interview room door and
yelled for Collier to show the gentleman out.

He sat down again and finished his cigarette. 'I
reckon he's in the clear.'

Morgan's eyes glazed. Still lost in erotic thought, he
muttered, 'I'd happily go to prison for an hour with
that Samantha, guv.'

'I wouldn't,' said Frost. 'I'd make certain I locked
the door first and wedged a chair under the handle.'

'Yet another false lead?' said Mullett, as if it was
Frost's idea to bring in Hadleigh in the first place.

'I reckon so,' replied Frost. 'We'll keep an eye on him though.'

Mullett held up the return Frost had given him. 'This is not my idea of a progress report. I want facts. Where do we stand with the prostitute killings?'

'We're following up leads,' said Frost vaguely. What few leads there were had proved worthless, but let Mullett think the inquiries were ongoing.

'And the skeleton? Have you found out who he is yet?'

'He's the least of my worries,' said Frost. 'He can wait.'

'No murder inquiry can wait,' snapped Mullett. 'I've been approached by the solicitor acting for the couple who own the property where the bones were found. Our delay in bringing this to a conclusion, plus all our paraphernalia in the garden, is stopping them from selling the house.'

'Tough,' said Frost.

Mullett waved away the interruption. 'He demands immediate action or they will sue for damages.'

'I hope you told him to get stuffed,' said Frost.

A scowl from Mullett. 'I did no such thing. He's a personal friend of mine. As you have done absolutely nothing, I have circulated details of the skeleton to all forces asking them to check their missing person files of some thirty or forty years ago.'

'Brilliant,' said Frost. 'They'll dump all their old missing person files going back to the year dot . . . We'll have files on Glenn Miller and Amelia flaming Earhart. How are we supposed to cope with that?'

'County are releasing four men back to us,' said Mullett, 'including DC Burton, and Inspector Allen should be back next week so you won't be able to use shortage of manpower as an excuse any more.' He tossed the progress report over to Frost. 'Do this properly and let me have it back tonight.'

'Sure,' said Frost. He chucked it in Mullett's secretary's waste-paper bin on his way out.

He was right about the missing person reports. He peeked into the incident room on his way up to the canteen. The fax machine, screeching like a fingernail scratched down a blackboard, was spewing out yard after yard of paper. Next to it, looking fed up, PC Collier was sorting the faxes out.

Frost gave them a desultory thumb through. 'Flaming hell,' he croaked. 'They've emptied all their rubbish on us, missing men, women, kids and dogs.' He lifted one up. 'And here's a bloke who only went missing last week. That stupid git Mullett!' He dropped the fax back on the desk. 'We haven't got time to sod about with these,' he told Collier. 'Bung them in a box file, hide them away somewhere and forget where you put them. I'm off to the canteen for a chip butty.'

He didn't make it to the canteen. As he passed through the lobby he was called over by Bill Wells. 'Lady to see you, inspector.' Frost froze. Not Doreen Beatty claiming to be raped again? Wells jerked his head to indicate a young woman in her mid-twenties with a three-year-old boy in a pushchair. Frost's heart plummeted. Please God, not another missing child! 'Thinks she might know who your skeleton might be,' said Wells.

'Bully for her,' grunted Frost, without much enthusiasm. He led her to the interview room. 'I'm probably wasting your time,' she said, manoeuvring the pushchair through the door.

He pointedly studied his watch and frowned, indicating he was pushed for time.

'I'll be as quick as I can.' She slipped off her thick coat under which she wore a tight, knitted blue woollen dress. To Frost's delight, beneath the

294

figure-hugging dress there was an awful lot of quivering breast and nipple fighting to get out. 'Take as long as you like, love,' he croaked, as she bent over to tighten the straps round the child and a pert little bottom waggled under his nose.

She smiled and sat down opposite him. He tore his eyes away and winked at the little boy. 'So what can you tell me?'

'My name's Mrs Vivian Tailor.' She waggled a finger to show him the wedding ring which looked a lot newer than the child. 'It's about that skeleton they found in Nelson Road. This may not have anything to do with it . . .'

'I'm sure it has,' he said. She was leaning over, her breasts supported by the table top, and his hand brushed them as he stubbed out his cigarette in the ashtray. 'Don't rush it.'

'Well, my mum used to have a friend in Nelson Road when she was a girl. I'm going back some years, of course. Anyway, there was this woman she used to chat to over the garden fence. She was a bit older than my mum and she had a son, a great lolloping boy.' She lowered her voice. 'Mum said he was a bit simple, but he couldn't help that, could he?'

'No,' agreed Frost. 'His name wasn't Mullett, was it?'

She frowned. 'No – Aldridge. His mother was Nelly Aldridge. Mum said she was a bit fast. She used to sunbathe topless in the garden – very flighty for those days.'

Frost nodded happily. This was getting interesting.

She leant further across the table, nearly pushing the pen from his hand. Her voice was even softer. 'Mum reckoned she was over-sexed.'

Me and her both, thought Frost. Cor, he could feel their warmth seeping into his knuckles.

'Anyway,' she continued, 'the whole point of this,

according to my mum, was that one day the son wasn't there any more. Whenever Mum asked about him, Nelly Aldridge would say, "He's in the house, not feeling well," that sort of thing. Then later she told my mum the boy had gone off to live with relatives, but she'd previously said she was all alone in the world without any relatives living.'

'And the boy was never seen again?'

She shook her head firmly. 'No, and she got all uptight whenever Mum mentioned him. Mum always reckoned she'd done away with him and I reckon that's his skeleton you've dug up.'

'She could have had him put away in a home?' Frost suggested, not entirely convinced there was any point in this.

'Then why not say so? Why all the mystery?'

'Is your mother still alive?'

She gave a sad smile. 'She died last year.'

'What about Nelly Aldridge?'

'No idea. She moved away long before I was born. One minute she was there, Mum said, the next the house was empty . . . not a word to a soul. She disappeared off the face of the earth.'

Well, at least it was a lead of sorts, something to waste the minimum of time on and keep Hornrim Harry quiet. He scribbled down the details, thanked her and accompanied her to the main door, watching her wiggling bottom as she pushed the child across the road. 'I wouldn't say no to a slice of that,' he told Wells.

'Bit young for you, isn't she, Jack?'

'I don't know, give me a week's notice and a fire in the bedroom and I think I could manage.' He hurried off to the incident room and dragged Morgan away from the racing page of the *Daily Mirror*. He quickly filled him in. 'So go and find out everything you can about Little Nell.'

Morgan didn't seem too keen. 'What number Nelson Road did she live, guv?'

'You want flaming jam on it!' snorted Frost. 'Knock on doors. She liked to sun her bristols in the back garden. Someone must remember. So find her, arrest her for the murder of her idiot son, then do all the paperwork and I'll buy you a beer in the pub tonight.'

'I was going to have my tooth out,' protested Morgan.

'Business comes before pleasure, Taffy,' reproved Frost. 'Find her first, then have your tooth out afterwards . . .'

He hurried Morgan on his way, then trotted upstairs to the canteen. 'All the bacon butties have gone,' said the canteen lady. 'Do you a nice cheese salad – much more healthy.'

He had the salad with double chips.

14

The scribbled message on his desk informed him that Forensic had found no traces of dog hairs on Jenny Brewer's clothing. He had forgotten he had asked them to test for this and stuffed the note in the case file.

He smoked and studied the cracks in the ceiling. Nothing was going well. A full stop on the murdered girls and a complete blank on the serial killer of the toms. He considered phoning Belton Division to see if they had had any luck with Big Bertha, but decided they would have contacted him if they had. The antique skeleton was simmering, but he doubted if they would get anywhere after all this time. He hated inactivity. He wanted to dash out and do something, even if it was pointless.

A tagged key was by his blotter. Puzzled, he checked the label. Of course, the key to Weaver's house, returned to him after they had tried to find those damned toilet rolls. He shuddered. The thought that he might have driven an innocent man to suicide made him go cold. He hooked the key on to his key ring to make sure he didn't lose it.

The internal phone buzzed. Somehow he knew it was Mullett and wasn't in the mood for him. Snatching his scarf from the coat peg he padded out to the car-park. He drove around aimlessly before realizing he was turning into the side street that led to Weaver's house. He sighed. This was no coincidence. Something was making him come here.

Turning the key silently in the lock he let himself in and stepped into the darkness of the hall. The house had a cold, empty, desolate feel. For a while he stood still, wondering what he was supposed to be doing here. Forensic had been over every inch of the place and had found nothing.

A tiny sound broke the silence. He stiffened, ears straining. There it was again, the creaking of a floorboard . . . someone moving about upstairs. Some bastard who knew the house was empty had broken in. He dug into his mac pocket for his torch. The battery was flat, but it was heavy and could be used as a cosh if necessary. Slowly and noiselessly he made his way up the stairs.

Light leaked from under a bedroom door – the mother's room. Holding his breath, he listened. Silence, then a rustling. Carefully he inched the door open. Someone was bending over the chest of drawers, rifling through its contents. He tightened his grip on the torch and raised it above his head. 'Hold it – you're nicked!' The intruder spun round. Frost gawped. It was a woman, grey-haired, in her early seventies. For a split second they just stared at each other, then she suddenly leapt at him, nails clawing for his face, screaming, 'Police. Help. Police.'

He dropped the torch so he could have both hands free and managed to hold off her talons, then hissed with pain as she kicked him sharply in the ankle. 'I *am* the bleeding police,' he yelled, pushing her roughly aside and fumbling for his warrant card. As she charged forward again he shoved the card in her face. 'Look at it, you silly cow!'

She blinked at the warrant card in disbelief, then at

him, keeping her distance. 'You don't look like a policeman.'

'And you don't look like a flaming mule, missus, but you've got the kick of one.' He rubbed his ankle. 'Who the hell are you and what are you doing here?'

'I'm Mrs Maisie White . . . Ada's sister.'

'Ada? Who's Ada?'

'Little Charlie's mother. I'm his Aunt Maisie.'

Frost dug in his pocket for his cigarettes. 'You've lost me,' he said, proffering the packet.

She waved it away. 'None of the family smoke – it used to affect Charlie's chest.'

Of course, thought Frost. Why am I being so thick? 'Little Charlie. You mean Charles Weaver, the bloke who lives here?'

'Lived here,' she corrected, dabbing her eye with a tiny lace-edged handkerchief. 'I can't believe it. First little Charlie, then Ada.'

'Ada? His mother? She's dead?'

The woman nodded. 'Early this morning. The nurse said she kept asking for him, but they didn't tell her . . . she never knew.'

'I'm sorry,' said Frost. He sat down, but realized he was on the commode chair, so quickly moved to the bed.

'A merciful release,' she said. Her expression changed. 'Are you the policeman who drove little Charlie to suicide?'

Frost winced. He wished she wouldn't keep calling the man that. It was hard to keep the image of Weaver as a child killer and rapist when he was called 'little Charlie'. 'We found photographs,' he told her. 'The little girl was in his house the afternoon she went missing and he lied to us. Until we could eliminate him, he was our prime suspect.'

She sat on the bed beside him. 'He didn't do it, Inspector. Believe me, I know. He was sweet, gentle

300

and kind. As soon as he knew his mother was ill, he had her moved in here. He devoted himself to her. A lovely boy.' Her lip trembled and she started to sob again.

Frost sucked at his cigarette. He saw Weaver as a murdering bastard, she saw him as a sweet little Charlie. 'The little girl who was raped and killed was a lovely girl.'

She dried her eyes. 'I know that boy. I brought him up. His mother wasn't married. It's commonplace now, but it was a dreadful thing then. The father deserted her and she had to go out to work, so I brought him up. Charlie loved children, not in a nasty way, but as a kind, gentle man. He didn't harm that little girl, Inspector, but you made him take the blame, and that was more than poor little Charlie could stand.'

Frost stood up. 'The case is still open,' he told her. 'If he's innocent, I won't keep it a secret.'

She looked at him. 'Too late for that now, Inspector.' She pushed the sodden handkerchief back in her pocket. 'It will be a double funeral. If you would like to come . . . ?'

It was the last thing he wanted to do, but he nodded his thanks and didn't ask for details. 'I'll leave you to it then. Sorry if I gave you a start.'

At the front door he hesitated, then, on impulse, retraced his steps to the back door, the door through which Weaver had told him Jenny had left the house on the last afternoon of her short life. Unbolting it, he stepped out into the tiny walled garden, squeezed past the dustbin and out through the door which led to a narrow alleyway, hemmed in on both sides by high brick walls. If, as Weaver claimed, Jenny was alive when she left, was the real killer waiting here for her to come out?

Doubt after doubt crowded in. Had he been wrong

about Weaver all the time? Mullett was right, he was always in too much of a hurry, making up his mind too quickly and then bending the facts to fit. He looked back at the house where the light was shining behind the curtains of the mother's bedroom. Auntie Maisie was tidying up for little Charlie's funeral.

The blue car! Weaver claimed the blue car, the car that brought Jenny to the house, was waiting outside all the time. Bernie Green claimed he had dropped the kid off and driven away after some ten minutes. Which of the two lying sods was telling the truth?

He hurried to his car and radioed through to Control, telling them he wanted Green brought in again for questioning right away.

A weary, fed-up Morgan was in the office waiting for him. The DC's jaw was swollen and his tongue kept finding the gap where a tooth used to be. 'I had the tooth out, guv.'

'Good.' Frost squinted through his in-tray. Nothing of interest. 'Bung it under your pillow for the tooth fairy.' He tried to remember what he had sent the DC out for. Ah yes, the bristol-flaunting woman with her simple-minded son. 'What joy, Taff?'

'None at all, guv. I've walked my feet down to the bone and knocked on every door in that street. I've been to the council, been through electoral rolls going back to the war. No Mrs Aldridge shown as ever living in Nelson Road.'

'The girl could have got the name wrong,' suggested Frost. 'It might be something similar like Shuffle-bottom.'

'I've checked everyone who ever lived in the street, guv . . . married women with kids, single women with kids, the lot.'

'What about widows with kids? I'd even settle for a man in drag without kids.'

302

Morgan rubbed his jaw. 'Take it from me, guv, I've checked everything.'

Frost nodded and yawned. Tiredness was creeping up on him and he didn't want to waste any more time on this. 'OK, Taffy, leave it for now. Go off home and get some sleep in your own bed for a change and we'll make an early start tomorrow.'

Morgan smiled gratefuly, but his early night was not to be. A tap on the door. PC Jordan looked in. 'We've picked up Bernie Green, Inspector. Where do you want him?'

'No. 1 interview room,' said Frost, grabbing the files. He jerked his head at Morgan who was trying to sidle out unnoticed. 'Come on, Taffy, suspect to interview. Shouldn't take more than a couple of hours . . .'

The interview room was cold: the radiator had died and had to be kicked into life. Frost gave a welcoming smile as Green was brought in, a smile that was not returned.

'Why have I been dragged here again?' the man demanded. 'I've told you everything.'

'We've got lousy memories,' said Frost. 'We want to hear it all again.' He waited while Morgan started up the tape. 'Right, Bernie boy, you're on talk radio, every lie you tell us is being recorded.'

'You're condemned before you open your bloody mouth in this place,' Green protested sullenly.

'I know,' beamed Frost. 'It saves all that sodding about getting evidence.' He took Green's earlier statement from the folder. 'Right. You say you took the kid to Weaver's place, watched her go in, then after ten minutes, drove away?'

'That's right.'

'But we have a witness, Bernie, who says you didn't drive off . . . you parked outside.' He didn't tell Bernie that the witness was the dead suspect.

'He's lying, Mr Frost. I drove straight off again.'

'Not straight off, Bernie. It must have slipped your mind, so let me remind you. You left the car and waited in that back alley. When the kid came out, you grabbed her, forced her in the car, then raped and strangled her.'

'As God is my witness, Mr Frost, she never came out while I was there. All right – I did get out of the car and waited round the back. I waited half an hour, but she didn't come out so I gave up.'

'You waited half an hour . . . in the freezing cold . . . Why?'

Green hung his head and drew little circles on the table top with his finger. 'Can this be off the record?'

'Anything you tell us,' said Frost, with an encouraging smile, 'won't go any further than these four walls and the Central Criminal Court.' The smile clicked off. 'This is a murder investigation, Bernie, everything is on the record. The only time we switch the tape off is when we want to refresh your memory with a few knees in the groin.'

Morgan winced. He wished the inspector wouldn't say these sort of things. If the tape was played in court, it might not be taken as a joke.

Unperturbed, Frost folded his arms and leant back in the chair. 'So come on, Bernie, spit it out. Why did you wait?'

'I thought she might like to come for a little ride with me. She looked the sort. I wouldn't have forced her, but you know . . . for a couple of quid . . .' He gave a weak smile. 'You know . . . nothing harmful . . .'

'Just a spot of homely fun,' said Frost grimly. 'You dirty bastard.'

'Well, it never came to it. After half an hour of standing in the freezing cold, I decided the bloke

304

inside was probably getting all the fun, so I called it a day.'

'You went home and took a cold bath?'

'I didn't need a cold bath. My dick was like an icicle.'

Frost grimaced. 'Bloody hell, Bernie, you've put me off frozen sausages for life.' He leant forward, his face inches away from Green. 'Let's try the truth for a change. You waited. She came out. You offered to take her for a drive in the nice blue motor car, you tried it on, but she screamed and yelled so you had to silence her.'

'No!' screamed Green. 'No!'

'You didn't mean to kill her, you just meant to keep her quiet . . . to stop her screaming, screaming, screaming . . .' His voice rose with each repetition of the word. 'It got on your nerves. You couldn't take it, so you put your hands round her throat and you squeezed and squeezed.'

'No . . . No!!' Green was standing and shouting. He suddenly stopped and sank down again in the chair. 'If they object, I stop. I don't want to know. It isn't fun if they object. I wouldn't have raped her. I don't do that sort of thing.'

'You're too good for this world,' murmured Frost. He showed him the photograph of Vicky Stuart. 'And when did you give her a lift, Bernie?'

Green shook his head. 'I've already told you, I know nothing about any other girl, Mr Frost. There's nothing else to tell. I've told you everything.'

Frost tapped a pencil on his teeth, then slipped the photograph and the statement back in the file. 'All right, Bernie. Give my colleague here a fresh statement, and you can go.'

Morgan followed him out. 'What do you reckon then, guv?'

Frost shrugged. 'If he's telling the truth and the girl

305

was in there for over half an hour, then what the hell was going on inside that house? Little innocent Charlie-boy said she nipped in, changed her dress, then legged it. That would take minutes. One of them is lying.'

'She could have nipped out the front way, while Green was waiting round the back.'

'Weaver said she went out the back way, why should he lie if she was only there a few minutes?' He yawned. 'I'm too tired to think. Let's leave it for now. Take his statement and get off home. See you tomorrow.'

He slept an untroubled sleep until two in the morning when the insistent ringing of the phone and the hammering at the front door woke him up.

The hot dog and pie and chip van, which catered in the main for the night trade – drunks rolling home from the local pubs, long distance lorry drivers, delivery men and cabbies – was parked in a cul-de-sac alongside the local comprehensive school. At half-past one in the morning it should have been a blaze of light, wafting out the greasy reek of fried onions, but it was now in darkness, and most of the onion smell had been blown away by the cutting wind. A little after midnight a crowd of noisy drunks from a nearby pub had amused themselves by distracting the owner's attention while two of them let down the tyres on one side. The van now drooped alarmingly.

The headlights of a minicab lit up the van and nosed in behind it as the owner, Ted Turner, a mournful-looking horse-faced man humping a foot-pump, clambered out and paid off the driver who had been chewing his ear-hole throughout the journey with good advice about always keeping a foot-pump handy in case anything like this happened.

As Turner went down on his knees to screw in the connection, he saw something underneath the van. A dosser, lying under some sacking, using the parked van as a temporary shelter. Just what he bloody needed!

'Oi you – out!' He hammered on the side of the van to wake the swine up, but was ignored. 'I haven't got all bleeding day. Out!' Still no response. He got down on his knees again and stretched out a hand to give the man a shake. He froze in horror. His outstretched hand was touching icy cold, hard, dead flesh.

'Bloody hell!' He snatched his hand back and wiped it down the front of his coat as he clambered to his feet. He kicked the foot pump under the van in case some bugger nicked it, then hared off to find the nearest phone box to call the police.

The area had already been cordoned off by the time Frost arrived. Arthur Hanlon scuttled across to meet him. 'Another dead tom, Jack. She's under the van.'

Frost rubbed his hands briskly. The biting wind was cutting right through him. 'Do we know her?'

'We can't get to her face until we can move the van.'

'Let's take a peep,' grunted Frost. 'I might recognize the rude bits.'

Watched by Hanlon and Collier he knelt and flashed his torch which picked out a naked arm, part of the torso, the rest covered by a piece of sacking. He straightened up. 'I don't recognize any of the bits I can see. Are we sure she's a tom?'

'I managed to squeeze part the way under,' Collier told him. 'She's naked, and she's been beaten and burnt, just like the others.'

Frost passed his cigarettes around 'This bastard is getting too bloody cocky. He's really taking the piss out of us and he's doing it too bloody often.' He accepted a light from Hanlon. 'This is what – number four or five, I'm losing count – and we're no nearer to catching him than we were with the first. Who found her?'

'The bloke who runs the stall,' said Hanlon. 'Some jokers let his tyres down and he had to go back home to fetch a foot-pump.'

'What time?'

'Just after half-past twelve. He checked the tyres then and she wasn't there.'

'And he got back when?'

'Half-past oneish. She was dumped between those times.'

'We've never been so close to the sod,' said Frost. 'He was here . . . less than an hour ago, he was right here.'

'I reckon he was a regular at the stall,' said Hanlon. 'Came for some grub, saw the place was deserted so decided to use it to dump the body.'

Frost chewed this over and shook his head. 'No, Arthur. If you've got a body on board, you want to get rid of it quickly, you don't stop on the way for a hot dog and chips. Besides, he had to be sure the owner was well away. He didn't want him coming back when the body was still being shoved underneath. I reckon he just happened to be driving past and saw the owner leaving in a minicab, so he grabbed his chance. If I'm right, we can pin him down to a time within minutes. This might be the break we're looking for.' He squinted down the street. Still a couple of houses with lights showing. 'Start knocking on doors. Not much chance there's anyone still up, but find out if anyone spotted a van, a car, a horse and cart, anything, coming down this road just after half-past midnight.' A long shot and he knew it. Cars and vans would be driving up here all the time to visit the stall and people tended to ignore the familiar.

308

He switched his attention back to the body. 'How do we get to her without dragging her out?'

'If we pumped up the tyres, we could move the van,' suggested Hanlon.

'Do it,' nodded Frost, looking up as headlights flooded the scene. He thought, at first, it was the doctor, but it was a minicab driver hoping for some fast food. PC Collier, guarding the cul-de-sac, was turning the driver away. 'Hold it!' yelled Frost, running across. The driver might have called earlier when the van was closed. 'Ask everyone if they were here earlier and if they saw anything suspicious.'

'Like what, Inspector?'

'Anything, son – I don't care how trivial. Even if they only saw someone stuffing a dead body under the van and happened to take down the registration number, it's little things like that that could help.' He turned away, spinning back as something else occurred to him. 'And take names, addresses and registration numbers of everyone you stop. We might want to talk to them again.'

Another car approached, but this time Collier waved it through. Frost grinned as Dr McKenzie, the police surgeon, climbed out. 'Over here, doc. We can do you a hot meat pie or a cold dead body.'

McKenzie waved his bag happily. He was always pleased to see Frost, even at three o'clock on a bitterly cold morning. 'Where is she?'

Frost pointed to the van where a perspiring Arthur Hanlon was working away at the foot-pump. 'Under there, doc. I keep calling, but she won't come out.'

McKenzie bent and squinted underneath the vehicle, aided by the beam of Frost's torch. 'How am I supposed to get under there?'

'Wait in your car, doc. We'll have the van moved soon.'

Leaving the doctor, Frost went over to the van and

climbed inside where Turner, a picture of misery, was drawing on a hand-rolled cigarette, its acrid smoke mixing with a strong smell of rancid fat and cold, fried onions. Turner's arm was resting on a fryer in which a dirty, oily brown substance had congealed. 'A dead body,' he moaned, kicking away a piece of broken cup on the floor. 'Just what I wanted, a bleeding dead body.' He shuddered. 'First some joker lets my tyres down, then a dead bleeding body . . .'

'Not your night, is it?' sympathized Frost, flicking ash on the floor. 'Tell me what happened.'

'I opened up just before ten as usual. All going fine until the pubs turn out, then a crowd of flaming drunks, singing and shouting, start rocking the bloody van. Next thing I know the van lurches over, cups smash and the fat's spilling out of the fryers. They'd let my flaming tyres down. Bastards! If I catch them . . .'

'Do you know who did it?'

'Yes, and if he turns up again he'll have a hot dog stuffed up his fundamental orifice.'

'Don't try and sell it to me afterwards,' said Frost. 'Right, your tyres were let down, then what?'

'A minicab driver turned up for some grub, so I got him to drive me back home so I could fetch a foot-pump.'

'You locked up, of course?'

'Too right I did. They'd pinch anything that isn't nailed down round here. If they'd spotted that body they'd have pinched that as well.' He shuddered again. 'Bleeding body, just under my feet. It's not hygienic.'

'She's dead, she won't notice,' said Frost catching sight of something black floating in the fat. 'That's not a beetle, is it?'

Turner gave a cursory glance, then stirred the oil with a nicotined finger, swirling the mess around. 'Bit of burnt onion.'

'With bleeding legs?' asked Frost. 'You sure she wasn't under the van when you left for the pump?'

'I'm down on my knees, staring at the tyres – I'd have seen her, and the jokers who let down the tyres would have seen her too.'

'The bloke who shoved her under there might have been watching you leave. Did you see a car or anything as you left in the cab?'

Turner shook his head. 'No.'

Frost took details of the minicab driver in case he had seen something. 'As soon as we get your van moved, do us mugs of tea and beefburgers all round.'

'With onions?'

'Yes – and change that flaming oil.'

Hanlon, wiping the sweat from his face, straightened up as the last of the tyres was fully inflated. He disconnected the pump, stepping smartly back as the van was slowly driven forward, watched anxiously by Frost. It cleared the body by a good few inches and canvas screens were quickly erected.

Frost beckoned the doctor over. McKenzie made a brief examination. 'Female aged around thirty-five to forty, dead some twenty-four to thirty-six hours, probably asphyxiated, definitely sexually assaulted – you can see the blood – badly beaten and burnt, but you can see that for yourself.' He straightened up. 'Drysdale will fill in the details.' He scratched his chin and looked down at the body. 'Are you sure she's a tom?'

'The rest were,' said Frost. 'I don't recognize her though.' He stuck his hands in his pockets and took a good look at her. Short, dumpy, with straight black hair. The gag, which was cutting into her mouth, exposed near perfect teeth. He ignored the staring eyes and studied the face. No make-up of any kind. 'If she's a tom,' he decided, 'she's a bloody weird one.'

He stood back as SOCO took photographs, then watched one of the Forensic boys carefully move the sacking which covered most of the body, shuddering at the sight of the weals, burns and cuts. Frost pointed to the large refuse container fixed to the wall which was overflowing with used polystyrene food containers from the van. 'Someone take a look in there. He might have dumped her handbag or clothes.'

He jumped as the serving counter of the van suddenly thudded down with a bang and Turner pushed across a tray filled with mugs of tea. 'Here's your teas, beefburgers coming up.'

Glad of something hot, the team crowded round. Frost took a sip and nodded. 'Not bad.' He smiled at Turner. 'On the house?'

'No, it bleeding well isn't. That will be twenty-six quid.'

'I think I'll take a look at your tax disc,' said Frost.

'On the house,' said Turner quicky. He leant out to survey the canvas screen. 'How did she die?'

'Food poisoning,' said Frost. 'You're our number one suspect.'

'Bleeding funny.' Turner sniffed at something burning. 'The beefburgers are ready.'

Hanlon joined Frost at the counter and gratefully accepted his tea. 'Nothing you would want to know about in the rubbish bin, Inspector, and only two replies from the houses – neither saw anything.'

Turner began passing out the beefburgers which were eagerly grabbed. 'Don't know how you can eat with that dead body there.'

'She's a damn sight more appetizing than your beefburgers,' said Frost. He turned to Hanlon. 'I know it's late, but there might still be a few toms plying their lustful trade. Get some copies of her photo from SOCO and see if any of the girls recognize her.'

Another glare of headlights. Drysdale's black Rolls-Royce purred into the cul-de-sac. McKenzie pushed away his tea. 'Can't stand that toffee-nosed bastard, Jack,' he muttered. 'I'm off.'

As he hurried back to his car, Drysdale got out. The two men bared teeth at each other.

'Burger and tea if you want it, doc,' called Frost.

Drysdale shook his head in curt refusal, then disappeared behind the canvas screens, followed by the inspector. He gave the body a cursory examination, flinching as Frost's teeth noisily sank into the beefburger. 'Must you eat while I'm carrying out an examination?' he snarled.

'Sorry,' said Frost, unabashed. He winked at the blonde secretary. 'Fancy a hot sausage, love?' She blushed, shook her head violently and busied herself with her shorthand notebook ready for the pathologist's findings.

Drysdale was brief. 'Died elsewhere and brought here, so not a lot of point in examining the body *in situ*.' He pulled on his gloves. 'Been dead at least thirty-six hours, suffocated, sexually assaulted, burnt and beaten.' A thin smile. 'A rather familiar pattern, Inspector.'

'Too bleeding familiar,' agreed Frost.

'I'll do the autopsy in the morning, nine o'clock sharp. I'm sure we will find a few things the good Dr McKenzie has missed.'

Frost nodded. 'That flaming place is becoming my second home. I'm thinking of moving my bed there.'

'I wish you would,' sniffed Drysdale, 'then you might turn up on time.' With a curt jerk of his head for the secretary to follow, he marched out to the warmth of his Rolls.

Frost urged him on his way with two fingers behind his back, then waved an arm at Jordan. 'Call the meat wagon, Jordan. They can take her away now.' Then he remembered something else he should have done and stuck his head inside the van. 'Oi, Fanny Craddock,' he called to Turner. 'Here a minute.'

Grabbing the man's arm, he steered him to the canvas shelter. 'You must get lots of toms, coming here for meat pies.' He pulled the sheeting from the face. 'Recognize her?'

Turner's mouth sagged, the spittle-soaked roll-up adhering to his lower lip as he jerked his head away. 'Never seen her before.' He backed away. 'You reckon she's a tom?'

Frost nodded.

'She'd have to fight bloody hard for my tuppence.'

Frost stared back at the body. Short and dumpy, she wasn't much of a looker. But she had to be a tom. All the other victims were toms and she had received the same treatment as them. He went back for one more look. Whatever she was, the poor bitch hadn't deserved this. He covered the face, bumping into the undertaker's men on the way out.

He took one last bite at the burger which was now greasy and cold and tasted of death then hurled it at the rubbish bin, but the wind kicked it to one side and it landed on the pavement. As he passed it, he gave it a savage kick. A quick glance at his watch: twenty past four. Another autopsy in less than six hours. He yawned. Nothing much he could do until then. 'I'm off home for some kip,' he told Hanlon. 'Post-mortem tomorrow at nine. If you turn anything up, give me a ring.'

But the ring that wakened him came from his alarm clock.

Quarter to eight and he felt like death. A twinge from his stomach told him that lousy beefburger was a mistake. He staggered to the bathroom, splashed his

314

face with cold water, decided a shave could wait, dressed, and made his way to the station.

As he paid for his bacon sandwich and mug of tea in the canteen, he spotted Arthur Hanlon at one of the tables and carried his tray over to join him. 'Never like attending post-mortems on an empty stomach,' he told him. 'Always like something hot to bring up.'

With a weak grin Hanlon pushed his unfinished plate away. He looked dead tired. 'No joy last night, Jack. Found a couple of girls still working, but they didn't recognize the photograph.'

'We'll have to try again tonight,' said Frost. The bacon sandwich was stirring last night's beefburger into offensive action, so he dumped it on his plate and pulled out his cigarettes. 'Are we knocking on doors in case anyone saw something?'

'All in hand, Jack,' Hanlon yawned.

'Go and get some kip, Arthur. You're not much use when you're wide awake, but half-asleep you're useless.'

Hanlon smiled, took a last sip at his tea and stood up. 'See you tonight, Jack.'

Frost was stubbing out his cigarette in the bacon sandwich when the tannoy summoned him to the phone. It was Bill Wells. 'Someone in the lobby wants to talk to you about the skeleton, Jack.'

'I've got the post-mortem at nine. Get Morgan to handle it.'

'It's that young bird you fancied with the baby.'

'They can't leave me alone,' sighed Frost. 'Put some bromide in her tea and I'll be right down.'

She hadn't put any make-up on and her hair flowed down her shoulders, making her look about fourteen, and Frost fancied her something rotten. She flashed him a warm smile that made things worse. 'Hope you don't think I'm becoming a nuisance, Inspector?'

'Of course not, love.' He sat opposite her. 'Where's the kiddy?'

'My sister's looking after him. I don't know if this would help.' She opened a small red and green plastic handbag and pulled out a dog-eared black and white photograph. 'I found this amongst my mother's things.' She passed it over to Frost.

The photograph showed two girls in their twenties, both wearing bathing costumes. One of the girls, dark-haired, bearing a strong resemblance to the woman facing Frost, had her arm linked round a ravishing long-legged blonde whose two-piece skimpy bathing costume was a mite too tight for Frost's comfort. A really sexy cow if ever he saw one. They were both grinning excitedly at the camera.

'That's my mum.' She pointed to the dark-haired girl. 'Taken a long time ago, of course. The other one is Nell Aldridge, the one I was telling you about. My dad took the photo – I think he fancied Nell.'

'I fancy your mum,' lied Frost, still staring at the blonde who simply oozed sex.

'Just behind them,' continued the girl, pointing to the fence they were leaning against, 'you can see her garden. That's where she used to sunbathe topless.'

'Disgusting,' said Frost, mentally stripping away the top of the swimsuit. 'Can I keep this?'

She nodded. 'I'd like it back, though.'

'If you find any more,' he told her, 'bring them in. I don't care how rude they are, I'll steel myself to look at them.'

He showed her out and watched for some time as her waggling bottom made its way across the road. 'She couldn't keep her hands off me,' he told Bill Wells as he cut through the lobby to his office. 'I had to give her a quick one to calm her down.'

A note in his in-tray from Mullett reminded him, with heavy underlining, that the promised progress report was very much overdue. He found the photograph more interesting than the memo. That blonde would have had more trouble beating off men than the poor cow whose post-mortem he was about to attend. He slipped the print in the file, then pulled it out again. Something he'd vaguely noticed. In the background, behind the two women, could be seen the spire of a church. It had to be St Aidan's, it was the only one in the neighbourhood . . . He rummaged in his drawer and found a street map. Yes – he was right. The fence the two girls were leaning against would have to be at the rear of the mother's house, not to one side. Nelly didn't live in Nelson Road, but in the road running parallel to it.

As he was unsuccessfully trying to refold the map, Morgan bounced in, all bright and breezy, a folded *Daily Mirror* poking from the pocket of his tweed overcoat. 'Sorry I'm late, guv . . . the damn car wouldn't start.'

Frost cut him short. 'I use that excuse myself, Taffy, so I know it's a bleeding lie.' He picked up the photograph. 'What do you want first – the good news or the bad news?'

'The good news, please, guv.'

Frost handed him the photograph. 'If you had your choice, which of these two would you pick?'

Morgan moved over to the window so he could study it better. 'No contest, guv – the blonde. I wouldn't say no to the other one, but just look at the blonde, those legs . . . that flat belly!'

'Did you notice,' said Frost, 'how tight her swimsuit is? How her lusty young nipples, full and firm like ripe wild cherries, are trying to fight their way through the thin fabric of her bra, how they are aching for the soothing, but rough rasp of a gentleman's thumb?'

'Pack it in, guv,' croaked Morgan. 'You know how responsive I am to that sort of talk. Who is she?'

317

'She's your next job, Taff. I want you to find her.'

A broad grin. 'You're on, guv!'

'Now for the bad news,' said Frost. 'That photograph was taken some fifty years ago. If she's not dead and buried, she will now be wrinkled, hairy in all the wrong places and stinking erotically of thermal knickers and wintergreen.'

Morgan's face fell. 'Oh!'

'You've been checking the wrong street, Taff. Old mother Aldridge's house was in the next street.'

'There's no next street, guv – just a through road and an estate.'

'That estate's only been up thirty years, they must have demolished the old street to erect it. There's some ancient street maps in the basement store room, go and dig them out.'

'Can it wait until I've had some breakfast?' pleaded Morgan.

'No, it can't. We've already waited fifty years. And hurry – I've got a date with a naked woman.' As the constable's eyes lit up, he added, 'She's dead and on a mortuary slab – so chop, chop.'

He was putting on his mac, ready to go, when Morgan returned smothered in cobwebs and dust from the basement store room and holding a yellowing map, its folds reinforced with brown sticky tape. 'Give it here, son.' Frost spread it out over his desk top. 'Where's Nelson Street . . . ah, yes. And look, there was a street running parallel . . . Beresford Street – that's where the girl with the wild cherry nipples lived. Back to the town hall, son.' He checked his watch. Ten minutes to nine. He was going to be late for the post-mortem.

Frost dragged the green gown over his mac and scarf. It was like the North flaming Pole in the autopsy room and he had to keep warm somehow. Drysdale,

318

hovering over the body, scalpel poised, stared pointedly at the clock on the wall. 'I've been waiting for you Inspector.'

'Sorry,' muttered Frost, 'damn car wouldn't start.' The body on the slab looked even less appealing than the night before, the bruises, weals and burns standing out in stark relief against the pallor of the white flesh.

'I take it we still don't have a name?' Drysdale asked.

Frost shook his head.

A deep dramatic sigh as if this was only to be expected with someone like Frost. 'Right, let's see if we can uncover any points that the good Dr McKenzie overlooked.' He turned to his secretary. 'Autopsy on an unknown woman aged between thirty-six and forty-two years.' The blonde's pen flew across the page of her shorthand notebook. Drysdale didn't believe in tape recorders ever since one let him down and details of a lengthy autopsy were lost.

As the pathologist droned away with initial findings that the inspector thought almost too obvious to mention, Frost's mind drifted on to other things, although his autopilot was ready to switch him back to full alert should anything of interest come up. He was suddenly switched back. Everyone was looking at him as if expecting an answer.

'Sorry, doc, what was that?'

'I asked if Dr McKenzie told you that this woman was a virgin before she was assaulted?'

Frost gaped. 'A virgin?'

'No doubt about it. You had her down as a prostitute?'

Frost just stared, open-mouthed. 'Bloody hell, doc. I didn't think there were any virgins left in Denton – present company excepted, of course.' He winked at the blonde secretary who was blushing fiercely. 'Are you sure, doc?'

319

'I am. Perhaps you'd like to call in Dr McKenzie for a second opinion?'

Frost shook his head, his mind in a whirl. They had put the killer down as a kerb-crawler, picking up toms. This required a radical rethink. No wonder she didn't look like a prostitute. Poor cow, what a lousy bleeding way to have your first sexual experience.

'Violent penetration, bruising, bleeding, but no trace of semen,' continued Drysdale.

Frost's gloom suddenly lifted. This was the odd one out, the victim that could lead them to the serial killer. The important thing now was to find out who she was. A dig in the back made him turn and there was Morgan, grinning all over his face.

'I've come straight from the town hall, guv . . . I've found that address.' He tailed off as he spotted the blonde secretary and flicked her a wink. She reddened once more and pretended not to notice. 'I couldn't half give her one, guv.'

'What for? She's got thousands pickled in jars. What have you found out?'

'Not a lot. She used to live at 44 Beresford Street. That almost backs on to the house where we found the skeleton.'

'So where does she live now?'

'Can't tell, guv, vanished without a trace. She could be dead.'

'Then check with the Registrar of Births and Deaths, and you can check if she ever registered the death of her son.'

'Do you mind not holding private conversations while I'm performing an autopsy?' said Drysdale peevishly.

'Sorry, doc.' Back to Morgan. 'On your way, son.'

But Morgan was staring at the body on the slab. 'Is that your unknown victim, guv?'

'Yes.'

320

Morgan stared again. 'I know her, guv. I'm sure I know her.'

'You can't know her,' said Frost impatiently. 'She's a virgin.'

'I've seen her, guv, and recently.' Morgan scratched his head in thought.

'I've asked you for silence,' snapped Drysdale.

'Sorry, doc,' said Frost. 'My colleague here thinks he can identify the body.'

Morgan moved forward for a closer look. He peered at the face. 'She's the spitting image of the receptionist from the dentist's when I went for the abscess injection.'

Frost frowned. This didn't seem likely. 'Are you sure?'

'It could be her, but she was wearing glasses.'

'Glasses?' Drysdale bent closer to look at the nose. 'She did wear glasses – there's an indentation across the bridge.'

'All right,' said Frost, still not impressed. 'Phone the dentist and ask if their receptionist is alive or dead on an autopsy table, and let me know either way.'

'Will do, guv,' said Morgan, giving the blonde another broad wink before trotting away.

'A dental receptionist?' mused Drysdale, picking up a scalpel.

'Don't get too excited, doc,' Frost told him. 'He's not as reliable as I am.'

'I wouldn't have thought that possible,' said Drysdale as he drew a red line with the scalpel across the stomach.

They both looked up as the swing doors crashed open and Morgan bounded back in, clasping his hands over his head sounding the 'Ta-ra' of a fanfare.

'No luck?' asked Frost.

Morgan smirked. 'She hasn't been in to work since Friday. They've phoned her flat but got no reply.'

'And no-one's been round to see what's up, or has reported her missing?'

'She had a row with her boss, so they assumed she'd walked out on the job.'

'All right,' said Frost. 'Then let's pay her a visit. If she opens the door, you can think of an excuse.'

15

The name on the neatly typed card pinned to the front door of the flat read 'Helen Stokes'. On the step were three bottles of semi-skimmed milk. 'You could be right, Taffy,' said Frost grimly as he hammered on the door with the flat of his hand, knowing that no-one was going to answer.

The door to the flat opposite opened and a bird-like old dear stuck her head out. 'I think she must be away. I haven't seen her for the past few days. Can I help?'

'Gas Board,' said Frost. 'Report of a smell of gas.' He sniffed. 'Cor, it's strong! Better keep your door shut, love.' The door slammed shut.

None of Frost's skeleton keys worked, so he stood back as Morgan kicked the door in. They stepped inside, Frost stooping to pick up the two letters on the door mat: a credit card statement and an envelope without a stamp. The flap wasn't stuck down so he thumbed it open and peeped inside. A scribbled note from the Ashby Dental Practice saying: 'Concerned you did not come to work today. Please phone.' He couldn't read the signature.

A tiny flat. The curtains were tightly drawn. Morgan pulled them open, letting in the morning sun. The same cold, chilling atmosphere that Frost had felt so many times before, almost as if the place knew that its occupant was dead. A quick nose around . . . kitchen, bathroom, tiny lounge and bedroom. The place had a clinical feel as if its owner had left no mark behind. Frost flopped down on the settee and lit up, treating the dark grey carpeting to the first shower of ash in its life.

'Look around, son. See if you can find a photograph.' He should have brought a Polaroid of the woman in the mortuary to show the old dear in the flat opposite, but hadn't thought of it. He soon got fed up watching Morgan grubbing through drawers and cupboards, so pushed himself up and wandered around aimlessly, not really knowing what he was looking for.

A thick winter coat was hanging in the hall. He went through the pockets. A petrol receipt, but nothing else. The front door had been fitted with a strong security chain and there were smoke alarms on the walls of every room. A cautious woman.

He wandered back into the lounge where Morgan, on his knees, was going through the contents of a drawer he had tipped out on to the carpet. 'It doesn't look as if she ever had her photo taken, guv.'

'It's the pretty ones who have lots of photos,' said Frost as he walked into the cell-like bedroom, its single bed made with almost military precision, a thick sensible winceyette nightdress neatly folded on the pillow. He sat on the bed, probably the first man ever to do so, and pulled open the drawer of the dark oak bedside cabinet. Handkerchiefs, spare glasses, and right at the bottom a photograph, the smiling face of a dark moustached man in his mid-thirties. There was something reddish across the surface. He lifted it to his nose and sniffed. Lipstick.

'Guv!' Morgan charged into the bedroom waving a passport. 'I've found it. The only photograph in the place.'

Frost flipped it open. The unsmiling face of the dead woman stared back at him to confirm what they already knew. 'Not the only photograph, son,' said Frost, showing Morgan the portrait from the drawer. 'She must have had the hots for him. It's smothered in lipstick.'

Morgan took the photo from Frost. 'I know who this is, guv.'

'Flaming heck,' said Frost. 'Don't start being useful for a change. So who is he?'

'He's the bloke she works for . . . Ashby the dentist. He pulled my tooth out.'

'Are you sure?'

'Positive, guv.'

'Then let's go and talk to him.'

He radioed through to the station asking them to send someone over to make the flat secure. 'Some silly sod's kicked the door in,' he told them.

The old dear opposite was hovering as they left. 'We've fixed the gas leak,' Frost assured her.

'I've just remembered,' she said. 'We're all electric.'

He pretended not to hear.

The dentist had a new receptionist, a cheery little redhead with bouncing breasts and perfect white teeth. She giggled nervously at the sight of Frost's warrant card. 'Mr Ashby's with a patient right now.' She nodded towards the surgery door from which the whine of a dental drill set everyone's teeth on edge. Frost winced in sympathy with the patient inside and ran his tongue round his own teeth. 'If you'll take a seat,' she continued, 'I'll let him know as soon as he's finished.'

They sat in the waiting area next to a stout woman and a man with a swollen jaw.

'I hate dentists,' muttered Frost. 'They give me the creeps.'

But Morgan had eyes only for the redhead. 'Did you see the size of her bristols, guv?' he whispered, but not quietly enough. The stout woman glared, and moved to another seat.

'I bet she thought you were talking about her,' said Frost, leaping to his feet as the surgery door opened and the previous patient, a pale-faced man, came unsteadily out. 'Won't keep you long,' he called to the woman who was indignantly muttering about people jumping the queue.

Ashby, the dentist, a little older and plumper than the photograph, was drying his hands on a towel while his dental nurse, a young, long-legged blonde, was disinfecting some shiny instruments before laying them out alongside the chair. The dentist's welcoming smile faded. These were not the patient he had been expecting.

'Police,' Frost informed him, flashing his warrant card.

The colour drained from Ashby's face. 'Police? What's happened?'

'Give us a moment, please,' Frost asked the nurse, waiting until she had left. 'It's about your receptionist, sir, Miss Stokes.'

'Helen? What about her?'

'Sad news, I'm afraid. Miss Stokes was found dead last night.'

Ashby stared at Frost, unable to take it in. 'Dead? An accident?'

'No, sir. We believe she was murdered.'

'Murdered? Helen? Oh my God, no.'

'I'm afraid so, sir. When did you see her last?'

'Eight o'clock Friday night. We are only open for emergencies weekends, so she wasn't due back until Monday, but she didn't turn up.'

'Didn't that surprise you?'

'Up to a point. We had a minor argument on

326

Friday. She left in a huff. I thought she had decided she didn't want to work here any more.'

'What was the argument about?'

Ashby shrugged. 'It was all so trivial. I don't know why she got so upset. I wanted my new receptionist to do the weekend duty instead of her. Helen had done it for years with my predecessor and thought it was her right.'

'When she didn't come in to work, didn't you check to see if she was all right?'

'Of course I did. We kept phoning the flat and got no reply. I popped round myself and put a note through the letter box.' His eyes widened. 'God, are you saying she was lying there dead, all the time?'

'Not in the flat, sir, no.' Frost didn't elaborate. 'We don't think she went back to her flat Friday night. Any idea where she might have gone?'

'Friday was her night for the Samaritans. She did voluntary work manning the phones.'

'Thank you, sir. I'll probably need to talk to you again.' Leaving the stunned dentist, they went back to the car.

'Did you get an eyeful of that dental nurse, guv?' asked Morgan as Frost slid into the passenger seat.

'Yes,' grunted Frost. 'Our dentist sure likes to have big tits around him. Poor flat-chested Helen must have stuck out like a sore thumb. Back to the station, son . . .'

Frost pinned up the photograph of dead Helen Stokes alongside the line of murdered prostitutes on the board in the murder incident room, then took his usual seat on the corner of the desk. 'Spot the odd one out. We've assumed our killer only went for toms, but this one wasn't a tom. In fact she was almost too good to be true. No vices, no boyfriends, went to church on Sundays, got out of the bath to do a wee and manned the phones at the Samaritans. But she was tortured and killed like the others, so why did he pick on her?'

'One consistent thing about our killer,' said Arthur Hanlon. 'He picks his victims up late at night, very late. All the dead toms were seen working while others had jagged it in.'

'Go on,' said Frost.

'What I'm saying is that our killer goes out late, looking for women on their own. Now usually that means a tom. Did Helen Stokes go out late at night?'

'I shouldn't think so,' said Frost. 'She looks the sort who would be tucked up in bed with a cup of cocoa at half-past nine.' He snapped his fingers. 'Wait a minute. The Samaritans! They operate twenty-four hours a day. Give them a ring, Arthur, find out what time she left them Friday night.'

His cigarettes went the rounds as he waited for Hanlon to make the call. 'Well?'

'She usually only stayed a couple of hours, but they were busy Friday with two of their helpers off sick. Just as she was leaving some nutter phoned threatening to do himself in and she was talking to him until well past midnight.'

Frost heaved himself off the desk. 'That's late enough for me! Let's talk to the Samaritans.'

The Samaritans were housed in two rooms over an empty shop that had once sold groceries before the big supermarkets opened up in the town. Its small team of men and women were devastated to learn about Helen Stokes. At a corner desk a plumpish lady was sobbing uncontrollably, comforted by one of the male helpers. Only Mervyn Adams, the leader of the team, a twitching, worried-looking man in a grey cardigan, looking as if he could do with some counselling himself, was of any help to Frost, being the only person in the room who was actually on duty the night Helen

328

was killed. He kept jerking his head nervously every time a phone rang, not relaxing until one of his team took the call. He removed his glasses and dabbed his eyes. 'Such a loving person. I just can't believe it.' He shook his head sadly. 'Who could have done such a thing?'

Frost nodded sympathetically. 'That's what we're trying to find out, Mr Adams. What time did she leave here on Friday?'

'Gone one o'clock, so it was Saturday morning, actually. We were short-staffed and very busy, phones ringing constantly, so she stayed on to help us out. She was all ready to go home when she got this long, distressing call. You can't cut people short, so it was quarter past one or thereabouts, before she was able to leave.'

'What was the call about?' asked Frost.

Adams was about to leap forward to answer a phone that had been ringing for some time when the wet-eyed, plump lady beat him to it. He smiled his thanks and turned back to Frost. 'Everything we are told here is strictly confidential.'

'I'm not asking for names at this stage, Mr Adams. I'm trying to find out who murdered this sweet, loving woman you seem so concerned about.' He retrieved the photograph from his mac pocket. 'Would you like to see what the bastard did to her?'

Adams turned his head away quickly. 'No thank you, Inspector. We see too much of the nasty side of life in here.'

'You and me both,' said Frost, stuffing the photo-graph back. 'So what was the call about?'

'A man in the depths of despair. He'd lost his job, the mortgage company wanted to reclaim his house and his wife had walked out on him. He was near suicidal.'

'I'd be near suicidal if I had to listen to that sort of

thing all the time,' sympathized Frost. 'I suppose you don't get many laughs?'

'No,' agreed Adams sadly, 'not many laughs, but sometimes, when we have been able to help some poor devil, it all seems worthwhile.'

'My job will seem worthwhile if we can catch this bastard,' said Frost. 'Did she talk him out of suicide?'

'I don't know. He suddenly hung up.'

'And then what?'

'She collected next week's duty roster, put on her coat and was ready to leave when her phone rang again. She answered it. At first she seemed frightened, then annoyed. She hung up abruptly – unusual for her – and left.'

'And what was that call about?'

'I don't know. I was meaning to ask when she came in again, but . . .'

'Could it have been a personal call?'

'I shouldn't think so. Helen didn't seem to get personal calls. Probably some crank.'

'Do you get many cranks?'

Adams gave a sad smile and nodded. 'We get more than our fair share. They are quite shocking to listen to at times, describing in graphic detail some obscene practice or some terrible crime they claim to have committed. Sick people who get their kicks from upsetting others.'

Frost stiffened. 'You get people confessing to crimes?'

'Yes. Mostly imaginary, of course.'

Frost's mind raced. What if the serial killer had phoned to boast about what he had done to those toms? What if he suddenly realized he had given too much away, something that could identify him? That would have made the person who took the call a potential danger. 'If you think people are confessing to a genuine crime, do you notify the police?'

'We have a strict code of confidentiality, Inspector. If it were learnt that someone had been arrested as a result of a call to the Samaritans—'

'But what if the call was from someone who had killed before and would kill again?'

Adams hesitated. 'I don't know. Fortunately the circumstance you describe has not yet arisen. If I was sure the call was genuine and the danger was real, then I might make an anonymous phone call to the police, but I just don't know.'

'Do you ever meet any of the people who phone you?'

'No.'

Frost worried away at his scar. 'Supposing, just supposing, that last call Helen took was from someone confessing to a crime. She urges him to give himself up. The caller says, "I'm outside, come and talk to me." Would she have gone?'

'At one o'clock in the morning, you do not meet complete strangers outside without telling someone. Helen was a very cautious lady. She would never have taken the risk.'

Frost scrubbed his face with his hands. He wasn't getting anywhere, but felt he was close, very close, to something. 'Thanks for your help, Mr Adams. I might want to talk to you again.'

As he made his way to the door, the plump lady beckoned him over. Her eyes were still puffy and red. 'I'm sorry I made a fool of myself, Inspector.'

'That's all right, love.'

'It was just the shock. I saw Helen's car outside and thought she was here, and when they told me—'

Frost stopped in his tracks. 'You mean her car is still here?'

'Yes, it's parked in the street outside.'

'Show me,' said Frost.

*   *   *

331

It was tucked away in the back street by a lamp post, a light grey six-year-old Mini. The doors when Frost tried them were locked. He bent to look inside. Absolutely clean, ashtrays empty and gleaming, only the driver's seat showed signs of wear, the rest almost as good as new. A lonely woman who probably had few passengers. He straightened up. 'She always came here by car?'

'When she was on nights, she did. There's no public transport in the early hours.'

'Thanks. You've been a great help.' He turned his attention back to the Mini. No buses, so why didn't she use the car? Was she waylaid before she could get to it? If so, she couldn't have been a random victim of the serial killer. This area was all one-way streets and cul-de-sacs. You would have to come here deliberately. He looked around. An area mainly of shops, not many with living accommodation above, so there would be few people about to see or hear anything at that hour of the morning. But just in case, he radioed Bill Wells for men to go house-to-house in the immediate area. He also arranged for the Mini to be towed back to the station for Forensic to find their usual sod all, and waited in his car to keep an eye on it until the tow truck arrived. Just his luck for some joy-rider to pinch it before they could examine it.

He sucked smoke, half listening to the dribble of messages over the radio as he turned over events in his mind. His theory that the killer had phoned Helen and given too much away was getting stronger and stronger. But how did he pick her up? The toms would willingly climb in a strange car, but nervous, cautious Helen Stokes, at 1.30 in the morning? She would have to be forcibly dragged with a knife to the throat. Make a sound and you're dead. But wait a minute. If the killer had only heard her voice over the phone, how could he recognize her when she came out?

The tow truck pulled up and he watched them remove the Mini. If she was recognized, the killer must have known her, perhaps from where she worked? He hadn't asked the dentist to account for his movements the night his receptionist was killed. Sod it! Why did he always forget the important things? He reversed out of the street and back to the dental surgery.

The surgery didn't seem to be open. The brass plate by the entrance confirmed it was closed for lunch between 1.00 and 2.30 p.m. He checked his watch. 1.45. Damn! He gave a half-hearted push and, to his delight, the entrance door swung back. The reception area was empty. From force of habit he went to the desk and had a nose through the papers. All boring dental stuff, letters, appointments, forms, but what the hell did he expect to find – a signed confession?

He was about to leave when he heard a sound, a faint sound, someone moaning. A woman, and it wasn't a moan of pain. The sound came from behind the closed doors of the surgery.

Tiptoeing over, he gently turned the door handle and peeped inside. The dental chair was in a reclining position, above it, a pair of pink buttocks pumped up and down and the long legs of the red-headed receptionist, whose bust Morgan had so recently admired, were wrapped tightly round a bare back.

He watched for a while, then cleared his throat. 'Sorry to interrupt your lunch, but could I have a word?'

A gasp, a squeal and the buttocks quivered to an abrupt halt.

'Who the hell is that?' The dentist was in no position to turn round and see.

Frost retreated to the reception area and waited. From the surgery came the sound of angry recriminations. 'I thought I told you to lock the door.' 'I thought I had locked it.' 'Well, you bloody well didn't, did you?'

After a few minutes a red-faced dentist emerged shrugging on a white dental gown, followed by an even redder-faced receptionist who, eyes averted, clattered past Frost to the ladies' toilet. 'I must apologize, Inspector,' began Ashby. 'Most embarrassing . . .'

'Never saw a thing,' lied Frost. 'A couple of questions I should have asked earlier. Where were you Friday night from the time Miss Stokes left the surgery?'

'I locked up and went straight home. I was dead tired. Then a meal, some television, and early bed.'

'Could this be confirmed, sir? Just routine, of course.'

'My wife will confirm it.'

Frost couldn't be sure, but he thought the dentist was looking a little uneasy. 'And where were you last night, from around midnight onwards?'

The dentist frowned. 'Last night?'

'That was when the body was dumped. As I say, just routine.'

'We had some friends in for dinner. They stayed quite late.'

'How late, sir?'

'It was gone midnight by the time they left. I then went to bed.'

'Your friends' names sir?' Frost scribbled details on the back of his cigarette packet. If the alibis checked he could wipe the dentist off his list of suspects. His list! That was a joke. The dentist was the only name on it. Please, he silently pleaded, please don't let his alibi check out otherwise I'm right up the creek. 'That's all for the moment, sir,' he nodded. 'I'll leave you to enjoy what's left of your lunch before it gets too cold.'

'Having it away in the dentist's chair?' croaked Morgan, spooning up his soup. 'Flaming heck!' They were in the canteen for a late lunch.

'He not only does extractions, he does insertions as well,' said Frost.

'I've done it in some strange places,' said Morgan in wonderment, 'but never in a dentist's chair.' He wrinkled his nose. 'A bit off-putting though, guv. All those pliers and drills and the spit suction machine gurgling away. Not very romantic.'

'Those spit pumps frighten the life out of me,' said Frost with a shudder. 'I'm terrified they're suddenly going to go in reverse and pump the last hundred patients' spit back into me.' He took another bite at his ham sandwich. 'Which reminds me, did I ever tell you the joke about the bloke who drunk the spittoon for a bet?'

Morgan's face went the colour of the spoonful of pea soup he was about to sip. He pushed the plate hurriedly away. 'Yes, you did, guv.' He had been warned to tell Frost he had heard it if ever he was asked, but curiosity had got the better of him and both he, and his stomach, had regretted it ever since.

'Right,' said Frost, disappointed. 'Go and see the dentist's wife and his friends, check his alibis, and run his name through the computer in case he's got form for murdering his receptionists.' As he washed down the ham sandwich with tea, the tannoy called him to the phone. The Scenes of Crime Officer, Ron Rawlings, was anxious to show Frost what he had learnt from Helen Stokes's car. Frost beckoned for Arthur Hanlon to join him and they both went downstairs to the car-park.

* * *

The grey Mini, doors wide open, was in the covered area to the side of the station car-park. Rawlings, beaming all over his face, came forward to greet them. 'Found a few things that might interest you, Inspector.'

'Dirty postcards?' asked Frost hopefully.

Rawlings grinned. 'Not as interesting as that. We checked it for prints. She must have cleaned and polished it every day. The only dabs on it were hers.'

Frost yawned. 'I hope it gets better?'

With a 'wait and see' smile, Rawlings continued. 'The car was locked and the alarm was set.'

'Wow!' said Frost. 'You'd have thought she would have left the doors open and the engine running in case anyone wanted to pinch it.'

Rawlings gave a patronizing smirk as he produced his trump card. 'We found this in the dash compartment.' He handed Frost a sheet of duplicated typescript which he had enclosed in a polythene cover. It was Helen Stokes's next week's duty rota for the Samaritans. Frost stared at it. 'This was locked inside the car?' he asked incredulously.

Rawlings nodded.

'But she wasn't given this until just before she left the place Friday night.'

'Precisely,' said Rawlings.

Arthur Hanlon, looking from one to the other, was puzzled. 'I don't see the significance, Jack.'

'We've been assuming she was waylaid before she reached her car, Arthur,' explained Frost. 'But we were wrong. She goes to her car, unlocks it, puts the rota inside, then locks it and sets the alarm. So why the hell didn't she just get in and drive off?' He noticed that Rawlings was grinning all over his face. 'You've got something up your sleeve, you smug bastard, haven't you?'

Still grinning, Rawlings nodded. 'I checked the

engine, inspector. The fan belt had snapped. The battery was as flat as arse-holes.'

'And you can't get much flatter than that,' said Frost. He shivered. It was cold out in the open and he only had his jacket on. He thrust his hands deep into his trouser pockets and walked round the car, kicking the tyres from time to time for inspiration. 'Half-past one in the morning. Freezing cold, the bloody car won't start, no buses. So what do you do?'

'You go back to the Samaritans to see if anyone knows anything about cars and can fix it, or can give you a lift back home?' offered Hanlon.

'That's what I would have done, Arthur, but she never reached there. So either some bastard forces her into his car, or she gets in willingly. You'd have to know someone bloody well to accept a lift from them at half-past one in the morning, especially if you were a nervous cow like poor Helen Stokes. So let's say she was forced into her killer's car. Why her? What was he doing there at that godforsaken hour? Those roads lead nowhere, so he'd have to be lurking for a specific purpose. Was he waiting for anyone, or just for her?'

'If he was waiting for her,' asked Hanlon, 'why did he let her get to her car in the first place? How was he to know her battery would be flat?'

'Don't start getting logical with me, Arthur,' snapped Frost. 'You're sodding up my theories.' He scratched his chin thoughtfully. 'We're back to our dentist. He phones the Samaritans boasting about how he killed those toms . . . Helen Stokes takes the call and he is terrified she could have recognized his voice, so drives round pronto and waits for her to come out.'

'Possible,' said Hanlon doubtfully.

'Come up with something better, Arthur, and I'll give you a jelly baby.' Back to Rawlings. 'Anything else you haven't told us about, like a set of false choppers that could have fallen from the dentist's pocket?'

'That's the lot,' Rawlings told him.

'You're bleeding useless,' said Frost. He jerked his head to Hanlon. 'Come on, Arthur, back to the office. Let's see what Morgan's found out about our prime suspect's alibi.'

They didn't have to wait long. 'Wow,' exclaimed Morgan, bounding in and warming his hands on the radiator. 'You should see his wife, a real cracker – boobs like melons . . .'

'I hope she didn't waggle it under your nose,' said Frost.

'No such luck, guv.' Morgan sat himself at his desk and went into a reverie of recollection.

'Well, now we know about his wife's bra size, perhaps you'd tell us if she confirms his alibi – assuming you tore your eyes away from her dugs long enough to ask?'

Morgan leant back in his chair. 'I think you're going to like this, guv. He never went out Friday night – they watched telly and went up to bed. Last night they had friends round, like he said, and they stayed until gone midnight, then up to bed.'

'I'm not liking it much up to now,' said Frost.

Morgan wagged a finger. 'Because I haven't told you the good bit. Some nights he can't get off to sleep, so he gets out of bed and goes out for a drive to make himself tired.'

'If his wife's the cracker you say, surely there were other ways of making him tired?'

'I think he does that as well, guv. But the point is, he got up and went out on both those nights.'

'How long for?'

'That we don't know. She always drifts off to sleep,

338

but he was there by her side when she woke up in the morning.'

'He wasn't covered in blood by any chance?'

Morgan grinned. 'Didn't ask her, guv, but I'm sure she would have mentioned it if he was.'

'We've getting somewhere,' said Frost happily. 'At last we're bloody getting somewhere.'

'There's even more good news, guv,' said Morgan, holding up a computer print-out. 'You asked me to check to see if he had form. He's never been charged, but he's received two cautions for kerb-crawling.'

With a yell of triumph Frost leapt up and punched the air. He jabbed a finger at Hanlon. 'What did I tell you, Arthur? We've got the bastard!'

'Shall I bring him in, guv?' asked Morgan eagerly.

'Not yet,' said Frost. 'We've got suspicion, opportunity and a possible motive, but no solid proof. If he picks up these toms, where does he take them? He can't take them back home. His busty wife is sure to wonder why there's another woman tied up in the bed. He must have another place somewhere, somewhere remote where nosy neighbours wouldn't see or hear anything suspicious.' He spun round to Hanlon. 'Arthur, check on all local estate agents, find out if he's bought or rented anywhere near here.'

'Supposing he used a false name?' queried Morgan.

'No, son. Respectable estate agents always want references, a bank or something, and they'd want an address to write to. If letters with a false name dropped through his letter box, his busty wife would start getting suspicious, tongues would wag and dugs would quiver.' He dragged an empty cigarette packet from his pocket and shook it pointedly. 'Ah, thanks, son.' He took one from Morgan. 'Next, I want a twenty-four-hour surveillance put on him, at least a double team. He mustn't be out of our sight for a single second.'

'That means more overtime,' said Hanlon. 'Mr Mullett won't like that.'

'Mr Mullett will have to bloody well lump it,' said Frost.

'More overtime?' Mullett shook his head firmly. 'I'm sorry, Frost, it just isn't on. We're way over budget now.' He held up the sheet of figures, then saw that Frost was not paying attention and was trying to read upside down the confidential memo from County in the in-tray. Mullett tugged the in-tray towards him and pushed it to the rear of the desk.

'Sorry, Super – I was miles away.' Frost blinked at the overtime figures Mullett was dangling and puffed out a stream of smoke to obscure them. 'If we're already over budget, a few quid more won't hurt.' His brain was whirling. He hadn't been able to read all the memo, but it was saying that, in answer to Mullett's request, County would be sending Chief Superintendent Bailey to Denton. What was that fat sod coming here for?

He switched his ears back to Mullett, who was droning away about everything having to be paid for and money not growing on trees. 'You're not even sure he's the killer, are you?'

'He's our number one, prime suspect,' said Frost firmly. He was their only bloody suspect, of course.

Mullett drummed the mahogany desk top with his pencil. He hated being pushed into making these sort of decisions. 'Surely there's another way not involving overtime?'

'Sure,' said Frost. 'We could wait until he murders a few more, hope someone spots him doing it, then, if the budget allows, we could send someone down to arrest him.'

Mullett was impervious to Frost's sarcasm. He shook his head and again looked at the list Frost had

340

handed him. 'Do we need all these men? Why a twenty-four-hour surveillance? All the murders so far have taken place at night.'

'He picks up his victims at night and dumps their bodies at night, but he holds them somewhere during the day. I want to find out where he takes them.'

'All right. So you follow him and you see him picking up a prostitute. Then what? Do you arrest him?'

'For what – kerb-crawling? We'd have to follow him and see where he takes her.'

The pencil drummed some more. 'No, Frost, I don't like it. Supposing you lose him and he kills the woman anyway? If it came out that we suspected him, watched him collect his victim, but did nothing to stop it, I shudder to think what County would say . . .' And just the thought of County's reaction made him visibly shudder. Mullett waved the overtime figures at Frost again. 'All of your investigations seem to require an inordinate amount of overtime and I'm not prepared to sanction any more.'

'Without twenty-four-hour surveillance, you can start clocking up more killings,' said Frost grimly. 'He's got the taste for it and he's not going to stop just because you won't sanction the overtime.' Seeing Mullett wasn't swayed by this argument, he played his trump card. 'I shudder to think what County would say if he killed again because you turned down my request.' Frost offered a silent prayer that this would do the trick as he had already sanctioned the overtime himself and would be in dead trouble without Mullett's authorization.

But the suggestion of County's disapproval tipped the scales. Mullett gave a grudging nod. 'All right, Frost, against my better judgement, but you are going to have to scale down the number of men involved. You can't have twelve; six at the very most.'

341

'Six?' shrilled Frost. 'That's bloody useless. To make sure we don't lose him we need two cars, two men in each. With eight-hour shifts that's twelve, minimum.'

'I don't care what your figures say, we haven't got the man power to spare. Apart from DC Burton, we won't be getting anyone back from County now until Monday. They're needed for the drugs operation.'

'And what about our bloody operation?'

Mullett winced. 'Please don't swear at me, Frost. Six men, maximum, and for four days only, not a second longer.'

Frost stared in disbelief. 'Supposing the silly sod doesn't co-operate? What if he decides to wait until the fifth day before killing another tom?'

'Then it will no longer be your responsibility, Frost, because you will be off the case.'

Frost gaped at him. 'I beg your pardon?'

Mullett twiddled with his pencil. 'County are very unhappy at the way you have conducted your investigations. Too much money expended without any sign of a result, and the suicide in the cell didn't help. Next week Chief Superintendent Bailey is coming down from County and will be taking over the investigation.'

Frost's eyes hardened. 'And you let them do it?'

Mullett clasped his hands together in mock sincerity. 'Believe me, Frost, even though you didn't give me any ammunition, I fought your corner . . .'

Frost stared at Mullett, not bothering to disguise his contempt.

The superintendent flushed and found the wording on his pencil of consuming interest. 'I fought your corner, Frost,' he repeated, 'but I was overruled.'

Fought my corner? thought Frost. The lying four-eyed bastard. That confidential memo he had been trying to read started: 'In accordance with your request . . .' Mullett had asked for him to be replaced and hadn't the guts to admit it. All right. He'd show the sod. Six men . . . four days. He'd get it all tied up before fat-guts Bailey could push his stomach through the door.

The curtest of nods to Mullett as he left. Outside in the corridor the doubts crept in. Face facts, he told himself. Mullett was right. What had he achieved? Sod all! He wasn't getting anywhere on any of his bloody cases. He was out of his flaming depth. But sod it, he'd try, he'd bloody well try.

16

DC Burton wriggled and tried to make himself comfortable in the darkened car. He brought his wristwatch up to his face. Nearly midnight. He yawned, and knuckled his eyes. Constant surveillance duty was taking its toll. This was his third, freezing cold night of watching outside Ashby's house, waiting for something to happen.

He poured the last of the coffee from the thermos and sipped without enthusiasm. He was dying to do a pee, but knew the minute he left the car, the dentist would come roaring out. He chucked the thermos on the back seat and listened to the burble of police messages over the radio, all from people sounding more alert and wide awake than he did. For three nights he had staked out the dentist's house and each night, dead on eleven, the front door would open, an empty milk bottle was deposited on the step then the house lights would go out one by one. Tonight had followed the same pattern.

His personal radio crackled. 'Frost to Burton. Any joy?'

'Not a damn thing, Inspector. Quiet as the grave.' But as he spoke a light came on briefly in the hall. 'Hold it, something's happening.' The light went out, then the front door opened. Burton's eyes flicked down to his watch. 'Time 23.59. Target leaving house . . . opening garage doors.'

A metallic grey Honda Accord rolled down the sloped driveway and coasted out into the road where the engine coughed into life and the car moved off. Burton waited a few seconds before following at a discreet distance, making sure he didn't lose sight of the Honda's red tail lights. Back to the radio. 'He's proceeding north towards the town centre. Am following.'

'Don't let him know he's being followed and don't lose him,' ordered Frost.

Burton grinned. What the hell did Frost expect him to do? But he knew the inspector was under pressure with Mullett breathing down his neck as the overtime figures mounted up. 'Target turning into Bath Road,' he reported, spinning the wheel to follow.

'We're in Bath Road,' said Frost. 'Drop back, we'll take over.' With so few vehicles on the road at that time of night it was important Ashby didn't realize the same car was behind him all the time.

Morgan slowed down to let the Honda get ahead of them. The night mist that had hampered previous operations was creeping back again, so he didn't want the dentist to get too far in front.

They drove in silence, Morgan squinting through the dirty windscreen of Frost's Ford, keeping the pin-pricks of red in sight At one point, just approaching a turn-off, he thought he'd lost him, but spotted the lights again in the distance. 'He's put on a bit of speed, guv,' he muttered.

'Eager for the bleeding kill,' grunted Frost. He frowned and scrubbed at the windscreen with his cuff. 'That's the wrong bloody car!'

'It can't be,' said Morgan.

'Well, it bloody well is,' snapped Frost as the mist thinned a little. 'It's a green Citroën.'

'Knickers!' spluttered Morgan, slamming on the

345

brakes. 'He must have taken the turn-off. I lost him for a while, saw the rear lights and assumed it was him.' He squealed into a U turn and headed back to the side road. 'Sorry, guv.'

Frost sat fuming. Bloody Morgan. They reached the turn-off. A long, clear road with no other vehicle in sight. 'Sorry, guv,' mumbled Morgan again.

'If he's after toms, let's try the red light district,' said Frost.

A bitter night with very few toms still about and the ones they asked hadn't seen a grey Honda. Frost radioed to Burton to report they had lost the target.

It was Burton who spotted the car parked down a side street to the rear of the red light district. It was locked and empty. 'Shit!' said Frost.

'Now what?' Morgan asked.

'You and Burton take a walk around, see if you can spot him, I'll watch his motor. He's got to come back sometime.'

A cutting wind made him shiver and he was glad to get back to the warmth of his car. He found a half-smoked cigarette in his mac pocket and lit up, drumming his fingers on the steering wheel, his eyes fixed on the Honda straight ahead. The night had all the makings of one of his first-class cock-ups.

A tapping at the driver's window made him turn. A woman in silhouette against the street lamp behind her. He wound down the window and a tatty, ginger-tinged fur coat opened to show a low-cut dress and yards of cleavage. 'Want to see the twins undressed, love?' asked a husky, sex-promising voice. 'Twenty pounds as it's cold.'

Frost's eyes moved quickly from the unappetizing twins to the face, heavily plastered with make-up, and the dyed red hair poking out from under a knitted bobble hat . . . 'Still on the game, Sarah? Can't you live on your old age pension?'

346

Sarah jerked back in dismay. 'The fuzz, just my flaming luck.' She backed away, but he reached out and grabbed her arm. 'Get in.'

He opened the door and she thudded down on the passenger seat, filling the car with the overpowering smell of cheap, musky perfume. 'You ain't going to run me in, are you, Mr Frost?' she pleaded. 'Not on me birthday?'

'Your birthday? Show us your telegram from the Queen!'

'Very funny.' She took the cigarette he offered and sucked at it gratefully. The glow from his lighter lit up a raddled face, heavily caked with make-up, and the smoke she exhaled was tinged with the smell of gin.

'You're getting a bit too old for this lark, aren't you, Sarah?'

She shrugged. 'The landlord wants his rent and I've got to pay it somehow.'

'Ever been approached by a bloke, mid-forties, little moustache, stinks of aftershave and drives a Honda?'

She shook her head. 'All I get is old men in Reliant Robins stinking of wintergreen.' She paused. 'A Honda? You don't mean the bloke who was in that Honda over there?' She indicated the dentist's car.

'Yes,' said Frost. 'Why?'

'I offered him my services and he told me to piss off.'

'And you took that as a "No"?'

'Supercilious bastard. Politeness costs nothing.'

'You didn't see where he went, by any chance?'

'Yes.' She pointed. 'In that house on the corner.'

Frost couldn't believe his luck. 'Are you sure?'

'Positive. He took out a key and let himself in.'

Frost beamed happily. 'I owe you one, Sarah.' He radioed for Burton and Morgan to return, then opened the car door for the woman to leave. 'On your way, love.'

She shivered as the cold hit her. 'I won't get much more trade tonight. I'm never going to get enough for my cab fare home.' She gave a pleading look. 'I suppose you couldn't see your way—'

Frost didn't let her finish. 'Sorry, love, you never paid me back the last time, or the time before that . . .' It was a waste of time giving the woman money. She'd go straight to the nearest pub and pour it down her throat.

She shrugged. 'Ah well. Thanks for the fag.'

He watched her lumber off into the darkness and waited for the two DCs to return.

'What do you reckon, then, guv?' asked Morgan for the eighth time. He was beginning to get on Frost's nerves. What did he expect – instant flaming solutions?

'We watch and when he comes out, we follow him.'

'What do you reckon he's doing in there?'

'How the flaming hell do I know?' Frost had taken a prowl around the house, but the curtains were all tightly drawn and there was nothing to be seen. He had squinted through the letter box into a darkened hall. Nothing to see, nothing to hear. He had asked the station to find out who lived there. The information supplied was that the premises were occupied by a Mr and Mrs F. Williamson who had lived there for some three years. Nothing was known about them.

'He could be in there with a tom now,' said Morgan. 'Got her tied to the bed and torturing the poor woman.'

'I know, I bloody know,' Frost snapped. 'If we burst in and he's just popped in to use their toilet, we've blown it. I don't think that's where he takes them. It's too public. He'd risk someone seeing him.'

'But you can't be sure, guv.'

'I know I can't be sure. For all I know it could be

packed floor to ceiling with dead toms. All we can do is wait until he comes out, then wherever he goes, we follow.' He yawned. 'No point two of us staying awake. I'm having a kip. Wake me in half an hour then I'll take over from you.' He pulled up his coat collar, hunched down in the seat and closed his eyes.

He woke with a start. Where the hell was he? The car. He was in the car. He brought his watch up to his eyes. 1.36. Flaming Taffy Morgan was supposed to wake him at 1.30. He stretched and looked round. Morgan, head back, eyes closed, was snoring softly. Frost snorted annoyance. Couldn't the silly sod do anything right? He jabbed the DC sharply in the ribs with his elbow. Morgan shot bolt upright. 'What's that?'

'Your early morning call,' began Frost and then his eyes widened and he swore violently.

The street lamp shone down on an empty parking space. The Honda had gone.

Morgan was rubbing his eyes. 'I nearly dropped off then, guv,' he murmured apologetically. He stared through the windscreen. 'Where's the Honda?'

'He must have driven it away when you nearly dropped off,' snarled Frost as he radioed through to Burton who was watching the rear of the house from a side street. 'You didn't spot Ashby driving off by any chance?' he asked hopefully.

'No,' replied Burton. 'You haven't lost him, have you?'

'Yes,' said Frost grimly. 'The lousy sod didn't have the decency to wake Morgan up as he left. Get over to his house and wait there. Let me know the minute he returns.' He radioed for all units to keep an eye out for the Honda, hoping and praying that Mullett wasn't listening in.

'I'm sorry, guv,' said Morgan again. Frost ignored

349

him, his brain whirling. What had Ashby been doing in that house? Was some poor cow even now tied to the bed, or had he sneaked a body out while Morgan was snoring his flaming head off? Frost gritted his teeth and stiffened to stop himself screaming out loud as, for the hundredth time, Morgan asked, 'What now, guv?'

'We've got to take a look inside that house.' He opened the car door. 'Let's see if we can find a way in.'

A forlorn hope but he tried the front door, just in case Ashby hadn't closed it properly. No joy. Another look through the letter box, this time shining his torch inside. Nothing. What did he expect to find – a dead tom swinging from the coat rack? He straightened up. 'Let's try the back way.'

An unlocked gate from the back alley led to the rear of the premises. A small garden with a tiny lean-to greenhouse. The back door was locked and the downstairs window catch stubbornly resisted the efforts of Frost's penknife to open it.

Morgan stepped back and pointed to an upstairs sash window which wasn't quite closed. 'I reckon I could get in through there, guv.'

With visions of Morgan slipping, smashing every pane in the greenhouse and waking up the entire street, Frost firmly shook his head. 'I'll do it.' He dragged the dustbin over and climbed on top, but even on tiptoe, the sill was just beyond his reach. Reluctantly, very much against his better judgement, he let the slightly taller Morgan try. The DC hauled himself up, full of confidence, just managing to hook his fingers over the edge of the sill. With a foreboding of disaster, Frost turned his head away. 'I'm there, guv,' called Morgan triumphantly just before he fell, his feet kicking, trying to get a foothold in the brickwork as he crashed down, sending the dustbin flying and the lid rolling and clanging. 'Sorry, guv,' muttered Morgan, picking himself up.

'That's your bleeding theme tune,' hissed Frost. For a moment, by some miracle, he thought no-one had heard the racket, then a light suddenly cut across the garden from the house next door. 'Let's get the hell out of here.'

Back in the car they stared at the house while Morgan sucked his bleeding fingertips and rubbed his grazed knees. 'I nearly made it, guv.'

'And Captain Scott nearly made it to the South flaming Pole.' Frost couldn't see any lights coming on in the house and wondered if it was empty. 'Sod it . . . let's take a chance. I'm going to smash a window and get in that way.'

Out of the car again. He was bending to pick up an empty milk bottle from the doorstep when headlights blinded him. A squeal of brakes and running footsteps. 'Hold it, you two.' He spun round, almost dropping the bottle. Two uniformed men, Jordan and Simms, were racing towards them, the flashing blue light of the area car in the road behind them. Frost gaped. 'What are you doing here?'

'Householder reports two men in her back garden trying to break in,' Jordan told him, wondering what Frost was doing here.

'Two men?' said Morgan. 'That was . . . Oow!' He hopped with pain as his ankle was kicked.

'We thought we heard something,' said Frost, 'so we stopped to take a look. You two go round the back, we'll go in the front way.' He hammered on the door. A light came on in the hall. 'Police!' he called. The door inched open on a chain and a hand took his warrant card. The door opened. They stared. Wearing a powder blue dressing-gown over a flimsy night-dress, the red-headed receptionist from the dental surgery was looking equally surprised at Frost. 'Thank goodness you've come. My husband's away and I'm in the house on my own. There were two of them.'

'We'll come in and look round,' said Frost. 'If they got into the house we'll flush them out. We've got two uniformed men round the back.'

They quickly went through every room, Frost lingering in the bedroom which held the unmistakable aroma of the dentist's aftershave. A heap of cigarette ends in the ashtray, but no shackles, no blood, no-one else in the house.

'No sign of them,' he told the woman. 'Probably miles away by now. We had a report of a man driving off in a Honda. Would he have been your husband?'

She looked confused and blushed. 'Er, no . . . a friend.'

'I see,' nodded Frost. 'Can you tell me exactly what time he left you?'

'Just before half-past one.'

About five minutes before Frost woke up to find the Honda had gone. 'Are you sure?'

'I checked the clock as I got back . . . er, got into bed. Why – is it important?'

'No,' said Frost, shaking his head. Bloody Morgan! They'd missed Ashby by seconds. 'It's not important.'

He sat in his office, moping. What a flaming night. There would be hell to pay in the morning when Mullett learned that after nights of fruitless surveillance, their target was actually on the move but they had lost him. He looked across at Morgan who was in a reverie of erotic recollection.

'I couldn't half have given her one, guv,' said Morgan, settling himself down at his desk. 'Red hair drives me mad. Did you see the love bites round her neck?'

'Is that what they were?' muttered Frost. 'I thought she had fleas.' He radioed Burton who was still stationed outside the dentist's house. Ashby still hadn't come back home and no patrols had spotted the Honda. 'What can the sod be doing?' asked Frost.

The phone rang. Control. Urgent message for Inspector Frost. The body of a woman had been found on the outskirts of the Denton Golf Course.

She was lying on her back, fully dressed, the unbuttoned ginger-tinged fur coat spread out beneath her, the low-cut dress pulled down, exposing her breasts. Sarah had looked old when Frost had seen her earlier. In death she looked very old.

He stared down at her, moodily smoking, getting in the way of SOCO and the Forensic team who were methodically searching the immediate area. She had been dumped in rough grass on the outskirts of the municipal golf course, no more than a couple of feet from a small cut-through road so her killer wouldn't have had far to move the body before driving off. He wouldn't have had to leave the road, just stop the car, dump her, then drive off within seconds. Forensic and SOCO were wasting their time looking for clues in the grass.

No attempt seemed to have been made to conceal the body, which had been spotted by an emergency plumber on his way to attend to a burst pipe at one of the local factories.

He realized Morgan was alongside him, also studying the body. 'I could have saved her life, Taffy,' he said. 'She asked me to lend her the money for a cab, I said no, so she went off to earn enough for her fare and this bastard picked her up.'

'It's a wonder anyone would want to pick her up,' said Morgan. 'I wouldn't fancy her myself.'

Frost expelled smoke. 'When I was a young copper, just joined the force, years ago – hansom cabs and Jack the Ripper – I often used to see Sarah plying her trade. She was a bloody cracker then.' He took another drag at the cigarette which was tasting hot and bitter. 'So where is our flaming dentist?'

'You reckon it's him, guv?'

'I hope and pray it is, Taffy. He's all we've got.' He moved back to let SOCO take photographs. Another look at the body. 'She's fully clothed. Why didn't he take her to his lair and strip her off like the others?'

'Probably picked her up in the dark and didn't fancy her when he saw her in the light?' offered Morgan. He nudged Frost. 'The doctor's here.'

Slomon, the duty police surgeon, annoyed at being dragged out of a warm bed at three o'clock on a cold, frosty morning, scowled a greeting at Frost, then knelt by the body and touched the flesh. 'Hasn't been dead long, a couple of hours at the most.'

Frost nodded. 'That fits in, doc. I was talking to her a couple of hours ago. She offered to show me her titties.' *Want to see the twins undressed, love? Twenty pounds as it's cold.* It was even colder now and everyone could see the twins for free.

Slomon made a brief examination, then studied the face. 'No sign of injuries. I think she had a heart attack.'

Frost frowned. 'Heart attack? All the others were suffocated.'

'Not this one.' Slomon stood up. 'She probably had a wonky heart to start with and when she realized what he meant to do with her, the shock killed her.'

Frost crouched and lifted the dress so he could study her stomach. No sign of cigarette burns. He checked the wrists and ankles. No rope burns.

'Could it be a different killer?' asked Morgan.

'I don't think so,' said Frost. Sod it . . . he had enough unsolved cases without a different bleeding killer being involved. 'He gets his kicks out of seeing women suffer and there's not many giggles if she's

354

dead and can't feel anything. That's why he dumped her so quickly.'

Slomon was scribbling out his expense claim. 'You anywhere near catching him?'

'Not so near that you'd notice,' sighed Frost. If only Morgan hadn't fallen asleep. If only he'd given the poor cow her cab fare. If only he was a better flaming detective. If, if, if . . .

One of the men from Forensic was examining the fur coat. 'This has seen better days, Inspector.'

'Better decades more like,' muttered Frost. He bent and rubbed the coat with his thumb. As he did so, wisps of fur floated off. 'It's moulting,' he told Forensic. 'If she got into anyone's car, or sat close to them, we'd find traces of rabbit's fur or whatever it is – right?'

'Without a doubt.'

Frost nodded his satisfaction. His radio called him. Burton reporting that Ashby had just returned home. Frost checked the time. 3.32 a.m. 'Where's his car now?'

'In the drive.'

'Right – stay there. If he attempts to leave the house again, arrest him on suspicion of murder. SOCO and Sergeant Hanlon will be with you in around fifteen minutes.' He clicked off and yelled to Detective Sergeant Hanlon: 'Arthur. The dentist has just returned home. I want his clothes, his car, and his house examined for traces of moulting fur – take SOCO with you. Then get Ashby down to the station, arrest him if necessary, but don't tell him about Sarah. Tell him it's about his late receptionist.'

'Aren't you coming?' asked Hanlon.

'No. I've got to wait for Drysdale. Just stick Ashby in an interview room with a warm cup of tea and let him sweat it out until I get there.'

No sooner had Hanlon and SOCO driven away

355

than the lights of Drysdale's Rolls-Royce cut across the golf course.

'Another one?' sniffed the pathologist, peeling off his gloves and handing them to his secretary.

'Kill one, get one free,' said Frost. 'Dr Slomon reckons she died of heart failure.'

'Brilliant,' said Drysdale coldly. 'Everyone dies from heart failure. It's what causes the heart to fail that matters.' His examination didn't take long. With much reluctance he agreed with Dr Slomon. 'A heart attack, probably brought on by shock. I don't suppose it will reveal much more than that, but the autopsy will be at two tomorrow afternoon.'

Frost sighed. 'I'll be there, doc.' He seemed to be spending half his flaming life at Drysdale's elbow in that miserable autopsy room. He left Jordan to oversee the removal of the body and let Morgan drive him back to the station. The aroma of Sarah's cheap perfume still clung to the interior of the car and there were bits of her tatty fur on the seat . . .

'You can't talk to Ashby yet, Jack,' Bill Wells told him. 'He's sent for his solicitor.'

'People are too flaming aware of their rights,' moaned Frost. The canteen was closed at that hour of the morning so he sent Morgan off to make some tea, then sat in his office to wait and draw doodles on one of Mullett's memos.

Morgan pushed the door open, bearing two mugs of tea. He was followed in by Detective Sergeant Hanlon. Frost fished the tea-bag from his mug, took a sip and shuddered. 'Cat's pee,' he said.

'Sorry, guv,' mumbled Morgan. 'Making tea isn't my strong suit.'

'Nothing done in a standing position seems to be your strong suit,' said Frost. He turned to Hanlon. 'What joy with Forensic?'

356

'They're still going through the house, Jack. They bagged up some clothes for examination, including the coat he was wearing in the car, but no obvious sign of any fur fibres.'

Frost looked worried. 'You sure it was the right coat?'

'His keys and his driving licence were in the pocket.'

'For all we know he went back to that red-haired receptionist's flat and changed. I should have left someone watching the place.'

'You think she's in it with him, guv?' asked Morgan.

'I reckon there's got to be two of them, Taff. He couldn't have carried Big Bertha's body from the car on his own, not without a fork lift truck.' He took another sip from his mug before grimacing and pushing it away. His cigarettes went the rounds. 'Knowing who did it is one thing – proving it can be bloody difficult.' He looked up hopefully as Rawlings, the SOCO, followed by Burton, came in and dropped into a vacant chair. 'This had better be good news,' said Frost, 'or I'll get Taffy to make you a cup of tea.'

Rawlings waved away the offer of a cigarette. 'Forensic are doing more thorough tests, but I haven't turned up anything either in the house, his clothes or his car. My guess is she was never in that Honda.'

'I'm not interested in your guesses,' moaned Frost. 'If you've nothing positive to report, then lie.' He turned to Hanlon. 'What happened when you went to the house?'

'I told him we'd like him to come to the station to answer a few questions. He said he'd come tomorrow. I said now. He told me to get stuffed, so I arrested him.'

'On suspicion of the murder of Helen Stokes?'

'Yes. He called us a load of incompetent fools.'

'He knows us too well.' Frost yawned. It had been a

357

long day and it wasn't yet over. 'Unless Forensic come up with something, we haven't got a lot on him; suspicion, but nothing concrete. We're going to bluff our way through this, pretend we know a lot more than we actually do.' His internal phone rang. Ashby's solicitor had arrived.

Ashby, dishevelled and furious, was seated next to his solicitor, a small balding man who looked equally annoyed. 'My client would have been perfectly willing to answer your questions at a reasonable time, Inspector. It's intolerable that you should drag him down here at this hour of the morning.' He glanced at the sheet of paper in front of him. 'I understand you wish to question him regarding the death of his late receptionist Miss Helen Stokes?'

'Bang on!' nodded Frost, settling himself down in the chair with his files, his cigarettes and his lighter. He checked that Burton was ready with the tape machine.

As soon as it was running, the solicitor said his set piece. 'My client wishes to state emphatically that he knows nothing at all about the death of his employee and he resents most strongly that you have arrested him without a shred of evidence.'

'Then let's try and clear this little misunderstanding up,' beamed Frost, leaning across the table to Ashby and making great play of studying his earlier statement. 'Miss Stokes was killed in the early hours of Saturday morning. You told us you went straight home Friday night, after the surgery closed, stayed in and didn't go out?'

'That's correct.'

'Is it?' asked Frost, sounding surprised. He pulled another sheet of paper towards him. 'So any witness saying they saw you out in your Honda in the small hours would not be telling the truth?' He had no such witness, of course and kept his fingers crossed that the solicitor wouldn't challenge this point, but to his relief, Ashby swallowed the baited hook.

'Saw me driving? Ah, yes, now I come to think of it . . . I suffer from insomnia, Inspector, and sometimes have to get up and take a short drive in my car. I find driving aimlessly around helps me sleep.'

Frost smiled happily. 'That clears up that little point, sir. We don't like to have these discrepancies.' He shuffled through the papers and pulled out a witness statement. 'Now what was the date that other witness mentioned . . . ? Ah yes . . . the early hours of Tuesday morning . . .' He raised his eyebrows enquiringly. More bluff. The statement was from a householder reporting they saw nothing at all at the time the body was dumped under the fast food van.

'Ah   ' said the dentist, as if suddenly remembering. 'I did go out for a late night drive . . . It slipped my mind before.'

Frost ticked the statement. 'Good. We know the body was dumped between half-past midnight and half-past one Tuesday morning. Can you tell us where your aimless drive had taken you between those times?'

'I'm sorry, Inspector, I don't stare at the clock as I drive, I just don't know.'

'Did you know Miss Stokes had a secret passion for you, sir?'

Ashby blinked in amazement. 'What . . . ?'

Frost showed him the photograph. 'We found this in her bedroom . . . the red marks are lipstick. She'd been slobbering all over it. Didn't you detect any signs of a smouldering passion?'

'No, I did not.'

The solicitor came to life. 'I can't see where any of this is leading, Inspector.'

'Bear with me, sir.' Back to Ashby. 'I'm suggesting,

sir, that Miss Stokes, with her secret passion, would have been insanely jealous if you gave your favours to someone else.'

'I'm a happily married man,' snapped Ashby.

'Yes, sir, but is it your wife who is keeping you happy or your new receptionist?'

The solicitor quickly intervened. 'Are you suggesting my client is having an affair with his receptionist?'

Frost gave the solicitor a knowing smile. 'I don't think your client will deny it, sir, especially as I caught them at it.' Back to Ashby. 'Did Miss Stokes catch you at it as well, sir? Did she threaten to tell your wife? Is that why she had to be silenced?'

'No, no, no,' shouted Ashby, his fist hammering on the table for emphasis.

'You had motive and opportunity, sir.'

Before the dentist could answer, the solicitor raised a hand. 'Just a minute, Inspector. A purely hypothetical motive which my client has denied, and as for opportunity, being unable to state definitely where he was at a critical time is hardly proof that he committed a crime.'

'You're right, sir,' said Frost ruefully. 'It's not enough, is it?' He lit up another cigarette and slowly exhaled smoke. 'Let's see if we can't bolster our case up a bit.' He put Sarah's file on the top of the heap and opened it up. 'Now here's coincidence. Death does seem to follow your client around. He was seen with another woman earlier tonight and now she's dead!'

The colour drained from Ashby's face. 'Jayne? Are you saying Jayne's dead? Oh my God!'

Frost's mind whirled. Jayne? Who the hell was Jayne? Then it clicked. She was the redhead. Clever, bloody clever. The man deserved an Oscar. 'Not your receptionist sir, a prostitute . . . Sarah Hicks, fur coat and bobble hat.'

Ashby's eyes narrowed as if he was trying to remember. 'You mean that old granny? She offered me her services and I told her to leave me alone. I then went into my receptionist's flat for a quick chat.'

'What time did you leave there, sir?'

'Round about half-past one.'

Frost nodded. That agreed with the time the receptionist had told him. 'And what time did you return to your house?'

A vague shrug. 'Around a quarter to two, I suppose.'

'That's the time I would have expected you to arrive if you had driven straight there, but in actual fact it was gone 3.30, not too long after we found the body.'

Frowning, the solicitor looked up from his notes. 'Who says my client didn't arrive home until nearly 3.30?'

'One of my officers, sir. Your client has been under surveillance all evening.'

'If he was under surveillance, you will know where he was during that time.'

Frost tried not to look uncomfortable. 'Unfortunately, sir, the officer concerned was called away to another incident for a while.' A tap at the door and Bill Wells came in. 'Not now,' hissed Frost.

Wells pushed a piece of paper towards the inspector and left hurriedly. Frost glanced at it. A note from Mullett, heavily underlined in red. 'Must speak to you urgently.' Damn. Was the sod still here? He crumpled the note and resumed his questioning. 'So what were you doing in that missing hour and a half, Mr Ashby?'

'Just driving around . . . I still wasn't tired.'

'And where did you drive?'

'Round the woods, along the trunk road. I don't know for sure. You may not be willing to believe this, Inspector, but I was still very upset about Helen. It's bad enough when a stranger is murdered, but when

361

it's someone you work with, you see every day . . .' He blew his nose loudly.

Hearts and bleeding flowers time, thought Frost. But he was worried. He wasn't really getting anywhere. He kept hoping Forensic would come galloping to the rescue at the last minute with solid evidence to nail the bastard. He pulled out the list of dates for the earlier prostitute killings and read them to Ashby asking where he was on those nights. To each date the reply was: 'I'm sorry. I don't remember.'

'An alibi we could check would be very helpful,' Frost told him.

'Had I known I'd need one I'd have made damn sure I got one. Prostitute killings! What else will you try to accuse me of – the Great Train Robbery?'

'Two people you were in contact with are now dead, sir. One of them was a prostitute. Our serial killer picks up prostitutes, and you have received two cautions for kerb-crawling, looking for prostitutes at night.'

The solicitor glared at his client. 'Kerb-crawling? You never told me about that.'

'I didn't think it was important.'

'Important? Of course it's important.'

'If I could continue,' said Frost, sounding almost apologetic for interrupting. 'One other question. Tell me about your phone calls to the Samaritans, Mr Ashby.'

Ashby stared incredulously. 'The Samaritans? Why on earth should I phone them?'

'Telling them about things you had done, and finding you were talking to your old receptionist and fearing she had recognized your voice.'

Ashby gave a scoffing laugh. 'This is really scraping the bottom of the barrel, Inspector. You're floundering. You haven't a clue and you're trying to come up

362

with a suspect, any damn suspect. You tried to pin the murder of those kids on that poor man who hanged himself. Well, you're not going to pin this on me.'

Frost winced inwardly but tried not to show it. Every tin-pot crook would be chucking that in his face from now on.

The solicitor cleared his throat. 'My client has denied your accusations which you clearly have no evidence to support. I demand that he be released from custody.'

'I'm sorry,' replied Frost. 'Our investigations are continuing and there will be further matters I wish to put before your client.'

The solicitor pursed his lips angrily and zipped up his briefcase with a flourish. 'Very well, Inspector. But if you hold him one second longer than the law allows without specifically charging, you will be in serious trouble.'

'I'm rarely out of it,' said Frost.

Harding from Forensic was waiting for him in the murder incident room. He wasn't smiling. 'You're just pretending it's bad news, aren't you?' said Frost. 'You've nailed him, haven't you?' He swilled down the dregs of cold tea on the desk, then spat it out hurriedly. He had forgotten he had dunked a cigarette end in it.

'Nothing on his clothes. Fibres from her fur coat adhering to the driver's window of the Honda, but nothing else.'

'She would have leant on the car to stick her titties through the window,' said Frost. 'You sure you found nothing inside – a 60B bra or a pair of open crotch knickers?'

Harding gave a tired grin. 'I wouldn't have kept it from you if we had, Inspector. I like to be frank and open.'

'I'd prefer you to be lying and bleeding devious,' said Frost. 'If she got inside that car there should be bits of fur all over the seat.' He had a sudden thought. 'He's got a place where he usually takes them. Perhaps he's got a car vaccum cleaner. Could he have cleaned it out before he drove back home?'

Harding shook his head. 'It would have to be a super vacuum cleaner to remove every trace, Inspector.'

'You're bleeding useless,' said Frost.

'We can't find what isn't there,' protested Harding, 'and you can take it from me, there was nothing.'

'Perhaps he's got a second car hidden away somewhere,' Burton suggested. 'Changes cars when he picks up toms, then changes back to the Honda when he drives home.'

'And changes his flaming suit as well?' said Frost, shaking his head. 'It's too complicated. Either we've got the wrong man, or we're missing something. In any case, it's too bloody late and I'm too tired to think.' He buttoned up his mac. 'First thing in the morning we contact all the toms who work in that area and find out if any of them saw Sarah going off with anyone.' He stretched his arms and yawned. 'I'm for bed before any more bodies turn up.'

He got as far as the corridor.

'Frost!'

He winced. Bloody Mullett. Half-past four in the morning and there was Hornrim Harry, uniform razor-creased, face all shining and squeaky clean, making Frost feel dirtier and more dishevelled than ever.

'Super?'

'My office . . . now!'

Frost followed him to the old log cabin and flopped wearily into the visitor's chair. Mullett marched to his desk and sat ramrod straight behind it, treating the inspector to a long, disapproving glare. What the hell have I done now, thought Frost, digging in his pocket for a cigarette and finding the note Bill Wells had given him in the interview room. Mullett demanding to see him urgently. Knickers! He'd forgotten all about it.

'I was just about to phone you when you called out,' lied Frost, thinking Sod it, a couple of minutes earlier and I'd have made it to the car-park and been off home. He put on his tired, overworked copper face. 'This won't take long will it, Super? It's been one hell of a night.'

'Not only for you, Frost. I too have had one hell of a night. Woken up in the small hours by the press demanding my comments on the latest killing and asking if it was true that we had arrested a man in connection with the serial killings. And I didn't know a damn thing about it.'

Frost frowned. 'I didn't know the press had got the story. They didn't phone the station.'

Mullett picked up his paper knife and beat a gentle tattoo on his desk top. 'Er . . . no . . . I had arranged that all press calls were to be diverted to me. I wanted to spare you the burden of having to deal with them.' He wouldn't look Frost in the eye as he said this. His concern was firstly that he didn't trust Frost to deal with the media, dreading seeing some of the man's more outrageous comments spread across the front pages of every London daily, but more important, it didn't do his own career any harm to have his name featured as spokesman in such an important case – and it also gave him the opportunity to deflect blame and misdirect credit.

'You spoil me, Super,' murmured Frost, who wasn't fooled for one minute.

Mullett modestly shrugged off what he took to be a compliment and returned to the attack. 'I couldn't give them answers, so I had to stall them. I asked you to phone me immediately you were free, and you ignored me. Then . . . then . . .' He banged the paper knife down on the desk to show the importance of his next point. '. . . the Chief Constable phoned me. The press had gone through to him. He demanded answers which, thanks to you, I was unable to provide.'

'Sorry about that, Super,' mumbled Frost, sounding just like Morgan.

'Sorry isn't good enough, Frost. I've been made to look a complete idiot.'

Frost bit his tongue and said nothing.

'I told the Chief Constable that the suspect you are questioning had, at my instigation, been under surveillance and that, although I didn't have the details, I was sure you had caught him red-handed and this was yet another feather in Denton Division's cap. He complimented me and is waiting for my return phone call to tell him we have formally charged this man with the serial murders.'

'You stuck your neck out a bit, Super,' reproved Frost. 'We're questioning Ashby, but he denies everything and we haven't yet got enough to charge him.'

'But you had him under surveillance. You must have seen him dumping the body?'

'We had him under surveillance,' said Frost, blandly, 'but we lost him.'

Mullett's face turned to stone. 'You lost him?'

'Yes,' agreed Frost. 'By the time we found the body, he was back home.'

'You lost him?' Mullett could think of nothing else to say. 'We set up an expensive surveillance operation, but at the vital moment, you lose him?' The enormity of how he was going to explain all this to the Chief Constable was tempered by the thought that he could put all the blame for this monumental mess-up on Frost's bungling. He waggled a reproving finger.

'There is no way County will overlook this, Frost. Heads will roll.'

'You mustn't blame yourself, Super,' said Frost, sounding very concerned. 'You meant for the best and it's not entirely your fault.'

Mullett blinked rapidly. His fault? How could the blame be put on him? 'What on earth are you talking about? You're the one who lost your prime suspect.'

'As I said to you at the time, Super, you hadn't given us enough men to do the job properly.'

'Not enough men? Three of you to tail one man?'

'At two in the morning there's hardly another car on the road. It was vital he shouldn't know he was being tailed. We had to keep well back so he wouldn't keep seeing the same two cars wherever he went. He suddenly put on a bit of speed and we lost him. Two more men in another car and we would have nailed him, but obviously, with County watching the pennies, the money angle took precedence over stopping another killing. Let's hope they see it's their fault and don't try to blame you. I'll back you up, Super.'

Mullett's head was in a flat spin. Frost always seemed able to wrong-foot him. How to wriggle out of this? 'But I've told the Chief Constable you would be charging him.'

'He has opportunity and motive. We just need a bit more evidence.'

'And how do you propose to get it?'

'We'll be questioning the local toms tomorrow. One of them might have seen him drive off with Sarah. If so, we've got him.'

'And if not?'

'If not, we let him go and hope we catch him next time.'

He left a stunned Mullett staring at the telephone, mentally drafting out his call to the Chief Constable.

'Frost seemed to think three men were enough. I urged him to take more . . .'

Frost didn't make it to the car-park. Bill Wells called him into the cell area. 'Ashby wants to speak to you, Jack.'

His tiredness evaporated. A confession. It had to be. He waited as Wells unlocked the cell door. Ashby was sitting on the bunk bed, arms folded defiantly. 'I'd like you to know, Inspector, that first thing in the morning, I am instructing my solicitor to instigate proceedings against you and this lousy police station for false arrest and wrongful imprisonment.'

'Is that all you wanted to say?' asked Frost, disappointed.

'Yes.'

'See you in the morning, then.' He turned to leave.

'You'll see me,' shouted Ashby. 'And I won't be hanging from a bloody hook.'

Pity, thought Frost.

17

A damp and misty morning. It was just pushing half-past eight as Frost turned into the station car-park. He'd had a phone call from Bill Wells telling him that Ashby's solicitor wanted to see him urgently at nine o'clock with his client.

He checked the cars in the car-park. DC Burton was in already but no sign of Taffy Morgan's motor. With a muttered curse he spotted Mullett's Rover in its designated parking space. Hadn't the sod got a home to go to? No sign yet of the solicitor's car so he had time to snatch something to eat.

As he pushed open the door, the siren smell of frying sausages and bacon wafted down from the canteen. A quick peek inside the murder incident room as he passed through. Sitting next to Burton, noisily slurping tea from a chipped canteen mug, sat one of the tallest women Frost had ever seen. Thin, with bleached blond hair, jangling curtain-ring ear-rings and wearing, below a short black jacket, a tiny leather miniskirt which made her long, skinny legs look even longer. Spotting the inspector, Burton hurried over.

'Who the hell is that?' whispered Frost. 'The giraffe woman?'

'You asked us to check on toms. Lily saw a bloke pick up Sarah last night.'

369

'From her height she could see for miles,' said Frost. He took one more look and shuddered. 'I can't talk to her on an empty stomach. I'll be down when I've had something to eat.'

He clattered up the stairs to the canteen, piled the full monty fried breakfast on a tray and sat down next to Bill Wells who was staring reflectively into an empty cup. 'Did you see what Burton's dragged in?' Frost asked.

'I reckon it's a man dressed up,' said Wells.

'Two men,' said Frost. 'One on the other's shoulders.' He cut off a chunk of sausage and dipped it in his fried egg. 'Did you hear the one about the midget who married the tall girl? His friends put him up to it!' He roared with laughter at his own joke, nearly choking on the sausage. 'Do you get it?'

'I got it, when you first told it to me,' said Wells glumly, 'but I was a lot younger then.'

'You're no fun any more,' said Frost. 'Do you know why Ashby's solicitor wants to see me?'

Wells shook his head. 'Ashby phoned him about eight o'clock. Half an hour later the solicitor phoned us, saying he wanted to see you urgently at nine.'

'Did he sound like someone whose client was going to confess and make a broken-down detective inspector very happy?' asked Frost hopefully.

'He sounded like someone who reckoned he had a broken-down detective inspector by the short and curlies.'

'Talking of private parts,' said Frost, 'I see Mullett's in?'

'He's got Wonder Woman with him.'

'Liz Maud? Back already? So I was wrong, it wasn't a heart and lung transplant?'

Wells leant over and lowered his voice. 'She's had an abortion.'

Frost's fork with a speared sausage hovered an inch

from his mouth. 'And Mullett's the father? Flaming heck. How do you know it was an abortion?'

'It stands to reason.'

'So does my dick . . . but how do you know?'

'She used to keep throwing up . . . that's morning sickness.'

'It could be the canteen food.' He cocked an ear as the tannoy blared out: 'Would Inspector Frost come to the phone, please.'

The solicitor had arrived.

Mullett took off his glasses and gave them a careful polish with a paper tissue, then smiled at Liz who was seated in the visitor's chair opposite him. 'So you are fully fit and ready to resume duties?'

'Yes, sir. It was only a minor operation.'

He nodded. 'Er . . . yes.' He found his eyes being drawn to her chest. If it was a breast enlargement operation as Frost had suggested, they certainly didn't look that much larger than he remembered them. 'If you could let me have your doctor's medical certificate – we need it for your sick pay, of course.' That should tell him what had been done.

'I didn't take the time off as sick leave, Superintendent. It was part of my annual leave entitlement.'

'I see.' He took another quick peek. Perhaps her chest was a bit bigger than before. These damn women with their mysterious female ailments, taking time off at crucial moments for trivial operations. 'Anyway, things should be a bit easier for you next week. Inspector Allen will be back and you will be able to revert to your proper rank as sergeant.'

Liz stared coldly. 'You did say you would see about getting my temporary rank of inspector made permanent.'

Again Mullett took off his glasses and held them up to the light, looking for non-existent smears. 'Ah, yes. I fought hard, Sergeant, but . . .' He shook his head sadly. 'In spite of all my efforts on your behalf, County wouldn't agree.' He beamed an insincere sympathetic smile. 'If you had achieved any good results, things might have gone differently, but as it was . . . !' He spread out his hands.

Her eyes spat fire. 'I see.' And she was out of the chair and his office without another word, her door-slamming pushing Frost's into second place.

Mullett shook his head and sighed. Damn woman! How right he was not to have recommended her promotion to County.

The bald-headed solicitor was seated next to his client in the interview room, his briefcase on the table. He nodded curtly as Frost, followed by Burton, came in to take their seats. 'An important development,' he announced.

You're looking too pleased with yourself, you smug bastard, thought Frost. Aloud he said: 'Oh?'

'As I understand it, Inspector, the mainstay of your case is that all these killings were carried out by the same person, including the murder of my client's unfortunate receptionist?'

'That's right,' said Frost guardedly. What had the sod got up his sleeve?

'And you feel the strongest link in your case against my client is the killing of Miss Stokes?'

Frost nodded.

'And whoever was responsible for her death, also dumped the body?'

Another nod. Get to the bleeding point, for Pete's sake.

The solicitor unzipped his briefcase and extracted a sheet of typescript. With irritating slowness, he took out his spectacle case and put on his glasses to refer to it. 'As the fast food vendor was away for such a short time, you can pin-point within a quarter to half an hour or so the time the body was dumped?'

'Yes.'

The solicitor turned to his client and they exchanged superior smiles. 'At first my client was unable to recollect what he was doing around half-past midnight or so, but this morning, he did remember.' He waved a hand for the dentist to take up the story.

'I needed cash, Inspector,' said Ashby, 'so I went to the automatic cash dispenser at Bennington's Bank in Lexton.'

Frost leant back in his chair. 'Lexton? Why didn't you use the cash point in Denton?'

'Because, Inspector, it was out of order – as I'm sure you will confirm when you check – so I went to Lexton and withdrew £50.'

'And what time was this?'

'Three minutes to one in the morning.'

'Which means,' the solicitor cut in, 'there is no way my client could have got to that fast food van between your window of times.'

Frost stared at the dentist. 'Did anyone see you there, sir – anyone who could confirm your story?'

'There was no-one else about at that time of the morning.'

'A pity,' said Frost, sounding relieved. He was afraid Ashby was coming up with a cast iron alibi. 'And why did you need £50 at that time of night?'

'The lady in question insisted on payment in cash, and I didn't have any on me.'

Frost frowned. 'Are you telling us that you drew money out to go with a prostitute?'

Ashby hung his head. 'I'm not proud of myself, Inspector, but yes.'

'After a session with your receptionist,' said Frost, 'I doubt if I would have had the strength to crawl back to my car, let alone go with another woman.' He pulled the cap from his pen. 'Details, please, so we can check.'

'I was out of luck, Inspector. When I got back, I couldn't find her, or anyone. I drove around looking for a while, then returned home.'

'Then we have nothing to corroborate your story, sir,' said Frost, trying not to sound relieved.

'On the contrary, Inspector,' smirked the solicitor. 'A timed receipt is provided with money withdrawn from the bank's cash machines. Fortunately, my client remembered he had retained his and it was in the pocket of his other suit. He phoned me this morning. I collected it, and here it is!' Like a magician asking 'Is this your card, sir?' he flourished the receipt at Frost. The date and time checked. The solicitor then produced his client's plastic credit card so Frost could see that the account number agreed.

'It does look fairly conclusive,' admitted Frost, grudgingly.

'It is proof positive,' smirked the solicitor. 'I take it my client will be released immediately? He does have a surgery to run.'

Frost thought hard for reasons to say no but couldn't come up with any. 'We'll need to make a few more inquiries, but at the moment he is free to go.'

Nodding with smug satisfaction, the solicitor zipped his briefcase and stood up. 'You will be hearing further about our claim for substantial damages for false arrest and unlawful imprisonment.'

'Fair enough, sir,' agreed Frost. 'We'll co-operate with you in every way. We'll even give the court full details as to why we suspected your client: his kerb-crawling, his late night excursions looking for nooky, his extra-marital affair with his receptionist . . .'

Ashby and his solicitor exchanged concerned looks, with the dentist shaking his head firmly. 'I'm not vindictive,' he told Frost. 'A full apology will suffice.'

'Then, sorry,' grunted Frost. He opened the interview room door and yelled to the custody sergeant: 'We're releasing this gentleman . . . no further action . . .'

Frost grabbed another mug of tea from the canteen and plodded back with it to the murder incident room, giving Mullett's office a wide berth in case the superintendent bounced out, as he always seemed to do at the wrong moment, to demand to know if the dentist had signed a full confession yet. Morgan was hovering at the incident room door and seemed reluctant to enter. 'What's up, Taff?'

Morgan pointed to the towering figure of the mini-skirted prostitute who was savagely applying fresh lipstick to replace that adhering to the rim of her mug of canteen tea. 'What on earth is that, guv?'

'You haven't met Mrs Mullett then?' said Frost, jerking his head for Morgan to follow, then sitting in the vacant chair next to her. In the corner of the room he could see Burton and Liz Maud in deep conversation. He introduced himself to the tom. 'I'm Inspector Frost. What can you tell me?'

She rammed the tube of lipstick back in her handbag. 'About bloody time! Is it true? Is Sarah dead?'

Frost nodded.

'The same bastard who did for the others?'

Again Frost nodded.

'And all you do is sit on your arse-hole drinking tea?'

'What else can I sit on?' asked Frost. 'My ear-hole?' He swigged from the mug. 'If you can help us we might catch the bastard, so tell us what you know.'

'Like I told the other copper, I saw Sarah last night going off with a punter.'

'What time was this?' Frost was giving her face a quick once-over: eyelashes heavily caked with mascara, make-up plastered on, but he was sure he could see dark stubble underneath.

'Late, ducky, getting on for two in the morning.'

'Are you sure about the time?'

'Bloody sure. If you're not one of Harry Grafton's girls you're not allowed out on that beat until all Harry's toms have packed it in for the night. He plays rough otherwise.'

Frost nodded. He knew this only too well.

'I gets there about half-past midnight and there was still a couple of his girls working, so I went to the pub for a drink, came back just after one and it was all clear. It's unfair, ducky, at that time of night all we get is the dregs of the trade.'

So do the punters, thought Frost. 'Right, then what?'

'Had a couple of customers and was standing there just before two when this car crawls up. I saw the bloke inside was giving me the eye, so I goes over to him. He looked the sort of bloke who only buys the reduced to clear stuff from the supermarket. "How much?" he asks. "Forty quid," I tells him. The bastard offered me a tenner. A tenner! I wouldn't even blow in his flaming ear for a tenner. I told him to get knotted.'

'I'd have thought you would have grabbed any trade that was going at that time of the morning,' said Frost.

'You're got to have standards, ducky,' she said, dragging up her miniskirt so she could give her thigh a vigorous scratch. 'I'd have come down to fifteen quid at a pinch, but a tenner, no way!'

'Then what?'

'Further down the road, leaning on that lamp post by the phone box, there's Sarah, wearing that moth-eaten fur coat of hers. He goes over to her in his car, they chat, she climbs in his motor, and he drives off.'

376

'And you didn't see her again?'

'No. For ten quid I'd have expected her back in five minutes – ten minutes if she was feeling generous – but she never came back.'

'Can you give us a description of this man?'

'Hardly took a look at him. Anyone offering ten quid wasn't worthy of my contemplation.'

'Come on, Fanny,' urged Frost. 'If we're to catch him, we want some sort of a description.'

'Medium age, medium height, black hair.'

'And distinguishing features?'

'No, apart from him being a stingy bastard.'

'Clothes?'

'Blackish coat, black jacket . . .'

'The man in flaming black,' snorted Frost. 'I suppose he had black fingernails as well?'

'Can't say, ducky – he had gloves on, black gloves I think.'

'Funny,' said Frost, 'I was going to say that. What about his car?'

She shrugged. 'An old banger, could have been black as well. I didn't pay that much attention.'

'Would you recognize him if you saw him again?'

'I doubt it.'

Frost sighed. They were getting nowhere. 'We're going to show you a few photographs, see if you can pick him out.' He went over to Burton. 'Show her some mug shots, slip in one of the dentist, you never know your luck.'

Morgan gawped as she strode out, towering over Burton. 'She's a big girl, guv!'

'Yes,' agreed Frost. 'She wouldn't waggle it under your nose, more like over your head.' He swallowed the last of the tea and thought he'd try his joke out on Morgan. 'Did I tell you about the midget that married this tall girl . . . Great big tart she was, just like Lily . . .' Morgan didn't think it funny either and was about to tell Frost a joke of his own when Burton returned, Lily traipsing after him. 'Flicked through the lot, recognized no-one,' he reported.

'Did you slip the dentist's photo in?'

'Yes. She passed it over, the same as the others.'

'Knickers!' said Frost. But it was only what he expected. He turned to the woman. 'Thanks for your co-operation. If you think of anything else that might help us, please let us know.'

She stared angrily at him. 'And that's it? What about some protection? If I'm out tonight and the same flaming bloke turns up, I could be lying on the slab next to Sarah.'

'If you're worried, don't go out on your beat until we catch him,' said Frost.

'And if you never flaming well catch him, how do I pay the lousy rent? If I was the Queen Mother you'd fall over backwards to protect me, but just because I'm a flaming tom you don't give a toss.' She snapped open her handbag and took out a ten pence piece which she banged down on the desk. 'For the coffee . . . so you don't waste your money on flaming toms.'

She stamped out, barging into Mullett as he came in, sending him crashing against the door post. Mullett glared his annoyance. 'What was that all about?'

Frost held out the ten pence piece. 'She brought your change back from last night, Super.'

Mullett's expression froze. The man was a disgrace and the sooner he could get rid of him, the better. He was now considering Liz Maud in a more friendly light. If he had her made up to inspector he might be able to get Frost moved on elsewhere. The thought was tempting. But he squeezed out a smile to show he enjoyed a joke against himself. 'What was that all about?' he repeated.

Frost explained. 'She saw last night's murdered tom going off with a client. We're hoping to trace him.'

378

'You think he could be the killer?'

'No,' replied Frost. 'He turned down the tall tom because she asked too much.'

'So?' asked Mullett.

'If you pick someone up intending to torture and kill them, you don't give a sod about the asking price. You wouldn't be paying it anyway . . . the poor cow would be dead.'

'So why are you trying to trace him?'

'I want to know where he dropped Sarah off. Her next client could have been the killer and our man might even have seen him.' A thought struck him. 'Actually, Super, you could help us with this.'

'Oh?' said Mullett warily.

'We need a TV and press appeal for this man to come forward. We say we know he's not involved, but his information could be vital to our investigation.'

Mullett mulled this over. The chance of appearing on TV always appealed, and he had his formal uniform in the office cupboard. 'Do we have a photofit picture?'

'No, and if we want him to believe we're going to keep him anonymous, the last thing he will want is his mug shot sprawled all over the telly. Can I leave that in your very capable hands, Super?' he smarmed.

Mullett beamed. 'I'll see to it right away.' He marched out, silently rehearsing his TV announcement, completely forgetting he had sought out Frost to tear him off a strip for not letting his Divisional Commander know the dentist had been released without charge.

Frost turned back to his team. 'Right. First, we're glad to welcome Inspector Maud back. I'll just go over what we've got so far in case she can spot anything we've missed.' He jerked a thumb to the photograph. 'There's our prime suspect. Ashby, the dentist. He's had cautions for kerb-crawling, his receptionist, Helen

379

Stokes, was murdered the same way as the other toms, he's two-timing his wife with his new receptionist and he was seen talking to Sarah Hicks the same night she too was abducted. Also, he claims to suffer from insomnia so is out of the house in the early hours which is when the murders have taken place. Lastly, he's got a little black moustache like Mullett. Now anyone with all that against him would have to be guilty.'

'He sounds a cert to me,' commented Liz Maud.

'That's what I thought when we brought him in, but the lousy swine has provided an alibi for more or less the exact time Helen Stokes's body was dumped.' He showed them the service till receipt. 'He never could have drawn the money out, then got back in time to shove her under the meat pie van.'

Liz Maud, who had been studying the service till receipt, raised a hand. 'Someone else could have used his card to withdraw the money.'

Frost stared at her, then grinned happily. 'You're right! His red-headed receptionist could have got the money out for him.'

Liz nodded. 'She uses his card to draw the cash out while he dumps the body. She gives him a phoney alibi.'

Burton looked doubtful. 'But how would they know he was going to need an alibi for that time? It was only sheer chance the fast food van happened to be deserted.'

Frost thought for a minute. 'Supposing it wasn't meant for an alibi at the time. It was only later, after we arrested him, that he realized he could use it as one.'

'The trouble is,' said Liz Maud, 'it's all theory – how do we prove it?'

Everyone went silent, but it was Frost, again, who came up with the answer. 'Wait a minute. Some of these banks have closed circuit TV cameras set up by their cash machines in case someone swears blind it wasn't them who drew the money out.' He jabbed a finger at Burton. 'Phone Bennington's Bank at Lexton and find out if they've got one.'

They waited anxiously while Burton made the call. As he listened, he smiled, then turned to give Frost the thumbs-up. 'Yes, they have.'

'Tell them we're on our way,' said Frost, rubbing his hands with glee. 'If it's anyone other than our teeth-pulling friend on candid camera, we've got him.' He was snatching his mac and scarf from the coat hook when Bill Wells came in with a face that telegraphed trouble.

'13 Denton Way, Inspector. Frantic mother on the phone. Her two six-year-old daughters have gone missing.'

Frost went cold. He had pushed the child killings right to the back of his mind. No clues and suspects. He had been hoping the killer had moved away to someone else's patch.

'How long have they been missing?'

'I don't know, Jack. She was almost incoherent and her English wasn't too good. I said we'd get someone over right away. Shall I send an area car or do you want to take it?'

Frost crushed his cigarette under his heel. This sounded bloody nasty. 'I'll take it if you like,' offered Liz Maud.

He nodded. 'Thanks. We'll join you as soon as we've checked the bank's video.'

He sat, slumped, sucking at an unlit cigarette in silence, as Taffy Morgan drove them to Lexton. He hoped that this, at least, would give him some good news.

*   *   *

381

The manager was busy with an important customer so he instructed one of his female clerks to get the videotapes out for the detectives to view. She was very young, sixteen or seventeen at the most, and wore tight jeans with an even tighter sweater. Morgan couldn't keep his eyes off her. As she knelt to get the tape from a bottom shelf, her sweater rode up as the jeans rode down, revealing the start of an inviting buttock cleft. Frost nudged Morgan who didn't need any nudging. 'I wouldn't mind swiping my credit card down that,' he whispered.

'Pardon?' asked the girl, turning her head.

'Nothing,' said Frost. 'Just hoping we weren't putting you to too much trouble.'

'No trouble at all,' she smiled, straightening up and tugging her sweater back into position, causing a sharp intake of breath from Taffy as it stretched and hugged. 'I've got what you want,' she told them.

'You certainly have,' muttered Frost through smiling ventriloquist's lips. Aloud he asked, 'Does the camera record all the time or only when there's someone using the cash point?'

'All the time, I'm afraid, so we'll have to run it through to try and find the right spot.'

'I'd love to find her right spot,' whispered Morgan as the girl fed the tape in the recorder and fast-forwarded. Smudgy, furtive-looking customers zipped across the screen poking in plastic, jabbing keys, removing money at high speed. A timer at the bottom counted through the hours and minutes. None of the pictures were very distinct. 'I bet the bank paid at least two quid for that camera,' said Frost.

The girl smiled. 'The bigger branches get the best equipment.' She checked the screen and slowed down the tape. 'Ah . . . this is what you wanted.'

But it wasn't what Frost wanted at all. There, on

the screen, taking his money and carefully checking it as the timer showed 00.57, was the dentist.

'Shit,' hissed Frost in dismay. 'We're right back where we bloody started.'

Detective Sergeant Hanlon was waiting in the murder incident room. He didn't look as if he was going to bring the smile back to Frost's doleful face. 'We've checked out most of the known toms, Jack. Very few of them were working that late, but we did find a couple who were around. Neither of them saw Sarah after midnight.'

'Have you ever considered how useless you are, Arthur?' asked Frost, dropping into a chair and fishing out his cigarettes. 'A serial killer of toms who loves inflicting pain, and we haven't got a single flaming lead.'

Hanlon took the offered cigarette. 'Most of the girls are demanding police protection.'

'They can flaming well demand. If they're that worried, they can stay indoors.'

'Couldn't we ask Mr Mullett to authorize extra patrols of the red light district?'

Frost exhaled smoke. 'And what good would that do? Uniforms in cars buzzing around every five minutes would scare the sod off. And what are they looking for? How would they know he was not a genuine punter?'

'We could take notes of all car registration numbers,' suggested Hanlon, 'then follow them up if there's another killing.'

Frost chewed this over. 'Better than sod all, I suppose. We could give it a whirl.'

The phone rang. Hanlon held it out to the inspector. 'Liz Maud for you, Jack.'

Frost went cold. The two missing kids. What kind of a bloody detective was he? He had completely forgotten about the kids. He snatched the phone, grabbing for his scarf with his free hand. 'On my way,' he began, but this time, for a change, it was good news. 'The kids are all right, Inspector. They were with the father although he's denied right of access. Uniform are dealing.'

A hot surge of relief flooded through his body. 'Thanks, Liz,' he croaked. His hand was shaking as he put the phone down. What if they had been killed and he hadn't even remembered they were missing? God! The thought made him shudder.

'Jack!' Bill Wells had poked his head round the door. 'Bloke called Scrivener in the lobby, asking for you.'

'Unless he's come to confess to something, I haven't got time.'

'He works for the Samaritans and said there was a message on his answering machine asking him to contact you.'

Scrivener was on duty Friday night with Helen Stokes and they had been trying to contact him. 'On my way,' said Frost.

Scrivener, a nervous, twitching individual, was furtively smoking a cigarette hidden in his cupped hand, like a man having a sly fag at a petrol dump. He kept shaking his head in disbelief. 'Shocking, bleeding shocking,' he told Frost. 'I was only speaking to Helen Friday night. Came home today and there she is all over the local paper.'

'You didn't know until today?' Frost asked.

'I've been away. After I finished my stint at the Samaritans, I drove straight down to my weekend cottage in Cumbria. It was a rough bloody night and I needed a break, otherwise I might have ended up doing myself in.'

'I know how you feel,' sympathized Frost. 'I've got

the Samaritans' phone number pasted inside my gas oven, just in case.'

'She never hurt a living soul, spent all her spare time helping these poor sods and this is what happens to her.'

Frost nodded sympathetically. 'We've been trying to get in touch with you.'

'Sorry about that. Mervyn left a message on my answerphone, but when he said the police wanted to talk to me I thought he'd reported me for the lousy five quid from the petty cash. I'd only borrowed it, for Pete's sake.'

'I know nothing about that,' said Frost.

'I wouldn't put it past the sod to call in Interpol,' continued Scrivener. 'He might be good for the Samaritans, but he does everything by the flaming book. I'd have paid that money back. Does he think I'm short of five lousy quid?'

'Yes, well . . .' began Frost.

'And he hates anyone smoking.' Scrivener's eyes flicked from side to side as he raised the cupped cigarette to his lips, looking as if he expected Mervyn to burst in. 'The minute you light up he starts coughing and clutching his throat and flinging windows open in the middle of flaming winter—'

'Yes,' cut in Frost. Talk of smoking opened a nasty wound. It was in this very interview room that Weaver had asked him not to smoke. 'You were probably the last person, apart from the killer, to see Helen alive, Mr Scrivener. Mr Adams tells us she had an upsetting telephone call just before she left. Any idea what it was about?'

'Yes,' said Scrivener. 'It was that flaming pervert again. If ever I got my hands on him I'd string him up by his flaming privates.'

'She told you about the call?'

'She was in tears. These bastards think it's a joke to

385

get you upset. If I get the call I always hang up on the sod. Mervyn doesn't like that, he says this could be the one time it's genuine, but I know a slimy faking bastard when I hear one.'

'You're losing me,' Frost told him.

'He phones, usually late at night when we're at our lowest ebb. Says he can't go on living, that he's going to chuck himself under a train – we should be so bloody lucky!'

'Why?' asked Frost.

'It's all a flaming act. He calls again, says he's on the railway bridge and is about to jump. You can hear the train getting nearer and nearer. Whoever he phones is yelling, "Don't jump – let's talk." Then there's a scream, the train roars past, then silence. The first time it happened Mervyn went berserk. He called the police and they traced the call to a public call box on a railway bridge. The phone was swinging from its cord, but no mangled body, no sign of the bastard. He's back home having a good laugh. He's done it to other Samaritans as well. Week before last he was on the phone to me. I said, "Jump, you bastard, jump" and got a right ear-wigging from Mervyn.'

'And this was Helen's caller?'

'Yes.' Scrivener lit up another cigarette from the stub of the old. 'Does this help you at all?'

'I don't think so.' Frost sighed smoke. Another dead end. 'And that was the last you saw of her?'

'Yes – except when she came back to phone for a taxi.'

Frost's head jerked up. 'She came back?'

'Yes – couldn't get her car to start so she called a cab. She didn't have any cash on her for the fare, neither did I, so I borrowed five quid from the petty cash box.'

Frost's brain went on overdrive. This knocked all

his previous assumptions to smithereens. 'Mervyn never told us she came back.'

'He didn't know. He was brewing up tea in the kitchen. He would have made such a stink about us borrowing from the petty cash, so I never told him.'

'She called a cab?'

'They said it would be along in five minutes, so she went down in the street to wait.'

'Do you know what cab firm?'

'Denton Minicabs.'

Frost scribbled this down on the back of his cigarette packet. 'She went down in the street and waited?'

'Yes. I kept an eye on her through the window. The cab was there in a couple of minutes. She got in and off it went.'

Frost stood up, almost shaking with excitement. A cab! She was picked up by a cab! This altered everything. 'You've been a great help, Mr Scrivener.' He called PC Collier in to take a statement and dashed back to the murder incident room. 'We've got a new lead.' He filled them in on Scrivener's statement. 'We could be on the wrong track looking for someone posing as a punter. Our killer could be a cab driver. Go out and chat up the toms again. Find out if any of them have had nasty experiences with cabbies. Inspector Maud and I will cover Denton Minicabs.' He nodded at Taffy Morgan whose hand was raised to attract his attention. 'Yes, you can do a wee, Taffy, but wash your hands afterwards.'

Morgan grinned. 'I've had a phone call from my contact in the council, guv. We could have a lead on Nelly Aldridge.'

'Wow!' exclaimed Frost. 'And who the hell is Nelly Aldridge?'

'The lady with the nipples in that old photograph,'

explained Morgan. 'The one with the missing son.'

The skeleton in the garden. He hadn't time to sod about with that. 'Make my day, Taffy . . . tell me she's dead.'

'Sorry, guv. It looks as if she's still alive and living in Denton.'

'If a lady wasn't present,' said Frost, nodding at Liz, 'I'd say, "Shit!" All right, follow it through. The rest of you, chat up toms.'

Max Golding, the fat and balding proprietor of Denton Minicabs, barely gave them a glance as they came in. He wore a dirty grey cardigan over a red and black lumberjack shirt and was chewing savagely on a soggy, unlit cheroot as he took orders from customers through his headset phone and relayed them over the radio system by means of a large, 1930s-looking chromium-plated microphone. 'A pick-up outside Marks and Sparks to the railway station. Who can take . . . Right.' He gave Frost and Liz a half-hearted enquiring glance before returning to the phone to take another call. Frost poked his warrant card under the man's nose, but he seemed unimpressed and began to take yet another call, yelling with annoyance as Frost dragged the headset from his ears. 'Hey!'

'Get someone else to take over,' snapped Frost. 'This is a murder inquiry.'

'And this is market day. We're too flaming busy for murder inquiries. Come back later—'

'Just do it,' hissed Frost.

Golding twisted round in his chair and yelled, 'Mavis!'

A fat, pudding-faced woman, a cigarette in her mouth, stuck her head through a hatch. 'I'm making the tea.'

'Leave it and take over. The fuzz are here.'

388

She waddled in and took over the headset from him. Golding jerked a thumb at the two detectives and led them through a door which had a piece of cardboard pinned to it with the word 'Office'.

Inside was almost a clone of Frost's office. An untidy desk spilling papers everywhere, a half-eaten cheese roll in the filing tray and squashed, soggy cheroot stubs in unwashed tea mugs.

Golding swept junk from two chairs and invited them to sit as he plonked down behind the desk, leaving the door wide open so he could keep an eye on the fat woman. 'So what's this about?' he asked, striking a match on the desk top and puffing away at his cheroot.

'We're interested in one of your pick-ups early Saturday morning.'

Golding burrowed through the mess on his desk and pulled out a wad of papers held by a bulldog clip. 'What do you want to know?'

'A pick-up around one in the morning outside the Samaritans' office in Marlow Street.'

A stubby nicotined finger travelled down the page. 'Got it.' He looked up. 'So?'

'You remember the call?'

'Yes.' He leant back in his chair. 'A woman, said her car had broken down and asked for a cab with a woman driver.'

'You sent a woman driver?'

'No. We've got women drivers, but they won't work after ten o'clock at night, it's too flaming dangerous. I told her I'd send one of our most reliable men.' His voice tailed off as he tried to hear what the fat woman was saying on the phone in the other room.

'And . . . ?' prompted Frost.

'I passed on the . . .' He suddenly leapt from his chair and dashed out to the woman. 'Don't send Jacko to Mrs Silverman, you silly cow. He's the one who ran over her pet dog when he collected it from the vet's after its expensive operation. She threatened to tear his balls out if she ever saw him again.' He stamped back to his desk. 'Pardon my French, love,' he apologized to Liz. He lowered his voice. 'I have to watch her all the time. She left her husband two months ago . . . for another woman!'

'I wish I had his luck,' said Frost, stretching out a foot to kick the door shut. 'Let's concentrate on the topic in hand, shall we – unless you'd like to finish this down at the station.'

Golding spread his hands in resignation. 'All right, all right, sod up my business. Why should I care?'

'Who did you give the job to?'

'Tommy Jackson . . . one of my most trusted drivers. I told the lady he'd be there in five minutes.'

'That was quick,' said Liz.

'It was going to be nearer a quarter of an hour, but I always say five minutes. If you tell them the truth they go somewhere else.'

A little bell tinkled at the back of Frost's brain. 'Jackson. Don't I know that name?'

Golding pursed his lips. 'Possibly. He's a good driver.'

Frost snapped his fingers and turned to Liz. 'Jackson! He was the bloke you arrested when that old dear reckoned he'd raped her.' Back to Golding. 'Do you know he's got form? Broke a woman passenger's jaw?'

A shrug. 'That was ages ago.'

'She wanted someone safe, you sent a bleeding jaw-breaker.'

'Beggars can't be choosers at one o'clock in the morning. It was Jacko or nothing.'

'Nothing might have been better,' said Frost grimly. Jackson was off duty, so Golding dug out his home address. As he followed them out he suddenly darted across to Mavis and jerked the plug from the switchboard 'I've told you before. We don't take bookings from that old girl. She thinks she can pay for cabs with her flaming bus pass . . .'

18

Frost and Liz Maud breezed into the interview room where a sullen, unshaven and bleary-eyed Tom Jackson greeted them with a scowl.

'Good of you to come in to help us, Mr Jackson,' said Frost, flopping down into the all too familiar chair.

'Don't give me that crap. I'm dragged out of bed with no word of explanation. It's not flaming right.'

'It's inexcusable,' agreed Frost. 'But while you're here, perhaps you could answer a couple of questions?'

'Questions?' frowned Jackson. He spotted Liz Maud who was ramming a cassette tape into the recorder. 'Not her again! Who am I supposed to have raped this time – Lily Savage?'

'Since you've asked,' said Frost, sliding across a photograph of Helen Stokes. 'Recognize her?'

'I never look at their faces when I rape them,' grunted Jackson. He squinted at the photograph, then pushed it back. 'I'm never that hard up.'

'She was one of your passengers,' prompted Frost.

'I don't doubt it. I have hundreds of passengers.'

'Just after one o'clock, Saturday morning, outside the Samaritans.'

Jackson picked up the photograph for another

look. 'I don't remember picking her up and I don't remember raping her. Can I go home now?'

'You *did* pick her up,' insisted Frost. 'Where did you drop her off?'

'If I picked her up then I dropped her off wherever she asked to flaming well go, and she would have left my cab with her handbag and her knickers intact.' He leant across the table. 'What the hell is this all about?'

Frost turned the cover of his file. 'Just looking at your form sheet, Tommy. You can be quite violent with your fares when you like, can't you?'

Jackson leant back and folded his arms. 'We having this again? Three o'clock in the morning, peeing with rain and on my way home when these two toms flag me down. Out of the kindness of my heart I agreed to take them to the railway station. When we get there, they've just missed the last train so they want me to take them to Lexton. "Don't worry about the fare, cabbie," they say. "Whatever it is, we'll pay it." We gets there, I hold out my hand for the money and they now tell me they've had a lousy night and they're skint. One of them lifts up her skirt and says, "Take your fare out of this, cabbie." '

'And you said, "Haven't you got anything smaller?" ' said Frost.

'Spare me the ancient jokes,' sighed Jackson, 'I've heard them all. Neither of them was worth the tip, let alone the fare, so I lock them in and tell them I'm driving them to the nearest cop shop. They then started attacking me and I had to defend myself.'

'You did more than defend yourself, Tommy – you broke her jaw.'

'I didn't break it, only cracked it. Anyway, what's all this got to do with her?' He nodded at the photograph.

'She got a bit more than a cracked jaw, Tommy. She was murdered.'

Jackson stared at Frost. 'Murdered?'

'She was seen getting into your cab, Tommy. The next time she was seen, the poor cow was dead.'

The man scooped up the photograph yet again. He studied it carefully, only to toss it back to Frost. 'I've never seen her before in my life.' His eyes narrowed and he jabbed a finger. 'Wait a minute! Saturday morning! Samaritans! Now I remember. The cow wasn't there. She orders a cab, I flog my guts out to get there in ten minutes, but when I arrive there's no sign of her.'

'Come off it, Tommy – you were seen picking her up.'

'Whoever saw me wants their eyes tested. I tooted my horn a couple of times, but no-one turned up, so I drove off. Lucky for me a bloke flagged me round the corner, and I took him instead.'

Frost lit up a cigarette. 'Then how come your boss has you logged in for doing this shout?'

'Because I was flagged in the street and it's against the law for an unlicensed cab to pick up passengers who haven't booked in advance. I didn't tell Max. He'd have screamed blue murder if he knew I was putting his business at risk.'

'Fair enough, Tommy. Give us your passenger's address and we'll check out your story.'

'I don't know his flaming address. I took him to the multi-storey car-park where I assume he'd parked his motor.'

'There's a pity,' said Frost, shaking his head in mock sadness. 'We could have checked it and cleared you.' His expression hardened. 'Gone one o'clock in the morning, vulnerable woman, car broken down. Why wasn't she there waiting?'

'How the hell do I know? Perhaps a licensed cab drove by and she hired that.'

Frost dismissed this with a snort. 'It's a cul-de-sac,

Tommy. Why should a licensed cab be cruising down there?'

'Perhaps he was dropping a passenger off,' suggested Jackson.

Frost grimaced ruefully. He hadn't thought of that. 'Where's your cab?'

'Why?'

'We'd like our Forensic boys to give it a sniff. If we find her blood all over the seat, it might refresh your memory.'

'You'll have to ask Max Golding where my cab is.'

'Why?'

'The cab doesn't stand idle just because I'm not driving it. When I get out, another driver gets in. The seat's red hot sometimes.'

Great! thought Frost. Bloody great!

He took one last swig from the mug of canteen tea, then committed his cigarette end to a sizzling death in the dregs. He was back in the murder incident room with the rest of his team. 'As you know, we've got yet another prime suspect. Tommy Jackson, minicab driver with form for violence. He was due to pick Helen Stokes up Saturday morning but claims she wasn't there when he arrived. He reckons another cabbie dropped off a passenger and picked her up. DC Burton has been checking all the cab firms to see if they had anyone in the vicinity at that time of the morning.' He raised an enquiring eyebrow at Burton who stood up.

'I've checked all the local minicab and licensed cab firms. None of them had cars in that immediate vicinity Saturday morning and none of them had drops anywhere near the Samaritans.'

'Right,' added Frost. 'I've been back to the Samaritans. Jackson said he tooted his horn when he arrived but there was no-one there waiting. Melvyn, the bloke in charge, thinks he might have heard a horn from the street, but he was on the phone and can't be certain of the time.'

'Which isn't much help to Jackson, or to us,' said Arthur Hanlon.

Frost grunted his agreement. 'Forensic are giving his cab the once-over, but I'm not optimistic. Other people have driven it as well as Jackson. However, Inspector Maud has been proving she's not just a pretty face.' He nodded for Liz to make her report.

She stood up. 'I checked the duty rotas at Denton Minicabs. Jackson was on duty every night the murder victims went missing.'

A buzz of excited conversation.

'Secondly,' continued Liz, 'I checked the pick-up records for the nights the victims were last seen. The firms don't always record destinations, only the pick-up points, but the night Big Bertha went missing, Denton Minicabs had a call from Downham Street, which is in the red light area, to Fenton Street, which is where Bertha shared a flat. Jackson was the driver, but, surprise, surprise, he told his firm there was no one there when he arrived.'

'We've got enough to charge him,' said Sergeant Hanlon.

'But not enough to get a conviction, Arthur.' The phone rang. Burton answered it. 'Forensic, Inspector. About the cab.'

Frost took the phone without much enthusiasm. Forensic hadn't been much help in the past. 'Right, give me the good news. You've found matching blood-stains, a pair of knee-length knickers and a signed confession?'

'No, Inspector,' said Harding patiently, 'but we did find a used condom so we can do DNA checks to see who used it and on whom. We also found fibres from that fur coat you were on about and traces of a considerable amount of dried blood on the carpeting which we are currently matching against the blood of the victims. Apart from that, little of interest.'

Frost squeezed the phone hard and stared up at the ceiling. 'Say that again.'

Harding said it again.

Frost beamed. 'The next time anyone says you're a lot of useless bastards, tell them I don't entirely agree.' He put the phone down and spun round. 'We've got him,' he said.

Jackson's scowl had deepened when he was brought back into the interview room. He snatched at the cigarette Frost offered.

'So you smoke cigarettes?' Frost commented, clicking his lighter.

'What else can you do with cigarettes,' snarled the cab driver, 'stick them up your arse? It's not a crime, is it?'

'Depends where you stub them out,' said Frost. He pulled out a wad of photographs of the murdered women and dealt them out, one by one. 'Recognize any of these?'

Jackson bent over to study them. 'I know most of them. They've used my cab quite a few times. They're prostitutes.'

'Dead prostitutes,' Frost told him. 'And by a strange coincidence, they all went missing on the nights you were on cab duty.'

'Hardly surprising, considering I only work nights.'

Frost flicked across the photograph of Big Bertha taken on the autopsy slab. 'Toms who phone for cabs on the nights you are on duty end up looking like that!'

Jackson screwed up his face and quickly turned his head away. 'That's sick. Just because they ride in my cab, it don't mean I murdered them. If they rode on a bus would you arrest the flaming bus driver?'

'If he was in the habit of beating up his passengers, I might, and if I found forensic evidence inside his bus, I damn well would.'

'Well, you found nothing inside my cab.'

'I'm afraid we did, Tom.' Frost tapped a finger on the photograph of Sarah. 'She was wearing a tatty fur coat the night she was murdered. We found fibres from it inside your cab.'

'I didn't say she'd never been in my cab. I just said I didn't pick her up the night she went missing,' smirked Jackson.

'At 2.36 last Thursday, this lady,' and Frost held up the photograph of Big Bertha, 'phoned for a cab to collect her from Downham Street. Max Golding gave the pick-up to you, but you claimed she wasn't there when you arrived, just as you claim Helen Stokes wasn't there when you arrived, and like Helen Stokes, the next time we saw her, she looked like this.' He waggled the autopsy photograph.

Jackson pushed the photograph away. 'If she wasn't there, she wasn't bloody there.' He clicked his fingers. 'I remember now. Yes, I radioed Max that the customer wasn't there so he gave me another pick-up just round the corner.'

'Another pick-up? I don't suppose you remember what it was?'

'No,' snarled Jackson. 'When you're murdering prostitutes all the time, you don't remember trifling little details like that. Max booked it, he'll know.'

Frost nodded for Liz to go and get the details from the minicab firm. 'Would you have any objection to giving up samples for DNA testing?'

'Why?'

'The killer raped the toms, using a condom. We found a used one in your cab.'

Jackson folded his arms and smirked. 'Take all the samples you like, Inspector. My bodily fluids are at your disposal.'

You're too flaming sure of yourself, thought Frost. 'So how do you suggest the condom got there?'

A pitying look from the cab driver. 'Don't you know anything about the late night cab trade, Inspector? If the tom hasn't a place to take the punter to, and the punter hasn't got a motor, how do you think they consummate their passion? They call a cab and have it away on the back seat, that's how. Some mornings, after a busy night, I'm cleaning out used condoms by the shovelful. But if you want to do a DNA test, be my guest.'

Frost groaned inwardly. His pile of hard evidence was shrinking fast. But there was still the blood to be tested . . . A tap at the door and Liz beckoned him outside.

'The call from Big Bertha,' she told him, 'came in at 2.36. At 2.50 Jackson radioed back to base to say there was no-one there. Luckily, Golding had another customer for him, a man in Felford Road who had cut his hand on a corned beef tin and wanted to be driven to the casualty department at Denton Hospital to have it stitched up. I went through to the hospital and got the man's name and telephone number. I phoned him. He says the minicab arrived about five minutes after he made the call and took him straight to the hospital.'

'Then there was no way he could have picked Bertha up and parked her somewhere before he took the other pick-up?'

'None at all. And there's more bad news. The man said he was bleeding like a stuck pig all over the back seat of the cab.'

'Shit!' said Frost.

*   *   *

'I can go?' asked Jackson in mock incredulity. 'Can't you think of anything else you can charge me with? What about that skeleton you dug up in that garden? Perhaps he rode in my cab.'

Frost ignored the sarcasm and tried not to show it was hitting home. He had nothing on Jackson and knew that the blood in the cab would turn out to be from the man who had the fight with the corned beef tin. 'Don't leave Denton. We may want to talk to you again.'

Shoulders slumped, he made his way back to the murder incident room but was waylaid by Mullett and led into the old log cabin.

'Have you charged him?'

'No . . . not enough evidence,' mumbled Frost, giving Mullett the details.

'This isn't good enough, Frost,' barked Mullett. 'You're arresting people left, right and centre, trying to make them fit the crime then having to let them go through lack of evidence. This has already led to one tragedy.' He shook his head reproachfully. 'I want a result, Frost. I want a result, quickly.'

'You should have said so before,' grunted Frost. 'I'd have tried harder.'

Mullett reddened. 'Don't give me your smart answers, Frost—' He was cut short by the phone. 'I told you to hold all my calls. Oh . . . I see.' He held the receiver out to the inspector. 'For you. A man on the phone in answer to my television appeal. He says he was with that Sarah woman last night.'

Another time-waster, thought Frost. These media appeals brought all the cranks and weirdos crawling out of the woodwork. He shouldered the phone to his ear as he poked a cigarette in his mouth. Mullett quickly skidded the heavy glass ashtray over before the carpet was smothered in ash.

The call came from a public phone box. Frost could

hear traffic roaring past in the background. 'Are you the detective handling that prostitute killing?'

'Yes,' said Frost, trying to sound interested.

'I think I'm the man you want to talk to. I was with her last night.'

'Oh yes?' said Frost, stifling a yawn.

'I picked her up in Fenton Street about half-past two.'

Exactly what we said in the telecast, thought Frost. We give these sods too many clues.

'I went to a tall tart first, but she was too dear.'

Frost sat bolt upright and signalled frantically to Mullett. He clapped a hand over the mouthpiece. 'Trace this call and get someone over there to pick him up . . . he's our man.'

Back to the phone as Mullett dialled. 'Sorry about that,' Frost apologized, 'I was looking for my pen. So you picked her up? Then what?'

'We drove down a cul-de-sac and we had it away. I don't like speaking ill of the dead, but she was rubbish. Then she had the flaming cheek to ask me to drive her home to Castle Street.'

'And did you?'

'No, I bloody didn't. I live near there and I didn't want anyone to see me with her in the car . . . she was hardly quality. I told her I wasn't going that way, so she asked me to drop her off at a phone box so she could call a cab.'

'What phone box?'

'The one by the railway arch in Vicarage Street.'

Frost looked hopefully across to Mullett who had the phone clamped to his ear. Mullett shook his head. 'Still trying to trace it,' he mouthed.

'Do you know what cab firm she was going to phone?' Frost asked.

'I didn't hold a conversation with her. I just wanted her out of my car.'

'Had you been with her before?'

'If I'd been with her before, I'd never have gone with her last night. She wasn't bloody worth it.'

'So you said,' murmured Frost, again raising enquiring eyes to Mullett who signalled back, winding his hand for Frost to keep the conversation going. 'Look, sir, I promise you'll be kept out of it, but it would be helpful if we could have your name.'

'No way.' A click and the purr of the dialling tone.

Frost slammed the phone down. As he did so, Mullett raised a finger. 'The public call box outside the main post office. Charlie Alpha is on the way.'

'I hope he'll have the decency to wait for them,' grunted Frost, heaving himself out of the chair. 'The bollocking will have to be put on hold, Super. I've got to follow this up . . .'

The phone in the murder incident room rang. Burton answered it. 'Charlie Alpha,' he announced. 'No-one in the phone box when they arrived.'

Frost gave a resigned shrug. 'I don't think there's any more he could have told us.' He was more concerned with getting a reply from British Telecom to tell him the number dialled from the call box in Vicarage Street. 'Come on, come on,' he moaned at the phone. 'I haven't got all flaming day.' He snatched it up on the first ring. British Telecom had the number, and it wasn't Denton Minicabs. Frost dialled it.

'Speedy Radiocabs,' announced a woman's voice.

'This is Denton police. You received a call around 2.30 yesterday morning to pick up a woman in Vicarage Street. Can you tell me which of your drivers handled it, please?'

A pause and the rustling of paper. 'Got it. Woman wanted to go to Castle Street. Our cab got there in ten minutes, but she wasn't there. We've had quite a few of these abortive calls lately.'

Frost put the phone down and spun round. 'She called for a cab. When it arrived she wasn't there. Jackson said the same thing happened for him with Helen Stokes and Big Bertha. This changes everything. We're not looking for someone pretending to be a punter. We're looking for someone posing as a minicab driver.' He got off the chair and paced up and down excitedly, teasing out his thoughts. 'A couple of years ago we had this pirate cabbie listening in to the other firms' calls on his radio so he could get to their pick-up before they did. I bet my flaming pension this is what our bloke is doing. He lurks about late at night, hears a call from a tart wanting a cab and gets there first. By the time the poor cow realizes he's not taking her where she wants to go, it's too late.'

'Possible,' acknowledged Hanlon.

'It's more than possible, Arthur. I've got one of my infallible feelings. Right, drop everything else. I want every minicab and licensed cab firm in Denton called on. Find out if they had calls the nights any toms went missing and if there was no show when they arrived. And I also want someone to check out the bloke with the pirate cab and see if he's up to his old tricks. The slightest suspicion, like a dead tom in the back of his motor, bring him in.' This was better. This was what he liked. Action.

The door crashed open and Taffy Morgan burst in. 'I've tracked her down, guv . . . Nelly Aldridge, the lady with the nipples.'

'Damn,' said Frost. 'I'd forgotten about her. What cemetery is she buried in?

'She's alive and well, guv. Lives in a smallholding at Hill Lane on the outskirts of Denton. No sign of a son.'

'She must be pushing eighty. I bet her nipples aren't worth looking at now.'

'She's a tough old bird by all accounts, won't let

anyone go near the place. The Social Services lady tried to call and got the chamber pot emptied all over her for her trouble.'

'We'll have to send Mr Mullett round in his best uniform. How long has she been there?'

'Over forty years. The previous owner died and the council had the place down in their records as empty and derelict. They only recently realized someone was living there.'

'How did they find out?'

'The old girl fell and broke her wrist. She got herself to Denton Hospital and they wanted to keep her in, but she refused. That's why they sent the Social Services lady round there.'

Frost checked his watch. If they could get this one tied up and out of the way they could concentrate on more important things. 'Right, Taffy. You and me will pay her a visit and see if she remembers burying her son in a neighbour's garden.'

Hill Lane was narrow, rutted and steep, and tested the car's springs to the limit. A bumpy, uncomfortable ride, so it was almost a relief when the lane petered out to a muddied footpath and they had to get out and walk, fighting their way, heads down, against a driving wind. A dank and desolate area with hostile branches and brambles scratching and tearing as they sloshed their way through rain-filled pot-holes. The lane twisted and started getting steeper. 'Are you sure this is right?' asked Frost. 'It doesn't seem to be leading anywhere.'

'It's definitely up here somewhere, guv,' Morgan told him. 'Not easy to reach, the lady said.'

'Ladies never say that to me,' said Frost. 'Ah . . .' They had reached the summit and were looking down on the untidy sprawl of the smallholding, mud dotted with piles of rubbish and battered corrugated sheeting.

Rusty wire held in a few scrawny chickens who squawked in protest at the invasion of the two detectives. From somewhere behind the chicken shed they could hear a goat bleating. The small house looked neglected with boarded-up windows, peeling paint and sections of guttering hanging limply down like a broken arm.

As they scrunched their way down a swampy cinder path, Morgan screwed up his face in disgust. 'What's that smell, guv?'

Frost indicated a small brick outhouse with a corrugated iron roof. 'That's an earth privy – a wooden seat and a bucket. If she offers us rhubarb and custard, say no.'

There was no knocker or bell push on the cracked front door so he thumped with his fist. They waited. Nothing.

'Perhaps she's out,' suggested Morgan, wishing they'd never started this.

'Perhaps she's filling up the chamber pot,' said Frost, stepping well back. 'You take over the knocking.'

Nervously, Morgan gave the door a tentative rap, then tried to look through the window, but the thick grime barely let him see through to the drawn, dirt-heavy curtains and all he saw was his own blurred reflection. He hammered the door again. 'Police – open up.'

'Clear off!' An old woman's voice. The upstairs window had opened.

Morgan hopped back quickly as a bucketful of something nasty splattered down. 'I don't think she's too keen to see us, guv,' he muttered.

'It's just her way,' said Frost as the window slammed shut again. He gave the door a savage kick. 'Open up, missus, or we'll kick the bloody door in.'

The window again creaked open. 'Go away. I'm sick.' The voice was weak and quavering.

'You'll be a bloody sight sicker if you don't let us in,' bellowed Frost.

They waited as footsteps slowly descended the stairs, then countless bolts were drawn and the front door slowly creaked open.

She was very old, leathery skin, wispy grey hair, wearing a bloodstained sacking apron over a faded floral dress. Her deeply wrinkled face was dirt-grimed and she studied Morgan's warrant card suspiciously with red-rimmed eyes, then jerked her head for them to come in.

Frost peered into the dark depths and sniffed gingerly. The earth privy seemed preferable. He took one last lungful of cold, clear air, then stepped inside. 'Thanks.'

They followed her over the bare boards of a dingy passage, their noses assailed by a mixture of smells, stale fat, ancient food, paraffin, and a lurking, earthy odour of something worse.

She led them into the kitchen, a smelly little room with a tiny window too high to see out of and too dirty to let much light in. A Primus stove stood on a rickety rusted metal stand next to a chipped, brown-stained sink piled high with dirty dishes encrusted with ancient food. Hanging from a nail on the wall, a recently killed, scrawny chicken dripped blood from its beak on to the gritty stone floor. She sat herself down at a scarred-topped wooden table, picked up a lethal-looking kitchen knife, wiped it on her sacking apron and started hacking away at the corpse of another plucked chicken which lay beside a pile of feathers. 'Sit down, if you like,' she grunted.

Frost glanced around. None of the chairs looked particularly appetizing. 'No thanks. You used to live in Beresford Street?'

'Yes.'

'When was that?'

'A long time ago.'

'When did you move here?'

'A long time ago.'

Frost raised his eyes to the ceiling in exasperation. 'Can't you give us some idea of dates?'

'No.' The knife crashed down like a guillotine blade and the severed head of the chicken dropped into a bin half-filled with food debris.

'Where's your son, Mrs Aldridge?'

For the briefest of moments the old woman froze, then the knife began sawing away as she dismembered the bird's legs. 'Haven't got a son.' The yellow, muddy legs joined the neck in the bin. She hacked off blooded chunks of meat and dropped them in a battered saucepan.

'Come on, love,' said Frost, through clenched teeth. 'You had a son when you lived at Beresford Street.'

'My son is dead,' she said bluntly, wiping blood from the knife with her sacking apron then dragging some carrots and onions towards her. The vegetables looked as if another wash under the tap wouldn't do them any harm.

'I'm sorry to hear that,' said Frost, not sounding it. 'When did he die?'

'A long time ago.'

'What, five, ten, twenty years?'

'I don't remember.'

'Let's have a look at his death certificate and we'll be off.'

'Don't know where it is.' She began slicing the vegetables, the knife a blur, barely missing her fingers as she pushed them under the blade.

'Then where is he buried?'

'Don't remember.' A handful of sliced vegetables

407

were tossed on top of the blooded chunks of meat in the saucepan.

Frost was losing patience. 'Come on, missus. You might forget a lot of things, but not where your only son was buried. Was it in Denton?'

She pulled more vegetables towards her. 'I'm old. I forget things. It might have been, or perhaps he was cremated somewhere.'

'Well, that narrows it down,' snorted Frost. He tried a different tack. 'What was his name?'

A sad smile. 'Boy. I called him Boy.'

'What was his proper name?'

She raised her head. 'Boy. That was his proper name.'

'Would Boy be buried in a garden in Nelson Road?'

Her head dropped. The hand holding the knife shook for an instant before she steadied it and slowly and deliberately gave all her attention to cutting up more vegetables, although already there seemed to be more than enough in the saucepan. 'No.'

'Only we found a body.' He was watching her closely.

'Nothing to do with me.' Chop, chop, chop.

'Do you have any living relatives who might have better memories than you?' Taffy asked.

'There's no-one.'

'What about Boy's father?'

'Dead. Everyone's dead.'

'What was his name?'

'Don't remember.'

'How old was your son when he died?'

'Don't remember.'

Frost was getting fed up with this. They were getting nowhere and he wanted to get out of the oppressive atmosphere of this tiny, dirty scullery. 'Just bloody concentrate. We found a skeleton of a man in a garden in Nelson Road. We're trying to establish who he is. Could he be your son?'

She gave the saucepan a shake. 'No.'

Frost dug into his mac pocket and pulled out the wrist-watch. He thrust it at her. 'Is this your son's watch?'

She jerked her head away. 'No.'

'Look at the damn thing before you say no.'

'Don't have to. Boy couldn't tell the time. He didn't have a watch.' She rose painfully from her chair and unhooked the other chicken from the nail and started to tear out its feathers. 'I want you to go now. I've got work to do.' The knife crashed down, completely severing the chicken's head and nearly splitting the table top in two. The old girl wasn't as frail as she looked.

She followed them out to the front door and banged it shut behind them. They could hear bolts slamming home.

Frost's nose twitched. 'Doesn't fresh air smell funny.' He shivered and tightened his scarf. After the fetid fug of that kitchen, the cold cut like a knife.

They trudged down the path. Morgan nodded at the potato ridges in the kitchen garden. 'She must be as strong as a horse, guv.'

'She smells like one,' grunted Frost.

'I mean, all on her own, digging the garden, tending the chickens and the goat. She must be as old as the Queen Mum.'

'I was wondering who she reminded me of,' said Frost.

'What's our next move?'

'We forget it, Taffy. She probably killed her son, but we're never going to prove it. We let it drop.'

But Morgan wouldn't let it drop. He kicked a lump of the dug-over earth. 'She could have more bodies buried here, guv.'

Frost groaned. 'What the hell are you on about now?'

'Where did she get the money from to buy this place? The council said they'd heard the old boy who used to live here had died, but they had nothing official. Perhaps she killed him, buried him, then pretended he'd sold it to her. I reckon we should dig the place up.'

Frost's hand flicked this suggestion aside. 'We've got enough flaming dead bodies without digging around to find more, Taffy.'

'If she killed her son and the old boy, guv, she should be made to pay.'

'The old cow's pushing ninety. She lives in a shit-house. Prison would be like the Mayfair Hilton in comparison. How is that making her pay?' He sighed. 'Sod it, Taffy. I hate it when you're keen. All right, you can do the ferreting. Get the old boy's name from the town hall and find out if he was still in the land of the living after he was supposed to have sold the place . . .'

It was chicken casserole for lunch at the canteen, but Frost didn't fancy it. He grabbed himself a sausage sandwich and was half-way into it when he suddenly remembered he was supposed to be attending the post-mortem of Sarah Hicks. Dropping the remains of the sandwich in his pocket, he dashed down to the car and was still wiping crumbs from his mouth as he charged into the autopsy room to be greeted by a scowling Drysdale. 'Just made it, doc,' he panted. 'I thought I was going to be late.'

'You are late,' snapped Drysdale. 'I said two o'clock.'

'Oh,' said Frost. 'I could have sworn you said twelve minutes past.' He shuffled on a green gown. 'If you could speed it up, doc, I've got lots to do.' He hoisted himself up on a stool and watched as the pathologist took a scalpel and scratched a preliminary

410

red line down the stomach. Suddenly it hit him. Only a few hours ago he had been talking to the poor cow. Only a few days ago he had sat on this same stool while Drysdale performed the autopsy on little Vicky Stuart. Someone was killing toms, someone was killing little girls, and he was supposed to be leading the hunt for the killers, but was getting absolutely nowhere. All his brilliant theories had proved false, all his dead cert leads had fizzled out. He no longer had any faith in his rogue cab driver theory, expecting it to blow up in his face like all the others. The responsibility was too bloody great. He was out of his depth. The pillow case flaming burglar was more his mark and he was getting nowhere with that case either.

'Are you still with us, Inspector?'

He snapped out of his mournful reverie. Drysdale was talking to him. 'Sorry, doc. What was that?'

'I said the condition her arteries were in, she could have suffered a heart attack at any time.'

Frost nodded gloomily. It didn't make him feel any better.

Four o'clock in the afternoon, dark as night outside and the pub was already crowded. The autopsy had depressed him and the awareness of his own inadequacy hung heavily over him. He couldn't face going back to the station without a drink inside him.

As he pushed his way through to the bar a familiar raucous laugh made him stop and turn. Leaning across the bar, chatting up the bespectacled barmaid, was Taffy Morgan clutching a beer glass. His back was to Frost, but some sixth sense told him he was being observed. Morgan turned and started guiltily. 'You looking for me, guv?'

As good an excuse as any. 'Yes,' lied Frost, 'I've been looking everywhere.'

411

'Sorry, guv. I was so busy getting the gen on that old farmer, I didn't have time for any lunch, so I popped in here for a quick sandwich.'

'Yes,' grunted Frost, 'I saw you drinking it. You can buy me one now, a pint!' He sipped the beer as the DC filled him in.

'I've tracked down that old boy's family, guv,' he began. 'It looks as if I was wrong about her killing him. The old girl bought the place from him for £3,500 in 1957 – paid cash apparently. The old boy died in his bed three years later. They showed me the death certificate.'

'Cash?' queried Frost. 'That was big money in those days – something over thirty thousand quid today.' He scratched his chin thoughtfully. 'In arrears with her rent, then suddenly comes up with that sort of money?'

'Tell you what I was thinking, guv,' offered Morgan. 'Suppose she had her son insured and killed him for the insurance money?'

'Insurance companies don't pay out without a death certificate and you don't get one if you dump the body in someone else's back garden.' He worried at his scar. 'We haven't time to sod about with ancient history, but we can't leave it like this. A body's planted in the garden next to her and her son goes missing. Then she suddenly comes into three and a half thousand quid. I hate to say it, but sometime or other we'll have to go back to Shangri-la, or whatever she calls the bloody place.' He downed the drink and wiped his mouth. 'But some other time, not now. Let's get back to the station.'

As they left, Morgan turned to wave to the dark-haired, bespectacled barmaid. 'What do you reckon to her, guv?'

Frost gave her an approving look. 'I wouldn't kick her out of bed on a cold night.'

412

'You know what turns me on, guv?'

'Every bloody thing turns you on,' said Frost, feeling a lot more cheerful now. Morgan always had this effect on him.

'What turns me on is the thought of making love to a girl who wears glasses. She strips to the buff, but keeps her glasses on.'

'Then you can breathe on the lens and she can't see how small your dick is,' said Frost.

He was about to dart through the lobby when he saw the grim, angular figure of Doreen Beatty in earnest conversation with Bill Wells. Frost froze and waited in the corridor until she left, then hurried across.

'What did old mother Beatty want?'

'She wanted you,' replied Wells. 'Reckons a man's been stalking her all around the town.' He glanced at the description he had noted down. 'Dirty, shifty-eyed, loose-mouthed and oozing lust.'

'Sounds like Mullett,' grunted Frost, pushing through the swing doors. 'He always fancied a bit of rough.'

He went through his usual ritual of riffling through the papers in his in-tray. The only item of interest was a copy crime report from Lexton Division concerning three robberies from private houses where pillows were found in the middle of the beds and the pillow cases missing. The pillow case burglar was working further afield, Frost hoped Lexton would have more luck than he did. If they caught the man it would automatically knock his outstanding crime figures down to a respectable level. There was also a request from Belton Division asking that the case of Big Bertha be added to the Denton Division list of unsolved crimes as the killing undoubtedly took place in Denton District, the body being simply dumped in Belton. A good argument, but it wouldn't help Frost's crime figures, so he buried it deep under all the other papers. He looked up as Detective Sergeant Arthur Hanlon came in.

'How did the post-mortem go?' asked Hanlon, dragging a chair over to the inspector.

'Told us nothing we didn't know already, Arthur,' grunted Frost. 'The poor cow died from a heart attack probably brought on from the terror of knowing what the bastard intended to do to her. There was something bloody weird there, though.'

'What was that?' asked Hanlon.

'It was when Drysdale scooped out her stomach contents.'

Hanlon pulled a face. He knew he wasn't going to enjoy hearing this.

'She'd been dead over twelve hours and yet in her stomach was this undigested sandwich.' He dug in his pocket and pulled out the remains of his sausage sandwich which he held up, parted the bread and looked inside. 'A sausage sandwich.' As Hanlon gaped in horror, Frost popped it in his mouth and gulped it down. 'Doesn't taste bad considering . . .'

Hanlon went green and shuddered, but Frost couldn't keep a straight face any longer and broke into a broad grin. 'You bastard!' Hanlon shrieked as Frost nearly fell off his chair laughing. 'You're having me on. I won't tell you what we found out from the cab firms now.'

Wiping tears from his eyes, Frost passed his cigarette packet over. 'If I couldn't find something to laugh at about that damn autopsy room, Arthur, I'd go stark, staring bonkers. The poor bitch lying there like so much meat and Drysdale slicing her open.' He flicked his lighter. 'Tell daddy about the cab firms.'

'We could be on to something, Jack. We've checked them all and on every night a tom went missing, one of them answered a call, but no-one was waiting for them when they arrived.'

Frost punched his palm with his fist. 'I knew it! He's listening in on an all band radio and if it's a call from a woman on her own, he gets in there first. We're going to nail him, Arthur. We're going to nail the bastard.'

'How?' asked Hanlon.

'We use decoys, Arthur. Lots of lovely, juicy, nubile policewomen as decoys.' Sod all the gloom. He was now feeling on top of the world.

19

'Decoys?' repeated Mullett, scrubbing away at the lens of his glasses to give himself time to think. 'I don't understand.'

'We want to lure this bastard into a trap,' explained Frost. 'We dress up policewomen as toms, plant them in the red light district, and get them to phone for cabs. We keep them under surveillance all the time. If the right cab turns up, we simply follow them to the destination, then bring them back to try again. But if it's a rogue taxi, we tail and get ready to pounce.'

Mullett pinched his nose and thought for a while. He was beginning to have nagging doubts about asking County to send a senior officer down to take over the case. He had been hoping for a chief inspector at most, but Chief Superintendent Bailey out-ranked him and would probably take command of everything, commandeer his office, spend way over Denton's limited budget, leave Mullett to take the blame, then hog all the credit if he was successful. For all his faults, Frost was now looking the much better option. If Frost could pull this off quickly, so County were kept out, there would be no question of the credit being shared. He tugged off the cap of his Parker pen and steeled himself for the worst. 'How many people would be involved?'

'Not too many. Crowds at that time of night would

arouse suspicion. Say two or three girls and four or five, maybe six cars to watch and trail.'

Mullett jotted some figures down and winced. 'And all on overtime?'

'Yes,' agreed Frost. 'The sod doesn't like raping and killing in office hours.'

Mullett added up the sums again, but couldn't make them any less. Perhaps he should let Bailey come after all, and let him take the responsibility for spending all this money. But it would still come out of Denton's budget. 'We've got to keep costs down. When the girls book a taxi, I'm only paying for the minimum distance – and no tipping.' He scribbled some more figures down. 'Eight men – three women per night – maximum. And I want receipts, receipts for everything.'

'Of course,' Frost assured him, standing up quickly before the superintendent changed his mind. 'It's all agreed then?'

'No, it's not all agreed,' said Mullett. 'Sit down.' He took off his glasses and pinched his nose. Sanctioning large sums of money made him nervous and when Frost didn't put up objections about it being too little, it made him feel he was giving too much away. 'If I'm to justify this sort of expenditure, I've got to show it's cost effective. I want a result.'

'You shall have one,' said Frost. The result could well be that the whole operation was a disaster, but it would still be a result even if it wasn't the one Mullett wanted.

'And this isn't open-ended. I'm agreeing three nights only, then I pull out the plug.'

'Agreed,' said Frost, knowing that if they needed more time, he'd argue about it when it happened. 'We might even get a result tonight.'

'That would make a pleasant change,' said Mullett, sourly. 'Results are something sadly lacking from you at the moment. What is the position with the child killings?'

'We've come to a bit of a dead end there, Super,' admitted Frost. 'All our leads seem to have fizzled out.' Mullett pulled a knowing face, implying this was only to be expected from Frost. 'And the skeleton in the garden? I understand you've tracked down the woman with the missing son?'

Frost told him about the visit to Nelly Aldridge.

Mullett's eyes gleamed. 'We're on to something there, Frost.'

'Ancient bloody history,' said Frost. 'Not worth wasting our time on.'

Mullett's lips tightened. 'You're so damned negative. No wonder you're making no headway. We've found a skeleton, her son is missing and she has no satisfactory explanation. On top of which, she has acquired, apparently out of nowhere, money to buy a smallholding. Bear down on her. She's your best bet for an early clear-up, and goodness knows, you need one.'

'All right,' sighed Frost. 'I'll see her first thing in the morning.'

'You've wasted enough time,' snapped Mullett. 'Do it today. If she doesn't come up with a satisfactory explanation, bring her in.' He picked up his pen and began signing his correspondence to signal that the interview was over.

Frost slouched out, passing through the outer office where Ida Smith, Mullett's faithful secretary, who had overheard everything, was smiling smugly to herself at the way her superior had put that awful man in his place. Frost gave her a nod as he passed. 'I quite agree with you, Ida – he's a real right bastard.'

'I don't think this is a very good idea, guv,' moaned Morgan as his foot squelched in a rain-filled pot-hole.

'It's a bleeding lousy idea,' agreed Frost, 'but we're flaming well stuck with it.' They were slithering and sliding in the pitch dark up the muddied lane leading to the smallholding. 'Not far now – I can smell the privy.'

They stumbled on and soon could see a feeble orange glow from a flickering oil lamp fighting its way through a dirt-caked window. Frost hammered at the door. 'Open up, Mrs Aldridge. It's the police.' They waited. He tried the door handle, but the bolts and chains inside held firm. 'Let's try our luck round the back.'

They picked their way round to the rear of the house. No lights showed and the door was again firmly locked.

'No-one in, guv,' said Morgan.

'She's in all right, Taffy – probably straining over the slop bucket even as we speak.' He rattled the door handle and yelled again. 'Open up, Mrs Aldridge – police.'

A bitter wind suddenly roared round the house. Morgan shivered. 'Let's leave it until the morning, guv. This place gives me the willies.'

'Talking of willies,' said Frost, 'yours is going to have a rest tonight. I've booked you in for overtime.' He banged the door again. 'Sod it,' he grunted. 'After coming all this way I'm not going back without chatting up the old cow.' He shook the door. 'I don't think it's bolted.' He tugged a key ring from his pocket and, with a bit of wiggling, the second key he tried did the trick. The door swung open. 'Oh, look,' he exclaimed in a loud voice. 'This door's been left open. We'd better check to see if the occupant is all right.'

They stepped inside, Morgan's torch beam probing the darkness. 'I'm not happy about this, guv.'

'You didn't join the force to be happy,' Frost

told him as he led the way through to the hall. He pushed doors open and steered Morgan's torch inside. Miserable, dank rooms stacked with junk.

'Guv!' Morgan, at the room nearest the front door, was calling him over. 'I think there's someone in here.'

The room was pitch dark, but there was the sound of breathing and the smell of a recently extinguished oil lamp. Tentatively, Morgan stepped inside. 'Mrs Aldridge?' called Frost, following him in.

Suddenly a cry from Morgan as the torch was knocked from his hand. Pitch darkness. Another cry from Morgan as he was sent crashing to the floor. A plea for help: 'Guv!'

Frost couldn't see a damn thing. Frantically he scrabbled for the light switch and as he realized there wasn't one, he was sent crashing against the wall as two bodies cannoned into him. His torch! Where the bloody hell was his torch? It had slipped through a hole in the lining of his mac and was refusing to come out. At last he yanked it free and clicked it on. It flickered fitfully, dimly lighting up the figure of a wild animal of a man, all matted beard and greasy hair, stinking to high heaven. He had Morgan in a bear hug and was crushing the life out of him.

Morgan's face was distorted with pain and he was gasping for breath. Frost crooked an arm round the attacker's neck and tried to yank him back, but was smashed against the wall as the man effortlessly shrugged him off. Frost grunted as all the air was forced from his body. 'Police!' he croaked, as if he expected that to make the man immediately surrender. He just managed to jerk his head to one side as an elbow missed him by inches and smashed into the wall.

Frost gripped the torch and brought it down with all his might on the man's head. A cry of pain as the torch went out and the sound of a heavy body

420

crashing heavily to the floor. Pitch dark again. He shook the torch and, to his surprise, it flickered back on illuminating the lifeless form sprawled out on the floor, a big, dirty, hairy smelly beast of a man. The beam moved to Morgan who was staggering to his feet and rubbing his ribs. 'You all right?'

'Just about, guv.' Morgan looked down at the man. 'Who the hell is he?'

'He didn't say,' said Frost, rubbing his own bruises. 'Get the cuffs on him quick before he comes round.'

The man, whoever he was, was out cold. Morgan knelt down and, with an effort, rolled him over so he could lock the handcuffs behind his back. He glanced up and his eyes widened as he saw something behind Frost. 'Look out, guv!'

Frost spun round. Eyes dimly accustomed to the dark made out the figure of the old girl charging towards them. Her arm was raised, holding something that flashed silver. A knife. The wickedly sharp, long-bladed knife she had used to dismember the chicken. She screeched and lunged, looking like the mother from Bates Motel. Frost flung himself to one side as the knife hissed through the air, missing him by a hair's breadth. Morgan leapt across to take the knife from her, then gasped with pain as she wildly jabbed and the blade slashed through the sleeve of his jacket. She raised the knife again, but Frost managed to grasp the skinny wrist and shake it from her grasp. As it thudded to the ground he kicked it well out of reach. 'What are you playing at, you silly, bloody cow?'

She glared at them, hatred spilling from her eyes, then backed away out of the room.

Frost shone the torch on Morgan's arm where a sticky red stain was spreading fast over the upper sleeve of his jacket. 'You all right, Taff?'

The DC squeezed his arm to stop the flow of blood. 'Just a flesh wound, I think, guv. Nothing serious.'

'You were right, for once,' said Frost. 'This wasn't a good idea.' He shone the torch down and swore violently. 'Oh shit!' The handcuffed man was no longer on the floor. 'Where did the bastard go?'

They raced to the back door just in time to see a dark figure disappearing into the night.

'Shit,' said Frost again. He leant against the wall and pulled out his packet of cigarettes.

'Aren't you going after him, guv?' asked Morgan.

'No fear,' said Frost. 'The bastard would kill me. He won't get far. We'll let the uniformed boys earn their keep for a change.' He pulled his radio from his pocket and called the station, requesting urgent assistance. Back to Taffy. 'And we'd better let the doctor look at your arm – you're dripping blood all over the lady's nice shitty floorboards.' The old lady! She was in the house somewhere and she could tell them who the hairy bastard was. Then he saw Morgan's face was chalk white; he had lost a lot more blood than Frost had realized. The old girl could wait, he'd winkle her out when the area car arrived. 'Come on, son.' Supporting him with an arm round his waist, he sat Morgan down in a chair, then poked a cigarette in his mouth, lighting up for them both. They smoked silently as they waited.

The car was heard whining up the incline long before the torch beams flashed at the window.

'We're in here,' called Frost. Simms and Jordan stumbled in, their boots and trouser legs muddied from their scrambling up the lane. Frost quickly filled them in, then steered them to the back door. 'He's out there somewhere. Go out and get him.'

'What does he look like?' asked Jordan.

'Like flaming King Kong only hairier. You can't mistake him, he's wearing handcuffs.'

He watched them make their way out into the bleak, moonlit landscape where leafless trees shivered in an icy wind, then returned to check on Morgan before going to look for the woman.

She was in a cold, upstairs room, lit by the flickering orange flame of a smoky oil lamp, seated in an ancient rocking chair which creaked a loose floorboard as she rocked forwards and backwards. She was humming tunelessly to herself, her vacant eyes staring at nothing. She didn't turn her head as he approached. He gently laid a hand on her shoulder. 'Sorry, love. You've got to come back to the station with me. There's lots of questions to be answered, like who's that hairy sod?'

No reply. Just the tuneless drone and the creaking of the floorboards.

'I'm arresting you for assaulting a police officer,' he began, reeling off the standard caution. He tailed off, leaving it unfinished. Why was he bothering? She wasn't listening and probably wouldn't understand a word if she was. 'Come on, love,' he urged. He gently gripped her arm. She snatched it away.

He had noticed a drab grey coat hanging from a nail in the passage and went down to fetch it. 'Put this on, love, it's cold.' She looked at him, then held out an arm like a child waiting to be dressed. He slipped the coat over her shoulders, put her arms through the sleeves, then buttoned it up. 'You got a scarf?' She shook her head. He took his own off and wound it round her neck. It was freezing out there. He didn't want another prisoner to die on him.

Footsteps and muffled voices from downstairs. 'Inspector!' called Simms. 'We've got him.'

'Coming.' He dashed down the stairs. 'Did he give you any trouble?'

'No,' Simms told him. 'He was huddled up by that big oak tree. He was crying.'

Frost looked at the man, whose arms were tightly gripped by the two policemen. His head was bowed and little of his face could be seen through the long matted beard and shoulder-length grey-streaked greasy hair. He wore shabby well-patched clothes, stiff with dirt.

'Who are you?' asked Frost.

The man didn't answer.

'What's your name?'

Slowly, the man's head came up. Tears had cut white channels through the dirt. 'Boy,' he said. 'My name is Boy.'

The area car had left, taking mother and son to the station. Frost took a torch and went for a look around the damp and musty-smelling house. He shuddered. What a place to live. Now that the woman's coat had been removed from the nail, he could see a small door under the stairs. He opened it and shone his torch inside. A filthy mattress and some dirty bedclothes. Boy's bedroom and a place he could hide on the rare occasions visitors were allowed inside the house. He must have been hiding here when Frost and Morgan had called earlier that day.

He closed the door firmly, extinguished the oil lamp in the kitchen and stepped outside. He paused. A flutter of wings from the henhouse, then silence. He looked at his watch. A few minutes past six. Was that all? He could have sworn it was nearer midnight. One last look at the house, then he scrunched down the cinder path to the car where Morgan was waiting.

Bill Wells was liberally squirting air freshener around the cell area. 'Where did you dig those two up from, Jack? They're stinking the place out.'

Frost grinned. 'If they don't talk I'm going to threaten them with a bar of soap.' He pinched out his cigarette. 'Did you hear the one about the two flies on the heap of steaming horse-dung? One says to the other, "I saw a bottle of disinfectant yesterday." The other one says, "Do you mind . . . I'm having my dinner." '

'Yes, I have heard it,' grunted Wells. 'How's Morgan?'

'I've packed him off to Denton Hospital. He might need some stitches. Where's the old girl?'

'No. 1 interview room. She looks harmless enough.'

'As long as she hasn't got a carving knife in her hand. And the bloke?'

'I've stuck him in a cell for now. Is he her son?'

'Apparently. She's been telling everyone he's dead. He smells as if he is, but she's been keeping the poor sod hidden away under the stairs.' He lit up a cigarette and took Burton with him to the interview room.

The mug of tea the WPC had brought her was left cold and untouched on the table. Frost moved it out of reach in case she decided to chuck it over him in lieu of a slop bucket. 'The officer you attacked. He's in hospital having stitches,' he told her.

She stared blankly ahead. Her face registered nothing.

Frost puffed out a lungful of smoke and watched it weave its way up to the ceiling. 'The sooner we get this over, the quicker you can go home. Is that hairy sod your son?'

She slowly turned her head towards him. 'My son is dead.'

'I've never been kneed in the groin by a dead man before,' said Frost. 'Why did you keep him hidden away all these years?'

Her mouth twitched a secretive smile, then she began rocking backwards and forwards in the chair, humming that same tuneless dirge, ignoring all further questions until he gave up and terminated the interview. A WPC gently took her arm and walked her back to a cell.

'She's off her head,' said Burton.

Frost worried away at his scar. 'She's a crafty old cow. I don't think she's as daft as she's making out.' He decided to ask Bill Wells to call in the duty solicitor to sit in next time he questioned her in case it was suggested he had taken advantage of a feeble old woman who couldn't defend herself unless she had a dirty great carving knife in her hand. 'Let's chat up Hairy Horace.'

The man wasn't looking so wild now. He looked frightened and was watching PC Collier mop up the tea that had spilt from the mug in his violently shaking hands.

In the harsh light of the unshaded cell bulb his face looked more dirt-grimed, his hair more matted and straggly than before. His long, ragged coat was flapping open. Bill Wells had removed the knotted rope used as a belt in case he decided to hang himself like the previous occupant of this cell. They took him to the interview room where he sat uneasily in his chair, shrinking back as far away from Frost as possible. He flinched when Frost lit up a cigarette and cowered away from the flame of the lighter.

'What's your proper name?' Frost asked.

'Boy,' he muttered. 'My name is Boy.' He repeated 'Boy' a few times as if he liked the sound of it. He grinned. 'Boy,' he said again.

'This is a police station. Do you know why you're here, Boy?'

A solemn nod.

'Tell me.'

The man hung his head and shook it.

'You've got to tell me,' insisted Frost. 'It's the law.'

426

Boy looked up, tears again cutting paths through the grime on his face. He wiped a running nose with the back of his hand. 'If I tell you, Ma says you'll hang me.'

Frost gawped at him. 'Hang you? We stopped hanging people years ago. Why should we want to hang you?'

Boy stared down at the table. 'I mustn't say,' he mumbled.

'We used to hang people,' said Frost, 'but only if they had killed someone. Did you kill someone?'

The man stared at his hands and rubbed the red marks round the wrists where the cuffs had bitten. 'Ma says I mustn't talk about it.'

'Talk about what?' asked Frost, softly.

Boy shook his head firmly from side to side. 'If I tell you, you'll hang me. I'm not going to tell you.'

Beaumont, the duty solicitor, had arrived; a small fuzzy man who didn't approve of Frost. 'You're charging her with assaulting a police officer?' he asked.

'It could be a bit more serious than that,' Frost told him.

They went into the interview room and waited for the WPC to bring her in. She scowled suspiciously at the solicitor. 'Who is he?'

'I'm a solicitor,' said Beaumont, carefully sounding all the syllables as if speaking to a young child. 'I'm here to protect your interests.'

Her head swung round to Frost. 'Get him out!'

'You'd better have him,' said Frost. 'He's free, and things are a bit more serious now. I've had a chat with Boy.'

'Boy's dead,' she snapped.

'He told me a lot of things, but he didn't tell me that,' said Frost. They settled down in the chairs. The solicitor sat next to her, then his nose twitched and he

427

decided his best position would be at the far end of the table. He usually objected when Frost smoked, but this time was happy to see the inspector light up. Tobacco smoke was preferable to other aromas!

'We've spoken to Boy,' Frost continued. 'He's told us everything.'

She shook her head. 'He doesn't know anything, he's simple.'

'He knows enough to tell us where you buried the body, the precise spot, exactly where we found it.'

Her eyes narrowed. She thought for a while. 'What did he say?'

Frost smiled sweetly. 'Never mind what he told us. Let's hear your version.'

The solicitor intervened. 'I think I should have a word in private with my client before she makes any kind of a statement.'

She glared at him with contempt. 'You shut your mouth!' Back to Frost. Lips pursed, looking shrewd, she didn't seem so simple now. 'His father deserted me as soon as he knew I was pregnant. I had to bring him up on my own. You didn't get any help from the government in those days, you were on your own. I had to get money any way I could.'

'And what way was that?' asked Frost.

'I let men stay the night.'

Frost looked at her through the blue haze of cigarette smoke. Wrinkled, scraggly grey hair, dirty and unwashed, it was difficult to imagine that this smelly crone was once able to get men to pay for her services. She read his thoughts. 'I was quite good-looking then.'

'I know,' nodded Frost. 'I saw a photograph.'

'This man – he was one of my regulars . . .'

Frost pulled out a pen. 'His name?'

She looked down at the table. 'I forget.'

'Come on, love,' Frost urged. 'It's difficult to forget the name of someone you buried in your neighbour's garden.'

'He said his name was Derek. He didn't tell me his second name.'

'Did Boy know about your men friends?'

'No. He was always asleep when they came. But that night Boy woke up. He'd heard noises and he was frightened, so he crept into my bedroom. He must have thought Derek was hurting me and wanted to protect me. Boy had this cricket bat thing. He hit Derek on the head with it and when Derek yelled, he hit him again and again . . .' She shuddered, her eyes glazing over as she recalled the horror of that moment. 'I screamed for him to stop, but he wouldn't. There was blood everywhere, on me, all over the bedclothes . . . I snatched the bat from Boy, but Derek wasn't moving and I knew he was dead.'

'You didn't phone for an ambulance?'

'We didn't have a phone.'

'You could have got help.'

'If I told anyone, they would have told the police. They hang murderers by the neck until they are dead. I didn't want Boy to be hanged.'

'How old was Boy?'

'Eighteen. If you're over sixteen they hang you. We had to get rid of the body. Boy was strong. He carried Derek down the stairs and into the garden. It was dark . . . no lights, no-one watching. We squeezed through the fence of that empty house and Boy dug a deep hole. We buried him. His clothes were still in the bedroom, so I burnt them . . . then we cleaned up the blood.'

'Then what?'

'Boy kept talking about it, about how he had hit the man and how we had buried him. I daren't let him out of the house in case he told everyone he met. Then

429

this smallholding came on the market, so I bought it and we moved.'

'Where did you get the money from?'

'From what I'd earned from the men.'

'So all these years you've kept him hidden away, sleeping in a cupboard, no friends . . . no contact with the outside world. What sort of life was that for the poor sod?'

'A much better life than being strung up by his neck.'

'The death penalty was abolished years ago. Don't tell me you didn't know.'

She stared at him, eyes slitted with suspicion, then turned to the solicitor. 'He's lying!'

'No, Mrs Aldridge. The officer is correct. Surely you read about it in the newspapers?'

'I can't read, neither can Boy.'

'The radio then, or television?'

'Ain't got them.'

'You've kept that poor bastard hidden away under the stairs for nothing,' said Frost.

Her shoulders twitched a shrug. 'You can't turn the clock back. Can I go now? I've got chickens to feed . . .'

Mullett was beaming from ear to ear. 'So, thanks to my insistence, we've got a result. It was a good thing I took this case over from you.'

Frost perched his cigarette on the large glass ashtray Mullett had hastily skidded across the desk top. 'It was a near thing, Super. I might not have solved it, then it would still be my case.'

This sounded like insolence to Mullett, but Frost always looked so sincere when he made these dubious remarks, he would have to give him the benefit of the doubt. 'And the son has admitted to killing this man?'

'Yes, Super. The poor sod was having it away when

430

the son welted him with a cricket bat. He died of a severe case of coitus interruptus.'

Mullett wrinkled his nose. He couldn't take Frost's crude attempts at humour. 'So what's the current position?'

'We've released your prisoners on police bail.'

Mullett's eyebrows soared in surprise. 'Released them?'

'They were stinking the place out,' said Frost. 'The council have been round twice to dig up the drains . . . We know where they are. We can always pull them in when we want them.'

'But this is murder, Frost. We've got a confession. I want them arrested and charged.'

Frost took another drag on his cigarette. 'The son's given us a statement, but it's all a bit vague and he hasn't got all his marbles. We'd be wasting our time taking him and the old girl to court.'

'That's for the Crown Prosecution Service to decide, not you. Do we know who the victim was?'

'Not yet. All we've got is his first name and we know the approximate date he had his last leg over, but that doesn't help much.'

'Doesn't help much?' echoed Mullett in mock incredulity. 'It narrows things right down. Do something positive for a change. Go through the old records until you find him.'

'We've been through them once,' said Frost.

'Then go through them again,' snapped Mullett. He smiled inwardly. He was feeling pleased with himself and was already mentally composing the conversation he would have with the Chief Constable: *Yes, I took the case over, sir. Frost was getting nowhere so something had to be done. We've got a confession, we know who the victim is, all 't's crossed and 'i's dotted.*

* * *

431

Hanlon and Burton came into Frost's office and sank wearily into chairs. Their clothes were dusty and they looked fed up.

'We went through all the missing persons for the year before and the year after,' said Hanlon. 'Only two Dereks, one a fourteen-year-old kid, the other a married man, both returned home after a couple of days. I didn't expect to find anything. We've already been through them once.'

'Never mind, Arthur,' said Frost. 'If you had found something the second time round I'd have chucked it away. Mullett's bloody smug enough as it is.' He rubbed his chin thoughtfully. 'But who the hell was he?'

'He might not have lived in Denton,' suggested Burton. 'We could circulate other Divisions.'

'I can see them wasting their time digging through ancient records for us,' said Frost. 'They'd do what I would have done – not look and say they couldn't find anything.' He squirted a salvo of smoke rings up to the ceiling. 'My gut feeling is that he lived or worked in Denton. He had to be within travelling distance of his bit of nooky. The old girl wasn't a bad looker in those days, but even if you were a nipple buff, you wouldn't travel too many miles for a leg over.'

'He could have come by car,' suggested Hanlon.

'Then it would have been parked outside the house, Arthur, and neither the woman nor the son could drive so they wouldn't have been able to get rid of it.' He opened the file and flicked through the pages, then abruptly slammed it shut. 'Why are we sodding about with this? He's been dead forty years and no-one's missed him and we've got a serial killer to try and catch tonight. You two go home and get some kip. I'll see you back here just before midnight.' He stuffed the file back in his drawer, put his feet up on the desk, leant back in his chair and closed his eyes. He'd have a couple of hours' sleep in the office, then get things ready for the night's decoy operation.

He didn't hear the door open. 'Working your fingers to the bone as usual, Frost?' sneered a sarcastic Mullett.

Frost opened his eyes and dragged his feet from the desk. Flaming Hornrim Harry had a genius for turning up at the wrong moment. 'You want me, Super?' he grunted.

'I've been expecting you to report back to me with the identity of the skeleton.'

'Oh, sorry, about that,' yawned Frost. 'We had no joy. Couldn't trace him.'

'Rubbish,' snapped Mullett. 'No-one goes missing without it being reported. I want a name and I want it tonight!' He spun on his heel and stamped out.

'I'll give you a name!' spat Frost to the closed door. 'Four-eyed bastard!' He froze as the door opened almost immediately. To his relief it wasn't an angry Mullett coming back, it was Liz Maud.

'Tonight's operation, Inspector. You want women as decoys?'

'That's right,' nodded Frost.

'Put my name down.'

Frost hesitated. He already had enough volunteers, but knew the poor cow was itching for a chance to prove herself before going back to her old rank.

'All right Liz, you're on. Tart yourself up and we'll see you in the incident room at midnight.'

20

The incident room was filled with a fog of eye-stinging cigarette smoke. Frost, on his usual perch at the corner of the desk, was on his second packet of the day. As he smoked, his brain churned over and over again his strategy for the night's operations, testing the seams, looking for the flaws that always seemed to be lurking in anything he was involved in.

A chorus of wolf whistles dragged him from his thoughts . . . WPC Polly Fletcher in a short tight skirt and an even tighter sweater swaggered into the room. She wiggled and gave Frost a suggestive wink. He winked back at her, his nose twitching at the pungent perfume she had doused herself with. 'Where did you get the scent? It smells like the stuff they use to deodorize cats' litter trays.' She grinned. Inwardly he was a ferment of doubts. God, what if it all goes wrong and we end up finding Polly's mutilated body dumped in a ditch somewhere? Too many people were relying on him, and reliability was not one of his assets.

He was snatched out of his introspective gloom when Liz Maud, a long blond wig concealing her dark hair, made her entrance and the wolf whistles soared. Heavily made up, she had squeezed into figure-hugging red trousers and a clinging black sweater, over which she had draped an artificial

434

leopardskin coat. Swinging a long strapped handbag from side to side, she sauntered over to Frost. 'How do I look?'

'I'm selling my Viagra,' said Frost. 'I don't need it any more.'

'Only two girls?' asked Hanlon.

Frost nodded. 'We keep this tight and simple. We don't want to flood the area with maverick toms, it might get Chummy suspicious. And thanks to Mullett, we've only got two cars per girl which is the absolute minimum if we're going to play it safe.'

At that moment Mullett strode in. Everyone, except Frost, sprang respectfully to their feet. 'Come to inspect the troops, Super?' Frost indicated the two girls. 'You're the expert, what do you reckon?'

Mullett squeezed a sour smile. 'They look very . . . er, nice,' he said weakly. He turned to the assembly. 'A few words. This is an important and expensive operation. I've had to go on my knees to County to get the expenditure authorized and my head will be on the chopping block if we fail. So let's have a successful, cost-effective and speedy outcome.' To a thin ripple of applause and what sounded suspiciously like a slow hand clap from Frost, he gave a brief nod and marched out.

Frost slid off the desk. 'The fact that Mr Mullett's head is on the chopping block must make it very tempting for you all to want to sod things up, but we've got to deny ourselves that pleasure. There's an even more sadistic bastard out there, torturing and raping, and it's up to us to stop his larks once and for all.' He turned to the large street map of Denton pinned on the wall behind him. 'This is how we're going to play it. If anyone spots any weaknesses in my foolproof plan, for Gawd's sake shout; sometimes my infallibility goes pear-shaped.' He pointed to six

435

coloured pins. 'There are six public phone boxes in the red light areas and we're going to use them all in turn. We don't want Chummy getting suspicious because all calls come from the same two phones. We've got two pseudo toms.' He nodded to Liz and Polly. 'And four cars, which is all that the cheese-paring budget generously donated by our Divisional Commander runs to. Liz and Polly, you've each got a list of cab firms to phone and destinations to be taken to. When we are all in position, and not before, you each phone the first firm on your list and ask to be taken to the first destination on your list. When the cab turns up, surveillance car number one will follow you every inch of the way. At your destination, you will get out and wait until the cab drives off, then the tailing car will pick you up and take you back to the next phone box, and so on. We've got two cars on stand-by in case anything goes wrong. From time to time we'll swap cars so it won't always be the same one tailing you. But these spare cars have another important function. If, at any time, the tailing car sees that your cab is deviating from where we know you asked to be taken, the other cars will be called in to augment the tail. All clear up to now?'

Nods and murmurs of assent.

'Good. Now, we've got one prime suspect.' He waited while photographs were circulated. 'That's Tom Jackson. Liz arrested him once, so she won't be calling his cab firm. That pleasure goes to you, Polly. If Jackson answers a call, I want both cars to follow, and I want you to be on your guard, Polly. I don't think he's our man, but I've been wrong before, so we don't take any chances.' He jabbed a finger at Detective Sergeant Hanlon who had raised his hand. 'Yes, Arthur?'

'The two cars you've got in reserve, Jack. Wouldn't it be safer if they both tailed the cabs all the time, then if anything happened to one, the other could immediately take over?'

'It would be safer, Arthur, but it might blow the whole operation. At two in the morning there's hardly any traffic on the road. A cab with two cars following its every move could stick out like an eager dick. If our bloke has the slightest suspicion there's something funny going on, he won't play ball.' He turned to Liz Maud who now had her hand up. 'Yes, Liz?'

'When we get in the minicab, do we sit in the back or next to the driver?'

'That's a good point,' said Frost. 'I hadn't thought of that.' He looked around. 'Anyone got any views on this?'

'It's safer if they sit in the back,' said Burton firmly.

'Yes,' agreed Frost, 'but we're not going for safety. We want the bastard to make his move.' He shook the last cigarette from the pack and stuck it in his mouth. 'Unless it's obvious he's expecting you to sit in the back, then take the seat next to the driver. Now, it's important you don't show your hand too soon. If he squeezes your titties, or ventures above the stocking top, don't flash your warrant card. Do what any self-respecting girl would do, knee him in the goolies and get out without paying. The odds are it won't be our bloke; titty-squeezing is small beer when you lust for stubbing fags out on a soft white belly.'

Polly's hand shot up. 'You say don't jump the gun, Inspector. At what point should we let him know we're policewomen?'

Frost expelled smoke. 'At no point, Polly. He shouldn't know you're a cop until we make the arrest. We need hard evidence. He takes these girls some- where, ties them up, tortures and rapes them. Unless we know where he takes them, we've got nothing. Ideally, we want to follow you right up to the point where he drags you into his hideaway. And then, providing Mr Mullett doesn't decide we can't do any more overtime and calls us all back, we burst in and rescue you.'

'Will we have radios?' asked Liz.

Frost shook his head. 'They'd be a dead giveaway. You'll each have a mobile phone. Many toms carry them, so it won't look out of place. Any trouble, use it. I don't care if it means you blow your cover, your safety comes first. Any more stupid, time-wasting questions?' He looked around. 'No? Right, we've got an hour before we need to move off, so let's all nip up to the canteen and get ourselves something to eat.'

He watched them file out, chattering excitedly to each other, then took one last look round the empty incident room before switching off the light. There was a sinking feeling in the pit of his stomach. Something was going to go wrong, he just knew it. Something was going to go terribly wrong.

Frost stifled a yawn and looked at his wrist-watch. Getting on for a quarter past three, time when all the decent toms were tucked up in their beds and the rubbish emerged to pick up any rough trade that might be going, jackals after the lion's leavings. Not much point spending Mullett's overtime money by hanging around any longer. Despite Frost's forebodings, everything had been going like clockwork; the girls made their phone calls, were picked up, tailed to their correct destinations, then brought back again. Things had gone so well, he just knew nothing important was going to happen tonight and good-looking toms, swinging their handbags at this hour of the morning, were going to look very conspicuous.

DC Burton, at his side, was staring through the windscreen, watching Liz Maud who had just been dropped off by the tail car and was waiting a couple of minutes before making her next phone call.

'Let's call it a night,' Frost began when Burton's fingers suddenly tightened on his arm. Frost's head came up. 'Yes, son, I see it.' His radio paged him. The other surveillance car. They had seen it also.

A metallic grey Peugeot slithered round the corner, stopping at the end of the road. Its lights went out.

'Can you clock the registration number?' Frost asked, scrubbing at the windscreen with his coat cuff. Burton shook his head. It was too dark. Very slowly, the Peugeot began to inch forward. Frost frowned. 'What's he up to?' The car shuddered to a halt by the phone kiosk and a burly man in a black zip-up jacket got out and approached Liz. They could see him talking to her, but she was firmly shaking her head. Suddenly, he grabbed hold of her arm and tried to drag her towards the car.

'This is it,' exclaimed Frost excitedly, clicking on his radio. 'All units stand by. Be ready to follow a metallic grey Peugeot 605, no registration details yet.' He squinted through the windscreen, puzzled at what he saw. 'What is she playing at?' Liz was resisting. She had pushed the man off and was walking quickly away. 'Go with the nice man,' pleaded Frost.

Burton, his hand on the door handle, was getting ready to run across to her assistance. 'No,' ordered Frost. 'Wait!' As he spoke the man chased after Liz and grabbed her again and again Frost had to restrain Burton. 'Wait, son.' He couldn't make out why Liz wasn't going quietly. She knew they would be tailing. Then a shrill, animal-like scream of pain shivered the air. Liz and the man were struggling and he hurled her to the ground.

'Sod tailing him,' said Frost. 'Get him.' He chased after Burton, yelling into the radio for assistance as he did so. A second man had now got out of the Peugeot. Something silver flashed in the moonlight. A knife. Another bloody knife! Two in one night.

439

Burton put on a spurt of speed. 'Drop it!' he screamed.

The second man spun round, seeing the DC for the first time. He jabbed the knife menacingly. 'Stay out of this, sonny!' Then he gave a grunt, his eyes rolled upwards and he dropped like a stone as Frost's torch cracked down on his head.

They didn't give him a second glance as they ran over to the black-jacketed man, who was straddling Liz and had his fist raised ready to smash into her face. Burton grabbed the wrist, feeling with his free hand for the handcuffs in his pocket. As the man threatened to buck Burton off, Frost grabbed a handful of hair, yanked the man off Liz, then smashed his face hard against the pavement. As Burton snapped on the cuffs, Frost gave it another bang for luck, before turning his attention to Liz Maud. 'You all right, love?'

'I'm fine.' She rose to her feet and brushed down her clothes, then she prodded the black-jacketed man with her foot. 'Do you see who it is?' Frost rolled him over and shone his torch on a bruised and blooded face. 'Mickey Harris!' he said. 'Nice to see you again.' Frost looked at the other man who was rising unsteadily to his feet, shaking his head and rubbing the bump on his scalp. Harry Grafton. 'Which of you bastards hit me?' he demanded.

'No-one hit you, Mr Grafton,' beamed Frost. 'You tripped and fell.'

Burton had dragged Mickey Harris to his feet. The man was spitting blood and wincing with pain. 'I want a doctor. That bloody cow kicked me in the goolies.'

'Was it you screaming?' asked Frost. 'I thought it was her.'

'And I'm suing for assault. You handcuffed me, then you smashed my face on the pavement.'

'Tut, tut,' reproved Frost. 'Policemen don't do

things like that. We tried to stop you falling but you tripped and accidentally banged your head on the pavement three times.' His expression hardened. 'I thought I told you to leave the toms alone, Mickey?'

'She offered me her services and I refused. That's why she kneed me.' He spat out bloody saliva. 'My tooth's broken.'

'There's a coincidence,' said Frost. 'That young tom you beat up, her tooth was broken as well.' He turned to Liz. 'What happened, love?'

'He threatened to cut me up if I didn't move off of Harry Grafton's territory,' said Liz.

'Just a minute,' called Grafton, pushing his way between them. He tugged a wad of notes from his wallet and stuffed them in the pocket of Liz's coat. 'There's a hundred quid there, darling. Keep your mouth shut, stay stum and I'll double it.'

Frost snatched the wad of notes and shook his head in mock reproof. 'Oh dear, oh dear, you've done it this time, Harry. Bribing a police officer to withold evidence, in front of witnesses too.'

Grafton blinked in astonishment. 'Police officer?' He peered at Liz, who pulled off the wig. 'Remember me?' she asked Mickey Harris.

Grafton turned to Frost in protest. 'There's no way you'll get away with this, Frost – this is entrapment.'

'We are going to get away with it,' Frost replied. 'We didn't entrap you. We were here on an entirely different case.'

'Anyway, I never knew she was a police officer.'

Frost 'tut-tutted' again. 'She called out, "I'm a policewoman." ' He pointed to the group of police officers who were now watching the proceedings. 'In the earshot of all those unimpeachable, unbiased witnesses who will swear on stacks of bibles—'

'You're a bastard,' snarled Grafton.

'You're upset,' smiled Frost, 'so I shall put that

441

down to a momentary lapse of good taste.' He jerked a thumb. 'Take them to the nick: armed with a deadly weapon, assaulting a police officer, attempted bribery of a police officer and dropping blood and bits of broken tooth on a public footpath.' He watched Jordan and Simms bundle them into the car and drive off. 'Well, not a bad result, even if it wasn't the one we were after. Let's call it a night and try again tomorrow.'

Police Superintendent Mullett studied the overtime claim form Frost had presented and winced. The third consecutive night without a result and the overtime bill was soaring. 'This isn't good enough, Frost. All this money expended and nothing to show for it.'

'We can only dangle the bait,' said Frost. 'We can't force him to swallow it . . . he picks his own time.'

'Well, he's now left it too late. I'm pulling the plug on Operation Decoy as of now. Heaven knows what County is going to say when they see this bill.'

'County knows we can't give guarantees,' said Frost. 'One more night. I've got a feeling in my water that tonight's the night.'

'No,' said Mullett firmly. 'You've had that same feeling the past three nights.'

'I'll cut out one of the cars and use mine instead,' Frost offered. 'Just think of the praise you'll get from County if we pull it off . . .'

'And the flak I'll get if we don't . . .' Mullett wavered. If Frost could pull it off and he could get on the phone to the Chief Constable to modestly announce that Denton Division had done it again . . . 'All right, Frost. One more night . . . but this is the limit and if your lack of success continues, then I'm taking you off the case.' He skimmed through the wad of receipts Frost had handed over to support the claimed expenses. Some of them looked decidedly dubious. Many of the cab fare receipts seemed to be signed in the same hand although the names were different. He stared hard at Frost, but the man seemed completely unconcerned. Damn. If only he could prove it. He pulled out his pen and signed the authorization. Frost, face impassive, suppressed a sigh of relief and snatched the authorization back before Mullett could go through it more thoroughly. 'I'll get this off to County now, Super.' He had a few more receipts to slip in and a final total to alter now that Mullett had obligingly signed the covering authorization. He rose to go.

'Wait,' ordered Mullett. 'Where do we stand with the murder of the two little girls?'

'We stand nowhere,' Frost told him. 'My only suspect topped himself.'

'I am only too aware of that,' sniffed Mullett. 'The inquest is coming up next week and your job is on the line. I suggest you find yourself a more likely suspect and fast.'

A half-hearted nod from Frost. He had reached an impasse on this. No other suspects, no more clues, no helpful witnesses coming forward. *You're working so hard on this one, Inspector*, Vicky's mother had said, and he was doing sod all. 'And the skeleton,' reminded Mullett. 'I'm still waiting to learn his name.'

'Still working on it,' lied Frost, who had better things to do.

'My patience is wearing thin, Frost. I want a name . . . today . . . without fail . . .'

'Stitches come out today, guv,' announced Morgan when he returned to the office.

'They should have stitched up the flies on your trousers while they were about it,' grunted Frost.

'So I'll need time off to go to the hospital . . .'

443

Frost stared at him, light dawning in his eyes. 'The bloody hospital. Of course!'

'Guv?' frowned Morgan, puzzled.

'Mullett wants us to name that skeleton! We know the poor sod broke his ankle a couple of months before putting his leg over for the last time. Here's your starter for ten. Where do you go if you break your arm?'

'Hospital, guv.'

'Precisely, and Denton Hospital keeps records back to the year dot . . .' He snatched his scarf from the hook. 'Get the car out.' On the way past the incident room he yelled for Burton. 'Come on, son, we're off to Denton Hospital.'

The hospital porter, a miserable-looking man in dirty overalls, led them down endless flights of stone stairs and unlocked an olive green door. A musty smell of damp papers wafted out to greet them. He fumbled for the light switch and clicked it on. A long, narrow room, almost like a corridor, its sides lined with ceiling-high racks jam-packed with ancient files running far into the dark distance, all gradually coming into view as light after light clicked on.

'Should be down the far end somewhere,' said the porter, leading them past shelves labelled with the dates of the files they held. It was like walking back in time as the files got yellower and yellower and the years rolled further and further into the past: '80s, '70s, '60s . . . Frost shivered and tightened his scarf. The far reaches of the corridor were damp, cold and mildewy just like the smallholding.

'There you go,' said the porter, waving a vague hand at the 1957 section where shelves groaned under the weight of files and bundles tied with string held in fossilized knots. '*If* he came here with a broken ankle and *if* it's been filed correctly, which doesn't always

444

happen, you should find him amongst this little lot.'
The racks of 1957 files seemed to go on and on. 1957
was a bumper year for people going to hospital.

'This could take all bloody week,' moaned Burton.

'At least,' grunted the porter. 'Turn out all the
lights when you've finished.'

'A helping hand would be nice,' said Frost hopefully.

'That's what I thought when you bastards nicked
me for speeding,' said the porter.

They waited until he was out of earshot, his footsteps fading in the distance. 'Find out the number of
his car and nick him again,' said Frost. Ignoring the
'No Smoking' sign, he passed his cigarettes around
and lit up. 'It's so bleeding damp, nothing would burn
down here,' he muttered, 'but I've half a mind to give
it a bleeding good try.' He pulled out a bulging file.
The string broke and the contents spewed out on the
floor. 'We're in for a flaming good time,' he moaned,
kicking the file to one side. He nodded at an overflowing rack behind Morgan . . . 'What are those big
green envelopes?'

Morgan pulled one out and looked inside. 'X-rays,
guv.'

'Right,' said Frost. 'If he broke his ankle he'd have
it X-rayed. Ignore all the other files, just get the green
envelopes out.'

Frost and Burton looked through the envelopes
while Morgan dragged them from the shelves. The
pile of discarded files grew higher and higher.
'Didn't people have anything better to do in 1957
than break their flaming arms and legs?' complained
Frost, adding yet another file to the discard heap.

'You realize he might not have come to this
hospital, guv,' said Morgan.

'If you haven't got anything helpful to say, shut up!'
snarled Frost. There were very few green envelope

445

files left and he was beginning to give up hope, when 'Bingo! This is it! Derek Fernley, aged twenty-six.' He skimmed through the patient's record card . . . 'Single. Address: 3a St Clement Road, Denton. Occupation, Assitant Manager.'

'Damn!' This as the tottering pile of discarded files suddenly toppled over and ancient string snapped, sending the contents all over the floor in an untidy mess. The two DCs bent to pick them up, but were restrained. 'That's what hospital porters are paid for,' Frost told them, tucking Fernley's file under his arm and marching out, deliberately neglecting to switch off all the lights.

The phone in the incident room rang. Harding from Forensic. 'Yes, Inspector, the break in the ankle of our skeleton corresponds exactly with the X-ray photograph. It's him all right.'

'Thanks,' grunted Frost. 'I'd have settled for him even if the X-ray didn't match.' He hung up and scratched his chin thoughtfully. The assistant manager of what? A shop, an office, a factory? An assistant manager goes missing and no-one reports it? Surely someone would have noticed by now that he wasn't at his desk? He took a look round the room. 'Where's Taffy?'

'He's still checking that address in St Clement Road,' said Hanlon.

'If Derek Fernley opens the door to him, we're back to square one,' grunted Frost. 'And if a nubile young tart opens the door we won't see Taffy back here today.'

'And who's taking my name in vain?' Taffy had returned, his clothes smothered in dust, an ancient police file tucked under his arm. He plonked a black and white photograph in front of Frost. 'That, guv,' he said proudly, 'is Derek Fernley.' The photograph

446

was of a man in his early twenties, arms folded, dark hair glossy with brilliantine, an over-large nose and a small, neatly trimmed moustache.

Frost studied it, then checked the photograph of the skeleton before shaking his head. 'Nothing like him, Taff. Our one hasn't got a moustache.'

'It is him,' insisted Morgan. 'I went to his old address. They couldn't help, but I found someone in the street who remembered him.'

'So where did you get the photograph?'

'From our store room. We've got a file on him. Look!' He dumped the file in front of Frost and opened it. A yellowing newspaper cutting clipped to the top had headlines that read: SUPERMARKET MANAGER AND TAKINGS BOTH GO MISSING! Below the headline was a reproduction of the photograph of Fernley. Frost picked up the cutting and read the story out aloud:

' "Derek Fernley, twenty-six, Assistant Manager of the large Superwise Supermarket in Denton, is being sought by the police in connection with the disappearance of some £6,000 from the store's safe.

' "Denton police are anxious to interview Fernley who has not reported for work since the money went missing. Neighbours said Fernley did not return home on the Friday and has not been seen since." '

Frost looked again at the photograph. 'Call me a suspicious old sod, but I reckon Fernley took that money.' He flicked through the investigating officer's typed notes. Small sums of money, between £5 and £10 a week, had been disappearing and it was obvious that Fernley had been milking the supermarket's petty cash float. Checking his flat they found he had cancelled the milk and drawn the balance from his bank account. There was no sign of his passport.

'They never found him,' mused Frost. 'They should have looked in that old cow's back garden.' He closed the file. 'So why wasn't he listed as a missing person?'

'Missing isn't the same as absconding,' explained Burton.

Frost handed the file back to Morgan. 'He was milking the petty cash. The auditors are coming which means he's bound to be found out, so he empties the safe and legs it, pausing only for that last fatal grumble and grunt with big-nippled Nelly and her creamy white belly. But what happened to the six thousand quid and how did big-nippled Nell suddenly find the money to buy the smallholding? Do we see some sort of a connection?'

'You're saying she took it?' Morgan asked.

'Yes, I am,' said Frost. He stood up. 'Come on, Taff. Let's go and ask her.'

She was in the kitchen, still preparing vegetables, chopping them into small pieces with a knife.

'We've found out who your last client was,' Frost told her. 'Derek Fernley, assistant manager of a super-market.'

Her eyes flickered briefly, then she concentrated on dicing the vegetables. 'I didn't know his name.'

'He paid a bit over the odds for his last bit of the other, didn't he? And he didn't even get a cup of tea afterwards.'

She kept her eyes down, the blade of the knife chopping, dicing, missing her fingers by a hair's breadth. 'Don't know what you mean.'

'Where did you get the money to buy this place?'

'Don't remember.'

Frost dragged a chair out to sit down, saw the state of the seat and decided against it. 'I'll jog your memory, shall I? He comes round for his usual Friday night nooky, but this time he's got a suitcase with him. After his unfortunate demise, you take a look inside

448

and there's more money than you've ever seen in your life, over six thousand quid. So here's a chance to move out, to hide away somewhere, to keep little Sonny Boy under wraps in case he blurts out about the naughty man he and mumsie planted in someone's garden. You buy this place for cash, poke Sonny Boy under the stairs and if anyone asks about him, you dab away a tear and say the angels grew lonely and wanted him for a sunbeam. Is that it?'

She shrugged. 'I don't know nothing about any money.' Chop, chop, chop.

The door creaked open and Boy lumbered in. He started at the sight of the two detectives.

'Go and chop some wood, Boy,' she snapped.

Obediently, like a well-trained dog, Boy went to the sink and pulled out an axe from under it. He shouldered it like a rifle. 'I'll chop some wood,' he announced, as if he had just thought of it. They watched him march out.

'You told us your son kept hitting Fernley on the head again and again.'

'That's right.'

'The pathologist reckons he was only hit once.'

'It was a long time ago. I don't remember it clearly.'

'Did you know Derek had the money with him when he came?'

'I don't know nothing about no money.' She scooped up the diced vegetables in a gnarled hand and dropped them into a saucepan.

Frost sighed. They weren't going to get anything out of her. 'All right, Mrs Aldridge. We'll leave it for now.' He jerked his head for Morgan to follow him out.

'You let her off the hook pretty easily, guv,' said Morgan.

'Maybe,' grunted Frost.

Outside, near the coop of squawking chickens, Boy

was chopping a fallen tree trunk into sizeable pieces, the axe blade flashing in the dying sun as it hissed through the air. Morgan nudged Frost. 'I reckon I could get him to talk, guv.' He wandered over to the man, who stopped his chopping and eyed him suspiciously.

'Go away. Mustn't talk to you.'

'Just a couple of questions,' wheedled Morgan, but Frost tugged him away.

'Leave it, Taffy.'

'But, guv—'

'I said leave it!'

Frost spun on his heel and marched off to the car, leaving a puzzled Morgan trailing behind him.

'So she wouldn't admit to taking the money?' asked Mullett when they reported back to him.

'We pushed her as hard as we could, Super,' said Frost. 'She denied all knowledge of it.'

'What about her son? Did you question him?'

'No, we didn't – Aww!' said Morgan, cut off in mid-sentence as a well-aimed kick from Frost hacked his ankle.

'We really put him through it,' said Frost. 'He says he knows nothing about any money and I don't think he's capable of lying. My guess is that Fernley hid the cash somewhere and we'll never find it.'

Mullett nodded his satisfaction. 'A loose end that needn't concern us unduly. Now, we know his name, I can forward the papers to the CPS. Like you, I very much doubt that they will prosecute, but that is their concern.' His hand reached out for the phone. 'If you'll excuse me, I'll let the Chief Constable know of my – er, our success.'

'I don't understand, guv,' said Morgan when they got back into Frost's office. 'You told Mr Mullett we talked to the son and we didn't.'

Frost kicked the door shut behind them. 'We didn't talk to the son, Taffy, in case he told us something we don't want to hear.'

'Like what, guv?'

'Like what really happened with Fernley.'

'We know what happened. The son killed him.'

'No, Taff. I reckon the old girl killed him.' He flopped down at his desk and lit up a cigarette. 'Did you clock the knife the old girl was using to dice up the carrots?'

'Yes, guv. It looked very similar to the one she stuck into me.'

'And it also looked very similar to this.' Frost opened his desk drawer and took out the plastic bag containing the rusty knife that had been found buried near the skeleton. 'In fact it could be its bloody twin, the same ring at the end of the handle for hanging it up.'

Morgan examined the knife carefully. 'It does look similar,' he admitted grudgingly.

'Similar? It's flaming identical. One of a pair, I reckon.'

'So what are you suggesting?' Morgan asked.

'I'm suggesting, Taffy, that this knife, which we found buried with the skeleton, came from her kitchen. Now why would she bury a perfectly good knife? She's too bleeding mean to throw anything away; she probably uses her toilet paper on both sides. She chucked it because there was blood on it, and not chicken's blood . . . Derek Fernley's blood.'

'You're saying she stabbed him?'

'Yes, I am. She said there was blood everywhere. You don't get that amount of blood from a crack on the nut. The boy might have been involved somehow, but she killed Fernley, probably to get the money, and that makes it murder.'

Morgan stared at him. 'Where's your proof, guv?'

451

'I haven't got any proof, son. I just know she did it.'

'Then why didn't you let me question her son? I could have got the truth out of him.'

'And suppose he told you that mummy stabbed the naughty man with her knife? Mullett wouldn't let it rest and we'd then have to start wasting our bloody time investigating an ancient murder case that would be thrown out of court, and I've got better things to do.'

'But you can't turn a blind eye to murder,' protested Morgan.

'Just watch me, Taffy. That old cow kept her son hidden away for years just to save her own skin. I'd like to get her for that, but she's too old and it happened far too long ago and I'm too flaming tired to care.' He exhaled smoke. 'Let this be a lesson to you, Taff. Stay away from women with big nipples and long knives.' He yawned. 'Let's get our heads down. I get the feeling we're going to be in for a rough night.'

21

PC Collier yawned and knuckled his eyes. Three in the morning, his fourth consecutive night on overtime and it was hard to keep awake. This was going to be yet another boring night with nothing happening. He closed his eyes for a few seconds and wished he was back home in bed, then his eyes snapped open as he became aware there was someone in the seat next to him. Jordan back with the big Macs? No. It was Detective Inspector Jack Frost.

'Sorry, sir,' Collier muttered, trying to look alert. 'Must have closed my eyes for a few seconds.'

'About two hundred and forty bleeding seconds,' said Frost. 'I know it's a bore, son, but there's little point to the exercise if you fall asleep just as the killer picks her up.' He took a look through the car window. 'Where is she?'

With a start of panic Collier snatched up the night glasses and scoured the area near the phone box. Polly wasn't there! He'd missed the pick-up, he'd bloody missed it! Then he saw her, leaning against the railings in the shadow. 'There, sir!' He passed the night glasses to Frost, trying to sound as if he knew all the time.

Sensing she was being watched, Polly moved forward to the light-splash from the lamp post and gave her bottom a little wiggle for Collier's benefit. He blushed, but Frost gawped with delight. 'Cor, I couldn't half give her one.' He turned to the PC. 'Shouldn't there be two of you? Where's Jordan?'

Before Collier could think of an excuse, Jordan appeared clutching two yellow polystyrene containers. His dismay showed when he saw Frost. 'Just popped out for some refreshment, Inspector.'

Frost took one of the boxes and looked inside. A beefburger, oozing fat and reeking of fried onion. 'You should have got one for Collier as well,' he said, sinking his teeth into it. His head jerked up. 'What's this?'

A flare of headlights as a beige minicab marked 'Dave's Taxis' drew up by the phone box and honked its horn. Collier consulted his list. 'The right cab, sir.' He focused the night glasses. 'And the right driver. He's picked Polly up a couple of times before.'

'OK, son. Follow it, then take her back to the station. I'm calling it a night.' He climbed out of the car, fatigue and depression weighing him down. He was so sure tonight was going to be the night. Now he'd have to face Mullett again in the morning and talk the cheese-paring bastard out of stopping the exercise. He took another bite at the beefburger but realized he didn't want it and chucked it into the gutter, giving it a savage kick as it fell. Round the corner to his own car and off to the other phone box. He had left Morgan watching Liz Maud but wasn't too happy at leaving the DC on his own in spite of the man's earnest protestations. 'You can rely on me, guv.' Taffy was the last bleeding bloke you could rely on.

Half-way there when his radio squawked. 'Control to Mr Frost. Urgent. Come in, please.'

He lifted the handset. 'Frost.'

'Urgent assistance required. Ram raid in progress at Conway's Jewellers in the High Street. One officer injured, ambulance on way. We need all your men, now!'

He radioed his team as he spun the car round. 'All units, abandon operation. Ram raid, Conway's Jewellers, officer injured. Get over there now.'

Morgan radioed back. 'I'm watching DI Maud, guv. There's a cab pulling up for her now. Can't see the registration number, but it's a woman driver. Looks all right. Safe to leave?'

'No, not safe to bloody leave,' snapped Frost. 'Might be a man in drag. Follow, pick her up at the other end, then both of you get over to Conway's pronto.'

Skidding round the corner, he was the first on the scene, the other two cars close on his heels. A Panda car was slewed across the road. The pavement outside the jewellers sparkled with broken glass and the alarm was shrilling with no-one to take any notice. He ran over to the still shape of a uniformed officer sprawled in the gutter, his head in a puddle of blood.

A slamming of car doors and the clatter of footsteps behind him. He knelt by the officer and touched the icy cold, chalk white face of twenty-year-old Peter Adams who had been with the Division a few months only. 'Get a blanket or something. The poor sod's freezing.' He moved to one side as WPC Polly Fletcher shucked off her tart's fur coat and gently laid it over the injured constable. Frost could smell the incongruous aroma of the heady scent she had been using.

'Hey!' A man was running towards them from a house opposite. 'It was me who phoned your lot,' he told them proudly. 'I saw it all.'

Frost took the man's arm and moved away. 'What happened?'

'I was watching a film on the telly when I heard this crash. I looks out the window and I sees this van ramming through the jeweller's plate glass window. There were three of them, youngish, in their twenties I'd imagine, all with balaclavas hiding their faces. They were scooping jewellery from the window when the cop drives up. He charges over and one of them welts him with this baseball bat. Poor sod went down like a stone. They ran back in the van and roared off.'

'Which way did they go?' asked Frost.

He pointed. 'Down the Bath Road, speeding like the clappers.'

'What sort of van?'

'Little grey delivery van. There had been a name on the side but it was blacked out.'

'Registration number?'

The man shook his head. 'Couldn't get it. The plates were covered in mud.'

Frost called for all units to be on the look-out. He had no sooner clicked off when Morgan radioed through, very excited. 'That van. It just passed me by the Denton roundabout going towards Exley . . . light grey, three men. Am in pursuit, assistance required.'

'Stick to the sods like glue,' said Frost, calling in all units to assist. He found himself having to shout over the noise of the shrilling alarm. 'Can't someone turn that thing off?'

'Key-holder's on the way,' Jordan told him. Another sound sliced through the night. The warble of an ambulance siren. Frost looked down at the unconscious man. Adams was really too inexperienced to have been out on his own at night. Sod the bloody budget cuts. And Adams had been too keen, too anxious to prove himself. He should have stayed in the Panda and waited for assistance, not gone rushing out when there were three of them, armed with baseball bats.

In seconds the paramedics were gently easing Adams on to a stretcher. 'Looks like a fractured skull,'

they told Frost, adding ominously, 'Could be nasty.'
Frost detailed Polly to go with Adams to the hospital,
the paramedics expressing surprise as she tottered up
the steps in her short skirt and high heels. He didn't
bother to explain.

As the rear lights of the ambulance dwindled to
pinpricks as it sped down the Bath Road, Frost
scrunched over broken glass to examine the shop
front. The metal grid used to protect the display was
crumpled and had been cut with heavy duty cutters.
The display shelves were stripped bare, except for
a solitary diamond necklace which hung forlornly,
its price ticket string caught on a drawing pin. Un-
hooking it, he checked the price tag. £4,500. He
whistled softly. He'd have guessed a couple of quid.

Morgan radioed through. 'Still on their tail, guv.
They're going at a fair old lick. Any chance we could
head them off from the other direction before they
reach the turn-off?'

'I'll check.' He called Control, but Morgan was out
of luck. The only available vehicle was over the other
side of Denton and would never get there in time.
He was pocketing his radio when a black Honda
Accord braked to a halt outside the shop and a short,
tubby man in a sheepskin driving coat clambered out.
'The name's Conway . . . it's my shop,' he told
Collier, then surveyed the wreckage of the window
with mounting indignation. 'Bloody hell! Look at it!
The third time in four months. I've only just had that
window put in.'

'My heart bleeds for you,' grunted Frost, intro-
ducing himself. 'You're insured, aren't you?'

'Top rate premiums and I have to pay the first
£5,000 of any claim, but after that I'm insured, yes.'

'Tough,' said Frost. He jerked a thumb at the
alarm. 'Can you turn that flaming thing off?' Conway
scowled. 'I can turn it off if it offends your ears,

Inspector, but tell me something, would you? Where was your bloody lot when it went off?'

'Our bloody lot was lying in the gutter with his skull smashed in,' snapped Frost. 'He was welted with a baseball bat.'

The man's eyes opened wide in concern. 'My God! I didn't know. Is he all right?'

Frost shrugged. 'He's unconscious. We're waiting to hear from the hospital.'

Conway covered his face with a hand and shook his head. 'I'm so sorry. I didn't know.'

'We'll want an inventory of what's been taken.'

'That's easy,' said Conway, bitterly. 'It's everything that was in the window.'

'As soon as you can,' said Frost, moving away as his radio paged him. Morgan again.

'We've lost them, guv.'

Frost stared at the radio open-mouthed. 'You've what?'

'Not our fault, guv. They swerved in front of an articulated lorry. The lorry driver slammed on his brakes, skidded and jack-knifed. We couldn't get past.'

Frost sighed. 'There's not many places they could have gone. Keep looking!'

The clock on the interview room wall clunked its way round to 4.12. The radiator still wasn't working properly in spite of Frost's kicks and the room was cold. Frost thumbed through the list of stolen items then raised his eyes to Conway. 'Nearly a quarter of a million. What were you stocking – the Crown Jewels?'

'It was all good stuff: gold, silver, jewellery, Rolex watches. It soon adds up.'

'Why wasn't it in the safe?'

'Good question. The flaming safe's jammed. We can't open it. The locksmith's coming tomorrow to fix it – too flaming busy to come today. I had to get special dispensation from the insurance company to leave it in the window overnight.'

'That was good of them.'

'Yes . . . very generous,' replied Conway with heavy sarcasm. 'All they charged was an extra premium of £500. £500 for twenty-four flaming hours.'

Frost glanced at the list of stolen items again. 'I bet they wish they'd turned you down, now.' He took out a cigarette. 'Was tonight the first time the stuff was left in the window?'

'Yes. These crooks were either bloody observant or bloody lucky – tomorrow night the stuff would all have been nicely locked away in the safe.'

Frost thumbed his lighter. 'At least you were insured.'

'Oh yes, and if I live long enough, and they can't find anything in the small print so they can wriggle out of paying, I'll get the wholesale price less £5,000 excess and treble the premium for next time.' He blew his nose noisily. 'But here am I ranting on and forgetting about that poor devil in hospital. Any news?'

'Still unconscious. It doesn't look too good.'

The jeweller's face creased. 'I'm so terribly sorry. I owe him. If there's anything I can do . . .'

'Thanks,' said Frost, rubbing his hands together to restore the circulation. 'And thanks for coming. We'll keep you informed.'

Conway zipped up his briefcase and pulled on a pair of leather gloves.

'Half a mo!' said Frost. As Conway sat down again, Frost beckoned Collier over. 'Nip out and see if there's any news from the hospital, would you, son?' He waited until the constable had left before leaning across the table to Conway and lowering his voice. 'Wanted him out of the way for a minute,' he said, tapping his nose conspiratorially. He pulled a brown paper bag from his pocket and shook the contents into his hand. A necklace which sparkled in the overhead light. 'I bought this from a bloke in a pub today, paid fifty quid for it. He swore blind it was worth £400. Was I caught?'

Conway stripped off his gloves and examined the necklace. A sad shake of his head as he handed it back. 'You got exactly what you paid for, Inspector. It's worth £50 top whack.'

With a rueful grin Frost tucked the necklace back in his pocket. 'The lousy bastard!' he said. Then he clicked his fingers as if he had suddenly remembered something. 'I'm a silly sod. This isn't the necklace I bought in the pub. This is the one I took from your shop window tonight. It had this £4,500 price ticket on it.' He swung the price ticket backwards and forwards.

Conway went white. 'I don't understand . . .'

Frost grinned back at him. 'Don't you, Mr Conway? Your bank manager does.'

'My bank manager?'

A cheerful nod from Frost. 'I phoned him a few minutes ago. It might have been my imagination, but he didn't sound too pleased at being woken up from a sound sleep. Anyway, it seems you're overdrawn like mad, the bank want to repossess your house and your shop, and there's quite a few of your cheques bouncing like the Dambusters' bomb. He said you had a profitable little business there until you let your son start running it.'

Conway stared, mouth agape, then, with an effort, pulled himself together. 'This is all beyond me, Inspector. I'm going—'

'Sit down!' barked Frost.

Conway's shoulders slumped. He dropped down in the chair.

A tap at the door and a grim-faced Collier returned.

He whispered something to Frost whose lips tightened. 'Thank you, Constable.' He stared at Conway. 'A fractured skull, extensive brain damage. They rate his chances as lower than fifty/fifty, but even if he does pull through, they doubt if he will ever be able to lead a normal life.' He bent forward, his face nearly touching Conway's. 'You bastard!' He spat out the words.

Conway jerked back as if he had been hit. 'How dare you!' he spluttered.

'An insurance fiddle. I can smell them a mile off. A fake raid, then claim on the insurance. And thanks to your scam a bloody good police officer who was trying to protect your property has been ruined for life.'

Conway flushed. 'This is preposterous. You're making wild accusations without a shred of proof. I am not saying another word unless my solicitor is present.'

'Good,' said Frost, opening his folder. 'You can show him this when he gets here.' He pulled out a printed form and handed it over. 'It's a search warrant . . . I took the liberty of getting one ready in advance. We're going to search your house.'

'My house?' croaked Conway, the search warrant shaking as he tried to hold it steady.

Frost nodded. 'Who knows, we might find a lot of the good stuff hidden away somewhere that you forgot to stick in your shop window.'

The jeweller's face crumpled. He stared down at the scratched and scarred table top. 'You've got to believe me, Inspector. I didn't mean for anyone to get hurt.'

Frost signalled for Collier to start up the cassette recorder, then gave Conway a warm, encouraging smile. 'Tell us all about it,' he said.

Frost watched Wells lock the cell door on Conway. 'His son and two mates carried out the fake raid.

461

We've sent a couple of cars to pick them up, so get the other two cells swilled out.'

'Conway's son was behind it all, then?' asked Wells.

'Yes,' agreed Frost. 'Conway put him in charge of the shop. The worst mistake of his life. Sonny Boy's been selling off the stock to pay for his gambling and drug habits and replacing it with cheap swag, hoping no-one would notice. Conway was going to sell the business and had the buyer coming in next week to appraise the stock, so Sonny Boy had to come clean. They thought this would be a good way out of their troubles. Let this be a lesson to you, Bill – crime does not pay!'

'Not a wasted night after all, then?' said Wells as they walked back to the lobby.

'If you overlook the poor sod in hospital and the fact that our serial killer is still on the loose, then by my lousy standards it was an unqualified success.'

In the lobby a worried-looking Burton was waiting for them. 'Anyone seen Liz?' he asked.

'Detective Sergeant Maud, to you,' snapped Wells. 'And I haven't seen her. Try the ladies' toilets – she spends most of her time in there.'

'She's probably in the incident room,' called Frost as Burton hurried off. To Wells he said: 'What's the world coming to? They get their leg over, then start calling senior officers by their first name.' But on the way back to his office he found himself worrying. He couldn't recall seeing Liz since early on in the operation, and now he thought about it, she wasn't at the scene of the jewellery raid. He found Burton staring into an empty murder incident room.

'She might have gone straight home, son,' he suggested. 'Have you phoned her?'

'I've phoned: she doesn't answer.'

'Let's ask Morgan where he dropped her.'

The sound of raucous laughter from the rear doors

heralded the return of Morgan with Jordan and Simms, all escorting three sullen men in handcuffs, the ram raiders. Simms was carrying the bags of fake jewellery. 'We've got them, guv,' announced Morgan triumphantly.

'Where's Inspector Maud?' asked Frost.

'No idea, guv. Isn't she here?'

'Would I be asking you if she was? You picked her up after the cab dropped her. Where did you take her?'

'I didn't pick her up, guv. I stopped following the cab when I chased after these three in the van.' He pointed to the handcuffed men.

Frost stared. He couldn't believe what he was hearing. 'You just left her?' Morgan nodded. Telling Jordan and Simms to get their prisoners charged, Frost dragged Morgan into the murder incident room. 'You just flaming left her?' he repeated incredulously, an angry Burton looking on.

Morgan's head turned from one to the other, not understanding what the fuss was about. 'I couldn't chase the van and follow the cab at the same time, guv. I told you I was going after the van. You didn't object.'

'I didn't object,' exploded Frost, 'because I assumed you'd already picked her up. I didn't think you'd be so stupid as to abandon her.'

'Sorry, guv,' mumbled Morgan. 'A misunderstanding. But it was a woman driver. Inspector Maud will be all right. She probably got them to drive her straight back home.'

'I've phoned,' Burton told him. 'She doesn't answer.'

'She could be in bed with a sleeping tablet,' suggested Morgan hopefully.

'She could be in bed with a flaming serial rapist,' snapped Frost. PC Simms was walking past the door.

463

Frost called him in. 'Drive straight over to Inspector Maud's flat, kick the door in if necessary, but get inside, confirm she's there, and radio me immediately either way.'

'Hold on,' said Burton, digging into his pocket. 'No need to kick the door down.' He handed a key to Simms, then turned back to Frost. 'She wouldn't have gone home without reporting back here.'

'She might have got pissed off with us because Taffy didn't pick her up and thought, Sod them!' said Frost. But he wasn't even convincing himself. Doubt and self-guilt chewed away at his innards. Why the bloody hell didn't he check with Taffy that he had Liz on board when he phoned? He jabbed a finger at Morgan. 'Phone the minicab firm . . . find out where they dropped her off.'

A hot, liquid surge of relief as the phone rang. This had to be Liz. But it was Arthur Hanlon joyfully reporting from Conway's house. They had found most of the allegedly stolen jewellery and watches in the home safe. This didn't cheer Frost one bit. The ram raid wasn't important any more. 'We've got a problem, Arthur.' He told him about Liz and ordered him to get over to Sutton Street where Liz should have been dropped off by the minicab, in the slender hope she might still be impatiently waiting to be picked up by Morgan. 'If she's not there, keep an eye out on the return trip. She might be walking back to the station.' In high heels and a tom's outfit? What a bloody hope, but it had to be covered.

No sooner had he replaced the phone than it rang again and again his hopes soared. This had to be Liz. But it was Mullett.

'I understand we've got an injured policeman in hospital. Why wasn't I told?'

God, he should have told Mullett right away. 'Sorry, Super – so much going on.' He filled the

Divisional Commander in, but didn't tell him about Liz. 'They are operating on him now. We've got the men who did it.'

'Hmph,' grunted Mullett. 'Keep me informed.'

Frost hung up as Morgan finished his call to the minicab firm, his expression telegraphing bad news. 'They don't use women drivers at night, guv. They took the call and sent a man driver, but when he got to the pick-up point there was no-one there.'

'Did you check the registration number of the cab that did pick her up?'

Morgan looked anywhere but at Frost. 'It belongs to a VW Beetle sold as scrap six months ago.'

Frost dropped in a chair and stared into space. 'Bloody, bloody hell.'

A howl of rage as Burton, hearing the tail end of this, hurried over to them. 'What are you saying?'

'It doesn't look good, son,' Frost told him. 'Unless Simms tells us she's tucked up in her flat, we've got to face the possibility that our serial killer has got her.' The phone rang. Control. Simms had just radioed in. Liz wasn't in her flat and the tom's outfit wasn't back in the wardrobe . . . He broke the news to Burton.

Burton's face reddened with anger. 'And that Welsh bastard just abandoned her?'

'I thought she'd be all right,' muttered Morgan, stepping back quickly as Burton, swinging wild punches, lunged at him.

'You *thought*, you bloody Welsh sod? When have you ever thought in your life?'

'Pack it in!' Frost pushed himself between the two men, forcing them apart. 'I'm as much to blame as Morgan,' he told Burton. 'I was in charge so I'm even more bloody guilty. If you want to beat me to a pulp, son, fair enough, but let's find her first.'

'Find her?' snarled Burton, still glaring daggers at Morgan. 'Find her dead body, you mean?'

Frost poked a cigarette in his mouth and lit up, a delaying tactic to give him time to think. They hadn't the faintest idea where she was so where the hell did they start looking? All they had to go on was the minicab, a black Ford. He opened the door and shouted to Bill Wells: 'I want as many cars as we can get to go out on the road and look for this Ford. The fake registration plates have probably been dumped by now, so let them stop any minicab, any vehicle in fact: car, van, articulated lorry, I don't care what colour or make, and search it. I want everyone in on this, off-duty men as well.'

'I'll need authority,' said Wells stubbornly.

'Sod authority. I'll get the authority and if I can't get it, I'll carry the can.'

'And you'll have to let Mr Mullett know.'

Frost snatched up the phone. 'I'm letting him know now. Just do what I bloody ask.' As he waited for Mullett to answer he yelled for Burton and Morgan to phone all the minicab and taxi firms and find out if any of their drivers had noticed a maverick cab in the area and, if so, where it was heading. The ringing tone went on in his ear. 'Come on, come on,' he muttered. 'It's only four o'clock in the morning, you can't be in bed yet.' At last a disgruntled, still drowsy Divisional Commander answered the phone. It took some time for the import of what Frost was saying to sink in and when it did, Mullett was wide awake.

'What are you trying to tell me?' Mullett's voice soared to a screech.

Frost pulled the phone away from his ear and let the sizzle of accusation and fury crackle round the incident room. When the noise stopped for a while, he tentatively returned the phone to his ear in case the superintendent was simply pausing for breath, but he seemed to have finished his initial tirade.

'Couldn't agree with you more, Super,' said Frost. 'A proper balls-up. I presume I have your full authority to do whatever is necessary to locate and rescue Detective Sergeant Maud?'

'How much is this going to cost?' shrilled Mullett.

'Cost?' echoed Frost incredulously. 'What the hell does the cost matter? A police officer's life is at stake.'

'I've got to get sanction from County and the first question they will ask is "How much?" '

'£2,300,' said Frost, plucking a figure from the air. 'Might be less if we're lucky.' And a bleeding sight more if we're not, he told himself.

'Right,' said Mullett, seemingly content now that he had a figure. 'Hold fire. I'll get back to you.'

Frost hung up quickly. Sod holding fire. 'All agreed,' he told Wells. 'I've got carte blanche to do whatever is necessary. Oh, and get someone to keep checking her flat. We'd look proper prats if we had the helicopters and the dogs out and she'd only popped out for some fish and chips.'

But he knew she wouldn't be back. He knew the rapist had got her and his face creased with pain at the mental picture of Liz, naked, tied to a bed, while the sadistic bastard stubbed fags out all over her. Smoke from the cigarette in his mouth drifted up his nose. It tasted foul. He stubbed it out on the polished surface of the desk. *Don't worry, we'll be following you every inch of the way*, he had promised. God, he'd made some balls-ups in his time, but this . . .

Wells returned, only to be sent out again as Frost thought of something else. 'Get on to the other Divisions. I want all their off-duty men standing by in case we have to do a house-to-house.'

Wells hesitated. 'Are you sure Mullett's agreed to this?'

Frost gave the sergeant his most reassuring and

467

sincere smile. 'When have I ever lied to you, Bill?' he asked.

'Every bleeding day of the year,' said Wells.

As the off-duty men reported in, he found them jobs to do: phone all the hospitals for unknown casualties; get names and addresses of every minicab and taxicab driver from their firms and phone or knock them up to ask if they had seen a maverick cab lurking about at any time. He sent Burton out with Collier to call on all the local toms yet again to ask if they had ever been approached by this minicab with the woman driver. The place was a-bustle. He had given everyone something to do, but in his heart of hearts knew that none of this would do any good. They needed a break, one of his strokes of luck, but his guardian angel was refusing to do any more overtime.

The phone rang. 'Frost.' It was Arthur Hanlon. Liz wasn't at the drop-off point. He'd retraced the route back to her flat. No sign of her.

The phone hardly stopped ringing. Negative reports. Nothing from cab drivers, toms, the hospitals . . . A blaze of headlights in the grimy windows of the incident room. A car pulling into the car-park. Liz! It had to be Liz. It was Mullett, bloody Mullett, just in time to receive a 'Sod all' progress report.

Even at that unearthly hour of the morning, Mullett was a walking tailor's dummy in his immaculate uniform. 'My office!' he barked, flinging the words through the open door of the incident room as he marched down the corridor.

Frost heaved himself out of the chair. 'It's probably about my promotion,' he said.

In the old log cabin with its highly polished built-in wooden cupboards, Mullett sat stony-faced at his desk. 'A shambles,' he said. 'An absolute shambles.'

Frost said nothing. Mullett was right. Of course it

was a shambles, but what was the point in stating the bloody obvious? How was this helping to get the poor cow back?

'Against my better judgement I bled our overtime budget dry, on your unequivocal assurance that by doing so we would definitely catch the killer and that nothing would go wrong. Teams of men, on expensive overtime, but when the killer turns up, what happens?'

'We sodded it up,' said Frost blandly. 'I know what happened, Super, I don't need telling.'

'And in addition you have put the life of one of our officers in peril, the very thing you assured me would be avoided. How on earth am I going to explain this to County?'

'I know it's the last thing you'd think of doing,' said Frost, 'but you could always put the blame on me.'

'The fact that I had put my trust in you could still reflect badly on me,' replied Mullett. His eyes lit up as he found a solution. 'We put the entire blame on DC Morgan, a man foisted on us by County against my better judgement. He deliberately disobeyed your explicit orders.' With luck, Denton Division could come out of this comparatively unscathed.

Frost shook his head. There was no way he was having the buck dumped solely on Morgan. 'I was in charge—' he began.

Mullett cut him short. 'Technically in charge, perhaps, but you had given him explicit instructions and he would know the consequence should he disobey those instructions. I want no falling on swords here, Frost.' He jabbed a finger, happily recalling the phrase used by County. 'Damage limitation, that's what this is all about, Frost, damage limitation . . .'

Frost was about to snap, 'Sod damage limitation,' when there was a tap at the door and Bill Wells looked in.

Mullett scowled, annoyed at being disturbed. 'Can't it wait, Sergeant?'

'Urgent call for Mr Frost,' said Wells. 'Mrs Beatty.'

'Drawers-dropping Doreen?' protested Frost. 'Get shot of her!'

'Who is she?' asked Mullett.

'A sex-starved spinster who imagines she's being stalked,' Frost told him.

'I think you'd better get over there, Inspector,' said Wells. 'She's in a hell of a state. She reckons the stalker broke into her house and she's killed him.'

'Shit!' said Frost.'This is all we bleeding need.'

He took WPC Polly Fletcher along with him. 'Just in case she accuses me of raping her,' he said.

The young WPC gave a weak smile. She wasn't finding Frost very funny at the moment. It could have been her, instead of Liz Maud, who had been picked up by the killer. With her face wiped clean of the tart's make-up she looked about sixteen. Her hands on the wheel were shaking.

'Don't worry, love,' said Frost. 'We'll find Liz.' He wasn't even convincing himself. 'There's the house.' He nodded at the only one in the street with any lights showing.

He thumbed the doorbell. 'Come on, come on,' he muttered, urging the woman on as she fumbled with the locks and chains. The sooner he got this farce over and was back in the station, the better.

Doreen Beatty was fullly dressed, a thick grey coat over her skirt and cardigan. She looked distraught. 'I told you I was being stalked but you wouldn't believe me. He got into my bedroom. He would have raped me.'

They stepped inside and she closed the door behind them. 'I couldn't sleep. I went to the all-night supermarket for some milk. When I came back, there he

470

was, in my bedroom. I hit him with my walking-stick. I killed him.'

'Good for you,' murmured Frost, not believing a word of it. 'Where's the body?'

She pointed a trembling finger to an open door. Frost nodded for Polly to take a look as he yawned and consulted his watch.

'Inspector!' The WPC was trying to keep her voice steady. 'You'd better come in here.'

The man was lying face down on the floor, blood from his head staining the beige carpet. A pillow was half-way down the single bed, an empty pillow case on the floor by the sprawled man. Frost felt for a pulse. The pulse beat was strong, but the man was out cold. He straightened up. 'Not dead and not a stalker, Mrs Beatty,' he told her. 'You've knocked out the pillow case burglar.'

'More than half of our unsolved crime figures wiped out in a stroke,' he told Bill Wells bitterly. 'Any other time I'd be over the moon but tonight I don't give a toss.' Polly had gone with the ambulance to the hospital. Slight concussion, nothing broken and he'd be fit for questioning in the morning. 'Morning? It's bleeding morning now,' said Frost, mooching back to the murder incident room.

He steeled himself to push open the door. All heads turned, everyone expectant, waiting for him to come up with an instant solution so they could roar out and pick up Liz unharmed. He flashed a pleading glance to Burton and Morgan who had just finished their phone calls to cab drivers. They both shook their heads. 'Nothing,' reported Burton. 'What do we do now?'

Pray, thought Frost as he peeled the cellophane off yet another pack of cigarettes. Bloody hell. All these men at his disposal, plus – although Mullett didn't know it yet – men from other Divisions standing by on overtime, and nothing to give them to do. Fall on his sword? If he had a bleeding sword he'd skewer himself on it right now.

They were still looking at him, thinking his silence was deep, studied thought instead of blind panic. He sucked down a lungful of smoke. Then, suddenly, his guardian angel decided to soften her heart. He leapt to his feet. 'The mobile phone . . . she had a mobile phone!'

Burton sighed. What was the fool on about? 'I've tried calling her on it,' he said. 'No reply.'

Frost flapped an impatient hand. 'I know, it's in silent ringing mode. Get on to the mobile phone company. Tell them to pin-point its location.'

Burton frowned. 'Pin-point it?'

'I'm not sure how they do it,' said Frost, 'but they can pin-point the location of all the mobile phones on their network – cross-bearings from their transmitters or something. Never mind how they do it, just get on to them.'

They waited impatiently as Burton made the call. A lot of hanging on, then being transferred to someone else with even more hanging on and Burton getting more and more uptight. Frost crushed out a barely smoked cigarette and lit up another one. At last Burton put the phone down. 'They'll get back to us. It could take a few minutes.'

'You did tell them it's a matter of life or death?'

'Of course I bloody did,' snapped Burton testily. Then he flushed. 'Sorry, Inspector.'

'It's all right, son,' soothed Frost. 'We're all uptight. I was a prat to ask.'

Silence as they all stared at the phone, willing it to ring. Frost was constantly glancing at his watch. How long had the bastard had Liz? What was he doing to her now?

472

'Inspector!' The angry voice of a furious Mullett from the doorway. He had just been told by Sergeant Wells of the men from other Divisions standing by and the time bomb of a mega-overtime bill ticking away. 'My office – now!'

'Later,' grunted Frost, his eyes back to the phone.

Mullett's face furrowed with annoyance. 'I said now!'

'And I said later,' snapped Frost. 'When I can fit it in.'

Mullett's mouth opened and closed. He couldn't think of what to say. Conscious of all eyes in the room witnessing his discomfiture, he forced a smile and nodded. 'Keep me informed.' He stamped back to his office. Frost would pay for this.

Burton snatched up the phone on its first ring. The mobile phone company. 'What?' He spun round to survey the large wall map of Denton behind him. 'Are you sure? Thank you.' He banged the phone down. 'We're in luck. They've traced it.' They crowded round as he tapped a section of the map. 'The phone is somewhere in this area here – the outskirts of Denton Woods.' He peered again at the map. 'It's nearly all trees and scrubland, but there is one house. There!' His finger jabbed the position. 'That's got to be it!'

'Right,' said Frost, rubbing his hands briskly. 'First thing is to find out who lives there. If it's a nunnery or a home for castrated clergymen, we could be sniffing up the wrong tree.'

Burton dashed out to the computer in Control to check. 'Occupants a Mr and Mrs Gerald Vernon,' he informed them. 'Vernon's had a couple of parking tickets . . . nothing else known.'

'Anyone know the house?' Frost asked.

Jordan pushed forward. 'I do, Inspector. We were called there a couple of months ago for a suspected burglary. Big, posh place, dirty great lawn at the front, double garage, massive garden round the back.'

Frost chewed this over. 'We'll all go. The more the merrier. If he manages to get out, we could be combing the woods for the sod, so we hem the place in tight and block all escape routes.' He squinted at the map. 'We don't want them to know we're coming, so once we get to this point . . .' he tapped the map, '. . . headlights off. We'll park well away from the house . . . here.' Again he tapped the map. 'We go the rest of the way on foot and we keep very quiet, so no talking, no torches, no car doors slamming and no bleeding sirens.' He snatched his scarf from the hook and wound it round his neck. 'One other thing. If he listens in to taxicab radios, he could listen in to police broadcasts, so we maintain radio silence.' He buttoned up his mac. 'Let's go.'

Burton was the first out, dashing to his car. Frost hung back for a quick word with Bill Wells. 'Get a doctor standing by, Bill. If we get to the poor cow in time we might need one. And if we don't get to her in time . . . the bastard who did it is going to need one because he's going to be seriously injured while resisting arrest, come what bloody may!'

22

It was freezing cold in the car. 'You didn't fix the heater,' Frost grunted.

'Sorry, guv.' Morgan spun the steering wheel and turned off the main Bath Road into the side road that skirted the solid black mass of Denton Woods.

They weren't saying much to each other, both caten up with guilt, Morgan for abandoning Liz, Frost for letting him do it. Frost tried to close his mind to self-recrimination so he could concentrate on the task ahead. What state would the poor cow be in when they found her? Would she still be alive? From time to time he twisted round to make sure the other cars were following. Morgan was driving much too fast and nearly missed the lay-by, having to brake hard and reverse into it.

The rest of the team joined them, some having to park up on the grass verge. Only one forgetful, silly sod slammed his car door and had to be hissed into silence.

The night was dark with clouds obscuring the moon, but as they reached the top of a slight rise, the moon found a gap in the clouds and slid through, dousing the landscape in silver and black. Before them stood the house, imposing and isolated . . . *Scream as loud as you like, love – no-one can hear you . . .* In front of the house a gravelled drive cut through a large lawn which had in its centre a fountain in the shape of a nude nymph, trickling water from a cornucopia into a circular fish pond.

Frost looked anxiously up at the night sky. Everything was too flaming bright. They needed the cover of darkness to get across that expanse of lawn unseen. Then, to his relief, heavy black clouds scudded across the moon face and friendly darkness returned.

'Here's where we split into two groups,' whispered Frost. 'Take your lot round the back, Arthur, the rest come with me.' Burton grabbed Frost's arm and pointed. A gleam of light suddenly splashed out of an upstairs window, then a figure in silhouette drew the curtains together and all was black again. 'The bastard's still up,' whispered Frost, 'so let's be extra quiet. Arthur, signal with your torch when you're in position.'

A cold, anxious wait until the torch flashed its signal. Frost jerked his head to the others. 'Let's go.'

The scrunch of their running feet on the gravel drive decided him to veer across the lawn. A mistake. Half-way across, a ring of security lamps suddenly clicked on, flooding the lawn with blinding light. They froze stock still, holding their breath. They had triggered a sensor. Frost could hear his heart drumming away as he looked towards the house, waiting for the shaft of light from the window. Nothing. 'Back to the path,' he hissed. As soon as they left the lawn, the lights went out, leaving them with a brief attack of night blindness. Frost blinked and rubbed his eyes.

An estate car parked by the front door was locked, but the radiator was still warm. It had been driven recently. 'That's not the car that picked her up, guv,' whispered Morgan.

'They'd have swapped cars,' said Frost. He looked up the ivy-covered wall to the upstairs windows where the light had shown. 'That's the room we try first.'

476

'I reckon I could climb that ivy, guv.'

Frost's withering stare was sufficient answer. 'We go in through the front door.' He looked round for Burton who had the pneumatic battering ram. 'Sod the noise, son – it's all speed from now on.' He stood back to give the DC room. The noise was deafening, but at the third blow the woodwork splintered and the door crashed back. Led by Frost they charged down the passage and up the stairs.

The first room they burst into was empty, but a muffled scream sent them hurtling into the next one. Curtains drawn, the room was lit only by the glow from an electric fire. The smell hit Frost, cloying tartish perfume mingled with sweat and stale cigarette smoke. His torch picked out white, naked flesh as he fumbled for the light switch.

On the bed, wide-eyed with terror, a naked woman. Leaning over her, a hand clamping her mouth to silence her cries, a man, also naked, his head twisted round, blinking at the night. Frost snatched the man's hand from the woman's mouth. It wasn't Liz.

'There's no money here,' said the man, trying to keep his voice steady. 'I've called the police. They'll be here any minute.'

'They're here already,' snapped Frost, flashing his warrant card. He went to the door and shouted to the others down the stairs: 'She's not in here. Look everywhere.'

The man grabbed a dressing-gown from a chair and slipped it on. 'Police? What the devil do you want with me?'

'I think you know what we want,' said Frost grimly. He turned to the woman. 'Are you all right, love?'

'I was all right until you bastards came charging in.' She blazed angry eyes at Taffy and pulled a sheet over her naked body. 'Seen enough?' Morgan pretended he had been looking past her at something on the wall and frowned as if he didn't understand what she was getting at.

'Pardon?' he asked.

'Dirty bastard!' she snarled.

Crashes and thuds from below as Hanlon's team joined in the search. The man barged past Frost and glared angrily down the stairs. 'You've smashed the front door in. Someone's going to pay for this!'

Ignoring him, Frost pulled Morgan to one side and nodded towards the angry woman on the bed. 'Is she the one who was driving the cab?'

Morgan shook his head. 'Don't think so, guv – wrong colour hair.'

'Could have been wearing a wig,' muttered Frost.

The man thrust himself between the two detectives. 'Would you mind telling me what this is all about or is it a state secret?'

'You are Mr Gerald Vernon?'

'Yes.'

'And this lady is your wife?'

A slight pause. 'Yes.'

'One of our female officers was abducted tonight. We have reason to believe she is in this house.'

Vernon's stunned surprise looked genuine. 'I don't believe what I'm hearing! Have you gone stark staring mad?'

'Have you been out tonight?' asked Frost.

'Yes.'

'Near the Fenton Road area?'

'Nowhere near the Fenton Road area. If you must know, we've been to the Coconut Grove night-club.'

'What time did you get there, sir?'

'About ten o'clock.'

'And what time did you leave?'

Vernon consulted his wrist-watch. 'A little after three.'

Frost turned to the woman on the bed. 'Is that correct, Mrs Vernon?'

She shot a quick glance at the man before nodding. 'Yes.'

The sound of something falling and smashing made Vernon turn to Frost in fury. 'I hope the police are well insured, Inspector, because whatever damage your ham-fisted, loutish oafs have caused will be added to the extensive claim for damages I intend to make against you.'

Burton came into the bedroom, brushing dust and cobwebs from his coat. 'We've been through all this floor and the loft – nothing!'

He was followed by Sergeant Hanlon whose men had been searching the downstairs and the grounds. 'Nothing down there, Jack.'

Frost's confidence was fast ebbing away. This was their only lead and if it led nowhere, they were left with absolutely nothing, and with time ticking away, they wouldn't have a snowball's chance in hell of finding Liz alive.

'Inspector!' Collier burst into the bedroom. 'I found this behind the hat-stand.' He held aloft Liz Maud's handbag. Frost's spirits sky-rocketed. He opened it and took out the mobile phone.

With a bellow of rage, Burton hurled himself at Vernon, smashing him against the wall. 'Where is she, you bastard? What have you done with her?'

With difficulty Frost and Collier managed to drag him off, but not before Burton had managed to bloody Vernon's nose. 'Go and check the two cars downstairs,' ordered Frost.

Burton scowled sullenly. 'I've checked them.'

'Then check them again – now!' As Burton slouched out, Frost turned to Vernon who was trying to stem the flow of blood from his nose with a handkerchief. 'I apologize for my colleague's over-enthusiasm, sir.

Like us, he's anxious to know where she is.'

'I don't know where she is,' hissed Vernon, each word making him wince with pain, 'and I don't particularly care. But you are going to pay for this. My God, how you are going to pay . . .'

Frost waved the handbag. 'When our colleague went missing she was carrying this. So where is she?'

'Why don't you ask him how the handbag came to be here, you bloody bullies?' The woman was shouting at them from the bed.

'All right,' said Frost sweetly. 'How did the handbag come to be in your house, Mr Vernon?'

Vernon folded the blooded handkerchief and stuffed it into his dressing-gown pocket. 'We found it in the road as we were driving home from the Coconut Grove.'

'What time was this?'

'I've already told you – three o'clockish.'

Frost sent Morgan to check this with the night-club, then signalled for Vernon to continue.

'As we turned from Bath Road into the side road, there was this car ahead of us.'

'What sort of car?'

'I only saw the back of it. Darkish, could have been black, nothing special.'

'It was black,' chipped in the woman from the bed. 'Black, one person driving, two in the back.'

Vernon glared at her. 'Do you want to tell this bloody story, or shall I?'

She pouted and stuck her tongue out at him.

'We're driving behind it when she sees something in the road and yells for me to stop. So, being a good citizen, completely unaware that I would be beaten up by the police for my trouble, I stopped and retrieved it.' He jerked a thumb. 'It was that handbag.'

Frost turned to the woman on the bed. 'You spotted it?'

She nodded. 'Yes. I think it came from the car in front of us.'

'You *think*? Didn't you see?'

'I wasn't actually looking, but I got the impression it had been chucked out. I wanted Gerry to go after the other car and give it back. He drove ever so fast, but there was no sign of it.'

'I was going to drop it in at the police station in the morning,' said Vernon. He winced and ran his tongue along his mouth. 'I think he's broken one of my teeth.'

'I'm sure he hasn't,' said Frost dismissively, hoping and praying he was right. They were in enough trouble. If Vernon's story checked out and he didn't leave the Coconut Grove until after three, there was no way he could have swapped cars and picked Liz up. Frost looked up hopefully as Morgan returned.

'I've contacted the club, guv. They confirm Mr Vernon didn't leave until just after three.'

'Shit!' said Frost.

'Yes,' said Vernon, smiling malevolently, 'and that is exactly what you've dropped yourself in, Inspector. I'm suing you, and that thug and the Denton police force for malicious damage and criminal assault.'

Where have I heard that before, thought Frost mournfully as he sent the rest of the team back to their cars. He put on his contrite look. 'I appreciate your feelings, sir, but it would be a nice gesture if you could overlook this error of judgement on our part. We were concerned for our colleague.'

Vernon shook his head. 'I don't make nice gestures, officer.'

Frost sighed. 'Fair enough, sir. If you and your lady wife would come down to the station with proofs of identity, we'll get the wheels rolling.'

Vernon frowned. 'Proof of identity?'

'It's just that your good lady wife, flashing her dugs over there, is a dead ringer for one of the high class

481

ladies of the night from the Coconut Grove. I'm sure I'm mistaken, but if she isn't your wife and your real wife finds out . . .'

Vernon's eyes blazed. 'You bastard!'

'Not such a bastard, sir,' smiled Frost. 'We'll accept your claim for damage to property – we're insured for that – and if it would spare you any embarrassment, I won't query it if you say you were alone in the house when it happened. But I want the assault accusation dropped.'

'You bastard!' repeated Vernon.

Frost beamed. 'All agreed then, sir? Don't bother to come to the door, I'll find my own way out.'

As he closed the front door behind him, the gloom returned, not helped by the weather. The black clouds had opened and rain was bucketing down. Liz Maud was out there somewhere, at the mercy of the serial killer, and he didn't know what the hell to do next.

Screwing his eyes against the stinging smoke drifting from his cigarette, he stared unseeing at the large-scale map on the wall of the incident room. The cigarette tasted hot and bitter, and his head ached from smoking too much, but it was something to do while he waited for an elusive, long absent, flash of inspiration to whisper in his ear, telling him what to do next. A tramp of footsteps as the team he had sent to search the spot where the handbag was found returned. As he feared, they had found nothing, but at least it had given him some respite, some relief against them all sitting staring at him, waiting for him to come up with the magic answer. He was all out of magic answers.

To add to his misery, an angry, all bright and shining Mullett brisked in. 'Four Divisions have men standing by, Inspector, all on overtime to our account, and no-one has told them what to do.'

482

Frost barely gave him a glance. 'As soon as I know what they can do, I'll tell them,' he snapped. Sod Mullett, sod the budget and sod everyone.

Mullett glared and stamped out.

Frost turned to the wall map and studied it closely, scratching his chin in thought. 'The bag with the phone was found here.' A nicotined finger marked the spot. 'Vernon slows down, unclicks his seat belt, gets out and picks it up. Back to the car, a quick nose in the bag, seat belt back on and away. That should take him what – thirty seconds?'

Burton shrugged. 'Depends how quickly he did it.'

'Of course it does,' said Frost, 'but he's got a hot bit of choice nooky in the car and he wants to get his leg over, so he's not going to dawdle. She wants him to go after the other car, so he puts his foot down – the foot on the end of the leg he wants to get over. He drives like the clappers, but no sign of the other motor.' Back to the map. 'Once you get round the bend here, the road runs straight as a die. You should be able to see the rear lights of the other car for miles.'

'What are you getting at?' asked Hanlon.

'If he didn't see it or overtake it, the other car must have turned off down one of the side lanes.' He indicated them on the map.

'There's a hell of a lot of them,' said Burton.

'But if it was out of sight before Vernon turns the bend, then it's got to be one of the early ones otherwise Vernon would have seen it.' He pointed this out on the map as they crowded round. 'This gives us three side road possibilities. This one, which leads to those farms and smallholdings where old mother Nelly Nipples lives. This one, which ends up at the new estate, or this one which goes through to the factory area. I'm going to call in all our resources from other Divisions and saturate these three areas, house-to-house, the lot.'

Burton, leaning over his shoulder to study the map, was doubtful. 'If he took the road to the factory area, he could have gone straight through and out on to the Bath Road at the back and be miles away by now.'

'He was on the Bath Road to start with, son. If he'd wanted it, he wouldn't have come off it in the first place.' Burton was beginning to get on his nerves. Maybe this wouldn't work, but it was all they had. 'We're going to have to get people out of bed and search their premises. They're not going to be very pleased. Lie to them if you like and tell them it's a three-year-old kid we're looking for – they might be more helpful than if we said it was a police officer. And if they still refuse to let you in to search, tell them that under the 1997 Police Act you have unlimited powers of entry and if they resist they will be arrested and charged.'

'What Police Act is that?' Jordan asked.

'Any bloody Police Act you like,' said Frost. 'It doesn't exist. If that doesn't work, knee them one in the groin and go in anyway. I'll carry the can for any come-backs. If you knock and get no reply, smell gas and break in. I want every single property searched.'

'It could take hours,' said Burton.

'Then don't hang about,' said Frost. He picked up the phone and told Bill Wells to call in the other Divisions. 'Of course it's authorized by Mr Mullett, but whatever you do, don't bloody tell him.'

The lorry that passed them was travelling at speed down the wrong side of the road to overtake. Frost's convoy of four cars had turned the bend, just past the point where Vernon found the handbag, and the dead straight stretch of road was ahead of them. Frost watched the rear lights of the lorry dwindle to pin-pricks of red, but still clearly visible. Vernon was right.

If the cab had stayed on the road, he would have seen its rear lights. It was the lorry driver's lucky night, speeding on the wrong side of the road past four carloads of coppers and getting away with it. Then he blinked. The red lights suddenly disappeared then, after a brief pause, appeared again. He went cold. Shit! He should have realized. As the map showed, the road went dead straight, but it also went up and down. Was that why Vernon didn't see the cab? Perhaps it hadn't turned off one of the three side roads he was going to search after all. It could have taken any of the many other side roads further ahead. He shot a quick look at Burton who was driving the car, but he hadn't given the lorry more than a passing glance. Frost's brain churned. They didn't have enough men to search all the possible side lanes. Right or wrong, he'd have to stick to his original plan and concentrate on the three nearest, but all the optimism he had when they set out had now evaporated.

They parked on a piece of scrubland and huddled round the inspector, coat collars up, getting drenched in the heavy, thudding rain. Even the weather was conspiring against him.

The area they were to search was bleak and remote with isolated ramshackle houses and bungalows, some empty and decaying, a few smallholdings and a couple of farms struggling to survive. In the distance, silhouetted against the night sky, they could see the house where old Nelly Aldridge lived with her idiot son. Not much point searching there but just to be thorough they'd give it a going-over after everywhere else had been covered.

'We look everywhere, houses, barns, sheds, the lot. When you've searched, radio Sergeant Hanlon and he'll tick it off on the map to make sure we don't miss anywhere. Start with the most likely – places with a good access for a car. He's going to have to drive his victim right up to the door not drag her half a mile up a hill. Off you go, and good luck!'

Frost, accompanied by PC Collier, began a search of some deserted farm buildings, all rusting corrugated iron, rancid hay and oily puddles. He had a feeling of having been here before, then remembered he had – when they were searching for the missing Vicky Stuart. Rain trickling down his neck, he shone his torch through a shattered window – broken floorboards, rotting rubbish and the scurrying and squealing of rats. He moved away. He couldn't see their killer bringing his victims here.

His radio called him. PC Collier from the rear of the farmhouse reporting signs that someone had been in there recently. Collier met him outside and took him into a room, pointing out a dirty mattress, some empty bottles and cans, and the remains of a fire in the grate. Frost shook his head. 'Some tramp's been using it. Have you checked upstairs?'

Collier nodded. 'Nothing. The rain's pouring in through the roof.'

Frost wrinkled his nose. The tramp had been using the corner of the room as his toilet. 'Hardly a love nest, is it, son? More like a sewage worker's beano site. Let's get out of here . . . and mind where you tread.'

As they were leaving, a radio call from Jordan: 'At a house now, Inspector. We've been hammering at the door. A dog's barking inside, but no-one answers.'

'Kick it in,' Frost told him. 'I reckon there's drugs on the premises.'

And then reports started coming in thick and fast, all negative, intensifying his doubts that they were looking in the wrong area, but, right or wrong, he was committed.

His radio called him again. Yet another negative report. He poked a cigarette in his mouth and surveyed

486

the area. Through a solid curtain of rain lights from dozens of torches bobbed in the dark. Anyone looking out would know the police were in the vicinity, but they couldn't search blind. The cigarette was sodden and wouldn't light. As he hurled it away another radio call, this time from Burton, sounding excited: 'Might be on to something Inspector. I'm at a bungalow at the foot of the rise, talking to a Mrs Jessop. She reckons she often hears a car, very late at night, coming from that smallholding on the top of the hill.'

'What does she mean by "very late"? Some of these old dears go to bed at six.'

'She doesn't sleep well. Says the car wakes her up as it goes past her place. About two o'clockish or thereabouts, she says.'

'Did she hear it tonight?'

'No, she took a sleeping tablet, but she's definite about the other nights. Do you want to talk to her?'

'No time for that, son. We go straight to the smallholding. Meet me outside.' He radioed for Morgan and Jordan to join him. They followed him up the steep hill. No chance of a stealthy approach. The whine of their engines straining up the steep rutted slope would waken the dead.

The smallholding was a collection of ramshackle structures around a two-storeyed house. Outside the main building a black car was parked and a light gleamed through curtains from a downstairs room. Surveying it, Frost felt the hairs on the back of his neck rise. This was it. This was bloody it.

As they squelched to a halt by the front door, Frost clambered out and ran over to the car, a black Ford, the windows wound down and the driver's door wide open. He stuck his nose inside and sniffed for traces of the pungent perfume Liz had been wearing. All he could smell was carbolic disinfectant. He checked the number plates. Not the ones Taffy had noted, but too much to expect the false plates still to be there. He rejoined the others and pounded at the front door with his fist. They waited. Nothing. Frost gave the door handle a tentative turn and, to his surprise, the door swung open. Collier was sent round to the back, while Frost and the other three entered the house.

They stepped into a long passage. Frost jerked a thumb to Burton and Jordan. 'Upstairs.' He and Morgan followed the passage to a large, stone-flagged kitchen where a cream-coloured Aga stove belted out heat. A long wooden-topped table was laid out for breakfast with bowls and cups. In front of the Aga a grey and black tabby cat in a wicker cat basket gave them bemused looks while her six tiny kittens, eyes still not open, suckled noisily. A peaceful, innocent domestic scene.

'I think we're on the wrong track, guv,' said Morgan.

'You can be a bastard and still like animals,' said Frost, although his frail certainty was now wavering. 'Hitler had a dog and Mullett's got a cat.' He opened the back door to let Collier in, then they checked all the downstairs rooms. All neat and tidy. Footsteps from above as Burton and Jordan returned.

'Nothing,' reported Burton. 'One double bed, but it hasn't been slept in.'

'So where are the people who live here?' asked Frost. 'Let's try the outbuildings.'

They split up, Morgan and Frost going to a wooden-walled structure with a corrugated iron roof. Pitch dark inside, but over the drumming of the rain they could hear rustling. Someone was inside. Frost fumbled round the door frame and found a light switch. Some twenty cats in cages blinked angrily at him. His heart did a somersault and he shivered, but not from the cold. *Déjà vu* again. Cats, and that smell!

488

Old Martha Wendle's cottage all those years ago when eight-year-old Tracey Uphill went missing.

'You all right, guv?' asked Morgan.

'Yes,' lied Frost, shaking off the memory. Tracey was dead when they found her.

A quick look round. Metal cupboards filled with tins of cat food and bags of cat litter. Nothing else.

On to the next building, a windowless barn-like structure. Frost stiffened and held up a finger for silence. The murmur of voices from inside. Carefully, he turned the door handle and gently opened the door. Inside, about half-way down, a hurricane lamp lit up two figures wearing oilskins, their backs to him. They were bending over something on the straw-lined floor, something whimpering in pain. He charged towards them. 'Stay where you are. Police!'

A squeal of alarm as they spun round. Two women looking terrified. Both were in their mid-fifties, one quite fat with uncombed dark hair, the other thin and sharp-featured.

'Police!' said Frost again, trying to find his warrant card. Morgan got his out first and flashed it in front of their faces. They blinked at it, not understanding.

Another whimper from the floor. Frost pushed them aside. On a bed of straw, a red setter, body heaving and shaking, tongue lolling, whites of eyes showing.

'She's in labour,' the thin woman explained. 'There's a blockage there, or something. We're very worried about her.' She blinked again at the warrant card. 'But why are you here?'

Frost quickly explained about Liz. 'We're searching everywhere in this area.'

The two women seemed genuinely concerned. 'How dreadful,' exclaimed the fat woman. 'She can't be here, Inspector. We've been up all night with the dog and we'd have heard a car. But please search anywhere you like – anywhere.' The dog whimpered again. 'We've got to get the vet,' said the thin woman. 'Can one of your policemen carry her to the house?'

Frost nodded to Morgan who bent and gently humped up the dog. As soon as the two women had left Frost called the rest of his team over. 'I've got one of my feelings. Get some more men in and give this place a right going-over. She could be alive, she could be dead, so look everywhere.' Burton and Collier were detailed to accompany him back to the house. 'I'll keep Little and Large talking while you search every nook and cranny.'

He slumped down in the chair alongside the Aga, the dog, eyes closed, panting heavily, in a basket at his feet. He ruffled its fur and watched the thin woman ring the vet's emergency number on a mobile phone, letting the Aga bake dry his sodden clothes.

'He's out on another call, Mavis, a calving, but he'll phone back when he's finished so we can take Jessie straight to his surgery. He thinks he'll have to do a Caesarean.'

Mavis, the fat one, looked worried. 'I hope the calving doesn't take long, Lily.' She shuffled over to the sink and filled a brown enamel kettle, stepping carefully over the cat's basket to plonk it on the Aga. 'Would you like a cup of tea, Inspector?'

'If you twist my arm,' yawned Frost, loosening his scarf. The heat was making him sleepy. He nodded at the mobile. 'Aren't you on the phone?'

'The phone company quoted over a thousand pounds to run a line up here and the electricity people wanted double,' Lily told him. 'We haven't got that sort of money, so it has to be the mobile.'

'We look after cats for the Cats' Defence League,' added her companion. 'So a phone is vital.' She frowned at the noise of dragged furniture coming

490

from above. 'You surely don't think she is in this house?'

'Not really,' smiled Frost. 'But we have to search everywhere, just to be thorough.' They each took one of his offered cigarettes. He lit up. 'One of your neighbours mentioned she often hears your car late at night.'

'Oh dear,' said Mavis, sounding very concerned. 'I hope we don't wake her up. We're always having to dash off to the vet's. Animals seem to have a habit of being taken ill in the middle of the night.' She slurped milk into the cups, the cigarette dangling from her lips. Frost's eyes narrowed. He had seen her somewhere before. She bent and poured milk into the cat's saucer. The cat eyed it blearily and decided she would leave it until later.

'All the doors and windows of your car were wide open as we drove up,' said Frost.

Mavis smiled and nodded. 'One of the cats made a mess inside it. I'm hoping the smell has gone by now.'

An explanation for everything, thought Frost, then suddenly his see-sawing spirits soared. He remembered where he had seen the fat woman before.

Their mobile phone chirruped. Mavis snatched it up. 'The vet,' she told the thin woman. 'On his way to the surgery now. He wants us to bring the dog over.'

'I'll get someone to go with you,' said Frost. They protested that it wasn't necessary, but he insisted. He called Burton down and drew him to one side. 'Go with them to the vet's. Don't let them out of your sight for a second and bring them straight back. I'll explain later.'

He saw them out to the car, then dashed back to the house just as Detective Sergeant Hanlon returned from searching the outhouses. 'Nothing, Jack, not a sniff.'

'Then we'll just have to sniff a bit harder, Arthur.

Bring in everyone – pull them off what they're doing. I want every inch searched again. She's here, alive or dead – Liz is here, I'm bloody certain!'

Hanlon stared at him. 'How can you be so sure?'

'That fat tart. She works in the control room of Denton Minicabs. Left her old man to live with her lady lover – that'll be skinny Lizzy. I spoke to her at Denton Minicabs, told her what we were investigating, but she never said a word about it today. She was hoping I wouldn't recognize her until they got Liz out of the way.' He turned to Morgan. 'Could Fatty Arbuckle have been driving the cab that picked Liz up?'

'Could have been, guv. I didn't really get a proper look.'

'It was her, I'd stake my last packet of fags on it. They said they would have heard a car if it came to dump Liz, but we come straining up the hill in two motors making one hell of a row, and they pretend to be taken by surprise. They'd seen the torches, they couldn't miss them from up here, and the fat tart would have recognized Liz. They knew we were coming. They were ready for us.' He rubbed his hands together briskly. Action, this was what he liked, action. 'Get everyone in, Arthur. We are now going to search on the basis that Liz is definitely here and we are definitely going to find her. Pull out cupboards, rip up floorboards, sieve the cats' flaming litter trays, never mind the damage, just find her.'

He watched for a while in the pouring rain as the teams went through the outhouses and sheds, then returned to the dryness and warmth of the house, getting in everyone's way as he mooched around. Back to the kitchen where he swilled down his mug of tea, watched by the nursing cat with its sleeping kittens.

The all too familiar negative reports rattled in,

non-stop: nothing . . . nothing . . . nothing . . . His gloom returned. She was here, he knew she was here, but what was the bloody good of knowing if they couldn't find her? Then he went cold. Up against the wall, near the sink, draped with a cloth and stacked with crockery as if it was a table, a large chest freezer, amply big enough to hold a woman's body. He piled the crockery in the sink and tried to lift the lid. Shit! It was locked. A tuppenny-ha'penny lock, but none of his skeleton keys worked. There was a poker by the Aga. Leaning over the cat, he snatched it up and levered off the lock, taking a deep breath before raising the lid, then forcing himself to look inside. Fish, meat, loaves of bread. No body. He let the lid drop with a thud, not knowing whether to feel relieved or dejected. He sank back in the chair and stared through the window to the night sky. Already daylight was scratching at the edges. He was sucking moodily on his fifth cigarette when Hanlon returned, looking as tired and dejected as Frost. 'We've torn the place apart, Jack. She isn't here.'

Frost scrubbed weariness from his face with his hands. 'I've sodded it up again, Arthur. We've been wasting our time, looking in the wrong place.'

'It was our best shot, Jack.'

'Which missed the bleeding target by miles.' Wearily, he pushed himself out of the chair. 'Nothing to do now but wait until someone reports finding a body.' His mobile rang. His heart skipped a beat. Good news? Bad news? It was Mullett asking, 'What progress?'

'None,' reported Frost. 'Not a sodding thing.' He clicked Mullett off in mid-moan and dropped the phone back in his pocket, now feeling almost suicidal. Another death on his conscience. Well, he'd give Mullett the treat of his life when he got back to the station, his resignation with immediate effect.

Hanlon sensed his mood. 'You did your best, Jack. You couldn't have done more.'

'I let it happen, Arthur. If that's doing my best, I'm bleeding useless.' Shoulders slumped, he made his way outside where the rain-soaked teams were assembled, waiting for his further instructions. He was about to send them all home when he stopped dead in his tracks and clapped a hand to his forehead. 'What a bloody, bloody fool! The generator!'

Blank expressions.

'They're not on mains electricity, yet they've got a fridge, a deep freeze, lights. They must have a generator. Did anyone find it?'

Heads were shaken. 'We looked everywhere,' said Hanlon.

'We couldn't have looked everywhere. You can't make electricity out of thin air. There's got to be a generator.' He stared upwards. No overhead power lines. 'It's got to be inside the house.'

They followed him back into the kitchen where the mother cat yawned annoyance at having her sleep disturbed yet again. He looked around. 'Where the hell is it?' As he spoke the thermostat on the deep freeze clicked and the motor started to hum. 'Switch that thing off and listen. If there's a generator we should be able to hear it.'

Morgan clicked the switch. The humming stopped. They strained their ears. Silence broken only by the mewing of one of the kittens. Hanlon shook his head. 'Can't hear anything, Jack.'

Morgan dropped to his knees and pressed his ear to the stone-flagged floor. 'I can!' he called excitedly. 'It's coming from underneath.' Frost joined him. He could hear it too. A low, throbbing sound just about audible through the thick slabs. 'There must be a cellar!'

Frost straightened up, eyes darting round the

kitchen, stopping at the cat and its offspring in the basket, bang in front of the Aga. He remembered fat Mavis stepping over it with the kettle. 'If I had a cat with kittens, I think I'd stick the basket in that recess alongside the stove, not bang in front of it where I'd have to step over it every time.' He tugged at the folded blanket on which the basket rested, sliding it, with the cat and kittens, to one side. 'Bingo!' The blanket had been covering a wooden trap door. Morgan heaved it open. Wooden steps led down to darkness. Frost fumbled and found a light switch.

A large cellar stretching the length of the kitchen. In one corner a diesel-powered generator throbbed away. Up against one wall was a single bed with a mattress and pillow. Frost sniffed the pillow. Perfume. Liz's perfume. She had been here, on this bed. He thudded up the wooden steps and yelled to the men outside. 'She's been here . . . search again.'

She had to be somewhere near. The two women would have spotted the police teams crashing about and would have had to get Liz out of the house quickly. She had to be within walking distance, but there was no trace of her.

'We need those two cows back here now!' said Frost, but before he could radio Burton headlights and the sound of a car straining up the hill. Burton and the two women returning.

He waited in the kitchen. Burton was in first, humping in an exhausted-looking red setter bitch in its basket. 'Mother and kids doing fine,' he announced proudly. Behind him the two women, beaming all over their faces, carried in a large cardboard box which they lowered gently to the floor. Frost looked down on five newly born red setter puppies. 'Panic over,' smiled Lily. 'Jessie didn't need a Caesarean after all.' The smile abruptly froze on her face. With his foot,

Frost was slowly pushing the cat's basket to one side. The two women watched as if hypnotized.

'We've found the cellar,' said Frost grimly.

The thin woman shot a warning glance to Mavis, clicked her smile back on and turned to Burton. 'Put the basket there, please.' She indicated the recess by the Aga. 'They must be kept warm.'

'I said we've found the cellar,' repeated Frost.

The two women busied themselves putting the puppies in the basket with their mother. 'There's nothing down there,' said Mavis, in a matter-of-fact voice. 'Just a spare bed and the generator. No-one could have got down there without our knowledge.' She held out a puppy to Frost. 'Isn't he a little darling?'

'Don't sod me about,' snapped Frost. 'Where is the woman police officer you brought here tonight?'

Mavis gave him a look of puzzled innocence. 'We haven't been out at all tonight, Inspector. How could we pick anyone up?'

'You're a lying bitch!' snapped Frost.

The thin woman came forward. 'Inspector, I appreciate you are concerned about your colleague, but you are wrong if you think she is here. We know nothing about her, I give you my word!'

The word of a bitch who tortures and kills, thought Frost. We've searched everywhere, so where the hell is she? He creased his face in thought. The women would have spotted the search party and had to get Liz out of the house bloody quickly. Where could they hide her? And then it hit him. 'Of course,' he exclaimed. 'Of bloody course!' The one place they hadn't looked and it was so flaming obvious. The boot of the car. What a prat he was. The car doors had been left wide open and he hadn't thought of looking in the boot! He held out his hand. 'Your car keys, please.'

Mavis nestled the puppy next to its mother, then dug deep in her coat pocket. Frost hurried out with the keys, but didn't like the relieved look which had returned to both the women's faces.

The boot was empty.

He was now at the brink of utter despair. Back to the house. 'Where is she?' he shouted.

Mavis shook her head and gave him a pitying smile. 'I'm afraid we don't know, Inspector.'

Frost tugged Burton to one side. 'Did you let either of them out of your sight even for a bloody second when you went to the vet's with them?'

'No,' said Burton.

Frost raised his head and swore bitterly at the ceiling. 'Shit, shit, shit. Tell me exactly what happened.'

'We drove to the vet's—'

'Who drove?'

'The skinny bird. I was in the back with Fatty and the dog. When we got to the surgery, the lights were on inside and the main door was open. It was peeing with rain, so she drove the car right up to the surgery door. I humped the dog out, the fat one came in the vet's with me while the other woman parked the car.'

Frost's eyes glinted. 'She parked the car? Where?'

'The parking area just round the back of the surgery.'

'She'd have to walk back through the peeing rain. Why didn't she leave the car where it was?'

Burton frowned. 'I don't know. I was more concerned with getting the dog inside. But she was only out of my sight for a minute or so.'

'That's all she'd flaming well need to drag Liz out of the boot, hide her somewhere and when we'd left, go back and pick her up again.'

Burton stared at him. 'Do you think she's still alive?'

'I hope so, son, I bloody hope so.'

He quickly briefed the others, then jerked a thumb at the two women. 'You're coming with us.'

Mavis looked concerned. 'Jessie—' she began.

Frost nodded at Collier. 'The constable will look after the dog.'

He hustled them into his car where they sat pressed together in the back seat gripping the armrests tightly as Morgan drove at speed down the bumpy incline. The car lurched and juddered, rain hammering on the roof, the windscreen wipers squealing as they tried to cope with the downpour.

At the vet's, now in darkness, Morgan swung the car into the rear car-park and braked violently. He and Frost were out, shoulders hunched against the driving rain as the following cars skidded to a halt behind them.

Frost opened the passenger door and leant in. The two women smiled up at him, seemingly not in the least concerned. 'We're going to find her anyway, so why not speed things up and tell us where she is?'

Mavis oozed with sincere concern. 'If we knew, Inspector, don't you think we would say?'

He slammed the car door and turned to meet the others.

'Where do we start?' asked Burton.

He surveyed the empty expanse of car-park, putting himself in the place of the skinny woman who would have been frantically searching for somewhere to hide the body in the boot. There weren't many places. His eyes fastened on the row of dustbins and large metal rubbish containers stacked along the rear of the surgery. 'Try over there.'

Much activity. Jordan and Simms managed to clamber up and get inside one of the large containers which held a mass of black plastic sacks, too small for a woman's body. They ripped a couple open. Dead animals for disposal. They climbed out, shaking their heads.

He'd got it wrong. He'd got it bloody wrong again. He tried to conceal the surge of panic building up inside. From the car the two women watched impassively. 'She's got to be somewhere near,' he said. 'That skinny bitch couldn't have carried her far.'

'Assuming she was here in the first place,' muttered Burton, voicing the unspoken opinion of most of the team. Like so many of Frost's hunches this was going to prove a disastrous waste of time.

The rain showed no signs of easing up. Frost's scarf, a sodden mass around his neck, added to his mood of misery and depression. He screwed his eyes against the stinging rain and took one last look around. Then he smiled. 'We've been too flaming clever. The skinny bitch wouldn't have had the strength, nor the time, to hump her up to those bins. She'd just drag Liz out of the boot and dump her.' He pointed to the long wet straggling grass just beyond the low, chain link fence forming the perimeter of the car-park. 'She's over there.'

No-one had any confidence in him any more. They slouched across and did a half-hearted search. It was Jordan, yelling and waving frantically, who found her. 'Over here!' He was shuffling off his greatcoat to cover her as they reached him.

She was naked, rain-soaked, blue with cold and not moving. Her wrists and ankles were bound with wire and a gag bit deeply into her mouth. There were angry red marks on her stomach – cigarette burns. Next to her was a plastic carrier bag. A quick look inside revealed Liz's clothing and other objects. Frost dropped to his knees in the muddy ground and felt for a pulse. He could have cried with relief. She was still alive. His penknife sawed through the wire and cut the binding to the gag as Jordan swaddled her in his greatcoat.

'Get her in the car,' ordered Frost. 'We'll take her straight to the hospital.'

They went in Burton's car, their clothes steaming with the heating turned up full and Polly Fletcher vigorously massaging ice cold limbs to try and restore the circulation. The sudden jolt of the car hitting a pot-hole made Liz's eyes snap open. She looked from side to side in terror. 'It's all right, love,' soothed Frost. 'You're safe. We're taking you to hospital.' She stared at him, then shook her head violently, muttering something he had to bend his head closer to hear. 'What was that, love?'

Her teeth were chattering as she forced the words out. 'I don't want to go to hospital.'

The WPC patted her arm. 'We want the doctor to examine you.'

'No.' She struggled to sit up. 'I don't want to go to hospital. I don't want to be examined.' Near hysterial, she leant over and tried to reach the door handle. Her voice was shrill and insistent. 'Stop the car. I'm not going to the hospital.'

'All right, all right,' murmured Frost, gently restraining her. 'What do you want to do?'

'I want to get back home. I want a shower. I want to get clean . . .'

'All right,' nodded Frost. 'If that's what you want.' To Burton he said: 'Take her home, son, take her home.'

From the canteen above the murder incident room came sounds of drunken singing, thuds and the glass shattering, almost a replay of the night the coachload of drunken football supporters had been brought in. The teams were celebrating the successful outcome of the search and the solving of the serial murders. Frost had looked in briefly just to show willing, but was in no mood to celebrate.

He put the plastic carrier bag on a desk and took out the tom's clothes Liz had been wearing, then removed the other items. A coil of wire identical to that used to bind all the victims, a roll of adhesive tape, a thin cane still wet with blood, and at the bottom of the bag, a large dildo. 'Bloody hell,' muttered Frost. 'No wonder we thought a man was involved.'

He was disturbed by Mullett, who frowned at the noise from above. 'They're not still on overtime, are they?'

'No,' lied Frost. Sod it, he had completely forgotten to book them out. Trust this to be the first thing Hornrim Harry would think of.

Mullett gaped at the dildo. 'What on earth is that?'

'Don't touch it, Super,' warned Frost. 'You don't know where it's been.'

He quickly explained as Mullett, the puritan, went scarlet and backed away in disgust. 'Nasty business. What's the position with the prisoners?'

'They won't say a word until their solicitor gets here, but Forensic are digging up so much evidence from that cellar, we won't need a confession.'

Mullett remembered what should have been his first query. 'And how is Detective Sergeant Maud?'

'Bearing up, but badly shaken,' said Frost.

'What did they do to her?'

Frost looked at the contents of the carrier bag and shuddered. 'She won't say.'

Mullett frowned. 'Won't say? Don't be ridiculous. We need her statement.'

'We can get a conviction without it.'

'We need to tell the court how we got on to the two women, why we arrested them. She will have to give evidence.'

501

Frost rubbed his chin and yawned. God, he was tired. 'I'll try and persuade her.'

'Tell her it's an order,' barked Mullett.

Frost reached for his wet scarf. 'Like I said, Super, I'll try and persuade her.'

It was Burton who opened the door to Frost's knock. 'She's showering,' he said.

Frost followed him into the tiny living-room with the electric fire glowing. He flopped into an armchair. 'How is she?'

Burton shrugged. 'Very uptight. She doesn't want to talk about it.'

'Did she say what happened in the cab?'

'The skinny one was driving. The fat tart was sitting in the back. Skinny says, "You don't mind sharing, do you, love?" Liz smelt a rat, but she knew Morgan was tailing her, so she didn't worry. Next thing she knows, Fatty has a knife to her throat and Morgan is nowhere to be seen. Later she tried to get to her handbag and the phone, but they chucked it out.'

'Mullett says we need Liz's evidence.'

A door clicked open and Liz, in a white bathrobe, glowing from the hot shower, came in, damp hair flowing down her back. Frost gave her a sympathetic nod as she pulled a chair nearer to the fire and sat down. 'We're going to need a statement.'

She shook her head. 'I don't want to talk about it.'

'What did they do to you, love?'

Her eyes spat fire. 'I don't want to talk about it, subject closed.' She hissed the words through clenched teeth.

'We need your evidence.'

'If you think I'm standing up in court and saying what those bitches did to me, then having to face the sniggers back at the station . . .' She stared down

502

at the carpet. She was shaking violently. 'I'm not returning to duty. I'm leaving the force.'

'No,' said Frost, firmly. 'We need you. You're a bloody good cop.'

'And look where it's got me.' She was on the verge of tears.

'I know,' said Frost gently. 'It's not been a ball of laughs, has it?' He tugged out his cigarettes. She took one and sucked the smoke down hungrily. 'I'm the one who sodded it up, love. I'm the one who should be leaving. The only thing stopping me resigning is the joy I know it will bring to Mr Mullett.'

She forced a smile and knuckled her eyes. 'I'm sorry, but I am not going into the box to tell the world what those bitches did to me.'

Frost dribbled smoke through his nose. 'Tell you what, let's bend the facts a little. They pick you up, they bundle you into the house, but before they could do anything, we arrive so they bung you back in the boot and dump you off behind the vet's. You weren't examined medically so no-one can dispute it and those two cows are going to keep their mouths shut.'

She studied the glowing end of her cigarette. 'I'll think about it.'

'I'll get a statement typed out. All you need do is come in tomorrow and sign it.'

'I'll think about it,' she repeated.

Frost grinned happily. He knew she would do it.

Coda

Frost stared out of the window. Snow, driven by a blustery wind, had coated the car-park in white and from the state of the sky there was a lot more to come down. He didn't want to venture outside in such weather but he and Morgan had been ordered to attend the coroner's inquest and he had been warned that the solicitor for Weaver's family was after his blood. Also, he had been tipped off that the London press would be there in force to witness the humiliation of an officer who had hounded an innocent man to his death.

He went back to his desk and yet again studied the transcript of the last interview he had with Weaver, the one they were going to read out in court.

FROST (Showing photograph): Recognize her? That's how we found her. Were her eyes open like that when you raped the poor little cow? Seven years old, you bastard – seven years old.

WEAVER: You're trying to incriminate me. You want a suspect, so you're framing me.

FROST: Did you give her one of your green sweets first? 'Here little girl, have a sweetie while nice Uncle Charlie rapes you then chokes the bloody life out of you'?

WEAVER (Sound of sobbing): You framed me. You

planted that body . . . you . . . (Sounds of choking: asthma attack brought on by questioning)

He was aware of Morgan's chin digging into his shoulder as the DC read the transcript with him. 'Doesn't read too good, does it, guv?' said Morgan. 'Perhaps you did push him that bit too hard?'

'Thanks, Taff,' grunted Frost, pushing the transcript back in its folder. 'You've cheered me up no end.' He was missing something, but what the hell was it?

'I'll still change my evidence if you like, guv,' Morgan offered. 'I owe you more than one. I'll say I never searched that shed in the first place.'

'No thanks,' muttered Frost. He was thumbing through the file and had come across Mrs Weaver's death certificate with brief details of her illness, which had been requested from the hospital by the Police Federation's lawyer in case the family's solicitor tried to suggest that the mother's death was hastened by Weaver's suicide. Something on the death certificate screamed at him. He pulled it out to study it more closely, then leant back in his chair and smiled. 'Who's a silly sod?'

'Me?' answered Morgan, cheerfully.

'Apart from you, Taff. Me! I'm the silly sod.' He tossed the death certificate over. 'Look at the address.'

'Danes Cottage, Fern Lane, Denton,' read Morgan. He frowned. 'They've got it wrong, guv. She lived with Weaver in Argylle Street.'

'She only moved in with him when she was taken ill, Taff. She had her own place. I should have bloody realized.'

'I don't see the point,' said Morgan.

'I'll tell you the point,' said Frost. 'When I told Weaver we'd found Jenny's body, he didn't ask where. He just started screaming and shouting that we'd planted her body to frame him.'

'Perhaps I'm a bit thick, guv . . . ?'

'There's no "perhaps" about it, Taff. Weaver didn't ask where we found it, because he assumed we'd found it where he'd left it. He accused us of planting it because he had left it in a place that would point the finger straight back at him.'

Morgan's eyes widened as the light dawned. 'You mean his mother's place?'

'Yes. No wonder we found no evidence in Argylle Street.'

'Then who moved it?'

'I'm not sure,' said Frost, 'but I've got a bloody good idea . . .'

His windscreen wipers had cleared a hole through the snow-plastered glass. It was still snowing heavily and everything was blanketed in white. Danes Cottage with its lop-sided 'For Sale' sign was the only property in Fern Lane. A brown estate car was parked outside.

He scrunched over thick snow to the front door and knocked. He hadn't expected anyone to be inside, and had been prepared to smash a window if necessary.

The door was opened by an old woman. Mrs Maisie White, little Charlie boy's Aunt Maisie. At first she appeared disconcerted, then resigned, to see the inspector. She knew why he had come. 'You've left it too late,' she told him.

He stepped inside. The place had been stripped bare. Furniture removed, carpeting taken up, floorboards swept and scrubbed clean. She followed him as he wandered from empty room to empty room, no lampshades, no curtains, nothing. In the kitchen a large chest freezer stood alone and forlorn. He lifted the lid and looked inside. It had been defrosted and it, too, was empty.

'You've done a bloody good job of removing all the

evidence,' he told the woman. 'Where did you find the kid's body?'

It took a long time for her to reply. 'Upstairs,' she said at last, leading him up the stairs to a curtainless room. 'In here.' She stood by the door. 'This was his mother's bedroom. If she knew what her darling son had been doing . . .' She shook her head. 'Charlie was her little angel, he could do no wrong.' She walked into the room and shivered. 'That poor little mite.' She closed her eyes and screwed up her face. 'The terrible things he had done to her!'

'Why did you cover up for him?' asked Frost.

'I always covered up for him,' she said. 'It would have broken his mother's heart if she knew what he was really like. There were photographs . . . filthy photographs . . . Charlie and children . . .'

'Where are they?'

'I burnt them.'

'And you sent the anonymous letter with the button?'

'Yes.'

Now Frost was shivering as he looked round the room where Jenny and Vicky had spent the last few terrible moments of their short lives. 'I want you to come back to the station with me and make a statement.'

She shook her head firmly. 'No. I told you for your own peace of mind, Inspector Frost, but I'm not making any statements. I shall deny everything I've told you.'

'Why?' asked Frost. 'Charlie's dead, his mother's dead.'

'I'm not bringing shame on the family.'

'Sod the family! In half an hour's time I'm going to be pilloried in the coroner's court for hounding an innocent man to death. I could be kicked out of the force.'

507

She lowered her head. 'I'm sorry, Inspector, but that is how it has got to be.'

Frost stared at her. She raised her head and stared back, lips tight and determined. She wasn't going to change her mind. Without her statement and without a scrap of evidence in support, he had nothing.

'All right,' he said bitterly. He was about to go when he saw it. On the window ledge, the window ledge of the room where she had found Jenny's body. A toilet roll. He walked across and picked it up. Nearly new, just a few sheets torn off. He smiled. 'On the other hand,' he said cheerfully.

Outside it was now blowing a blizzard. He was going to be very late for the inquest. But he didn't care.

THE END

A TOUCH OF FROST
by R. D. Wingfield

'A funny, frantic, utterly refreshing brew'
Sunday Telegraph

Detective Inspector Jack Frost, officially on duty, is nevertheless determined to sneak off to a colleague's leaving party. But first the corpse of a well-known local junkie is found blocking the drain of a Denton public lavatory – and then, when Frost attempts to join the revels later on, the nubile daughter of a wealthy businessman is reported missing.

Sleepy Denton has never known anything like the crime wave which now threatens to submerge it. A robbery occurs at the town's notorious strip joint, the Coconut Grove, the pampered son of a local MP is suspected of a hit-and-run offence and, to top it all, a multiple racist is on the loose. Frost is reeling under the strain, his paperwork is still in arrears and now, more than ever, his self-righteous colleagues would love to see him sacked. But the manic Frost manages to assure his superior that all is under control. Now he has only to convince himself . . .

'What impresses most is the extraordinarily vivid interplay between the police characters. Frost himself is splendidly drawn'
The Times

0 552 13982 3

NIGHT FROST
by R. D. Wingfield

'Multiple cases, multiple bodies and lashings of police in-fighting. Fast, furious and funny'
Daily Telegraph

A serial killer is terrorizing the senior citizens of Denton, and the local police are succumbing to a flu epidemic. Tired and demoralized, the force has to contend with a seemingly perfect young couple suffering arson attacks and death threats, a suspicious suicide, burglaries, pornographic videos, poison-pen letters . . .

In uncertain charge of the investigations is Detective Inspector Jack Frost, crumpled, slapdash and foul-mouthed as ever. He tries to cope despite inadequate back-up, but there is never enough time; the unsolved crimes pile up and the vicious killings go on. So Frost has to cut corners and take risks, knowing that his Divisional Commander will throw him to the wolves if anything goes wrong. And for Frost, things always go wrong . . .

'Meaty police procedural; bawdy, funny . . . enough material here for cult hero status'
Literary Review

0 552 13985 8

HARD FROST
by R. D. Wingfield

A young boy is found dead in a rubbish sack, suffocated and with one finger cut off. Another boy of the same age, Bobby Kirby, is missing. A psychopath is stabbing babies as they lie sleeping in their cots. Enter Detective Inspector Jack Frost, scruffy and insubordinate, foul-mouthed, intuitive and fearless.

The next problem for the understaffed Denton force is the abduction of Carol Stanfield, a fifteen-year-old who's found naked by the roadside, her father having paid a ransom. Robert Stanfield is a dicy customer, and Frost has his doubts . . .

The corpse of a petty criminal, Lemmy Hoxton, is discovered, with the tops of three fingers chopped off. The small children of a carpet-fitter are murdered; his wife's body is found on the railway line. A super-market MD is sent a ransom demand for the missing boy Bobby, accompanied by one of the child's fingers.

Jack Frost, brought to magnificent life by David Jason in the TV series, staggers from crisis to crisis, his bumbling *modus operandi* disguising his extraordinary powers of detection.

'Frost is a splendid creation, a cross between Rumpole and Columbo'
Marcel Berlins, *The Times*

'Inspector Jack Frost (is) deplorable yet funny, a comic monster on the side of the angels'
Matthew Coady, *Guardian*

0 552 14409 6

A SELECTED LIST OF CRIME NOVELS AVAILABLE FROM CORGI BOOKS

THE PRICES SHOWN BELOW WERE CORRECT AT THE TIME OF GOING TO PRESS. HOWEVER TRANSWORLD PUBLISHERS RESERVE THE RIGHT TO SHOW NET RETAIL PRICES ON COVERS WHICH MAY DIFFER FROM THOSE PREVIOUSLY ADVERTISED IN THE TEXT OR ELSEWHERE.

14221 2	WYCLIFFE AND THE DUNES MYSTERY		
		W. J. Burley	£4.99
13433 3	WYCLIFFE IN PAUL'S COURT	W. J. Burley	£4.99
14205 0	WYCLIFFE AND THE THREE-TOED PUSSY		
		W. J. Burley	£4.99
14116 X	WYCLIFFE AND DEATH IN A SALUBRIOUS PLACE		
		W. J. Burley	£4.99
14437 1	WYCLIFFE AND THE HOUSE OF FEAR		
		W. J. Burley	£4.99
14661 7	WYCLIFFE AND THE REDHEAD	W. J. Burley	£4.99
14043 0	SHADOW PLAY	Frances Fyfield	£5.99
14174 7	PERFECTLY PURE AND GOOD	Frances Fyfield	£5.99
14295 6	A CLEAR CONSCIENCE	Frances Fyfield	£5.99
14512 2	WITHOUT CONSENT	Frances Fyfield	£5.99
14525 4	BLIND DATE	Frances Fyfield	£5.99
14526 2	STARING AT THE LIGHT	Frances Fyfield	£5.99
14223 9	BORROWED TIME	Robert Goddard	£5.99
13840 1	CLOSED CIRCLE	Robert Goddard	£5.99
14224 7	OUT OF THE SUN	Robert Goddard	£5.99
54593 7	INTO THE BLUE	Robert Goddard	£5.99
14225 5	BEYOND RECALL	Robert Goddard	£5.99
14597 1	CAUGHT IN THE LIGHT	Robert Goddard	£5.99
14622 6	A MIND TO KILL	Andrea Hart	£5.99
14623 4	THE RETURN	Andrea Hart	£5.99
14584 X	THE COLD CALLING	Will Kingdom	£5.99
14561 0	THE SLEEPER	Gillian White	£5.99
14563 7	UNHALLOWED GROUND	Gillian White	£5.99
14564 5	VEIL OF DARKNESS	Gillian White	£5.99
14555 6	A TOUCH OF FROST	R. D. Wingfield	£5.99
13981 5	FROST AT CHRISTMAS	R. D. Wingfield	£5.99
14558 0	NIGHT FROST	R. D. Wingfield	£5.99
14409 6	HARD FROST	R. D. Wingfield	£5.99
14047 3	UNHOLY ALLIANCE	David Yallop	£5.99

All Transworld titles are available by post from:

Bookpost, PO Box 29, Douglas, Isle of Man IM99 1BQ

Credit cards accepted. Please telephone 01624 83600, fax 01624 837033, Internet http://www.bookpost.co.uk or e-mail: bookshop@enterprise.net for details.

Free postage and packing in the UK.

Overseas customers allow £1 per book.

'FROST IS A SPLENDID CREATION, A CROSS BETWEEN RUMPOLE AND COLOMBO'

Marcel Berlins, *The Times*

Denton is having more than its fair share of crime. A serial killer is murdering local prostitutes; a man demolishing his garden shed uncovers a long buried skeleton; an armed robbery at a local mini-mart; a ram-raid at a jewellers and a series of burglaries.

But Detective Inspector Jack Frost's main concern is for the safety of a missing schoolgirl. Nine weeks ago, Vicky Stuart, eight years old, didn't return home from school and in spite of exhaustive enquiries and extensive searches, has never been seen since. Another little girl from the same school is reported missing. Her body is found...raped and strangled.

Frost's prime suspect, strongly protesting his innocence, hangs himself in his cell, leaving a note blaming Frost for driving him to suicide. Subsequent evidence points to the man's innocence.

Coarse, insubordinate and fearless, DI Jack Frost is in serious trouble.

'If you enjoy crime fiction at all, read this. If you've never read a crime novel in your life, start with this one'
Morning Star

'R.D. Wingfield has created possibly the most accurate picture of police work in crime fiction today...*Winter Frost* is an absolute cracker. Maybe not what you would expect if you have only met Frost on television, but a must for any crime fan worth their salt'
Mike Ripley, *Sherlock Holmes*

Also by R.D. Wingfield:
A TOUCH OF FROST • FROST AT CHRISTMAS
FROST • HARD FROST
Published by Corgi Books

ISBN 0-552-14778-8

9 780552 147781 >

Distributed by
Trafalgar Square
N. Pomfret, VT 05053

Cover photograph by Michael Wildsmith